Praise for
WARPATH by Tony Daniel

"Disembodied intelligences both artificial and not so, interstellar travel by canoe, mass minds, totemic aliens, and a small-town newspaperman whose lost love is part of the environment. It is an achievement to produce a successful amalgam of such disparate items. But Tony Daniel has done it, in this, his impressive first novel. Remember his name, and keep watching for whatever he does."

–Roger Zelazny

"An original premise, interesting characters, and stylish writing distinguish this first novel."

–*Publishers Weekly*

"Tony Daniel is without a doubt the most lyrically gifted writer to enter the field in many a year. WARPATH, with its echoes of Sturgeon and Bradbury, is more than a first novel; it is a powerful and passionate act of the imagination."

–Lucius Shepard

"Daniel's first novel uses Native American lore and hard science to create a compelling visionary tale that is part adventure and part dream quest. This impressive debut belongs in most SF collections."

–Library Journal

"WARPATH is a stunning blend of buckskin and Buck Rogers, with a sophisticated surreality that sets it miles above other attempts to blend the outer frontier with the western frontier. Set on a world named Candle, where they call the wind Sarah, WARPATH is incandescent."

–Elizabeth Ann Scarborough

"What makes WARPATH a success isn't simply the engrossing plot, but the fact that Daniel has provided us with many captivating characters who cause us to care...they all seem real and true, more living creatures than words on a page."

–Science Fiction Age

WARPATH

TONY DANIEL

TOR®

A TOM DOHERTY ASSOCIATES BOOK
NEW YORK

WARPATH

Copyright © 1993 by Tony Daniel

Cover art by Nick Jainschigg

A Tor Book
Published by Tom Doherty Associates, Inc.
175 Fifth Avenue
New York, N.Y. 10010

Tor® is a registered trademark of Tom Doherty Associates, Inc.

ISBN: 0-812-51966-3
Library of Congress Catalog Card Number: 92-41280

First edition: April 1993
First mass market edition: April 1994

Printed in the United States of America

0 9 8 7 6 5 4 3 2 1

For Mapes, of course

Thanks to family and friends who helped me write this book: My parents, Martha and Jerry Daniel, my brother, David Daniel, my grandmother, Louise Montgomery, my great-grandmother, Lecter Cooley, Kevin Mims, Wendy Counsil, Carolyn Gilman, Adam Bridge, Greg Gutfeld, Maria and Gene Bottoms, Noemi Daniel, Edward Turner and Diane Mapes, without whom, nothing. A special thanks to my grandparents, Myrtice and Emmett Daniel, for giving me a cabin and a summer to write the first chapters, and to the Clarion West class of 1989.

Thanks to the people who taught me the craft: Ann Barker-Boozer, Dee Gorey, Catherine Hoff, Carter Revard, Andrew Ferguson, Paul Lucey, the inimitable Michael McInturff, and my instructors at Clarion West: Orson Scott Card, Connie Willis, Amy Stout, Roger Zelazny and Karen Joy Fowler.

Gardner Dozois edited a bunch of words into the original novella, and Greg Cox did the same for this novel. And you may hold Lucius Shepard personally to blame for everything else.

Every day is an animal, you know. You can wake up in the morning, stick your nose out the window, take a smell. Feather musk of raven? Wired electricity of weasel? Clumsy thickness of cow? There will be a trace in the air. Then, as the day progresses, as Candle's old sun strains and pulls itself across the blue-black sky, as she wearily passes around the planet, over the horizon, the animal in the day takes shape, manifests itself, until you *know* You know.

And I knew very well what animal *this* day was turning out to be. There was a scurrying in the wind, a clever quickness to the air, like the smell released by quickly crinkled paper. A smell fast and mean. A flat-out *carpe diem* smell. Clouds hung close to the ground, moving behind the mountains, through the icy passes, like hunted things on the run—or hunting things on the stalk—misty, sneaking scavengers. This day was a rat. Unquestionably a rat.

I stood in a small clearing, on the very top of Canoe Hill. My down parka flapped in the breeze, and I pulled it close around me. The hill rose halfway between Jackson, where I lived, and the Indian village of Doom. I could take it all in, all the human settlement on Candle, with one sweeping turn. After nine years on this flicker of a world, I still couldn't assimilate the sight, though, couldn't find a way to analyze and categorize it.

* * *

The view from the hill reminded me of one of those prints of gay little towns in the nineteenth century, where the artist fills in the streets, the homes and businesses, with exacting detail. It was kind of like one of those prints, only the guy they got to paint the towns on Candle was evidently demented.

Imagine *this* print, if you will, a postcard to send home to your folks on Earth, to show them the quaint surroundings you find yourself in. Only, if you're me, your folks are long dead and these are not just your surroundings, they are where you will spend your remaining days. This print will always be a reminder and register of your absolute surprise that first day when you climbed Canoe Hill, and saw what humanity had made of itself in the last five hundred years.

It is a painting made, you might think, in the late 1830s on Earth, in the old United States of America. It depicts, in the rich, textured oils of the day, a frontier town. On the western edge of Missouri, you'd guess. Under a brindled sky. Almost a nineteenth-century town, but not quite. The streets are not gold, or brick or dirt. The roads are hard and smooth, but made from silky-white, engineered bacteria-shit.

There is a small break in the clouds above Jackson, and the spider-silk streets of the town are shining white along this narrow slice of light where the sun strikes them directly. Many of them, however, are still a dull, glowing gray in the more common diffused light. The streets spread out from the town square like radials in an imperfect spiderweb. In the mixed lighting, the streets look very much like a *true* spiderweb, but a spiderweb at night, when you shine a flashlight on it from the side and catch only a swath of strands.

You can just make out dots and clumps that are the good citizens of your adopted home. The streets are not truly made from the spinnerets of giant spiders, though, and the people below are not bugs caught in the city's sticky web.

They move with speed and purpose along the streets, riding in hovers, or walking. The brick-and-wood buildings of the town shine dully where the light strikes them, and they all send cottony trails of steam toward the sky. You might have imagined this steam to be the dissipated heat of commerce and industry, if you hadn't been told that the buildings were warming up their thermal coatings and melting off last night's snowfall.

On the left side of the old painting, in the west, is the Indian village, Doom, under overcast skies. Not that sunlight would brighten it up much. Doom has only walking paths between the houses, no streets. Anywhere farther than walking distance, the Indians go by canoe—just as the Mississippians had been doing since they discovered the mental trick that allowed them to travel to the stars, almost 1,400 years ago. Standing twice as high as the dwellings, like some king-building before which the houses lie prostrate, is the Gathering Hall, the center of religion and government for the clannish Indians.

You look above the buildings of Doom and feel a little disgust, for you find that the painter has got his perspective all wrong (unless he is trying deliberately to be primitive). A few canoes are crowded above the village, as if they are hanging in the sky. You know they *must* be farther away, to the north of the village on some large blue lake, going out for hunting toward the woodlands, or toward Jackson, for trading. The painter has just neglected to make them smaller, to reflect their greater distance. A child's error. You mentally try to correct it, to put everything in its proper position.

Boom—epiphany: this is *not* a painting after all; it is your new life.

The canoes will not budge. They *are* hanging in the sky above the village and you watch, amazed, as the two Indians at the bow and stern in each canoe paddle them easily through the air, as if they are gliding upon still water.

And now that I have observed the Indians and settlers, it's time to place myself into that quaint print. If you look carefully, toward the center of Jackson, you will see my office, steaming along with all the rest. You won't quite be able to make out the wooden shingle hanging at the entrance. The Candle *Cold Truth,* it says. It's the best newspaper in the Territory, if you ask me—but then, I'm the editor and publisher.

* * *

This morning I was taking some time off, however. I'd climbed Canoe Hill to meet a man who was returning from a long journey. And, yes, I certainly expected him to bring news I could put in my paper—but I'd walked the long way from Jackson because he was my friend. Gazing above me, into the cold blue morning, I watched as Thomas Fall returned, descending from the stars, paddling his birch-bark canoe. And even after nine years on my new planet, I still thought the sight was damn near the most strange and wonderful thing I'd ever seen.

But this rat of a sky did not want Thomas to paddle his canoe down through it to get back home. Candle is known for bad wind storms, despite our attempts at weather control, and they're especially bad here at the equator, near the geothermal vents. This wind storm was worse than most. Thomas descended through an evil wind that few Indians and no settlers could have survived in, much less piloted with skill. He made it look easy, negotiating the swells and buffets of the atmosphere with a sureness which came from long years traveling to many worlds. He was only thirty years old, but there wasn't much he hadn't seen.

Since I am the reporter who was supposed to have been everywhere, seen it all, I was a bit envious. Truth to tell, Earth and Candle were the only places I'd managed to visit in my thirty-five years, and I hadn't seen half of either planet. Thomas visited something like a world a month, and he could relate a seemingly bottomless stock of details about each of them. Well, such is the memory and storytelling ability of an Indian Wanderer. Me, if I don't write it down, I can't remember when Justice Day is, or even the anniversary of my own instantiation.

Sometimes I wonder if the old neural structure was scrambled just a bit during those five hundred years I spent being a radio wave.

When Thomas was about a hundred feet from the ground, the wind slammed into his canoe with redoubled force. There was a spray of mist in the air, and I could actually make out what looked like swirling tendrils, clawing at the gunwales of the canoe, like some panicked, drowning swimmer, frantic for a handhold. This was no ordinary breeze, no backwash that the weather algorithm had to kick in here over the hill so that the old sun would keep shining over Doom and Jackson. This wind shook the canoe with a malevolent force.

Sarah is the name of our weather algorithm, though only I and a few others call her that. This wind sure as hell wasn't Sarah. How was I so sure? I don't tell many people this, but I knew Sarah a long, long time ago, when she was a farm girl from Oregon. So I knew that this wind wasn't Sarah in one of her friskier moods. Too mean-spirited. Instead, it felt more like a bug in the system. Or, what I was really afraid of, like a programmed assault on Thomas Fall.

Tricksters tamper with the weather more than you'd think, especially out here in the boonies. Candle's security is not so good. What's the use of it, people think, when everybody knows everybody else and folks are basically trustworthy and good? What they don't realize, no matter how many times I editorialize about it in the *Cold Truth,* is that bad guys know we are thinking this way and are prepared to take advantage of us. Or one of us could turn bad, and not care what anybody thinks anymore. It wasn't Sarah's fault. She wasn't self-aware, at least not like you and I. At least, so the people told me who programmed her. Weather algorithms can be confused by a clever person.

Take that Clerisy indwelling on Aeolus two years ago, the one that got wiped out when some priest read a little too much Mao Tse-tung, Willibus, and Saint Paul, and went renegade. He seeded a tornado half-sentient, and told it there was food buried under all those little buildings with steeples on them. Wiped out a gaggle of monks and nuns. The guy who did it got away. Or was it a woman? I just remember running the wire story. Come to think of it, my friend Frank Oldfrunon, who owns a bar in town and happens also to be the mayor of Jackson, told me a joke about that story: what do you call it when fifty priests get crushed under falling chapels? A good start. Frank and the Clerisy are not exactly on sharing-spit kissing terms.

Anyway, this harsh wind kicking up made me worry for Thomas. He yawed heavily to one side, sure enough, but then the silver in the silver-black birch bark which lined the outside of his canoe began to glow with a luminescence that was almost blue. Thomas was putting his mind to righting the problem. Above and around him, there was a gathering of light, a swirl of shimmering lines and flashes—coming together, congealing, into the face of a great black bear.

This was Thomas's chocalaca, his Indian pet—or, as some would have you believe, his familiar. Thomas had named him Raej. People have called a Wanderer's relation with his chocalaca a kind of symbiosis. Thomas just called it friendship.

I could feel the nasty rat of a day snatching at the canoe, mean and hard, trying to get a bite of the soft human-meat inside, or to pitch Thomas one hundred feet below, to die crashing through the trees and into the frost-hardened ground. Raej's great bear head looked around, turning like a huge holographic representation twisted from tubes of blue and green neon. The chocalaca looked like an advertisement, a three-dimensional billboard over the line to an amusement park ride—Bear Mountain, say, or the Black Forest of No Return—attractive, scary, but, of course, you knew it wasn't real.

Then Raej growled.

The sound seemed to come from somewhere deep in the chocalaca's being (who can say if they have throats?), with the sound of thunder on the horizon, of a winter avalanche down the high pass of a mountain. For an instant, there was silence. No rat wind, no Sarah. Just the empty wash left after the passage of sheer power through the world, the brush of some demi-god's wing. Was Raej pure order, drowning out the patterns about him as a boat's wake will obliterate the spreading wrinkles of a small stone dropped into water? Or was his growl the ragged cutting edge of Chaos incarnate, grinding order to nothingness?

It was *something* terrifying and awesome, one way or the other, and I sure as hell was glad he wasn't mad at *my* little gray-celled algorithm. He could probably wipe my mind clean with only a sweeping look from those glowing eyes.

Then the rat wind returned slinking back in to surround the canoe, maybe to examine what had frightened it so. Again, Raej roared. Splinters of blue and white light shot out from the phantom bear's maw, like ice crystalizing in veins of rock. I imagined the rat wind beginning to split apart under that on-slaught of power, breaking into disparate breezes.

All rats are cowards at heart—which is why they are survivors—and this wind was no different. It went scurrying away, leaving behind a stink like the smell of damp leather shoes. The canoe quickly worked itself upright, and Thomas was smiling at me as he brought it gingerly down into the grass of the meadow where I was standing. Raej was gone—gone back to whatever place or company chocalacas keep when their Indians aren't paying attention to them.

Thomas rose from the canoe, and there was a faint crackle (it has always sounded like the crinkling of fine, white paper to me) as Thomas allowed the Effect to collapse and dissipate. He drew his green coat tighter about him as the perpetual chill of Candle's air, air which no weather algorithm can warm, rushed into the place formerly protected by Thomas's bubble of awareness. Or, as Indians and old-time ship captains say, as Thomas came back into the universe.

Thomas sat still for a moment, sniffing the air.

"Your weather's being bad today," he said. Then, after a pause, "But it's good to see *you*, Will James."

"Likewise," I said. "I don't think that was Sarah, making that wind."

"No harm done."

Thomas reached into the canoe and took out a backpack of blue and gray cloth. Green, blue, and gray were colors that went with Thomas, as the reds, yellows and browns of deciduous tree leaves fit the autumn. It was late autumn on Candle, which, as Frank Oldfrunon says, means that when you piss, it freezes halfway down to the ground. In summer, it waits until it puddles a little, at least. In winter, you just hold it until spring.

Most of the trees here are evergreens the Indians brought with them, or the local sponge trees, although there are plenty of scraggly hardwoods in the forests—those that the settlers planted two generations ago, and the birches the Indians use to make their canoes. I miss the bright red maple burning across the Ozarks, in Missouri, where I grew up. At least *there* you knew that, though winter came, it would pass and warm weather would come back again. On Candle, it just goes from cold to colder.

I helped Thomas swing his pack onto his back. He lived for months out of that thing, and the outside pockets were full of mail and messages from other Indian-settled worlds. Everything a Wanderer needed for his physical survival was jammed into its guts, because *most* of what a Wanderer needed, he carried packed up tightly in his head.

"You going to see Janey first, or go down to Doom?" I asked.

"Doom," he said. "Have to let them know I'm here, so that they can get the Gathering Hall ready."

"Janey's not doing so well."

"How bad?"

"I saw her a week ago. Not good."

"I'll go there first, then."

There was a tautness to Thomas's bearing. You wouldn't call it tension, not in him. More like a controlled state of readiness.

"You're infected to the gills, aren't you, Thomas?"

"It's for Janey. You know that."

Thomas spoke coldly, but smiled when he said the words. There was a dangerous undertone playing around the edges of his voice.

"Besides," he said, laughing low and harshly. "Nobody thinks I'm bringing her rhythm. They just think I'm fucking her. They always have."

I'd gotten to be friends with more Wanderers than just Thomas, and I knew that, according to custom, they were supposed to be celibate. One passed through every month or so. Mostly I talked to them because they were my best sources for news, but also because being a Wanderer and being a journalist were not so different. Those that I knew had discrete and meaningless affairs with locals. Like I said, not really so different from

journalists. Thomas and Janey had grown up together. Since
Wanderers couldn't officially marry, anybody who had a clue
thought Janey Calhoun was Thomas's lay when he came home
for Gathering. I knew differently.

"Yes, nobody suspects, really. I just worry about you sometimes."

Thomas didn't answer.

"There's trouble coming up, amigo, I may as well tell you,"
I said. "Real bad blood coming to a boil. Mostly over the clay,
and rhythm, but also over other things. Clerisy isn't helping
things."

A look of sadness, of weariness, came over Thomas. He
swallowed, closed his eyes. Then he raised his shoulders and
smiled at me.

"When has there *not* been trouble, Will?" he said. "Every
time I come back, there's something new—but it's really the
same old thing. And there's some bad news I'm bringing from
Etawali. Some Indians got killed there. Then some settlers got
killed. Over clay. Over smuggling."

My journalist's instincts kicked in, and I mentally called up
my reporter's menu, selected the notepad pop-up, and turned
on the memory-banker in my visual cortex. The little red tell-
tale began to blink in my right peripheral vision. I began pump-
ing Thomas for details. We'd heard nothing about this in the last
wire dispatch. But then Wanderers were faster travelers and
were always scooping the Territorial Wire Service.

"Over clay ownership?" I said. It wasn't really a question,
though.

"What do you think?" Thomas said. "Westpac's about to
legalize rhythm."

"I'm not so sure about that."

"Doesn't matter. Settlers are convinced of it. They're getting
greedy."

"And the Indians aren't?"

"Things are getting out of hand."

Rhythm is a drug. Yeah, like Jupiter is a planet. It's an
algorithm copy of a human personality—complicated far

beyond most such copies, like the halfsent and quartersent algorithms. But that's not the secret ingredient. Slavery is what makes it work—and *work* and *work,* for whatever lucker dancer flashes it into his brain. Manacle loops hold the algorithm, while programmed prods force it to intelligently seek out the dancer's pleasure centers and supply them with the best fantasy simulations it can come up with. The smarter the algorithm, the higher the quality (and the price) of the rhythm.

Thomas had been looking away from me, over Jackson and Doom. Now he turned and looked me straight in the eyes, and I suppressed a shudder. Looking into Thomas Fall's eyes could be disconcerting—like a bell is disconcerted by a clapper. And it wasn't the drug in his system that did it.

Get a picture of the man: very tall, the kind of tall that you remember, that is kind of, well, *metaphysically* tall. He had the rounded features of his Mississippian Indian mother, the copper skin, encrypted with the black curl and jag of his Ordeal tattoos. But his eyes were startling in that dark, tangled face. Where you thought there was only unthinking force of presence, thick and oppressive as a jungle, you suddenly discovered native intelligence in them. They were the same gray-blue as Thomas's pack.

Thomas was not a man given to very many words, and what he said was usually short and to the point. But you couldn't mistake this for lack of depth—not if you knew him. He saved his words for when they counted, in the Indian Gathering ceremonies, where he shared news and told stories.

Yet his eyes belied the fact that he had his father's settler blood in him, and he'd lived much of his childhood in Jackson. Was Thomas Indian or settler? It depended, really, on the light, on the mood. At the moment, Thomas had the Indian feel about him, thick as leaves in an Ozark forest: the quick attention to details that did not seem important to anyone but Indians, like the way he'd sniffed the air before he got out of the canoe, and pawed the ground when he'd stepped over the boat's gunwales. Like the way he carefully cupped his hands when talking about other worlds, Etawali in this case, as if, by this action the planet would be kept safe and warm. And mostly, the air of brusque

indifference Indians couldn't help radiating toward settlers—
even though, in my case, Thomas and I had been friends for
years.

If I'd met him for the first time this day, I might have tried
to speak the Loosa patois—the common language of the scattered Mississippian Indian tribes—rather than English, thinking
I'd have a better chance of being understood.

Thomas started walking toward the edge of Canoe Hill, to the
trail down into the valley below. He spoke over his shoulder,
not looking at me.

"Will you come with me to Janey's?" he said. I didn't have
to answer. I was always the one who set up the exchange of the
drug. We usually did it at my place, so that Janey's sisters
wouldn't discover us, and I was the one who watched over them
to make sure nothing bad happened, though I had precious little
idea what I would do if Thomas had come into a bad batch of
rhythm and both their brains burned out in a quick flash.

We went down the hill into the green and white stillness of
autumn near the equator. The evergreens and sponge trees in-
termingled to form a green and brown curtain on either side of
us. The trail switchbacked down the hillside like the flick of a
cat's tail. Snow patches were smeared along the forest floor, as
if some painter had spattered a brush full of white paint in a
generally westerly direction. Here and there, big granite rocks
jutted through the snow. The air was cold, but still, so that the
chill very slowly, but inexorably, pulled away the warmth surrounding our bodies.

"I've really missed this place," Thomas said.

"Yeah, right. How many planets did you visit this year? Last
year it was twenty-seven."

"That many?"

"Damn right. And every one of them different. All they share
is the same language and a mistrust of settlers."

"That much is true."

I was about to say more, but Thomas raised a hand and cut
me off.

"It's just that I have a special place in my heart for cold worlds," he said. "For ice and snow."

Thomas's face was full of something very like pain. Then he softened.

"And a place for those good warm fires in the evening. These trees, Will, these mountains."

I knew exactly what he meant. I didn't *have* to stay here when they brought me back from the dead, from the void. I could have taken the next ship back in. But back to *what*? An Earth still suffering, in places, from the biologic fallout of wars that had happened a hundred years ago? And the rest of Earth? I'd seen pictures, read descriptions. Earth was changed beyond my comprehension. I, too, chose to remain on Candle.

"So, how long you planning to stay this time?" I said.

Thomas walked on through the morning. The sun was about halfway up the sky, red in the east. A little wind began to kick up, to play with wisps of snow. This was more like Sarah—playful, sometimes tricky, but never dangerous, never deadly. I was even more convinced that there was a bug in the system, and none of the rat-day, rat-wind stuff had been Sarah's doing. The day had been more like a mean-ass, sneaky city rat anyway, rather than like a wild-but-free country rat of the kind that Sarah might have known and painted. Sarah was a painter. Did I tell you that? She made a living as an artist for a little while, before the Broadcast Project. Sometimes I imagined Candle's daily weather as a series of her paintings. Well, even if somebody *had* been messing with the weather, Sarah was back in control again.

"I don't know how long I'll stay," Thomas said vaguely, paying attention to something else. "Maybe I'll settle down."

He looked off to the side of the trail, stopped, then shrugged and kept on walking. I looked also, but didn't see or hear a thing.

"Then maybe Doom'll appoint *me* Wanderer," I said.

"You? Leave Candle's wind behind?" he said with a smile. I'd told him about Sarah. "Not likely."

Somewhere in the woods, snow fell from a limb. Thomas stared intently into the forest gloom.

"Some kids out playing?" I asked quietly.

After a moment, he replied. "Yes." He didn't sound very convinced.

We went on without talking, and the breeze picked up. Sarah loved moths—the bump of them at night, their softness against the hand, their mute, intense desire for light. The zephyr surrounded me like the cool beating of many moth wings. Snow began to sift down from the sky like butterfly scales, just like Sarah's breath used to feel against my bare skin. Snow caressing and then stinging, like a shrill voice calling from a great distance through a thick blanket of atmosphere. *Or like a breathy, whispered warning.*

The leaves rustled more loudly, and I tried to fit a stronger wind in with Sarah's personality, finally decided it was just some utilitarian function, a compensation for somewhere else that demanded calm weather. Frank Oldfrunon had a habit of taking late-morning strolls, and a worse habit of using his status as mayor to override weather programming for his own convenience. When I first started the *Cold Truth,* I'd thought this an outrage, and editorialized about it a couple of times stridently enough. But everybody liked Frank, and nobody really minded that much, so I let it drop.

But it was not the wind; the leaves were crackling, but it was not the wind that stirred them.

"There's someone to the right," Thomas said softly. "I'm afraid—"

Then they were upon us. I saw a brilliant yellow flash, then red and green. Parkas. The air around me suddenly crackled and the world got more blue. Then I felt a most unsettling wrench. Down deep, like it was my soul being jerked around. My feelings of surprise, fear, a small edge of anger—all of them, all at once—were yanked into my complete consciousness like a knife being unsheathed. I heard a growl, all around outside me, and, impossibly, a growl *inside* my mind as well, a growl that was completely alien.

Raej. Coming into being around Thomas and me.

My brain rang with the beginning of the growl, and the world suddenly got *more intricate.* That is the only way I can possibly describe it. Everything about me took on a deeper texture, became more complete. I watched, almost hypnotized, as some men came running toward me. They shimmered and shifted in space like bits of glass in the barrel of a kaleidoscope. Their faces were burning like the sputtering wicks of candles. I have no idea how I knew they were male. There was a third figure, nearby but not moving toward me, whose face also glowed, but steady and bright, more like a detonating fuse than a candle wick. Somehow this meant femininity.

I'm seeing the world like a goddamn Impressionist painter, I thought. One of the men had something in his hand that burned like a blue-green jet of lit propane. The man's own bright redness swirled down his arm to join the thing in his hand, meeting in a white-hot glare where they joined, looking like one of Van Gogh's "Starry Night" stars.

Then the man hit me over the head with the propane jet. The pain told me that it was actually something very solid, like a blackjack.

I felt the jolt of Raej leaving my mind, of my vision of the world returning to normal. What I saw was the ground coming up to meet me. Flashes of light that accompanied a head-splitting pain. The beginnings of Raej's roar. Two sets of legs beside me. The roar stopping, cut off like some switch was flipped. The rushing of air from my lungs as I slapped into the ground. Thomas falling beside me. My own surge of anger. Then another crack of wood against my skull, curiously distant. Then nothing. Then hands on my shoulders, pinning me down. I turned, bit a hand, felt a loosening, and rolled free. Only to sit up with a pistol pointing between my eyes. Too much. Too much to handle. I raised my hands to my temples and cradled my head against the throbbing pain. I sat very still for a while, with my eyes tightly closed. When the throbbing subsided a bit, I looked around.

The man with the gun wasn't taking any trouble to hide who he was and I recognized him almost immediately. Hell, I'd run his picture in the *Cold Truth*, standing beside an ungainly piece of impressed sculpture. It was one of those artsy publicity shots, so the lighting was all contrasty and I had a hell of a time scanning it into the paper's template with my rather archaic hardware. Ran a little story about him opening his art gallery and bistro in the trendy part of Jackson—as much as a town of twenty-five thousand can be said to have a trendy part—something I do free for new businesses, hoping they'll think of me when they get established and want to advertise. The man's name was Kem Bently. Apparently, he hadn't appreciated my services.

Two other guys were nearby, one holding his bitten hand and stomping around cursing. The other was grinning, uncontrollably it seemed, and holding Thomas down. He didn't need to. Thomas was out cold. A woman stood above him, dangling a nightstick from her hand. It had a smear of blood on it that corresponded to the bloodied bruise on the side of Thomas's forehead. The two guys I recognized as hired help at Bently's place. I'd never seen the woman before. Her hair was long, straight, and midnight-black. She was muscled like a settler from some high-gravity world like Grendel or Tashitara. Dark-skinned—maybe Mississippian, but more likely just latter-day Amerind. She looked like a bad-ass broad.

Bently was tense, like he might get a muscle cramp from all the tightness in him. I just hoped he didn't get it in his trigger finger.

"You hit him too hard," Bently said to the woman.

"I know what I'm doing." She kept her eyes on Thomas.

"Morning, Kem," I said, showing him my hands were empty. I tried to keep the tremble out of my voice. "You still angling for a lower rate on your ad in Friday's entertainment section?"

This got him to crack a smile, and I felt a little safer, for the present. In fact, once he saw that Thomas was really knocked out good, but not about to die, he loosened up quite a bit and threw a swagger into his manner, reminding me of a terrier that has killed his mouse or bird or whatever, and keeps looking at you for confirmation and a nice pat. I'd have liked to pat Bently really nicely on the top of the head. With a good stout piece of hickory.

"Nestor Marquez isn't much of a sheriff," I said, keeping a smile on my face. "But even *he'll* bounce you off-planet quicker than a cleric quotes Trotsky once he finds out what you've done here."

Bently just winked at me. He turned to the woman, who was now kneeling over Thomas, efficiently rifling his pockets and pack.

She found what she was looking for in the inner folds of Thomas's cloak—a bit of hardened clay, about fist-size. It was brownish-white, probably fired in one of the wood-burning groundhog kilns the Indians used for their pottery. She showed the clay to Bently, who turned to examine it.

And I dove for the pistol. The guy I'd bit on the hand whacked me across the shoulders and the back of the head with his blackjack and I collapsed, holding my temples, trying to squeeze the pain out of my brain. I decided not to try the hero bit anymore.

Bently trained the gun on me again, then saw I was sitting on my rump, moaning, and turned his attention back to the clay. He took it, looked it over very carefully.

"That's it," said the woman. "Let's go."

Bently didn't answer. He dropped the clay onto the ground and ground it into dust with his boot.

"Oh, *shit,*" said the woman. She moved toward Bently, not raising her club, but she wasn't the sort who had to threaten. She looked ready to kill him.

Grin-face, the man who was holding Thomas down, shuffled uneasily and watched the woman, but Thomas was out cold and couldn't take advantage. My guard didn't take his eyes off of me.

"Don't worry, Verna," said Bently, gripping the pistol tighter. "That was just his damned chocalaca pet. Indians carry them in the clay. This boy's too smart and too good to use clay for smuggling rhythm anyway."

"Well, you could *tell* me," said the woman. She eased back over to Thomas.

Not a lot of trust here, I thought.

Bently turned to Grin-face.

"You don't have to do that anymore. Go get me the slurper."

The man, still unable to keep his face out of a taut grimace, went into the woods, then came back with a gray cylinder. Maybe it was just the name of the instrument, the slurper, but that thing surely looked evil to me. The gray was black-gray, and the top and bottom were rounded, like a can bloated with botulism toxin.

Grin-face handed it to the woman, Verna. She took it from him with a sneer, and turned it the other way around, like the fellow was some kind of idiot for carrying it wrong. As far as I could tell, there *wasn't* any up or down on it. But Verna did something and the end she had up sort of retracted, leaving what looked for all the world like a pair of false teeth displayed on a little pedestal. But I'm from A.D. 2041 originally, and *you* don't know what the hell I'm talking about, do you?

"Wait," said Bently, and knelt down next to Thomas, putting the gun to Thomas's head. "You can wake him up now."

Verna turned Thomas's head sideways and put the two mandibles of the slurper around his exposed neck, right at the spine. I wasn't liking this at all, but couldn't see what to do about it.

Verna touched something, and Thomas shuddered, then opened his eyes. For a moment he tried to sit up, but then Thomas felt the cold of Bently's pistol and relaxed. In fact, he relaxed a great deal. As if he understood what was going on and would bide his time.

"Gonna relieve you of some contraband, Mr. Wanderer," said Bently.

"You don't know what you're doing," said Thomas, evenly, with resignation—like he felt a moral obligation to tell these people the consequences of their actions. "You're going to kill a woman by doing this. And maybe hurt a lot more people. Do you want to start a war?"

"Oh, the dancers will get their jangles, you needn't worry," said Bently contemptuously. "Only from a different supply house. I'm surprised at you, Fall. You Indians have enough slaves as it is. What do you need with all this rhythm?"

Bently sounded like some low-rez actor reading from a prompter pop-up. Thomas closed his eyes and sighed.

I hadn't liked the bastard when he first came into the office. Shortish, bowl-cut hair that was supposed to be some sort of mockery of the Clerisy, even though Bently belonged to the Church. Most of the bar customers on his side of town were Cell members, but I figured he just went to Cell for the business connections. Bently wasn't exactly oozing with social justice and heavenly virtue, at least on the face of it. Now, while I have my reasons for liking the local Clerisy more or less, there's no love lost between me and Managua—but Bently wasn't just making fun of priests. His whole attitude was one of amused contempt, hidden behind the put-on of an easygoing good old boy. He'd compared his inner vision to the world and found humankind wanting. Small-town artists. I can smell 'em at five hundred paces, and they just get more rank the closer they get.

Verna pulled back her hair, and put her eye to the other end of the slurper. She touched something, and the slurper started making the noise from which it got its name, pulling the drug from Thomas and injecting it naked into Verna's optic nerve. So Verna was one of those soulless rhythm-techs who were the scourge of the known galaxy, at least according to the Westpac Steering Committee. Personalities so empty that the drug couldn't find a purchase in them, couldn't find a pleasure or fantasy they would want. I didn't waste any time feeling sorry for her.

But Thomas was another matter. I watched, and winced as the teeth dug into his skin. He felt no pain, I later learned, because the thing stung him with a local anesthetic first, but I didn't know that then. And the pain Thomas was feeling was in his heart, in his soul at that moment. There is no anesthetic for that anguish.

The slurping sound continued for about five seconds. Then the machine disengaged and retracted back into its engorged cylindrical shape. Verna stood up, looking intently at a gauge or something on the slurper.

"Prime fullsent," she said, almost in awe. "It doesn't get any better than this. Just like the real thing."

Then she closed her eyes for a moment and twitched a little, as if she were feeling around inside her own body. She opened her eyes again, held the cylinder up to the sunlight, as if that would help her read the thing better. She looked mighty perplexed.

"There's not any security. No A.I., no basic manacle loops. Nothing!" she said, almost to herself. "This is too easy."

Bently frowned, backed away from Thomas slowly, then stood up. He kept his eye on the Wanderer as he spoke to her.

"You *can* contain it, can't you?" he said.

"Sure. I'm stone, baby. And I've got better AIs than Westnet," Verna said. "But it'll be a job making this algorithm usable. I don't know what we've got here, but it's potent as hell."

Now Bently smiled. Like a terrier will, before it humps your leg.

"Good. Excellent," he said, then turned to Thomas and me. "Gentlemen, you come by the gallery anytime for a free drink." He spoke to his goons. "Tie them up."

My guardian goon bound up our arms and legs mean and tight while Bently covered us with the pistol. They set us off to the side of the trail, up against an old sponge tree.

"I'm warning you, stinkard," said Thomas, using the worst of Indian epithets. "You're starting a war."

Bently just smiled.

"I'm just a simple businessman," he said. "What Indian is going to fight over some half-breed Wanderer's stolen firewater?"

"Let's go," said Verna, who was standing behind Bently. "This stuff in me is getting restless."

Bently just kept smiling at Thomas and me.

"By the way," he said with a sick little laugh, "Give Janey my regards, and thank her for a wonderful evening last night."

I didn't see Thomas's reaction to this. I was watching Verna.

Her eyelids began to flutter.

"Oh, no," she said.

Then she let out a scream, which began high-pitched, but deepened as it continued—it seemed to go on forever—until it ended up deeper and louder than I would have believed a human's lungs capable of. Somehow, that scream was familiar.

Bently spun around and shot her in the chest.

He looked frightened and amazed that he'd pulled the trigger, like he wanted to apologize, but didn't have anybody to whom he could say he was sorry. Apparently he'd loaded the pistol with halfsent flechettes, the burrowing kind. There was a muffled grinding noise, and Verna's chest arched outward and oozed a little blood through her shirt. She slumped to the ground. Bently stood over her, staring, not quite believing what he'd done. The goons had stopped in their tracks, and were staring at their boss like stunned children.

"Still time to get the rhythm out," he whispered. "Have to hurry."

He told the two goons to pick her up. They followed Bently as he left the way he'd come.

"Oh Christ," said Thomas, as soon as they'd gone crashing through the woods. He jerked violently at the ropes, but didn't get free. "Damn them to hell, I've got to get Raej."

The wind begin to pick up again, like Sarah was both urging us on, and blowing about in impotent fury. What could she do, with air for hands?

Again he pulled at the ropes, and again they held.

In the woods, I heard a hover's rotors begin to chop. But this noise was masked by a huge deep-throated yell from Thomas as he pulled his hands free of the bonds. He left behind a good deal of skin and blood in the mass of ropes, but this didn't concern him.

"Thomas, the bastard said he *stepped* on Raej," I said, realizing how stupid that sounded.

Thomas paid me about as much mind as he did to the cuts on his arms. He stormed off through the woods after Bently.

But the hover was above the trees now. It buzzed over me on

the trail, turned down the hill, and was soon gone toward Jackson.

Thomas lurched back out of the woods, ran down the trail a little, then saw the speck of the hover just before it disappeared. Thomas's shoulders slumped, and he hung his head. If only Sarah were truly sentient, could *really* understand, I thought. Then she could bring down that fucking hover with one good swipe. But no. There were security routines that would always hold her back. And Sarah wasn't sentient anyway, just a moaning wind.

"Oh damn," Thomas said, almost in a conversational tone. "Oh damn."

I'd worked my own way out of the ropes by then, less drastically, and I came to stand beside him. It may not have been proper Indian etiquette for one man to put his arm around another for consolation in defeat, but what the hell. I put my hand on Thomas's shoulder, felt the quiver of a sob run through him.

What to say? Something was flashing red to the side of my field of vision. The memory-bank tell-tale. So I had it all banked, for all the good it would do us. That memory bank was just as incriminating for us as it was for Bently and crew.

"We can get more rhythm for Janey," I finally said. "Some-where."

He looked at me sadly, with more care on his face than a thirty-year-old man ought to have lines to express.

"That wasn't just rhythm, Will."

"What?"

I tightened my hand on his shoulder, but he would have no comfort. He walked away, and my hand fell back to my side. A line of leaves whipped up nearby, as if Sarah had come back to check on us, like some hunting dog who has lost the trail.

"Some new copying equipment just came out. They had it on Etawali. Not many people know about it. I had to make a deal with the Clerisy indwelling there. I did them a favor once. The equipment is sophisticated enough to copy a chocalaca."

Thomas took a deep breath, shook his head in a cross of sadness and fury. "Raej volunteered to be morphed. For Janey. He was the rhythm I was carrying inside me."

For a moment, I did not understand. Wasn't the rhythm just a copy, not the real thing? Then I remembered Verna's astonishment at the copy's intricacy. *Just like the real thing.* I, too, felt a great sadness come over me. Raej could be copied, and re-copied, made to perform like an animal in a circus act. I pictured the great and powerful bear-thing, chained with iron-logic, put to work inside the head of some addict to provide mental masturbation. A slave.

The day darkened, even though it was still mid-morning, and Candle's old sun, never much of a source of warmth to begin with, burned like white ice in the sky, seeming to radiate a chill, rather than heat or light.

This world is so damned cold I don't know why *anybody* would ever want to live here, I thought. All the warmth, everything, gets lost, or frozen, or stolen away by the chill.

"Oh, Raej, Raej," said Thomas to himself, to me, to the empty air.

And the wind picked up again, slicing through Canoe Hill's trees like air across a woodwind's reed. You almost might think it was a dirge.

2

On Earth, they count a house's age in centuries. So everything on Candle is young to visitors from there, and they laugh—but oh, so politely—at our ideas of what is historic. Even folks from North America, which always startles me at first. When I was going to school at Washington U in St. Louis, I had a friend, Lukas Meyer, who was an exchange student from Germany. Now *I* thought St. Louis was *old,* with its brick houses and cobblestone waterfront. But Lukas had laughed, the way people from Earth laugh at us settlers nowadays. The house he grew up in in Tübingen, he told me, was over three hundred years old. And it was just a house, no historic landmark, no museum, nothing *special*.

I met a fellow from St. Louis a couple of years ago—worked for some contractor to the Sponge Factory, I think—who couldn't get over all the historic markers we've got scattered around Jackson. I mean, their Arch is nearly six hundred years old now, and is about the *newest* thing they consider a sacred memory of the past. But I returned the condescension when I told him that I'd covered the ground-breaking ceremony at Cahokia Spaceport. And did I cover the dropping of the A-bomb on Hiroshima? he wanted to know. For most Earthers, everything that happened more than fifty years ago seems to have happened all at once.

But settlers are fresh come into this world, both as individuals and as a culture. *Everything,* I mean everything, down to the portable johns the first Westpac expedition set up over at Lufson's Well, everything has a damn plaque slapped on it, with a halfsent in it to tell you precisely, down to the last ounce, how much shit the founding dads and moms were full of. So what if we don't have a real history? We carved a civilization out of the ice, didn't we? We damn well *will* have a past and purpose to justify us. Or something that looks mighty *like* one, anyway.

Janey Calhoun lived with her sisters in an old wooden house, with one of those plaques on it. It had that classic pioneer line to it, Frontier Revival it's called, modeled after what the founding families figured the buildings in the American West looked like back during the Westward expansion of the 1800s—except that the settlers of North America didn't have herds of engineered bacteria to make the wood, or molecule-sized carpenter machines to peg everything together and maintain it. The result was that the oldest houses on Candle were stylistically old, but *looked* new, like some meticulously preserved historic structure.

People lived in these structures, however, along with hordes of tailored biota and microscopic robots, which followed behind the humans to see to their needs and clean up their messes. Those of us who got here later, after building space was restricted by treaty with Doom, envied the rambling spaces in the old houses. But the founding families held on to them as if the houses were the last ecological niche left for their dwindling species. Some of those families certainly *were* dinosaurs, long past their time.

Hell, they should have put a historic plaque on the Calhoun family itself, let alone the house. Old blood, off the first ship, doers of great deeds. At least the original Calhouns: Jackson mayors, Westpac reps, Indian negotiators. Nowadays, three sisters kicked around in the old house, whittling away at the big pile of money and esteem that their grandparents and parents had shoveled up for them to sit on. Except for Janey. Janey actually earned her keep, and then some, making quilts.

"Go and stay with Janey," Thomas had told me as we came down off Canoe Hill. "Keep her safe until I come."

"And what will you do?"

"Go to Doom. Get some rhythm for her."

"From the Indians?"

"No, but they can help me get it."

"Don't do anything that will get you killed," I said. "That can't help Janey."

"I'm not the one who needs to worry about getting killed."

At the bottom of the hill, Thomas took the trail to Doom. Since the morning had started out fine, if cold, I'd left my hover at the office and walked to Canoe Hill from Jackson, about five miles. I jogged back to town, and, since the Calhoun place was closer than the office, I went there first.

I hated that house, no matter how much it reminded me of a Missouri farmhouse. It may be sided with white clapboards and have six gables, but the halfsent that marshaled all the microscopic house servants was copied off Georgia Calhoun, the oldest of the Calhoun sisters. To say I didn't like her would be a gross understatement. Georgia and I took to each other pretty much like a bullet takes to human flesh. But I had to get past the house to get to Janey.

"Will James to see Janey," I said at the door. The house waited a good while to answer. The afternoon sun, though feeble as usual, was at a killer angle, bouncing off the little glass window of the front door and straight into my eyes. The house made no move to polarize the glass, even though I was squinting something fierce.

"Janey is under the weather this afternoon, Mr. James," the house said in a brittle, hushed voice, like nurses use at the hospital when they are simultaneously speaking to you and trying to get you to hold your voice down. It was vibrating the window glass as the medium for speech, and, with each word, a hot flash of sun flicked into my eyes. I have trouble remembering sometimes that these house algorithms have no more real intelligence than, say, your average pig—that they are really no more than pencil sketches of the full-canvas personality they're copied from. *Bitch* must surely have run deep in Georgia Calhoun, in that case, for it to come through so clearly in her house.

"It's very important for me to see her."

"Her rest and recuperation are equally important."

"My business concerns her recuperation," I said. I turned my head away and shielded my eyes from the glare of words about to be coming off the door.

"What, exactly, do you want with her, Mr. James?" said the window.

Patronizing bitch, at that. Maybe I had to put up with this shit from the *real* Georgia, but I'd be damned if I were going to take it from some half-witted amalgamation of all her most grating mannerisms impressed on a heap of historic wood and steel.

"Tell Janey I'm here, house, and I'll talk to her about it," I said. "And please use something besides this window to talk to me. Get this sun out of my face."

If a building can let out an indignant huff, that house did so then, but I got what I wanted in both instances. Apparently there was no human override to prevent it from accepting my direct orders—nothing but sheer contentiousness on the house's part. So I was allowed admittance with a curt "Janey will see you now," but that was all. If I hadn't known the way to Janey's sewing room, I could have rambled about that lightless house all day, for all the assistance I got from the housekeeper.

I stumbled through the darkness of the living room, where only a faint trace of light made it through a crack in the heavy curtains over the window, and promptly cracked my shin against some piece of furniture. I let out a yelp of pain, and heard a surprised gasp, nearby. My eyes finished adjusting to the gloom, and I detected the still form of a woman in the corner of the room, one hand over her mouth, the other hand holding a half-full glass of some dark liquid.

"Hello, Wrenny," I said.

Wrenny Calhoun said nothing. She turned suddenly and went out through a side door. I continued across the room and climbed the stairs. The Calhoun sisters were a strange lot. Even Janey. *Especially* Janey.

"Under the weather" was a nice way of describing her condition. Without rhythm, Janey phased in and out of rationality. Even though Thomas brought her the best constructed rhythm he could find—and so, probably the best in the Territory—it usually started wearing off before he got back to Candle, and Janey started slipping. Sure, it wasn't ethical for her to use, and maybe it was really morally wrong, but Thomas and Janey had both told me that *something* truly horrible would happen if she didn't get it. I didn't fully understand what the horrible thing would be, but knowing that it involved Janey dying was justification enough for me. Yet Janey wasn't crazy, even without the drug. Janey was just *different*—not crazy.

She was feverishly working on a quilt when I entered the doorway of the sewing room, but when she saw me, she came up short.

"Will."

The sewing room was sparely furnished. Janey sat on a stool, with a little table in front of her. In a corner was a big wooden trunk. Janey wore a faded calico dress, more white than any other color, and supple brown moccasins that Thomas had probably given her. Her hair was at the red edge of brown, and fell to her shoulders unhindered. She seemed almost to blend in with the quilt she was making.

Now, I know about as much about quilts as *you* do about twenty-first-century America, but I can tell quality when I see it. Janey's design was not merely pleasing—in fact, you might not call it pleasing at all if you were in the wrong mood, but there was an energy to the whorls and stars and lines of stitches, an intricacy. There was feeling in those blanket folds, and intelligence. Somehow, they seemed familiar to me. Janey's quilts sold on Earth, in a North Carolina gallery. And also down the street, at Bently's place, goddamn him.

Janey stared at me intently, as if she had newly realized that someone named Will James existed and that conversation might be held with him. Every time I saw Janey, I got the feeling that for her the world was somehow always new and surprising from moment to moment, and you couldn't ever tell what to expect.

"I saw the edge of something this morning," she said, "and I'm trying to work it in here."

She pointed to a section of the three-quarters completed quilt. "Gnawing, running, biting, pulling down, hunger in the gut like baby spiders eating out of their nest."

You had to get used to Janey doing this. There was usually a point. Think of Emily Dickinson. On fast forward.

The patterns on the quilt coalesced. They started to make sense. I cocked my head, moved around behind Janey, so that I was seeing the quilt over her shoulder. A line of geometries, scattered by a single, formless patch of brown cloth, criscrossed with erratic, elaborate stitches. Should have looked like a mess, but instead it worked. I *recognized* what I was seeing.

"A rat," I said. "Feels like a scurrying rat."

"Yes. Yes. But a mean one."

"When did you get this idea?"

"I woke up with it. This morning."

Then she glanced up at me, saw my concern for her intensity, and laughed one of those Janey laughs that let you know there was a real girl in there that knew what was going on here, on Planet Candle. She set the quilt aside. Janey was still disturbed. She didn't seem to know what to do with her hands, now that she wasn't working on the quilt. She bunched and unbunched her fists, as if she were kneading the air in front of her. With an effort, she reached down and smoothed her dress.

"Is Thomas coming soon?" she asked. "It's just about time."

She brought her hands together with force, and clenched them tightly, trembling a little, on her lap.

"He got here this morning. But—"

"I'm so glad. Georgia is shining bright, lately. Hard and bright, like polished candle brass. But there's blood too—a little trickle running out of the top, red over the brass."

"She's been giving you trouble again?"

Janey swallowed hard, then rushed on, as if the subject frightened her. "She's very disappointed, I'm afraid, in how I've kept up the Calhoun name. Wrenny is not much help to wipe away the blood."

Wrenny liked her bourbon neat and frequently. Though I hadn't really seen her in the gloom of downstairs, I'd seen her before, and knew her a little. Wrenny was a lush, yes, but she could surprise you with her wit and charm. She was absolutely useless at anything, however. She was also strikingly beautiful, at least when she was sober; she reminded me of the Parthenon— partially preserved and stately on the outside, but crumbling to pieces, I imagined, behind the façade.

Then Janey looked at me—I should say, looked *through* me, as if I were a curtain through which she caught glimpses of the day outside. She gasped.

"You're all bunched and twisted, Will! Cocked like one of Grandaddy's old pistols. What has happened?" Then, after looking me over again with intensity, "What's happened to *Thomas*?"

"He's fine." I didn't want to say more, seeing as how the walls had ears in this house, so to speak. Janey noticed my reticence.

"House, leave us until I call," she said, not taking her eyes off me.

"All right, Janey," came that near-Georgia voice, deeper now, unlocatable. Probably using a loose floorboard for a tongue.

"Someone jumped us. They got your rhythm from Thomas."

"The rat?"

"Yes. No. It was some people, from Jackson."

Janey kept staring at me. I was getting uncomfortable, because I knew she was seeing things that I didn't necessarily want seen. Don't ask me how.

Thomas explained it once, that first time he asked me to watch over them while he flashed Janey with rhythm that he'd smuggled in. But he explained it in that way Wanderers have of discussing what you'd thought were the most simple of matters, and, by the end, leaving you so confused that you wished you'd just stayed simply ignorant.

We were at my house, in the living room. I'd opaqued the windows, and Janey lay asleep on my worn couch. The blue flicker of Raej's presence surrounded her, holding her, Thomas told me, in a kind of dreamless state. Raej was able to interact with Janey very much like rhythm did, Thomas said, better even. Only then, seven years ago, there hadn't been equipment sophisticated enough to make a decent copy of the chocalaca so that the halfsent might stay with her throughout the year while the original Raej traveled with Thomas. Instead, she had to use common rhythm—and it was the nature of rhythm to decay over time, so that she was really hurting for it by the time Thomas returned from his yearly Wanderings.

"Remember that raven in Poe?" Thomas had answered, in a low voice.

"The raven that won't shut up from saying 'nevermore'?" I said, gazing at Janey's sleeping form. She was quite pretty with her auburn hair spread in a crescent about her face.

"Yes. For Janey, the world is that raven."

He sat in the chair next to the couch, waiting for the rhythm's extraction routine to bootstrap the drug out of the labyrinth of his own mental pathways, and pack it for shipment down his optic nerve.

"Like a starship captain talks about?" I said. "What do they call it? Seeing into the *true* world, hearing it speak?"

"No. Janey's different from all us travelers and Wanderers. We can barely hear the raven, and most of us half believe we're making it up."

"Janey can hear it pretty loud?"

Thomas thought about this until I thought that there had been some kind of error, and that the rhythm had blown a fuse in there somewhere.

"Janey's raven sits on her shoulder, screaming in her ear, and never shuts up," he finally said.

"And rhythm makes it shut up?"

"No," he said. "Rhythm keeps her from turning *into* the bird, and clawing all our eyes out."

He turned his head as if someone had tapped him on the shoulder.

"It's ready now," he said. "We'll both be unconscious for a few minutes."

Just then it struck me, as it had several times since, that I was an accomplice in a highly illegal act.

"Why do you do this, Thomas? Are you in love with her?"

Thomas considered this. "I grew up with her. I can't remember a time when Janey wasn't there."

And that was all he said. The rhythm was ready. He pulled up Janey's eyelid, and made the transfer with eye-to-eye contact. The two of them looked like they were exchanging the passionate kiss of lovers, with Janey in a swoon from her agitated feelings. Janey's hand trailed to her side and rested on a cushion of my couch, her fingers relaxing into a loose curl. Janey was beautiful in a way neither of her sisters could match. There was no perversion of character to detract.

I suddenly felt like a voyeur, there in my own house. I turned away from the sight, embarrassed. When I returned, both of them were unconscious, asleep in each other's arms. After Thomas awakened, we did not talk about what had happened, or how he felt about it.

All mirrors and poetry, Thomas was. Sometimes I wondered if Thomas *himself* existed, or was just some whirlwind of leaves and twigs that the forest wind had kicked up.

And Janey? *Janey* surely existed, and was making me damned uncomfortable, I thought, as the silence continued and the woman peered into my soul. She'd done this before. I was not a frequent visitor to the Calhoun house—having to see Georgia most every time I came around took care of that. But Janey was no recluse, and she and I went out together occasionally. Well, I'll admit it: she was about the only woman I ever dated on Candle.

We'd even shared one evening of passionate, if confused, intimacy. But that ended with me telling, or her somehow divining, the truth about my long-lost Sarah. And there was always Thomas, our friend, overarching all that we did with the white constancy of the stars through which he traveled. Or was it the thought of *Thomas* that bothered Janey that night? All Janey had said when we pulled apart was "I haven't done very well with relationships."

She hadn't said anything when she found out about Sarah, only looked at me with the utmost sadness. Now she was seeing, in her way, a different emotion in me—my worry for Raej, mingling with those memories of first kissing her, of first kissing Sarah. Maybe the feelings then and now weren't so different after all. Sarah. Raej. Patterns enfolding, twisting into our lives like vines about old stacked lumber. Then you grab the vines, yank, and the lumber goes tumbling, clattering into a heap.

"Black paper ashes sifting down, down around you, covering you, Will," Janey said. "And the fire, low, but hot and angry."

I felt it, too, when I reflected on my mood, on the knowledge of what I had to tell her about Thomas and Raej, about the probable hopelessness of the situation. And, as much as the gentleman side of me said not to, the reporter in me had to ask her about that statement Bently had made, about thanking Janey for last night.

Then the door to the sewing room swung on its hinges, and from the squeak came the voice of the house.

"Pardon the interruption, Janey, but Georgia is here and wants badly to see you."

The door kept rocking back and forth on the hinge in order to complete its request, and each squeak made my teeth grind even harder together. I cannot abide an unoiled door.

Janey relaxed a bit, took her gaze from me.

"Tell her in a minute," Janey said. "And stop trying to annoy Will with that door."

"Very well," said the house, this time from a board almost directly under my feet.

Then, before I could say more, the house spoke again.

"Georgia says she must see you immediately. She's on her way up."

Janey began to fold the quilt she'd been working on. She did this meticulously, but quickly.

"Georgia thinks I'm quite crazy. That my quilts are crazy," she said. "And you'd better go, Will."

"Janey, I hardly think—"

"Georgia's mad. I was with a man, yesterday. Georgia found out."

"It was Kem Bently, wasn't it?" I said.

Janey was genuinely surprised by this. As if she hadn't even known herself who it was until I said it.

"Yes, that's who it was. Georgia said it was here, in the house, and I remembered it happening. Sometimes that happens when the rhythm starts to wear away. Now I remember *who*. I went to the gallery yesterday and—"

There was concentration on her face and she was rocking slightly, chopping the air with her hands, the rest of her very still for a moment, as if she were carefully trying to impose order on a scattering of objects in front of her, to force coherence on her thoughts.

"You men—with your wants dangling from you, burning in you. Sometimes I scarcely know what I'm doing when I'm out of rhythm. What I'm becoming."

Janey wasn't paying any attention to me now, just talking to herself. She darted to an old trunk in the corner and fumbled with the catch.

"My sister is a woman of honor. It's a morning-glory vine in her, twisted around a metal trellis."

"Janey, we have to get you the drug," I said, moving to help her.

Finally, I got the trunk open, and Janey flung the quilt inside, then slammed it shut. She spun around, looking wildly at the door. We could hear Georgia's high heels now, clipping up the stairway. Janey's hand found mine, squeezed. What is going on? I wondered. Georgia Calhoun was a dragon lady, but Janey's fear was excessive. Almost like she saw Georgia as some kind of monster, coming to eat her. *Almost like she could see Georgia's monstrous soul.*

"Disappointment in *me*. She despises me. It hangs from her honor-vine like scarlet blossoms, Will."

Georgia was at the top of the stairs.

"Bleeding blossoms," Janey whispered.

"Janey Calhoun, I should have known," said Georgia, standing in the doorway, very still, not entering. "Another cheap *tryst,* and in the *house,* again, Janey. In *my* house."

"Ma'am, I—" I said, but Georgia shot me a withering look.

"And with a *transmission,*" she said, pronouncing the double *s.*

"Georgia!" said Janey in dismay. She looked at me, trying to apologize with her eyes.

"Georgia, everything is quite innocent," I said, trying to sound as reasonable and mature as I could. I was, after all, five hundred years her senior.

"I think that you had better leave, Mr. James," she replied, looking at me now with a hatred I had only seen between, well, between Clerisy bigwigs and separatist Indians.

I had known there was a certain amount of prejudice against my type, a kind of gut belief that you couldn't really make a complete human out of instantiated gamma broadcasts. And I was from the very beginning of the Broadcast era, the mid-twenty-first century. Among the first twenty people in the old Radio Corps, as a matter of fact. Many of us hadn't *quite* made it. Take Sarah for instance. So I was doubly suspect.

Nevertheless, I knew in *my* gut that I was just as human as the next guy. Georgia had the worst attitude toward us radio personalities that I'd ever come up against. But I was damned if I was going to let her treat me like a halfsent.

"I will leave when Janey asks me to," I said, with a hard voice and an empty smile.

Georgia came into the room.

"House," she said. "Call the sheriff."

"Gladly," said the doorhinge.

I'm going to have to report my own arrest in my own goddamn paper, I thought. Georgia stepped to the side, motioned me out the door.

"No!" said Janey. "You won't. House, you won't do it."

"House," said Georgia quietly. "Do as I say."

For a long moment there was no word spoken. Then the house's voice filled the room.

"I am owned jointly by Georgia Lee Calhoun, Wren Warren Calhoun, and Jane Kildrey Calhoun. As per my legal containment algorithm instructions, I must consult Wrenny Calhoun to break the deadlock—"

"And *Wrenny,* she says that if you call the *police,* they are liable to find her nice little stash of duty-free hooch that her star captain friend is so kind as to drop by on his rounds about the Milky Way," said Wrenny, who leaned against the door frame. She spoke with the rushed, willowy voice of the very drunk.

"House, you are under no circumstances to call the sheriff," Wrenny said. She attempted to put her foot down firmly, but lost her balance slightly and sloshed the drink she held in her hand down her arm.

"Wrenny, you are drunk," said Georgia, her tone as flat as an overcast sky. Georgia turned back to Janey, and that sky flashed with lightning. "Janey, ask this man to leave."

"He's not wrong, Georgia. He's not dark and moist like the other one. He's bright sunlight on water. I'm better today, I promise."

"Ask him to leave."

I could see that Janey was becoming very upset. I must be getting really angry, too, I thought. The room was beginning to blur, as if I were looking at it through a sheen of tears.

"Georgia, I'm sorry you hate me so," Janey said. "I'm so sorry."

I felt my legs begin to give way. I looked down.

Oh shit. My feet are melting.

My feet were spreading *out,* like a pat of butter on warm bread. This wasn't right at all. For a moment, all I could think of was that Poe's raven had come to life and was calling out the end of the world like some croaking trumpet.

I leaned over and put my hand on the old trunk, to steady myself. What had been age-hardened wood gave way like the bark of a sponge tree.

"Nonsense, Janey. I'm your sister. I love you. I only want what's best." Georgia sounded like her throat was full of phlegm.

"Georgia, I don't want to hurt you," said Janey. "I'm *going* to hurt you."

I remembered what Thomas had said about the raven clawing our eyes out.

Georgia turned to Wrenny, rather desperately.

"It's one of her attacks. She's having one of her attacks. Help me calm her down, Wrenny."

But Wrenny just stood there, tottering back and forth, laughing nervously. I looked at Janey. She stood staring at her sister in anguish.

"I'm quite out of rhythm," she said. "Georgia, I'm quite out."

Georgia moved toward Janey, but the nearer she got, the more fluid her motions became. Her skin began to run like syrup. I looked at my own hands. They were peeling slightly, as if they were covered with wet scabs sloughing off. So *this* was what happened when Janey was out of rhythm.

And I'd figured that *Thomas* had the hard part of the bargain, going after more rhythm. At least he wasn't going to be the victim of a metaphysical meltdown. Or was he? Maybe the range of this was planetwide. Hell, maybe Janey was bringing the whole universe down around us, although I suspected not. Wrenny did not seem to be affected. Whatever the effect, I knew the cause. Georgia Calhoun.

I caught Janey from the side, before she saw me. Janey is tall, but thin. I picked her up in arms that felt like rotten wood, and ran from the room. I slipped and took most of the stairs on my butt—it felt like I was leaving part of my butt behind on the staircase, too—but I got up and out the door as quickly as possible. Janey had no softness to her at all. *She* wasn't melting. Evidently, she was immune from her own effect.

I ran down the street to the corner, where there was a small town park with a plaque commemorating some original settler structure or another. I set Janey down on the plaque and backed away. After I got about ten yards distant, I began to feel myself tightening up, coming back together, the way water must feel as it freezes in a container.

The plaque ran away from under Janey in a thin brown stream, and the ground around Janey slumped inward a good two or three inches. Then Janey began to cry, hard. I was mightily tempted to go to her, comfort her. But I figured it would be better in the long run for her state of mind if I didn't disintegrate before her eyes like an old-time leper. So I kept my distance.

After a while, Janey stood up.

"It's all right, now, Will," she said. "Come and tell me what has happened to Thomas."

We sat in the park, on a bench that had been next to the melted plaque. Its middle was curiously bowed. I pulled off my parka and wrapped it around Janey. I turned up the thermostat in the sleeve of my long underwear and was tolerably warm. The day was pretty mild for Jackson in autumn—maybe in the upper thirties. We are almost at the equator, after all.

"You tell *me* what happened just now," I said. "Should we call a doctor for your sister?"

"You got me out in time," said Janey. "People take a long while to boil away. When you turn off the heat, they go back to normal."

"You've done that *before*?"

Janey looked at me in surprise. Then a sorrow came over her, and she turned away.

"I killed a man that way. A long time ago, before you came. I thought I loved him."

She touched the edge of her eye, as if feeling for a tear. There was none there, so far as I could tell.

"He tried to hurt me. Then he just boiled all up," she said. "They knew he was bad to me and didn't press charges. And yesterday. I almost boiled the one away yesterday—"

"You remember now, all of what happened?"

"Oh." she said. "Oh, no. His face, like an old pumpkin. . ."

I was beginning to be glad that Janey hadn't spent the night with me that one time. But I was also starting to piece a few things together.

"When I get like this, I spin and spin."

"And you grab hold of whatever can stop the spinning," I said.

"I forget how the world is, and it starts falling apart."

"You used Bently's needs to hold things together, but there was a price."

"He *wanted* things, and so *I* wanted them too. But they were bad and they upset me. Everything started to fall apart."

"Georgia came in."

"Yes."

"And he left. Things went back to normal, and you didn't remember."

"Only what Georgia said had happened."

We sat there a long time, staring at the white space on the concrete slab, where the plaque had been. Evidently, the information algorithm they always put with those things had been wiped out along with the historic marker. The ground was silent.

"We have to get you some rhythm, Janey," I finally said.

This broke her reverie.

"What happened to Thomas?"

I told her about the morning. About Raej. First she said, very quietly, to herself, "Raej." Then she spoke to me.

"And where is Thomas now?"

"He went to Doom," I said, my mind just beginning to really work again. Had I gone soft in the head along with the rest of me? "To find a way to get more rhythm . . . Janey—" I could not stop my train of thought. "—that is weird-ass shit you do. Newsworthy, even."

Janey stood up, walked toward the park edge, stopped at its perimeter. She didn't seem to hear me.

"All this is my fault," she said.

Then she sniffled, sobbed a little.

"If only I could find a way to poke out my eyes, not to *see*."

"Janey, your eyes are beautiful," I said, not catching on too fast. Her beautiful eyes were tearing up now.

"It's the seeing that softens the boundary you know, that lets things leak in and melt away. In the true world, what you see is what you become."

I'd heard Wanderers and ship's captains talking about what they called the real, or regular, world—our everyday world—and the true world, about phenomena and noumena. About the Effect, and how it let you cross the boundary. It was the way that first the Mississippian Indians, then Westpac settlers, had traveled to the stars: build a mental envelope outside of space and time, stamped with and made from your captain's consciousness, then mail it through the true world postal service. A few weeks, or months, or years later—depending on the denomination of the captain's stamp, his agility at thinking his way across the galaxy—the letter will arrive at its destination, light-years from where it started, a metaphysical trick on the universe performed by that clever prestidigitator, humankind. Of course, this is a simplistic explanation. For one thing, it generally takes two Indians to fly a canoe, and starship captains rely utterly on being linked with a computer. But Janey was talking about the opposite, about things from the true world trying to come into the *real* world. She seemed to make it happen with alarming regularity.

"Go ahead and put me in your paper, Will James," Janey said. "I can see that's what you want."

I walked to her, turned her to face me, keeping my hands on her shoulders. She felt so frail beneath the calico dress, like a small bird, quivering.

"My strongest desire is for you to be happy and safe, Janey. How about trying to fulfill that one?"

She was startled for a moment, then she smiled. I'd seen that smile before. First, a couple of years ago, when we'd kissed, touched one another. Before that, I guess you'd have to go back five hundred years or so, to another girl, this one from Oregon, whose hair was just this color, caught the light just this way. I really shouldn't have kissed Janey. The timing wasn't appropriate, but nothing bad happened. The wind quickened a bit, and ruffled her hair fondly, as if she were a child. The wind. And five-hundred-year-old memories lit the edges of her hair with more radiance than Candle's old sun could ever provide.

"Will you come with me to my house?" I asked. "You can't go back home today."

"I'll come with you."

We went first to my office and picked up the hover. With some guilt, I set the paper's algorithm to work by itself on assembling the afternoon *Cold Truth*. Then I took Janey to my house. All the way there, she held my hand very tightly.

I don't live fancy, and though I could afford it, I couldn't get a house like the Calhouns' even if I wanted it, what with land use restrictions in Jackson. My housekeeper is mute, efficient, and discreet. It's a stock model based on some very proper gentleman's gentleman from a long-ago era on Earth. My house is pretty tidy, because I don't spend a lot of time there to mess it up. It's full of old comfortable furniture. Nothing fancy or valuable. But good stuff. I splurged on the bed frame and had it brought out from Earth. It had been mine, a long time ago. The mattress is made from the leaves of a native sponge tree. Nothing in the universe is so perfect for resting the human body upon.

We kissed again after the house let us inside.

"I really need something to hold on to," Janey whispered. She kissed me harder, with a directed desperation.

It was very still inside my house, and I heard the rustle of the parka Janey was wearing. It sounded like wind blowing through tree branches.

"I think we'd better stop," I said, pulling back. She kept a strong hold on me. I gently loosened her tight hands from the shirt of my thermal underwear.

"When you understand who I see when I look at you," I said, "you are going to get upset again."

"Sarah," she said.

"Always."

"I think I'm going crazy," Janey said. She went and sat on the couch.

"You just see the world differently. You know that."

"No, I think Georgia is right. I think I'm losing my mind."

"What do you mean you think Georgia is right?"

She reached into a pocket on a fold of her skirt and pulled out an impressed letter, coded on that blue plastic lawyers and doctors use.

I walked over and gently took the letter from her hand. I went to a chair, sat down, and activated the plastic.

The visual in my head was of a prim man, with very straight, brown hair, parted nearly in the middle, bowl cut just above the ear, Earth-style. I inverted my perception, the way those letters let you do. The man froze in mid-throat clearing and receded to the back of my perception. I watched Janey. She sat on the couch all bunched together and tight, as if she were an animal ready to start at any disturbance. My house is safe, I thought, and she will be all right. I turned my attention back to the letter.

The man had tanned skin—much too tan to have gotten it on Candle, unless he'd had it done cosmetically. His voice was nasally, as proper as his looks.

Dear Georgia,

Of course I remember those good old days at Emory. The parties in Atlanta, the raft trips down the Chatahoochee. And I with the very embodiment of the old State on my arm in its pretty namesake. I can only hope that those colonials appreciate the refinement and civility with which they were blessed when you returned to the stars.

There was more of such stuff. I hadn't known Georgia had been sent back to Earth for her education. That fact explained much.

In answer to your questions: yes, there seems to be a problem. Janey appears to be an ill woman.

More blither about the inadequacies of Territorial physicians to treat complex cases. Then he came down to his preliminary diagnosis.

> *The house-videos you sent to me show Janey exhibiting far-ranging emotional swings and incoherent speech patterns. Combined with the past history, which you reported, they suggest she may be very ill. I won't trouble you with the details, but I suspect she has what is known as Borderline Personality Disorder.*

Fortunately, he continued, the condition was treatable through his program at Bryce Hospital in Tuscaloosa. He was sure that Georgia would want the best care in Westpac for Janey, and Bryce was the place for it. There was just the matter of Janey's informed consent, and passage to Earth, and he'd be happy to admit her to the program. Then the picture was replaced by the shrink's signature—the Hippocrates snake, wrapped around a magnolia branch rather than a staff. Underneath was his name in frilly letters: Deason Allerby, Ph.D.

And then came a white sheet of paper, with a deep, comforting woman's voice reading what they said. All I heard was the first three words:

ARTICLES OF COMMITMENT

"Jesus Christ, Janey! She wants to put you away."

Janey shot up from the couch and stood quivering.

"It's cold in here," she said. I heard the house kick in the heater. My house was always the gentleman, and very unobtrusive. "I'm flowing farther away every day, farther away into the dark." My house, unfortunately, didn't have a remedy for that. The closest it could get was clearing the front plate glass window, letting the afternoon light stream in.

"You *are* sane; you just need the drug," I said.

"You've seen what I become. I can hurt people."

How could I answer her? I'd *felt* what she could do in my own body. And she said she'd killed a man, and almost did it again yesterday to that son-of-a-bitch Bently.

On the other hand, I hear just about everything that goes on on the surface of this planet, and quite a bit that goes on out in space comes in over the wire service. I hadn't heard of any unexplained deaths caused by some metaphysical disease. Only the usual kind, brought about by ignorance, accident, jealousy, greed. It was greed that had me worried now—not about Janey, but her sister.

I had a notion of what Georgia was up to with trying to browbeat Janey into signing those committment papers. Old Stephen Calhoun, Janey's grandfather, had been given Honored Man rank among Doom's Indians for helping them negotiate some treaty or another with Westpac. A parcel of land automatically went with this title. And Indian land meant one thing nowadays: Loosa clay.

Found nowhere on Earth, completely owned by the Indians in the Territory, it was worthless red stuff—except for one property. It was complex enough, in its natural state, to store sentient algorithms dynamically in a very small space. Something about the lattice of the suspended minerals being nonrecursive, and the minerals—aluminum, magnesium, silicon—occurring themselves in quasicrystal quantum-dynamic formations. I'm just quoting from my encyclopedia pop-up, folks. All I know myself is that Loosa clay allows programs big enough to run a city to move and breathe inside a clay ball the size of your fist.

It was the perfect medium for transporting information to new worlds. And perfect for smuggling rhythm. The Indians refused to sell it.

"Janey, who got the Indian property when your father died?"

"Me," said Janey. "I go there and work on quilts sometimes."

My house made the harumphing, throat-clearing noise that it used when it wanted to get my attention. Whatever it was could wait.

"Well, Georgia wants it," I continued. "For the clay. This thing that happens to you is not a mental disease. You don't need to be in an institution."

"Maybe yes and maybe no," she said with a smile—as rational a smile as I've ever seen. "But Georgia. I love Georgia. But something inside her, something that's scared, that's hungry.

That could be what wants me to go away. It's a little cockroach, peeking in and out of her honor-vine."

"I can see that plain enough in the real world, Janey," I said.

Janey took back the legal plastic. The light coming in through the window flickered, as if a large object had just crossed the face of the old sun. I figured it was Sarah, playing with her clouds. The house made the harumphing noise again.

"Clay," said Janey.

A human voice, raised in a vaguely familiar cry, came from somewhere. I looked around. The house opened the door, and gave a great, long throat-clearing, like some put-upon, extremely proper English butler. Janey and I started outside. Halfway across the living room, I remembered where I'd heard that cry before: the Indian games at Gathering. A war whoop.

"How curious," said Janey, stepping through the doorway, looking up into the ice-blue Candle sky.

I realized what Thomas had meant when he said that the Indians would help him get some rhythm.

There were about fifty canoes, each with two warriors paddling on either side, making their way through the afternoon sky, heading east. They were two or three hundred feet off the ground, navigating over swells and buffets in the atmosphere as if they were traversing a lake. A hundred Indians in the sky.

Thomas had raised a war party. The first to be seen on Candle in a hundred years. Tomorrow's *Cold Truth* would be a hell of a read.

I began to realize how the original settlers must have felt when they saw the sight for the first time. I felt a bit of it myself. I'd never seen so many canoes together before. It was wonder. Awe. And, if they were headed for *you*, fear.

I knew who would soon be feeling the terror in this case, if he was stupid enough to have gone back to his Bistro and Art Gallery. Yes, he'd be there, certainly, maybe still trying to extract Raej's algorithm from Verna, attempting to contain it. Thomas would have made sure that he was there before bringing the warriors in like this.

After the canoes had sailed farther east a bit, I could see some of their occupants. There was Thomas, near the lead, with another Indian in the canoe. Without Raej, he had to resort to the two-man traveling mode. He was paddling intensely, too far away for me to make out the expression on his face. But I knew that if I were Bently, I would run, I would hide, I would do anything to get away from him, to keep from looking into that tattooed Wanderer's face, into those tumbling-dice eyes that were rolling out my future.

3

What I haven't told you yet is what I do know about Thomas and Janey. They grew up together, before Thomas forsook Jackson for Doom, and then to become a Wanderer for his mother's people. Thomas's father, Jeremiah Fall, and Janey's mother, Margaret Dillard, were also close as kids. In fact, most everybody assumed that they would marry—which they *did*, only to different people: Margaret to Rex Calhoun, and Jeremiah to Metay-andi, Sun-sister of Doom. Some said Margaret Dillard Calhoun regretted her choice until her dying day, that Jeremiah had offered and she'd refused, settling instead for the security of a Calhoun. I never found out what the truth was. By the time they netted me down from out of the starry sky, Jeremiah and Metay-andi's son Thomas had finished his training with his uncle, Herbert Sandle, and was the Wanderer of Doom.

I actually met Janey first, when I decided to buy out the *Cold Truth*. The Calhouns owned a part share in the name—the newspaper had stopped publishing years ago, done in by the Jackson *Clarion*, which was in turn bought out and put under by the Westnet *Daily Local Editions*. Damned daily locals were run by unsupervised halfsents and printed month-old news and whatever line the local elite fed them. They destroyed many a good planetary paper. I was still fighting Candle's, ad dollar by ad dollar. Anyway, I would have handled the whole thing through a lawyer, but Georgia balked when she found out that I was a transmission. So I had to talk personally to Wrenny and Janey and convince them what a nice guy I was.

The money wasn't a problem. The "me" that remained after my copy was broadcast into space left about two thousand dollars in a trust fund for me when he died. When *I* died. In 2107. The principal grew substantially in five hundred years. I could probably buy the Calhouns out completely, if I'd wanted to. I am rich by *Earth* standards. But all I wanted was the paper—and I was determined to get it.

I thought Janey was nice enough when I first met her, if a bit flighty and difficult to get a handle on what with the quaint images that interlaced her speech. She reminded me of spring in Missouri. I told her I was interested in making a real newspaper for Candle, not just a PR sheet for Jackson. She said that if I really wanted to cover all the happenings, I should get to know the Wanderers, particularly Doom's Wanderer.

I was lucky. It was near Gathering time, and Thomas was back. I took him out for a beer. And began a long friendship. I am a pretty lonely fellow when you get right down to it, and there was something similar in Thomas. Both of us did not *quite* belong to our chosen culture, and never could, no matter what we tried. Thomas had renounced just about all the Westpac upbringing he could. But he never could forget the English language—or Janey Calhoun.

At first, I thought it was love . . . then when I found out about the rhythm Thomas smuggled in for her, I figured it was a parasitic relationship, sex for drugs, that sort of thing. But Thomas could find somebody to screw for much less trouble than that, and the more you got to know Janey, the less you could believe she was that sort of woman. Sometimes I figured that all Thomas wanted to feel for Janey was brotherly love—sometimes I just couldn't tell. But Thomas always came back, year after year, to bring Janey her drug.

I knew, in a vague way, that there was some factor I was missing, something that was present between them that I didn't understand. I always watched them carefully whenever I was with them, trying to puzzle it out. One thing was clear to me: Thomas was often tender with her, but sometimes he was brusque—like the way he'd been determined to go to Doom first, this morning, instead of going directly to her. I believed Thomas was fighting a war in himself over his feelings for Janey.

She was a part of everything he'd given up: arrogant, democratic Western society, animated with the frenetic energy of an electrified corpse, moving with only material purpose, containing no soul. But she was *also* just Janey Calhoun, who had somehow come into an uncontrollable sickness—or power—which Thomas was uniquely suited to help her understand and direct. He was a Wanderer; he spent most of his life journeying through the true world. He also went everywhere in the real world, and knew where to get his hands on the best rhythm in or out of the Territory.

Like I said, until I saw Georgia dripping like a melting wax figurine, and started getting all squishy myself, I didn't really understand what the rhythm was *for.* People who got jangled with rhythm didn't exactly use the drug for medicinal purposes. Rhythm's overseer program exists to see that the copied human algorithm finds ways of making its host happy if it knows what's good for it. The better quality the rhythm, the longer it lives, and the fewer side effects you feel from its death. But it always dies, from the feedback and the wear and tear.

As far as I could tell, for Janey, the rhythm didn't provide the direct cause-and-effect link between cerebral cortex and pleasure center that usually established itself in dancers. It didn't give her multiple mental orgasms, like it did for the tease dancers, or let her experience getting to the top of Mount Everest without the climbing, like it did for the exotic dancers and armchair travelers. The drug just gave her some very complex, organized process to hang on to. It kept her from generalizing, from spilling out of herself and affecting the world around her. Well, let's call a spade a spade: it kept her from turning all of us into primordial goo, is what it did.

So it was this strange love-need relationship between Janey and Thomas that was driving the desire that pushed the Indian canoes toward Bently's place. It was this bond that was about to start a war that could maybe inflame the whole Territory.

"Rain clouds, black with thunder," Janey said. "Red heart flames burning in them like lightning."

"The Indians are on the warpath," I said. "I have to cover this for the paper, but you have to stay here, Janey."

She wasn't paying attention, but kept looking up.

"Thomas," she whispered. She started to follow the canoes. I could feel something soften inside me, and I don't mean emotionally.

"No, Janey. I promised I'd keep you safe. You can't do anything about it."

As a matter of fact, I was thinking just what Janey *could* do about it. I pictured men and buildings melting, streaming away, sloughing into nothingness. Maybe after a critical mass was reached, the whole thing would keep going by itself. Reality unraveling. Jackson would melt, untwist to chaos, then Doom, then maybe all of Candle. Then maybe the galaxy. Maybe *everything*.

"If you follow, and get upset—and you *will* get upset—you may end up killing a lot more people than just that one man."

I could see that she agreed, but she was pretty unsettled right then. I resolved to get her inside my house and then to get the hell out of there. Janey clenched her fist, and then seemed to clench her whole body, struggling to stay in control. I bundled her in through the door.

The house obliged me by opaquing the windows. Janey sat on the couch, her jaw held too tightly to speak. The house rolled in a serving tray with water, some fruit, and what looked suspiciously like old-time smelling salts, though I couldn't imagine where the house might have gotten them. Janey reached for the water, and, with an effort, brought the glass to her mouth without spilling and drank half of the contents down.

"Promise me you'll stay," I said.

"Yes, all right," she said, with strain in her voice.

I kissed her on the forehead and started to go.

"Will."

I turned.

"Take care of Thomas. Help him get Raej back. Raej is more important than I am."

"I'll do what I can," I said, and left.

Other people were headed in the same direction as I turned my hover onto a main street. Lots of people were running down the sidewalks, and a couple of hovers passed me at breakneck speed. I popped up my notebook and activated my memory bank on the run. I was a little worried, because even the enhanced human mind can't store, pixel for pixel, too many hours' worth of stuff, and I hadn't dumped this morning's little encounter when I went by the office. It's not like I would be putting it in the paper, after all.

Jackson is a pretty town at sunset. The streets catch the red and shine like bloody roped silver. They are made of a matrix of silk, clumped together in unbroken lines, so that, to the touch, they feel like smooth, steel-hard corduroy. This texture causes a striated reflection that sparks and flashes as your position changes relative to it. The blood colors in the wood and stone of the buildings also reflect the sunlight, and everything glows with subtle gradations of red, as if all the buildings were flasks full of a fine cabernet sauvignon, and the streets ran with wine.

The sun burned bloody behind me in the western sky. I could picture Bently, hearing whoops and cries, straining to look into the sun, nearly burning his eyes out, seeing nothing but red brightness. Then *something*. A speck. Specks. Moving with deliberation, moving toward *him*. Indians, coming down from the sky. Then maybe they'd hear the hum of atlatl spears streaking in his direction.

I heard a muffled explosion off to the west, crackling through the late autumn air and echoing among the buildings—either gunfire or an atlatl missile-spear. Somebody was using powerful ammunition, whichever it was. More explosions.

I flipped the emergency manual override under my hover's dash to escape the town's speed damper. I'd just explain that I was chasing wild Indians, if I got caught and had to go to traffic court. I gunned the rotors and was at practically a ninety-degree tilt, roaring east down the silken streets. I saw the plume of smoke five or six blocks before I got there.

Bently's Gallery and Bistro was gutted. Firelight flickered through a broken window, where a Closed sign hung on one string and twisted about in the updraft from the heat inside. The outside wall was blackened with several six-foot circles where atlatl spears had hit and exploded. There were many blast holes in the ground nearby, and a few spear fragments. A crowd was gathered around the gallery's entrance, in a rough semicircle.

It looked at first like they were performing some religious ritual, but when I got there, I saw what they were looking at. Paintings, sculptures, one of Janey's quilts, all lay outside in a big pile. I wondered for a moment what the criteria were for saving a piece. Indians, I knew, had a strange aesthetic. But apparently they'd just dragged everything out.

Some of the people were picking through the items. I didn't worry too much about anything getting stolen. Not on Candle. It seemed like when we went in for crime, we did it on a grand scale, or not at all.

One man had his back to the gallery contents and was looking up into the western sky, his whole body shaking with rage.

"Fucking red cocksuckers!" he said, over and over.

A woman, nearby, was crying hysterically. A couple of other ladies, older, were not helping matters by trying to get her to tell them what she'd seen. What was more ominous to me were several clumps of three or four people talking in low voices. I looked at their faces, and didn't see just surprise and bewilderment, but active hate. And two words permeated the crowd, worming their way through the afternoon as voice after voice spoke them: *Indian massacre*.

I ran past the citizens of Jackson, around to the side of the building, and into the Bistro entrance. There was a low crying echoing through the rooms, punctuated by an occasional shriek. The house halfsent was burning to death. I found Verna, stretched out on a long table, her chest clotted with blood, her body stiff as a board, dead for hours. I felt the wooden door to the gallery: hot, the edges beginning to darken.

"House," I said, not having much hope that the halfsent was still coherent. "Is there anybody else in here?"

"Oh, God, to end this way," whispered a voice. "Flames, flames, licking my wounds, burning up my life blood."

Christ, I thought, he's got one of those poet amalgams for a housekeeper. A very bad poet.

"Where is Kem Bently, House?"

"Gone, everyone gone, taken by men, their skin like flame, flame in their eyes, burning me, burning. O captain, my captain. You are gone. Your words, your touch."

I wondered, briefly, exactly what kind of relationship Bently had had with his bistro and gallery. Then the house let out a bloody, unaffected scream, and all was silent.

Bently and his helpers, I figured, were probably on their way to Doom, trussed up in the floor of a dugout canoe. Unless Thomas had gotten the rhythm back. Then they might be dead. If not, they might wish they'd burned with the gallery; Mississippian Indians had the quaint custom of torturing their war prisoners. I got the hell out of the dead bistro.

And ran right into Mayor Oldfrunon, Sheriff Marquez, and Unit One of the Jackson Fire Brigade and Rescue Service. The big fire hover circled overhead, like a huge, inverted dragonfly, spraying water from its splayed legs down onto the gallery roof, which was rimmed with the blue-hot sheen of burning shingles.

"See anybody in there?" said Janet Kreel, our fire chief. She looked very much like she wanted to dart in and save someone. Firefighters didn't get to do much of that around here, what with the spark-proof polymer coatings on buildings nowadays. It usually took a concerted, intelligent effort to get a whole structure burning. The Indians had done a thorough job.

"I saw a woman; she's already dead. The house said there was nobody else."

Nevertheless, Kreel was set to lead a group in with her for a quick search, when something—probably alcohol—exploded, sending a blast of scorching air rushing over us, and setting whatever wasn't already on fire ablaze.

"Figuring out how Indians think is as hard as whistling when your spit's froze, but *damn*. Just *look* at this," said Frank Oldfrunon, as we watched the last of the roof trusses crash into the blaze below it. "The people who live around here are really worked up about it. They want blood, I can tell you."

"I figure it was a private matter between Bently and the Mississippians," I said.

Oldfrunon looked at me for a long moment. "That's what you figure, huh?"

"You know I can't leave it at that," said Nestor Marquez. "There's laws. I've got to answer to those people."

There was an even bigger crowd now than before. Marquez had two of his deputies keeping the crowd back and the other standing guard over the pile of artwork, putting out the occasional spark that landed on the pieces. The sides of the structure fell inward, creating a big bonfire centered about where Verna's body had been. I popped up my tell-tales. I was still getting all of this banked, with about fifteen percent storage space left.

"I'm too old to fight a war," said Oldfrunon. "Guess we'll just have to stop it before it starts."

"Nobody wants war," said a voice behind us, rich and deep, like strong Colombian coffee. "The Clerisy is at your disposal, Frank. We'll be happy to do all that we can."

I knew without turning that it was Gerabaldo Corazon, the Directing Priest of the local Clerisy indwelling. I was sometimes amazed at how quickly Corazon turned up when there was some way for the Clerisy to worm its way into a situation. He was a man with such a bright and shining end burning before him that it blinded him to the means he might use to achieve it—a potent combination of old-time Bolshevik and Jesuit. But I didn't necessarily disagree with his interests; if it hadn't been for Clerisy pressure a few years back, we transmissions might still be headed out toward the Milky Way's long arm.

The Clerisy was not officially a part of Westpac, though

plenty of Westpac citizens, including about a third of Jackson's population, were Cell members. Oldfrunon didn't draw a great deal of his political support from that one third.

"Baldy, so help me, if the Clerisy makes this situation any worse than it already is, I'll personally kick your priestly ass," said Oldfrunon, without even turning around.

Corazon and Oldfrunon hated each other from way back. I never heard what specific atrocities they'd committed against one another, but I knew what caused the general mistrust: Frank Oldfrunon was a territorial expansionist from the cradle. As far as he was concerned, Earth was like the dead heartwood at the center of a tree. Only the outer cambium of humanity was truly doing anything worthwhile to keep the tree alive, and to *stay* alive, we had to keep growing.

On the other hand, allegedly carved into the heart of every priest of the Church of Liberation and Global Justice was a fervent desire that we direct our efforts (and our cash flow) *inward*, toward social justice and spiritual wholeness (overseen by the Clerisy, of course). They thought it was a big mistake that we had ever left Earth in the first place, and a really big mistake that we ever had any dealings with Mississippian Indians.

"We only want to help," said Corazon evenly. "But just remember, Frank, a good percentage of Jackson belongs to the Church. And poor Mr. Bently was one of them. People saw the Indians drag him away kicking and screaming. That is, before they hit him over the head with a tomahawk."

Corazon's tone didn't change as he recounted the Indian actions.

"At least he got one of them before they got him," Corazon said, growing dramatic at the end, his voice hinting at the political consequences.

"What?" I said. "An Indian was killed?"

"Bently and the others that were with him shot one before they were overrun. Franz Wasal—he's a lay-reader for us and he owns that hover repair place across the street—he saw it all."

"I'll want to talk to him," said Nestor Marquez. "But I think we all know what I need to do next."

"Goddammit," said Oldfrunon. "I'm going with you."

"As will I," said Corazon. "Mr. Bently is, after all, one of my flock."

Marquez looked at them both for a moment. His mind was none too fast, and his police blotter had as much spice to it as plain tofu, but Nestor had a notion about what he'd be up against, and that it wasn't just a matter of law and order anymore.

"All right," he finally said.

"You're sure as hell not going to exclude the press," I said. "I'll get there one way or another, you know."

"Jesus fucking Christ," said Marquez, "all right."

He called up his hover, and we were in the air in ten minutes. I flicked off my memory bank to conserve space, figuring I could just write things down until I needed to switch back on. I spent most of the flight over to Doom looking for a pen, cursing myself for letting my software make me lazy and forgetful. Candle's below-zero night cold set in as the sun went down, and it was pitch dark when we got to Doom—without hope of brightening, because Candle has no moon. I really missed the parka I had given Janey. Electric underwear is no substitute for a good down jacket.

Doom is the oddest combination of stone-age and space-age clutter you could ever see. Most of the culture dates back to the 1200s, when the Mississippians first figured out the old faster-than-light trick, and took to the stars *en masse*. But they haven't been slow to assimilate whatever Westpac artifacts they've since found useful or admirable, either.

So there were dirt-floor wigwams with Westnet dishes on them. There were religious sunpoles at every corner, with carvings of snakes and that ubiquitous hand with the eye in its palm, proclaiming the divinity of their priest-king class—and doubling as supports for 500-watt arc streetlamps.

Beside most of the wigwams, wrapped up in worn skins and rags against the cold, working by porchlight or lantern, men and women burnished canoes with battery-driven polishers, repaired wigwams with hammer and nail, carried water in plastic jugs. They did not look up as we passed them, took no notice of us as all, as befitted their classes. Because, of course, they were stinkards and slaves.

If you want to picture it all, think of ancient Egypt, with the Jews milling about doing the dirty work, while the pharaohs are inside watching television.

"Exploiting despots," muttered Corazon. "History will deal with them one day."

What did you say to this? The Clerisy was completely opposed to dealing with a culture with indigenous slavery, and the Mississippian Indians had had a slave class since before they all left Earth—a century before Columbus had even arrived in North America. So why doesn't Westpac, in its infinite wisdom, mow down the masters, free the slaves, and put all the survivors on special reservations to keep them from ever keeping human chattel again? Didn't we try something like that *before*? Goddammit, I didn't like slavery any better than Baldy Corazon.

And you're wondering why Thomas Fall was all-fire mad about his chocalaca, Raej, being made into a rhythm slave, when he positively supports slavery among his own people? All I can say is that *Thomas* didn't own any slaves. And a rhythm program is much more complete than a halfsent program. You fully experience your bondage, and you never sleep, never have a free moment. You work for your host every *second* of your sorry existence. Being copied for rhythm use is a fate not even an Indian Noble would wish on a stinkard. And believe me, most of them despise stinkards.

"I suppose the best chance of finding Bently will be in the Gathering Hall," I said.

When we got there, I was pretty sure I'd been right. There was a guard at the entrance—armed with atlatls. The spears that were notched into the throwing arms were not ceremonial, however, but were those quaint guided missiles the Indians had adopted for weapons since their first contact with Westpac civilization.

A council fire's smoke rose thickly from the roof hole. Wedoweeta, the Trickster—my favorite constellation—shimmered in and out of existence as the smoke roiled upward, dimming and blotting out a vertical swath of stars. Bet you're having a laugh today, old boy, I thought, then wondered if the coyote was a male or female, or both. Thomas had pointed it out to me, years ago, but I never asked him about the gender. Do males or females love strife more? I wondered. Because strife was what we were going to get, and I suspected that the smoke wafting across the twinkling stars was a kind of laughter at human folly.

From inside the Gathering Hall came a shriek of complete terror.

Indian cries, male and female, competed with the scream, as if they were empathetically suffering some horrible torture along with their victim, or urging him on in the expression of pain.

"*Do* something, Sheriff," said Corazon.

Marquez stiffened his shoulders, and walked forward. The three braves guarding the entrance came to alert. When Marquez got five feet or so away from them, they swung their atlatls around, aiming straight at his midsection. Even Nestor Marquez figured out mighty quickly that these Indians weren't bluffing. He backed off.

"I have a semiautomatic in the hover," he said, as if it were a statement of fact completely unconnected with our present circumstances.

"Not an option," said Oldfrunon.

"A man is being tortured to death in there," said Corazon. "I should think your wonderful Westpac technology would give you something you could use to put a stop to it."

"Stun fields. They use them on Earth to stop rioting and such," said Marquez.

"Well?"

"Don't have one."

Another scream from inside, with accompaniment.

I was beginning to put two and two together.

"Gentlemen," I said, and walked toward the guards.

They lowered their atlatls for me. I popped up a phrase book I'd programmed in with my other reporter peripherals just in case I'd need it, but, even unassisted, my Loosa wasn't too shabby. Granted, Loosa was just a trade pidgin, but Indians on a hundred worlds conversed, argued, and—when it failed them—went to war using it. Come to think of it, maybe Loosa's inadequacies were to blame for all the warring Mississippians seemed to do. Whatever the case, it got me through the guards.

"You know me," I said to one that I recognized, Laylay Potter. He'd been the other brave I'd seen in the canoe with Thomas during the attack. "I'm Thomas the Wanderer's friend. Let me through."

They debated it a moment, then motioned me past them, closing behind me quickly so that none of the others could come. Laylay followed me in. I was in a little alcove, with a thick, woolly skin hanging over the door to the main room. Around its edges came the yellow flicker of bright firelight. The entranceway to the outside had no door, but the alcove was hot. It had to be sweltering inside the Gathering Hall.

"I'll get Thomas," Laylay said, and went behind a corner of the skin-door.

"Well," I said, as Thomas pulled the skin aside and stepped into the alcove. "So."

Thomas was stripped to the waist. He wore pants made of some sort of leather, and moccasins. His hair was matted with sweat and something darker than sweat trickled down his face, through the tangle of tattoos. His chest was covered with curves and whorls of red welts, accented by thin ink lines down their centers. These were new tattoos.

"We don't go to war very often anymore," he said. "So everybody's getting highly decorated."

"So that's what the screaming is about."

"It hurts."

Thomas seemed to fill the alcove, and for a moment I was sure he was using up all my air. I was gasping for breath. Then I realized it was smoke from the Gathering Hall interior leaking through.

"Just what are you burning in there?"

"No English for it. Sipsi. Makes you see the future."

"Uh huh."

Thomas looked past me, into the night. "Marquez. Politicians?"

"Oldfrunon's here trying to stop a war; Corazon's here trying to start one."

"How's Janey?"

I looked carefully at my friend before answering. Even half-jangled, he had a sort of magnetism to him, a patina of mystery and, at the same time, weary cynicism, as if coatings of dust from all those worlds he'd visited had built up on him, layer upon layer, filling the wrinkles of his skin with a network of experience, working itself in, under, as full of order and information as the tattoos which covered most of his body. But the planet dirt, the dust he picked up between the stars, it all went deeper, anchoring into his soul, like lichen into rock, transforming him from a man—albeit a man between peoples, a natural outcast, but a man nonetheless—into some sort of statement, some long sentence the universe was trying to say. What do *you* say to such a creature? What does it mean to be its friend?

And, at the same time, he was also just Thomas Fall, who loved a woman in a way I did not understand, maybe could not understand. A woman I, too, perhaps loved. I didn't even know if he'd ever slept with her, or if he even wanted to. All I really knew was that he and I shared an easy manner when we were with one another, that I did not have to guard my thoughts so much when I was with him and, I believed, that he felt the same way toward me—so much so that he'd shared his greatest secret and his greatest weakness, this attachment of his to Janey Calhoun. I knew that he was confident that I wouldn't betray him, and that, if I couldn't go along with the course he had decided to follow, I wouldn't use our friendship as a weapon against him.

"Janey," I said, "needs some rhythm."

"I know," said Thomas quietly. "Come inside."

The Gathering Hall was big, even by settler standards. It was about a hundred yards long, fifty wide, and had a ceiling that stretched at least three stories above us. Firepots were burning at each corner, and a huge fire in the middle of the floor, with five men and women continually feeding it with branches and seeding in a gravelly stuff which I figured was sipsi. The Indians used this place for games and for audiences with the Suns, the ruling class, who were, in addition to the heads of state, also the supreme court.

And once a year, at this time, there was the Gathering, when the Wanderer returned from the sky with news and stories of all the scattered clans. Everybody came, ate, drank, and listened: slaves, stinkards, Honored People, Nobles, and Suns alike. I'd attended several in my time. But what was going on now in the Hall was no Gathering.

I imagine that for Gerabaldo Corazon it would have been a vision of Hell—if he actually believed in such a place. As far as I could tell, most of the priests in the Clerisy held the turnings of history and the ethical evolution of man as their Deity. They didn't mention God much. Well, the Indians believed in a personal God, all right. One that occasionally enjoyed human sacrifices.

Most of the Indians sat in unkempt rows around the central fire. Directly in front of the fire, the tattooing ceremony was taking place, augmented by a kind of drunken dancing by the men who were the next in line. Working themselves up to face the pain, I supposed. They were all screaming as if they were being tattooed right along with the lucky Indian who actually *was* being tattooed.

Next to the tattoo ceremony was a large pyre, on which rested what looked like a body wrapped all in cloth patterned with brilliant reds and purples. The Indian who was killed today. I clicked on my memory bank. The room was contrasty as hell, with brilliant purples and reds, and deep, velvety blacks. You had to be there. I could memory bank it all, but there was no way I could reproduce the full range of lights and shadows in that room. Nevertheless, no journalist that I knew of had ever gotten a glimpse of this ceremony, or of Indians in this frame of mind, so I had to try.

All over the floor, particularly up next to the walls, tattooed braves lounged, some still moving, some passed out, some intertwined with women or with one another. The air was stiflingly hot, and full of the sweetish sipsi odor.

"I've been looking into the future," Thomas said, leading me towards the far corner of the Hall. "No matter what road I look down, I see trouble ahead, stretching across the horizon, eating its way toward us like gangrene."

I felt like I was walking down a set of stairs where each step was of a different height; I stumbled, caught myself, coughed. A purplish-red mist came out of my throat and formed itself into clouds before my face. It was moving, trying to form into images, faces. Goddamn sipsi, I thought, I don't *want* to know *my* future. I hurried through it, dispersing it with my hands.

Thomas laughed, as if he'd read my thoughts. Or maybe I'd spoken it aloud. Hard to remember, and my memory bank was recording things just as subjectively as I saw them.

"Well, even gods can have bad days," Thomas said, pointing to the man on the pyre. "The Great Sun went up against a machine gun."

"Your uncle?"

"Yes. He insisted on leading the attack. Died like a warrior. I wish I'd known him better."

"Who's in charge?"

"Nobody, until Sun-sister Metay-andi decides on a successor from among her children."

Succession is maternal among the Indians at Doom. If the Great Sun dies while his mother is alive, she chooses from among his brothers. If she's dead, his eldest sister chooses from her male children.

I looked hard at Thomas, put my hand on his shoulder, even though it made him flinch in pain.

"What do you see in the future, Thomas Fall?"

He kept walking.

"I don't want it," he said. "All I wanted was to get Raej back and get Janey her rhythm—then tell my stories and go back out."

"But you used your status to get what you wanted."

"I didn't see any other way. Goddammit, I'd have done the same if it were you. You don't let your friends be made into slaves. You fight. You sell your soul if you have to."

As he said this, he walked ahead, stopping at a large sack of potatoes in the corner. The sack stirred and I realized it was actually Bently. He looked at Thomas, moaned, and sat up. His hands were bound behind him.

"Stand up," said Thomas.

Bently struggled to his feet.

"Shit," I said.

Bently wasn't going anywhere. The backs of his ankles had been pierced and thongs of leather run around his Achilles tendon. One was tied off to one corner of the Hall, one to the other. If Bently moved much more than a foot, he would hamstring himself.

"Remembered anything new, Kem Bently?" said Thomas, looking directly at the trembling man.

"I couldn't get it out of Verna," Bently said, then began to whimper. "I told you; I told you. Ask Shed and Hank."

"Shed and Hank can't tell me. I saw the slurper in your gallery," said Thomas. "And some very advanced transmission equipment. I've only seen stuff like that once before. Where did you send my rhythm?"

"Shed and Hank," said Bently. His eyes widened. I guessed that he was talking about the two goons who helped him jump us. Bently was fighting his facial muscles, which were trying to twist into a sickened grin. "They're dead, aren't they?"

Thomas gave Bently a sharp push backward. He stumbled, and cried out in pain as his tendon came up against a thong. Thomas stalked away. I gave Bently a helpless shrug and followed Thomas.

"Kind of cruel and unusual, don't you think," I said.

"I didn't string him that way. They'd already done it when I got here."

"And Shed and Hank?"

"They're tied up in my house, with a friend of mine guarding them from . . . accidents like what happened to Bently. They don't know anything."

"Things are kind of getting out of hand," I said.

Thomas didn't reply, and the smoke was getting impossibly thick. After a moment, I couldn't even see Thomas in front of me. The smoke was billowing now, hanging in thick clouds like bloated sacs of toxin. I hurried to catch up. But my legs were melting, just like they had in Janey's sewing room. I flailed about, trying to catch something, to stop my fall. Indians crowded around me, their bodies slick with sweat, and I reached out to them, but my hands slipped away down their arms. I could feel the network of tattoos covering their bodies, and the tattoos were not drawings, but etched things, dug *into* the skin. It was like running your thumb over an old coin, but the ridges were not sharp enough, the skin-crevasses not wide enough, for even my fingernails to get a hold. I fell past them, into the mist, a long, long way. Then I slowed down, though still falling. A face formed in the red clouds, a woman's face. Sarah. She did not speak, but smiled at me wanly, like she had the day we parted. Her hair mussed, her lips sipsi-red from my kiss. She stepped into the transmission chamber. And stepped out again, copied, broadcast. Now it was my turn. Just a moment, the space of a breath, and we'd be together again. Like two lovers who pause at the edge of a pond, admire their reflections, then walk away to live the rest of their lives. But the *reflections* linger, like a rainbowed film of oil on the water. Until one of them is washed away. And the other finds that his soul is, in the end, just tar-black oil without her. Looking back, it was all so unutterably sad.

Then, gently, the floor came up to meet me. A strong arm steadied me. The red mist abated, but did not clear.

"Did you see the future, Will James?" asked Thomas.

I steadied myself, shook my head.

"No, the past," I said. "How do I get out of here?"

4

My memory bank filled up in the middle of the most secret and sacred ceremony that an Indian Wanderer is empowered to perform, which is just as well, because I would just as soon have torn up the Press Amendment to the Westpac Constitution than run pictures of the Calling of the Chocalaca, Raej, without permission.

But I can tell you about it.

We'd left through a back door, and, for all I knew at the time, Oldfrunon, Marquez, and Corazon were still at the Gathering Hall entrance, posturing and twiddling their thumbs. Thomas had a house which remained unoccupied most of the year. But when Gathering time came around, everybody in Doom pitched in to fix it up nicely, and stock it with provisions. Next to the house was a small, tightly built hut which covered a little outcropping of Loosa clay, and that was where we headed.

Thomas sat on a rough-hewn bench in the center of the hut, rolling a bit of kiln-baked clay between his palms, talking to himself in some Loosa-variant that I could not follow. It was nearing midnight and getting toward that piss-freezing point I mentioned. I stamped about, trying to get up the courage to go outside, into the biting wind, to empty my bladder before it was too late. Finally, I went. I dropped the waistband of my long underwear just low enough and long enough to do my business.

I wondered about the possibilities of frostbite, and pissed out onto the ground full of Loosa clay.

This clay was somehow necessary for the chocalacas' existence, and I knew enough about Wanderers to know that their chocalaca was essential to traveling alone, analogous somehow with the huge computers that starship captains were intimately linked with on their voyages through the true world. To lose your chocalaca in flight meant death, as surely as a computer malfunction would strand a ship in deep space, with nothing to do but drift until the air ran out.

In fact, *all* of the worlds the Indians settled on have substantial clay deposits. They couldn't have their solitary Wanderers without it. Sure, the Indians could travel without chocalacas, in a two-man canoe, with one man keeping up a ritual chant about the canoe's and its passengers' existence, and the other doing the mental work of forging *ahead*. That was how they got off Earth in the first place, according to legend. But it took a two-man canoe months to travel the same distance that a starship could travel in weeks—and that a Wanderer and his chocalaca could cover in a day. Some say that the chocalacas were always in the clay, that they, in some way, *were* the clay. Others said that they were a subconscious construct of collective Indian society. Not even the Wanderers were sure what was the truth.

One thing was certain: Westpac scientists had noticed, in a big way, that Wanderers were the fastest thing around, and that this was somehow related to the clay. Nobody had quite figured out how it worked yet, but clay speculation was the hottest game on the commodities market. The stuff was too expensive to use for bulk transporting of halfsents, but those few settlers who owned clay knew it wouldn't be long until it would be in big demand, and worth even more. There was one thing (not spoken of, but always a consideration) that it *presently* paid to ship impressed in Loosa clay: rhythm.

So settlers greatly resented the fact that, for all practical purposes, Indians owned all the clay. Back when everybody was first meeting each other, it hadn't mattered so much. We were all going to be friends, Westpac was going to make up for the shabby treatment of all the Native Americans who got left behind in the great exodus, or were, more probably, never invited in the first place. Western culture had progressed in twelve hundred years, discovered certain inalienable rights—and common decency. It took a big gulp, sure, to swallow the slavery thing. But then we found out about the clay.

And Candle was found in the nick of time, and space: 500 light-years from Earth, the nearest substantial clay deposit. The first planet on which Westpac settlers had run into Mississippian Indians, the biggest surprise in Western history. Of course, all this was a hundred years before my time, or three hundred ahead of it, depending on how you look at it.

So Thomas and I inhabited this nick of time, and were notched on old time's stick, standing at the finite meeting point of two infinities, past and future, precisely in the present, precisely and perversely at a logic gate in old time's flow chart, a point of forced decision, filled with prickly consequences. But ain't we always, all of us?

I finished pissing, then came back in, to find the interior of the hut bathed in a blue glow. The air smelled gamy, like I myself did after I'd been out backpacking for three or four days. Thomas finished shaping the clay, and put it back into the pocket from which Verna had taken the other piece. Suddenly, there was a flash that filled the hut, and Raej coalesced in the air around us.

Again I felt that alienness, that otherness, in my mind. A great restlessness, a need to be *out,* turning things over, looking into places. A bear's hunger. But for knowledge, for novelty.

"Chocalacas *eat* experience, don't they?" I asked.

The presence in my head—Raej—growled low and soft. It was gentle mockery, I somehow knew.

"It's a lot more than that," said Thomas, "but even I don't really understand them." Then, his voice in my mind, but not speaking to me, "How have you been, old friend?"

Raej let out a grouchy growl in reply.

"Thank you for coming back to me, after what I've done."
Raej didn't answer, as if the apology were completely un-

necessary. After a moment, a huge roar filled the hut, and I felt an old anger in my mind, a hatred of something silver-red, snakelike, but nearly transparent, empty—yet intelligent. Then Raej's flame died down and I felt him pull away from my mind like a great wave going back out to sea.

"What was that *thing* he's so mad at?" I asked.

"Don't know," said Thomas. "I know he hates that thing, whatever it is."

Thomas closed his hand around the bit of clay in his pocket, and closed his eyes, as if he were making a promise to himself never to lose it again.

"Now we have to get back the ghost of you that was stolen."

We walked back out, into the night, to try one more time to get Kem Bently to tell us what he'd done with the copy of Raej.

Halfway to the Gathering Hall, Nestor Marquez stepped from the shadows, his gun in hand. Behind him stood Oldfrunon and Corazon. Oldfrunon looked pained; Corazon looked pleased.

"Thomas Fall, you are under arrest for abduction and suspicion of murder," said Marquez. "And don't try anything with that pet of yours or I'll shoot."

Thomas just smiled. "I don't suppose I could tell you that I've renounced my Westpac citizenship," he said.

"Sorry, Thomas," said Oldfrunon. "Just checked the records. You never did anything legal about your citizenship."

"So, the half-breed is the only one you can arrest in all of Doom," said Thomas. "Well, you got your man."

We went to the hover. Marquez made no attempt to hide our exit from the slaves who were still out and about. Marquez and Thomas sat in the backseat of the hover. Marquez kept his rifle on Thomas and let the hover's computer drive. I sat across from Thomas.

"This is bad, isn't it?" I said.

"They know where I am," said Thomas. "Metay-andi chooses at dawn."

"What the hell are you talking about?" said Marquez.

"What you've got here," I said, "is the most likely successor to the Great Sun. The old man was killed this afternoon."

It took a second for this to sink in. But everybody knew what it meant. The priest-king of Doom wasn't just a leader, he was brother to the stars. The Indians *worshiped* the stars.

"Damn," said Frank Oldfrunon. "God damn."

Corazon was squirming around in the front seat, agitated as hell. All of this was just confirming what the Clerisy had been saying about Indians all along.

"Sheriff, I think you'd better have a force ready in the morning," said Corazon. "An armed force. To prevent a slaughter, a massacre."

"Or start one," said Oldfrunon.

Everyone was quiet while the hover sailed unerringly down the silk road to the Jackson jail. After Marquez got Thomas locked up, he was less concerned about Raej making an appearance and maybe scaring him enough to make him drop his gun. What he should have been afraid of was the chocalaca burning out his brain. But evidently Thomas had decided non-resistance was the way to go for the moment.

I was allowed to sit in the hall where Thomas's cell was. Hell, Nestor Marquez was barely noticing my presence at that point. He was a lot more concerned with getting the word out that the Indians were coming in the morning. He did this most effectively.

I picked up the day's edition of the Candle *Cold Truth* in Marquez's office and looked it over. Fluff and wire stories. Deadline for the *Cold Truth* was two o'clock; I ran an afternoon paper. I'd had nothing much that I could report on until midafternoon today, so my little algorithm gleaned what it could from the local halfsents and from the Territorial Wire Service. Halfsents were, well, half-sentient, and never quite got things right, no matter how much information they "knew." And the wire stories would, of necessity, be several weeks old, taken from the computer of whatever tramp freighter was in port at the Docks. The Wire was not actually a wire, of course. More like a packet service.

Oh, I had faith in my algorithm; I'd built it up myself, from specially imported programs made of bits and pieces of a good cross section of the great journalists since the mid-twenty-first century, back when translation first began. It's just that no software (or human being) can massage good stories out of sparse data. And the best data base on Candle, at the moment, was me. Tomorrow's paper, if I lived to put it out, would be a sight more lively and informative.

I went back to sit with Thomas and await the turning of our side of the planet back toward the old, red sun. Thomas wasn't talking much. He dozed occasionally, and awoke more than once with a startled cry. Along about three, Marquez came back. Janey was with him.

Raej flickered into reality for a moment. A blue light filled the half-lit darkness of the jail hallway.

"He's here," said Janey, excitedly.

Marquez pulled his gun.

"Keep that thing away or I'll keep it away for good."

For an instant, Raej flared, like the flash of paper when it hits a fire. Then he subsided, flowed away. Marquez lowered his gun, looked at Thomas suspiciously.

"The security algorithm is monitoring you. I'm just out in the hall, so don't try anything."

"What, and deprive you of your war?" said Thomas.

Marquez muttered some imprecation, then left.

"Why does there have to be a war? Raej is back," said Janey. Then she thought about it a moment. About the stolen rhythm copy. "Oh."

"How are you, Janey?" I asked.

"There was a long, white time at your house. Then I smelled the things your house gave me. Some colors came back."

Janey looked flush and rested. Apparently my dear old house algorithm had done a good job of keeping her calm and comfortable.

Thomas was standing now, leaning out from the bars of his cell, his hand extended.

"Janey."

She raised her hand toward his and his hand encircled her

wrist. A blue spark passed from Thomas to Janey, a faint shimmering of power. Raej was among them, joining them. For a moment I looked at this tableau. You would almost think them a family. Janey's face was radiant; it had an expression of utter bliss. I began to feel embarrassed. What kind of contact had she and I had compared to this complete connection of intellect and emotion that Raej provided Thomas and Janey? How could I have doubted what they really felt for one another? Through Raej, Thomas and Janey were practically one person. I turned and quietly walked away. No one noticed me going. Marquez merely grunted as I passed his desk and went out the door, to stand in the deep cold of Candle's autumn night.

After my eyes got used to the moonless darkness, I could detect a very, very faint glow coming from one of the jail windows that looked out on the town square in which I stood. It was surely Thomas's cell. I thought about going back in, standing watch over Thomas and Janey, as I had before. But what possible business could I have in there now? Thomas no longer needed me. I'd proved indifferent, at best, in taking care of Janey. Christ, I'd almost taken advantage of her while she was in a weakened state. Some friend. And Janey had Thomas and Raej to keep her steady, and to keep the boundary between the true world and the real world solid.

When I was first broadcast, I'd thought: what a wonderful thing to travel to the stars. What was most important, what was essential, was that I'd get to *see* the future with my own eyes. Maybe babies feel this way, tingle with some mute, innate yearning to get *out,* to explore. Then they find that you have to make a living in the out, make a life. At least, that was what I'd found out. Either that, or take a quick look around and then kill yourself.

Because the only way you ever really saw was to *do.* To see, to know, meant to live another day, to figure a way to stay alive and interested. That's all there was to it. But maybe I was not a babe, fresh from the womb of the twenty-first century. Can you yank a man from his culture, from everything that makes him what he is, and still call him a man? What was I contributing today? Nothing. Maybe I was like those cancerous skin cells that, shaved from the body, keep dividing and dividing into undifferentiated masses, useless. Merely a scientific curiosity.

Then there was snow on my nose, my lips, fluttering into my face like moths.

Funny the tricks the mind can play on itself. We humans have a most ingenious little algorithm packed into that gray matter between our ears. I thought I heard a voice. Her voice.

"Hush, Will, hush."

For a moment, I almost believed it. But all it could have been, really, was the sound the wind makes as it flows and ebbs along silent town streets. I stamped my feet against the cold, and went back inside. I stopped at Marquez's desk.

"Let her stay the rest of the night. I'll keep a watch on them."

Marquez scrunched his face up like he was about to deny my request. He looked at me for a long moment, then shrugged.

"You watch them, then," he said.

When I got back, Thomas and Janey were almost exactly as I'd left them.

"What will you do in the morning, Janey, when the Indians come for Thomas?"

"She can come with Raej and me," said Thomas, still looking at Janey intently.

"Do you want to do that, Janey? You may not be able to come back."

"I want to stay with Raej," she said.

"With Raej?"

But almost before the words were out of my mouth, I understood. I *knew*. It wasn't Thomas—or at least it wasn't *mainly* Thomas—whose return Janey awaited each year. Thomas was Janey's friend, yes, just as I was. Raej was something much more. Janey's lover?

Janey turned toward me. She still had that beatific air about her, but there was also a look of determination.

"I want to stay with my father," said Janey. "He always goes away. I want to stay with him for a while. I hardly know him."

I just stood there, in the hallway, for a long time, watching them. So it was not Raej who was the bond between Janey and Thomas. It was Thomas who was the bond, the conduit, for a father's love. And for a daughter's reflection of that love.

Finally, I spoke. "You're half-chocalaca, aren't you, Janey?"

"Yes."

Then Janey smiled at me, as a friend. I don't know if a smile can really accomplish that much, but I felt better. Still awkward, slow to understand, but included in the world she and Thomas shared.

"This will make a great story someday, won't it, Will?" said Janey.

"This is one whale of a story."

So old Maggie Dillard, Janey's mother, hadn't been satisfied with her staid Calhoun husband after all. Perhaps Thomas's father, her old friend Jeremiah Fall, had had something to do with introducing her to her chocalaca lover. What a story! The first human-alien sexual encounter in human history. And the day I printed this story in the *Cold Truth* and betrayed my friends would be the day I hanged myself.

But I got to thinking. The chocalacas had existed among the Indians for centuries by now, since the first exodus, when the Indians arrived on Candle. This was probably not a first. But I'd bet my poetic license that it was a first among Westpac settlers. A half-alien, misunderstood, fighting to find her place in society. That would sell some papers.

"Going to the Indians will solve the commitment problem with Georgia," I said. "But if you stay with them, Georgia gets the clay."

"Georgia's cockroach gets the clay."

"Yes. And maybe Wrenny's got more fight in her than most people give her credit for."

"I'll be happy to get away from that house," she said, very softly. "Even when I have rhythm, it's hard there."

"Raej helps you to control your mind while he's here?" I asked.

"Yes, and Father and Thomas bring me rhythm for when they're gone on their trips."

"But a permanent copy of Raej would be better, now that that's technologically possible?"

"Yes," said Thomas. "Now you know. Don't print it, Will."

I was taken aback and a bit hurt.

"Is that why you never told me?"

Thomas looked at me and smiled. "I always trusted you. It was Raej who didn't want us to tell anyone."

"He told you that?"

"Not exactly. I . . . . *felt* it. Until now. Things are coming to a head, and he probably thinks it's important that someone should know."

"That copy was transmitted from the art gallery to somewhere else on Candle before you got to Bently," I said.

"Something a lot bigger than a mugging in the woods is going on," Thomas said. "Raej probably wants you on our side."

"Or he's just a big old bear who's changed his mind. You don't really know what he *thinks*, do you?—or even if he *does*?"

Thomas's reply was a ritual saying among the Wanderers. He said it in Loosa. As close as I can get in translation and still get any of the multiple meanings is: "Chocalacas think otherwise."

Just before dawn, I called up the *Cold Truth* and dumped as much of my bank as I could over phone lines. All the sheriff's phone had was a standard optical flasher. I spent about twenty minutes transferring, and cleared out around fifty percent of my storage space. The paper's algorithm didn't say much. It was pretty much stunned by the load of information it had to start extracting news from. What I had left in my head was mainly the morning meeting with Bently, which would never make the paper anyway.

Outside, settlers were gathering. I could hear a large group milling around and, unfortunately, the clinking of what I was sure was gun metal. As the sky lightened, I could see that Marquez, whatever his shortcomings, sure could network. No wonder he kept winning his sheriff's position every year by a landslide. It looked like half the people in Jackson were lining the streets nearby, speaking in low voices, passing cups of coffee from hand to hand, the steam rising in the deep chill of Candle's morning. Living silhouettes milled among the shadowy hulks of the statues of their dead ancestors which were interspersed across the town square. Like their ancestors, they were about to meet one of the lost tribes of the Mississippian Indians. It was cold, and Janey still had my parka. I turned my longjohns up full blast.

I have never understood why the Indians of Candle choose to worship its sun. Even at noon, the poor thing reminds me more of an inflamed pimple than a nuclear fire. You can't really look into the sun on Candle for very long—but certainly for longer than you can look into Earth's sun. And it seems to take a long time before you get retinal afterimages. Some days, at sunset, we all look at the swollen red thing going down and a sigh passes through everyone; it's kind of the way you feel when a crushed bug finally pulls its carcass into a crack so that it can die in peace.

But the thing keeps coming back up, day after day. And once again, on this day, the sun rose. I flicked on the memory bank once more.

And the Indians came, sailing across a still sky. Even Sarah seemed to be holding her breath. In the town square, on the pedestal platform of the highest of the statues honoring Candle pioneers, Frank Oldfrunon stood. He stood at the huge greened-bronze feet of old Stephen Calhoun, the first Westpac settler to meet the Indians. When Oldfrunon spoke, I realized that he had ordered Sarah to be still, to funnel and amplify his voice like a megaphone.

"Nobody do anything we'll regret," he said. "Let's wait and hear them out."

"Yeah, like they heard out Kem Bently!" someone yelled. But such was Frank Oldfrunon's presence (and Sarah's dampening of the challenger's words) that nobody moved.

Still the Indians came on.

There were no war cries today. They formed a tight circle above the town square, and one canoe peeled off and came down to where Oldfrunon was standing. One of the Indians in the canoe was Laylay Potter. He gave a great heave, and dumped Bently over the canoe's gunwales. Bently landed in a heap on the stone platform. He tried to get up, couldn't muster the strength, then sat back down, quietly sobbing.

"Give us Thomas Fall," said Laylay. Everyone heard it. "Give us the Great Sun."

Gerabaldo Corazon emerged from the crowd below and climbed up to examine Bently.

Oldfrunon loosened up before our eyes, the old, easygoing bumbler-of-a-mayor seeping back into his body like a spring thaw in ice.

"We can do that," said Oldfrunon. "Seeing as how you've returned our citizen to us. Nestor, bring him out."

Thomas walked out, straight and tall, before Marquez. Marquez had, wordlessly, allowed Janey to remain with Thomas. Maybe I *would* vote for the fellow if he ever came up for election again. Janey was wearing my red parka, which caught the red of the morning sun and seemed to glow. But the glow didn't only come from the parka. I could still feel the presence of Raej between Thomas and Janey, the barely visible flicker, which might have been mistaken for the redness of the parka, the faint trace of ozone in the air, but that could not be mistaken once you knew it.

Marquez had a sidearm, but it was holstered. I followed behind them. I was feeling the effects of lots of running around, and no sleep. The early morning chill sent an ache through my legs and I limped a little. When the Indians saw Thomas, they let out a great whoop.

As Thomas and Janey began to climb the pedestal, the sun rose slightly and painted Stephen Calhoun's granite face a deep red. Corazon stood up when we were halfway up to the platform.

"This man has been mutilated," he said, with a resounding, dramatic calculation.

Sarah amplified his voice through the streets. I felt her recoiling, the sudden dampening of the air about us. But it couldn't be that Sarah was understanding any of this, realizing that she was being manipulated. She has half a mind, the mind of an animal, cunning but not intelligent, mostly emotion. The instantiation engineers the Clerisy had paid to have brought out from Earth told me this that first year, after I'd recognized her in the winds of a winter snow storm, after a hundred days of having her wrapped around me like some old familiar blanket.

We thought it would be better if you didn't know, they said. What we managed to recover is, to put it grossly, the right side of her brain. We can't even rescue elementary grammar functions. Still, she's complex. Perfect for inhabiting a large, extremely dynamic system. There's really nothing else we can do, and the town council thought that such a courageous pioneer of the Transmission Era deserved at least a sort of life. History and all, you know.

At least you can't slap a plaque on the wind.

So I actually *wasn't* feeling Sarah drawing back, I told myself, wasn't recognizing her dismay at being used by Corazon. Too much sipsi last night; too active an imagination.

"Someone is going to have to answer for this," said Corazon, pronouncing each word separately, distinctly, like it was imperative he get the syntax right. Like it was some kind of code phrase.

And suddenly Sarah wasn't there anymore. I knew. The rat wind was back—a pack of them, yanking canoes this way and that, blowing sneaking bites of frigid air over the backs of the Indians. Canoes were tossed violently while the Indians struggled to maintain mental control. One pair of braves in a canoe lost it, and plummeted about fifty feet. Below them, settlers yelled and pointed rifles. Then the two Indians, paddling furiously, pulled out of their dive and leveled off. But the Indians weren't going to be able to keep themselves aloft for long, I suspected.

Through all the screaming, I heard a whisper. It was Janey's, who was standing very still, halfway up the steps to the platform. *"No."*

Gerabaldo Corazon stood in the rat wind, his face flush, full of a manic glory. Bently was seated beside him, laughing like a little demon familiar. Thomas ran the rest of the way up to the platform. Marquez started to draw his gun, and I cracked him in the back of his head with my elbow. I caught him as he slumped and gently set him down. Nobody noticed; they were all looking upward, watching Indians being thrown around the sky. Marquez had a very hard head, and my elbow was humming like a thwacked hornet's nest. I'd probably done more damage to myself than to him.

Thomas reached Corazon.

"Call it off," he said, almost spitting in the priest's face. There was authority in Thomas's voice, along with an undercurrent of deep power that came from a ghost-bear haunting his syntax. I couldn't have resisted.

But Corazon just looked at Thomas and smiled, almost benevolently.

Bently lunged at Thomas. His face was twisted with more hate than I'd ever seen in a human being.

But we are, after all, creatures of flesh and blood—and tendons. Bently's torn ankles gave out on him and, with a cry of pain and indignation, he ended up prostrate at Thomas's feet. He didn't stay there long, though.

A huge, nearly transparent paw flicked out toward Bently. Above and behind Thomas's head, Raej's big bearish face, glowing with blue-tinged flame, flashed into a snarl. The see-through paw had substance enough, though. It picked Bently up and flipped him over backward, as if he were a log, with big, juicy grubs underneath. I hadn't known chocalacas could do that. Bently landed on his back, behind Corazon.

"Damn your holy ass to hell," said Frank Oldfrunon. "I knew you were up to something, Baldy. I just never thought you really wanted war. I should've never allowed you to ship that fancy equipment in. Algorithm upgrade! And I'm a goddamn suntan oil salesman."

"Call the wind off," said Thomas. Around him, Raej crackled and roared. "Stop hurting my people."

Corazon's righteous calm began to crack at the edges. Thomas reached for him. I knew also to some degree what Corazon was feeling in his head, because I'd felt something of the same thing myself. Corazon was realizing that Raej could burn out his brain like a jet of propane igniting magnesium, in one swift, white-hot flash.

"If you hurt me," he said, "your little devil-pet gets disseminated to every world with a Clerical indwelling. We'll work it until its mind falls apart, begging us to stop."

Bently squawked. He sounded like a chicken a fox has just pounced on, betrayed past all belief.

"You told him! You *shithead*! After what I went through!" Corazon paid no attention.

"That's right, Kem," I called up to him. "He used your sorry ass."

"They ran rawhide through my ankles!" Bently cried out.

"You made your sacrifice for History," said Corazon, primly.

"Yeah, and now Corazon's told *everybody*," I said loudly, putting the best derisive edge I could in my voice.

Bently was so enraged, he couldn't speak for a moment. He lay gasping for breath in his amazement.

"You *told*," he said. "It's all worth nothing."

"You were paid," said Corazon. "Now shut up."

And that was when Bently cracked.

"Paid?" screamed Bently. "I *believed*. I believed in your precious History. I used one woman. I *killed* another one. You fucker!"

"Shut the hell *up!*" said Corazon.

Again I heard Janey whisper.

"Stop it. Please, stop it."

Bently didn't need to use his legs to get at Corazon; he just rolled over, wrapped his arms around the priest, and dragged him down. They went tumbling down the steps of the pedestal, past Janey, who turned to watch them. On the way down, Corazon managed to get hold of one of Bently's ankles. He squeezed.

I had to jump to get out of the way. They rolled about five feet away from the pedestal's base. When they came to a stop, Bently was clutching at his legs, trying to dislodge Corazon. Corazon got both hands on the ankle and twisted mightily.

Bently arched backward, completely lost in pain, and Corazon pulled himself up and darted away. I started after him, but my legs were stiff from supporting me all night and didn't respond well. I heard a powerful rushing coming from behind me, growing louder. Raej's paw crackled past me, after the priest, but the range was just too great, I guess, or Raej didn't want to risk hurting anyone else, and Corazon disappeared into the crowd, trailed by the tang of Raej's electrical passing. I was worried. Raej was doing lots of things, but one thing I was pretty sure he was *not* doing was keeping Janey calm. And *that* was what scared the hell out of me more than anything. Maybe Janey was not in range for the more delicate care she needed. Maybe Raej just had too much on his mind, even for a chocalaca.

Returning to the edge of the pedestal, I felt my insides begin to lurch. I looked up. Stephen Calhoun was beginning to lean at a crooked angle against the sky. Apparently the shift wasn't great enough for the people standing up there to notice. Here we go again, I thought. There was nowhere to take Janey this time, no escape from the strife that surrounded her.

The rat wind blew on.

Some of the Indians had gotten back control over their canoes. They tried to land. Only there wasn't any space wide enough to avoid fleeing settlers.

Nobody knows who did it.

Somebody fired a shot.

An Indian's chest exploded. Without the two of them, his partner could not keep up the Effect. The canoe careened into a patch of settlers. Maybe it even crushed whoever fired that bullet. Indians who could pulled atlatls from the bottoms of their canoes, arming them with missile-spears. Settlers cocked their guns, took aim. Across a space of about a hundred feet I saw, unmistakably, an Indian taking a bead on *me*. There was nothing I could do, no time to find cover. I was about to get killed.

Then a voice filled the atmosphere, as alive as a farm full of animals and growing things, as vivid and full of feeling as a Van Gogh.

"Get out of here, rat," Sarah said. "Get on away."

The wind stopped short, like a dog that's reached the end of its chain. It squealed a little, straining.

"I'll sic the cat on you," said Sarah.

The rat withdrew quickly then, down the street of Jackson, sucking a trail of kicked-up litter after it.

"Nobody's going to fight," said the same voice, yet it was another voice, and located just underneath where Thomas and I stood. Janey Calhoun came up the stairs, to stand under her great-grandfather's statue. "This all started because of me, and I'm going to end it."

Everybody heard her. Her voice came out of Janey, yes, but it was also the whisper of wind around the edge of the buildings and canoes—and the modulated tones of a breeze blowing over the ends of gun barrels. Sarah's voice.

Janey was crying, very upset. But we weren't all melting.

"You've spread out," said Thomas, almost in awe. "More than you ever have before."

"I found a strong rhythm to latch onto," she said. "She's always been there, but I never knew she was so strong. There's so much *feeling*. She wants to be whole as much as I seem to want to fall apart."

"She's there," I said, or maybe I only thought it. "She's really alive."

A gun cracked and a bullet sank into Stephen Calhoun's left knee. There was a puff of down where the bullet had passed through an edge of the parka Janey was wearing. Janey turned to look below her like some flame-faced goddess with vengeance on her mind.

"Damn," said Bently. "Missed." He was standing next to the sheriff's still-unconscious form, Marquez's pistol in his hand. "I'm going to kill that fucking Indian. There's going to be a war."

So it was Thomas he'd been aiming at, not Janey. The man was seriously losing it, but there was no time for me to get to him.

"You knew I wasn't well, but you used me to hurt other

people," said Janey, quietly. But, through Sarah, Bently heard.

He steadied his hand, taking more careful aim—at Thomas.

Something ludicrous was happening. Bently's bowl-cut hair stood up on end, making a cup on his head, like the bloom of a tulip, if they'd had tulips on Candle. The morning grew dead quiet.

"You won't hurt people anymore," said Janey-Sarah.

At first I thought Bently had gotten his shot off, but no gun flashes like that. Most of the settlers instinctively covered their ears, so loud was the sound. Those near Bently were knocked flat.

Bently fell over, dead.

He'd been struck by a lightning bolt out of the clear blue sky; he lay on the ground, smoldering.

"Nobody's going to fight," said Janey again, still using Sarah's voice to be heard. Everyone hastily lowered their weapons, settlers and Indians.

"Now everybody go home."

A few people started to leave, some running in terror. A group picked up the four or five who'd been hit by the falling canoe. A couple of other people got Bently's body. Nobody touched the dead Indians. The settlers weren't moving fast enough for Janey, though. A quick, strong wind kicked up, and people began almost blowing away, chattering like autumn leaves tumbling down a sidewalk.

"Indians, too," said Janey.

Thomas called out to the braves in the canoes in Loosa, directing a couple to get the fallen ones from the ground, telling the rest to go on back to the village, that he would be there soon. He motioned Laylay over, and the Indian readied his canoe for Thomas.

Thomas moved around behind Janey, who was looking out over the streets. He took her by the shoulders and spoke softly in her ear. Janey seemed to recede back into herself a little, and the slight trembling and tension in her body slackened.

Whatever contact, whatever symbiosis, Janey had had with Sarah, it was gone now. I knew Janey—and I knew Sarah. This was Janey leaning into Thomas's arms; there was nobody else there.

Frank Oldfrunon came up beside me.

"We've stopped it for today, Will, but if this girl can't keep up her magic act, I'm still worried."

I was silent for a moment, looking inward, checking my memory bank. Bently's ambush of Thomas and me was all still there.

"This afternoon I'm going to run a story that might change peoples' minds," I said. "And it will probably get me in a lot of trouble."

"If you can hold off this war, I can keep you out of trouble," said Oldfrunon. "I've got more friends than you might suppose, me being the old geezer that I am."

"Then get that Clerisy indwelling sealed off as quick as you can," I said. "And don't let anyone in but Thomas Fall."

"I'll see to it. And I'll see about catching that damn priest, while I'm at it." Oldfrunon went down the stairs, then stopped by Nestor Marquez. He shook the sheriff awake. Marquez sat up with a groan.

"Well, I'll let it pass *this* time, Nestor," said Oldfrunon. "But if I catch you asleep on the streets of Jackson one more time, you'll have to quit sheriffing and run for mayor."

Marquez, of course, did not reply. Oldfrunon led him into the courthouse, looking for all the world like an old prospector leading a mule.

A faint blue aura surrounded Thomas and Janey, and I knew that, at least for the moment, the real Raej was within his daughter's mind, soothing her, sustaining her.

"I don't think it will be a hard thing to get the rhythm back from the indwelling," I told Thomas. "But I hope Oldfrunon finds Corazon. Corazon's clever, and he thinks he's doing the right thing. I say he's still a dangerous man."

Thomas nodded.

"Laylay and I will go to the indwelling. Do you want to come?"

I thought about it a moment. Maybe I should see all this to

completion, get it all in memory. But I had a feeling the Clerisy was going to give the copy of Raej back lickety split, and just as quickly call Gerabaldo Corazon a renegade, like they'd done with that priest on Aeolus. One thing the Clerisy has known how to do since its early days as a heretical movement in Third World jungles is to cut its losses. Still, I had a bad feeling that Corazon was going to be more trouble.

Yet, one thing was good. There was no question about it, today I was going to scoop the hell out of the Westnet *Daily Locals*.

"I'll stay," I said. "I have a paper to get out."

Janey pulled off my parka and handed it to me.

"Sorry about the hole, but you need this to stay warm, Will James," she said. Then she and Thomas got into the canoe with Laylay.

I had something I wanted to ask, something I *had* to ask, but I was afraid. I have skipped across time like a flat stone thrown against still water. I have seen the future. What have we made of ourselves? What have we discovered?

Clever people that we are, we've looked down the well of our own minds, taken a flashlight to the walls, and we've found, yes, that it's deeper than we thought, that there are other realities. But haven't we found that, after all, there *is* a bottom, dry and sandy, and that there's no water down there, no soul? Nothing but ashes, as we've suspected and feared all along—and that what we mistook for thoughts and feelings was only the sifting and settling of those ashes?

Welcome to the future, brave Radio Pioneer.

"Tell me, Janey," I said. "Does she remember me?"

Janey looked at me and smiled.

"She hasn't forgotten, Will James. Of course she loves you still."

I pulled on the parka, hugged myself against the cold. There is always the *possibility* that there's something real behind words and weather. It was enough to keep me going. It always is.

"Thanks for letting me hear her voice again," I said. "Even if it was just for a little while."

Janey didn't say anything. Raej's glow surrounded the canoe for a moment, followed by the papery crackle of the Effect enfolding them. The canoe rose into the blue air, and turned toward the east, toward the Clerisy's indwelling, and disappeared into the sun. I watched for a while, as the faint light struck my face, warming it just a little. No, worship is just not the proper relationship to be in with Candle's star. Something less grandiose seems more appropriate—something more like friendship. I stood in the old sun's friendly morning glow for a long time, among the statues of the dead pioneers, and listened to the whisper of the wind.

PART TWO

A Man of the West, Descending

Age is no better, hardly so well, qualified for an instructor as youth, for it has not profited so much as it has lost.

—Henry David Thoreau, *Walden*

5

The special edition of the *Cold Truth* had been out for two days, when Marquez came into the office, numbed my arms, and escorted me to the hoosegow. He brought me in with no more words than were necessary to inform me that I was under arrest. He impressed a "basic rights" information quartersent lawyer imprint to the back of my neck—one of those things people call a "shark's tooth." For a few minutes, my brain was teeming with a frenzied legal incantation, until I figured out how to mentally shut the damn thing off.

After the paper came out, I'd been getting sympathy from the town, more than opprobrium. They were still burying the casualties, and generally getting over being stunned senseless. Most everybody was grasping for *any* explanation of what had happened. I reported the story of what happened those two days pretty much uncut. I didn't, of course, include the moments of filler that are sprinkled through even momentous happenings like dud firecrackers, and I tried to order everything in a way that made logical sense, at least to me.

I normally can't afford to put out a daily newspaper on the fancy imprinted plastic like the Westnet *Daily Locals* and still break even with the *Cold Truth*. Mostly, I put the paper out on el cheapo text-and-image cards. I promised myself when I started that the paper would not become a rich man's hobby and cash drain. But this time I sprung for the good plastic, for a special edition—the imprinted plastic that gives readers a limbic, as well as a cerebral, account of what happened.

I wanted Jackson, and my not insubstantial Indian readership, to feel those days in the seat of their pants, and in their hearts, as well as see it in their heads. Especially during Bently's ambush of Thomas and me. Maybe then we wouldn't have to worry about a war. I was still not sure what it all meant, but figuring that out was not my job.

Which wasn't to say that I wasn't accountable. Marquez sure thought I was guilty of *something,* only he wasn't quite sure what, so he charged me with the obvious crime.

In more civilized places, rhythm smuggling gets you a compulsory trip to the rehabilitation psychologists, who bathe you in the warm glow of their thought correction processors. On Candle, it's five years in the thought correction processor known as the City Jail. And, of course, five years on Candle is seven Earth years.

I didn't do much time, however. I won't go into all the details, but the judge's name was Ezra *Fall,* and he was a second cousin to Thomas on Thomas's father's side. He was also Mayor Oldfrunon's partner in the Goosedown, Jackson's most comfortable, least talkative tavern. After I spent a night in jail, in the same cell Thomas had occupied, Judge Fall released me on my own recognizance. There was no thought of trying to arrest Thomas. As the Great Sun of Doom, he was now outside the bounds of Westpac law, and could not be touched.

What worried me the most was not Marquez or the local Justice of the Peace. The story of the ambush got picked up by the Territorial Wire's halfsent. Johan, the local Westnet tech, told me that he had fed the information into the computer of a little freighter that happened to be leaving the day after the story ran in the *Cold Truth.* Soon, the story would spread. Slowly, but inexorably, newspapers across the Territory and back on Earth would carry it.

Which meant that I might expect a visit from the Territorial Rangers any day now. Rangers were almost the mythical equivalent of Indian Wanderers. They piloted the fastest starships in the Westpac fleet, and, since Circuit Judges could take up to a year to get to some of the planets in the Territory, Rangers had quasi-judicial powers when it came to locking you up and setting bail.

If they decided to try me on the Territorial Circuit, Judge Fall couldn't do a damn thing about it. And Marquez would probably be only too glad to keep me for a year or so, if he were ordered to do so. It took him a while, but he finally figured out that I was the one who knocked him out.

But I was underestimating Frank Oldfrunon. Oldfrunon had been around the Territory. In his younger days, he'd been a representative on the Sector Steering Committee and had chaired the Under Committee on New Exploration. It was Oldfrunon who first pushed for development of Mumba's Reef, out on the very edge of the Wild at the time, which gave a lot of malcontents a home, and made a lot of people rich.

Those former malcontents were older now, and the Reef was a Territory member in good standing. One of those malcontents happened to be the current Subchair of the Territorial Steering Committee. Another was on the Westpac Board of Trade, as a Territorial Rep to Earth. Both of them remembered Oldfrunon fondly as the guy who'd given them chances in what they had once thought would be wasted lives. Oldfrunon sent messages out by the next ship. The Rangers did not come to lock me up for smuggling.

When Marquez first came in to arrest me, I had been pondering whether or not to go and see Thomas and Janey. I hadn't seen them since they'd left for the Clerical indwelling to try and recover the rhythm copy of Raej.

I asked Marquez about them, after he got me safely locked away, and the question seemed to break the dam inside him.

"I don't know *how* they are," he said, bringing a stool up to the outside of my cell, and sitting down with a coffee mug. He put the mug under a water-fountain spigot nearby and ordered up coffee from the jail halfsent.

He asked if I wanted anything, but I shook my head. "What

I really want is for you to explain what you mean by what you just said."

"Well, what I should have said is that I don't know *what* they are, after hearing about what that girl did in Pioneer Square." He took a contemplative sip. "And after what I saw with my own eyes, out at the indwelling."

He proceeded, in his rambling fashion, to tell me what had happened there, but I think I can piece it together a little more coherently for you.

Oldfrunon had been true to his words—for this first time among many, although I didn't know this yet—and the indwelling was pretty much sealed off by the time Thomas, Janey, and Laylay got there. In City Hall, from the manager's office, Oldfrunon had sent a message, via the optical fibers embedded in the town's roadways, to the microscopic road crew of tailored bacteria that bred and worked within the interstices of Jackson's spider-silk road like living darning needles. But this time, instead of re-questing a repair or an alteration, the order was to pull out *all* the stitching on the road to the indwelling.

The indwelling was on the eastern outskirts of town, a good ways past where Bently's Bistro and Gallery used to be. There was dense forest for about two miles between it and town. The road was the only quick access and, within minutes, the road was consumed by a mob of microbes officially running amuck.

The only other way to get there was by a hover large enough to sail over the treetops. Or by Indian canoe. Oldfrunon had Marquez issue a police warning to all airborne hovers to stay away from the indwelling. No one was using hovers that day, anyway. Most people had retreated to Jackson's restaurants or were gathered at home in their living rooms, discussing the morning's events.

Oldfrunon himself called up the indwelling and ordered the Assistant Abbot, Sister Dolgren Pitt, to admit Thomas, and to do anything he asked. If she didn't, Oldfrunon warned, whatever the political repercussions, he would send all the priests on Candle back to Managua in cement habits. As a final precaution, he sent Marquez out to nab Corazon. Marquez figured Corazon might try to make it back to the indwelling.

He didn't find Corazon. Marquez's head was hurting so badly when he took off for the indwelling that he was seeing things. He mistook a strangely shaped sponge tree that he passed over in his hover for Corazon and almost careened into it before he got close enough to make the crucial distinction. And, at the indwelling, he reported something even more strange, something that he put down to his blurred and affected vision.

The priests, perhaps assuming Marquez had come to arrest Thomas after all, happily directed him to a room lined with teak consoles covered with brass knobs and rheostats.

"It wasn't bug wood either," Marquez told me. "The wood in *that* room came out of a forest on Earth, as sure as hell is deep."

In the center of the room was a rounded wooden pedestal, about two feet high. Janey Calhoun stood at its center. This was the duplicating center, filled with advanced technology for making the prime halfsents that the Clerisy was famous for—and, from which it derived a good portion of its operating expenses.

Thomas was standing on the floor, beside Janey, and a blue-green aura surrounded them. Marquez later said that, in the room, there was the unmistakable odor of wild bear—though where he'd ever smelled a bear before that day, he couldn't say.

Marquez, in fact, saw *two* bears, or rather, the giant *heads* of two bears, both of them seeming to hang in the air about Thomas and Janey. The bears glowed as if composed of excited phosphorous, creating weird neon spirals and flares in the carefully polished wooden faces of the machinery housing. Each bear touched the nose of the other, as if they were snorting each other's breath, deciding whether or not to attack. Marquez could only watch—and wonder whether the knock on the head had permanently damaged his vision.

Then the bear above the platform—Janey's bear, which I took to be the rhythm copy of Raej—let out a great roar, and seemed to draw in upon itself, like an umbrella folding up and being pulled down for use as a cane. Janey, whose posture had been slack and relaxed, behaved as if she were jolted by a big current. She stood up straight and tall, as she had earlier that morning, just before calling the lightning down.

Marquez was not a religious man. His mother had been old-time Catholic, and he'd been to a few of the Clerisy's Cell meetings, but politics was what truly moved his soul. Nevertheless, he felt a sort of religious awe as Janey turned and looked upon him.

She had the cold, glacial eyes of the bear. Marquez couldn't help screaming in holy terror.

Then Janey laughed and smiled at him. Like a goddess toying with a mortal is how he described it. He darted from the room, out of the indwelling, into his hover, and back to the comfort of his secular office at the Town Hall. He didn't *want* to understand what he'd seen, and he told me about the experience more to expunge it from his soul, than to come to any comprehension.

What I believe Marquez saw, however, were the final stages of the recovery of at least one of the rhythm copies of Raej from the indwelling's advanced storage devices, where Bently had beamed them with the fancy equipment Thomas had discovered in his Bistro. Then Janey flashed the copy into her own brain, hence the two Raejes in the air. The one hanging over Thomas was the real chocalaca, and the one over Janey, the manifestation (perhaps aided by Janey's chocalaca nature) of the copy, which was now lodged within her, helping to keep her stable.

Marquez remained garrulous after he told me his story, and next he wanted *me* to recount what went on during the time he'd been in Never-never Land during the confrontation in Pioneer Square, which I did, leaving out the part where I cracked him out cold with my elbow. To his credit, he didn't spoil the atmosphere of good feeling by bringing it up.

But despite our getting to be on better terms, Marquez had no intention of releasing me. When he left for the evening, he put the silent lockup algorithm on-line, and I leaned back on my cot and prepared to soak in the prison experience.

Mostly what I did was think about Sarah.

She never was, I suppose, anything special to look at. Thin, almost translucent skin, always fresh, hardly ever having been darkened by a childhood tan, growing up, as she did, in the mists of the Oregon Cascades. But when she moved away from home—for school, then for work, then for me—she took a tan wonderfully. Not like some people do, as if it were the year's toil and life's accumulated grime made manifest in their very pores—but as fresh earth takes a crop. Sarah bloomed. Especially during the Radio Days.

Even then, this was what we called that time when we were preparing to be broadcast. The year was 2041. She had green eyes and brown hair, which burned red when the sun was right. In many ways, Sarah was like Janey, but unlike her, too. Where Janey was a small-town woman, Sarah was from the country. Even after coming to the city, she never lost her essentially rural ways—she merely adapted them to new circumstances.

Sarah was an artist by trade, a painter. I met her at Washington University, in St. Louis, where she was a graduate student. It was her paintings that first got to me, in an exhibit I happened to pass through on the way to my own classes. The paintings were farm landscapes—at least, according to the titles (Maple's Field, Silverback Orchard)—but of no farmland I'd ever seen. They were farms for the mind, strong acrylics thick on canvas. Chaotic, beautiful colors—maybe she invented some new ones, even. I thought the paintings looked like souls might, stripped of their bodies, stripped of their thoughts, left only with a burning will to live—an exposed roar of feelings.

Sarah was good. I spent days trying to meet her, and when I finally did, we took to one another almost immediately. Soon, we were seeing each other exclusively.

Yet, I found, Sarah didn't care much about souls. Even her own. She was not a believer in any sense of the word. Once, after we'd made love, I asked her if she thought she could paint *my* soul, as she had painted the soul of the farmland in her landscapes.

"It wouldn't matter much if I could," she said, as we lay on the messy covers of her small fold-out bed, in her tiny apartment. "Souls don't matter."

"I kind of like *my* soul," I said. "And I like yours, too." I kissed a pearl-white breast and reached for her foot to tickle some foolishness into her. But we were being serious now. She hid it beneath the sheets.

"All that matters is communication. That's what I think, Will. That's why I paint. It's a language. A better language than I can speak."

"Communication is *for* souls, so they can interact," I said—but that was enough philosophy for one afternoon. I pulled her on top of me, and, since we'd already made love once, I easily slipped inside her. In those days, I was pretty much insatiable. Sarah caught her breath, then moved with me.

"Souls. Don't. Make. Language," she said, turning *my* movement into her own with an almost terrifying deftness. "Not any more than neurons make thought. We're connections, you know."

"Connections," I said.

"Yes. Like wheat in a field. And language is the wind rippling through."

This was to be our fundamental difference, but the reason that we both signed up with the Broadcast Project—both of us with our different ideas about communicating. But that afternoon, and into that night, we were pretty much *as one* physically.

That day, I'd given her a present. A brass bracelet, a thin circlet. From then on, Sarah almost never took it off. As her fingers kneaded my chest, the bracelet rubbed again and again against one of my nipples—brass, and amber hair, and the red-orange of the sun, the real, Earth sun, slanting through the blinds behind her, ruddying Sarah's skin and haloing her as if she were some elemental demigoddess, arisen from deep and secret fires.

Language, I thought in my bare cell, on a planet five hundred light-years—and five hundred years—away from those days. You're nothing when you're alone. Just a neuron, sparking nonsense in some dumb petri dish. Just a piece of wheat chaff, scattered by the wind.

Sarah knew loneliness and she knew connection. She grew up the middle of five sisters. Her father was not terribly successful at farming, and had been a heavy drinker. "It wasn't what you'd think, though," she once told me. "When Daddy was passed out in the cucumbers, or driving around on the tractor with no clothes on at two in the morning, with Mom chasing him through the fields, it kind of drew us sisters together. We'd make up stories to tell the neighbors, make sure everybody had her facts straight, so we wouldn't be caught in a lie.

"And there was always work and the animals to keep us cheered up. We had the meanest Shetland pony in the known universe," she said.

We were in California then, in the San Bernardino Mountains. We had a house overlooking the L.A. basin. It was a nicer place than I'd thought we would ever have. I'd worked odd jobs for small papers since I'd gotten out of school, and made a little from freelancing magazine essays on the side. Sarah's painting brought in a little more, but we were not well-off by any means. That is, until we'd signed up and been chosen for the Broadcast Project. Now Broadcast Project money paid the rent. The living room in our big house had a glass wall, and below, the lights of San Bernardino twinkled through the smog. We were stretched out on the floor, trying out one of the new toys the project had provided us with. It was a crude mind link—one of the prototypes of that device. This was back when they were just beginning to experiment with impressing algorithms on micro-machine cultures, and the brain interface was all or nothing. The thing was still mostly a mass of wires and dials.

At the moment, Sarah was riding the Shetland pony over rough ground, along a ridgeline in the highest of the Cascades. I was with her, inside her thoughts, in the crude, unfiltered connection those early links made possible. The pony jolted beneath me/us, and I could feel the unfamiliar buzz of mild feminine arousal.

"This is the mean Shetland?" I asked.

"Yes." Sarah was concentrating on the feeling, intensifying it. There was only blue-black sky and the regular fall of hooves. I'd never felt this way before. I gently caressed her, as much for me as for her.

"Shetlands are always mean."

"But *I* could ride him. I let him bite me once in a while so he could keep up appearances."

In some ways, those old links are better than the perfect, no-wires-attached ones we use today, such as, for instance, the legal plastic that had contained Janey's commitment papers and the letter from Deason Allerby. You couldn't control what you transmitted very easily with the primitive links. Thinking to another person wasn't so much a performance as it was a revelation.

Having animals again was one of the reasons Sarah was glad when we both had gotten picked by the Broadcast people. We could move into that decent-sized house where she could keep a few pets in comfort. We had a dog, a cat, and a ferret. The ferret liked to bite *me,* but Sarah could handle her.

Like she'd handled the rat wind, with Janey's help. Or had that been Sarah? Had Sarah ever been on Candle at all? Things were strange here in the future. Indians with ghost bears, houses with ghost maids. I'd told Janey all about Sarah. Had her presence at Pioneer Square been some sort of creation of Janey's imagination, brought to life by whatever metaphysical power Janey was tapping?

What did it matter to me? I, myself, was nothing more than the creation of the peculiar workings of a queer universe, wasn't I? So I *felt* like a man, so what? Nine years before, they'd *made* me, with a handful of common elements and a translating computer, especially rented from Earth, that had cost as much to build as the Gross Planetary Product of Candle for a year. Without pressure from the Clerisy, who, I was convinced, were pretty much crackpots, I would have kept sailing on, like a song when there are no radios to receive it. And now, after they'd spent a fortune in bringing me back, they threw me in jail to rot.

Kind of perverse and malevolent, when you think about it—like I was stewing in the guts of some kind of smart-ass, wiseguy universe. Like I was bad beer for a cheap drunk.

This time, from outside the cell, there was no whisper of the wind. Absolutely nothing. Snow fell blankly on white streets.

"Sarah," I said softly. "Sarah. Can't we communicate? I want to so much, now." I didn't mean them to, but my words came out in a sob.

Outside, the night remained still and empty.

I returned to my memories. And, with nothing to do but reflect, I went over every detail of that last day, the day of the transmission, in my mind. And something occurred to me. Something terrible.

The Broadcast Project scientists had weighed us, graphed us inside and out, when we first joined up. When we stepped into the transmission chamber, their computers already had our bodies and genomes mapped to the last detail. The chamber was where they copied *minds*. We wore clothes, but the clothes were actually sensors, part of the machinery. They would not be a part of the signal that was broadcast.

Sarah stepped into the chamber with a faint, knowing smile. This was what she wanted more than anything in the world. To become pure communication. Pure art. To become a word in the universal conversation. She was happy. This was worth doing.

Sarah forgot to take off her bracelet.

During all the measurings, all the examinations, she'd taken it off. It was an excess, a complication the project didn't need. No one had asked her, but she wanted to make things easier for everyone.

It was the bracelet that had killed her.

I felt certainty about this. Sure, it *could have been* lots of things: planetary magnetic fields, the flares of uneasy suns, or merely the background radiation that permeates the universe like electromagnetic scattershot after the Big Bang. But it was the bracelet.

Nobody noticed that she was wearing it. It had never been an issue in the preparations; she'd always quietly removed it before, and slipped it on afterward.

Nobody told the machines that it wasn't part of her mind. They translated it, combined it with the rest of the code. And my Sarah lost the part of her mind that could say she loved me within a circlet of old brass that I had given her. I gave it to her because I loved her. I told her I would always love her.

"It's not *that* bad, son. You'll be out in the morning."

Frank Oldfrunon was standing on the other side of my cell's door. He was drinking something hot and steaming.

"Jail," he said. "Give Mr. James a warm cup of tea."

Oldfrunon's voice was law in the city complex; the jail complied. The microbial machines in the wall activated, and a standard-spec mug grew out of the stone. I picked it as I would a grapefruit. Tea ran from the spigot in my sink. I asked for a slice of real lemon, but that was one thing you couldn't get on Candle.

"I was just thinking about something sad," I said to Oldfrunon, pulling my stool over to the cell bars. One thing I didn't expect to find in the future was the same old barred cell doors. But, at least on Candle, here they were. I rested my cup in the middle horizontal slat that held the bars rigid.

"Strange days, these days. Wonderful times, but sad times, too."

"I was thinking about *my* time," I said.

Oldfrunon smiled a restrained smile. "This is *your* time, as much as it is mine, or anybody else's."

"Not to hear some tell it."

Oldfrunon didn't bother to answer this. I'd often felt, when around him, that I was missing a point entirely that he was patiently waiting for me to catch on to. This was not necessarily due to his silver hair and fox-brush-gray eyebrows. I suspected Oldfrunon had made people feel this way when he was a young man, as well.

"You *died* five hundred years ago, Will. There's no denying it was *you*. Yet here you are, alive again. Kind of makes you wonder whether time is the big tyrant it's cracked up to be."

"It is," I replied.

"I don't know. You can *choose* for it to be, that's for sure. You can submit to time's mastery."

"When you know the decision is not really authentic, then pretending like you have a choice is pretty hollow."

Again, Oldfrunon seemed to answer a question I hadn't asked, but *should* have.

"This world has known stranger than you, Will James. Don't think your circumstances are so damn special. Candle finds a place for us all."

I breathed out over the top of my cup, and steam rose before my eyes. Through the mist, in the dim, cool jail lighting, Oldfrunon looked like some ancient troll, come to do mischief in the night.

"How old *are* you, Frank?" I asked.

He drew back, arched his eyebrows. "Son, that is not such a simple question to answer. Traveling around the Territory can do odd things to a person's metabolism."

"How's that?" I said, sipping a long draught.

"That statue we were standing on the day before yesterday, the one that got shot in the knee—"

"Colonel Stephen G. Calhoun?"

"Yep. I knew him. As a matter of fact, I knew his father, Lincoln Calhoun, when he was an old man and I was a young boy."

"Lincoln Calhoun? The man who discovered the Mississippian Indians?"

"He was a boy at the time."

"But a genius." I'd read the history books. Lincoln Calhoun was Candle's George Washington, Ben Franklin, and Martin Luther King, Jr.—all rolled into one.

Oldfrunon leaned closer to me. He pulled something from the folds of his parka, which he'd left on when he came inside. People on Candle only take off their coats when they are going to stay quite a while. It saves a lot of time, because most of one's traveling time involves getting ready to face the cold outside.

"Do you know the story?"

"I've read the accounts and watched the old videos. That's where we got Justice Day, right?" Justice Day is Candle's celebration of the unspoken treaty that we would never do to the

Mississippians what we did to the North American aborigines.

Oldfrunon chuckled low and bounced his eyebrows up and down.

"There's more," he said. "That's the real reason I came to see you tonight."

I was silent. My reporter's instincts prickled, and I turned on the memory bank.

"Old Lincoln was kind of vain," said Oldfrunon, "in a respectable sort of way. He was also the best damn politician Candle ever produced. He was revered by those early settlers, Will, and what he said could influence the way the people *thought,* as well as how they acted. God, I remember, even as a boy, I felt some of that magnetism."

"What are you trying to say, Frank?"

Oldfrunon gave me a look of mock exasperation. "All right, Mr. Reporter. It seems to me that we've arrived at a crucial point in Candle's history. Hell, in the history of the Expansion. It's time to rethink some of our assumptions."

"As in . . ."

"As in the relationship of Indians and settlers. Maybe leaving one another alone isn't the answer anymore. I've got something here that kind of puts a new spin on things."

"What kind of 'new spin' could there possibly be?"

"Well, it's not so much the *facts,* as the interpretation of the facts. For years, Lincoln Calhoun had a vested interest in making us all believe that what kept the Indians and settlers from coming to blows was a mutual respect for each other's ways. And separatism."

"That's what it *had* to be, isn't it? I mean, neither really understood the other, right from the start."

"No," said Oldfrunon. "But I'll have to show you." He handed me a piece of imprinted material—the old-fashioned kind that was composed of some kind of exotic crystalline material, made back before they could use the weak atomic force to store data and algorithms, back in the 2500s. Oldfrunon wasn't lying; he *was* almost as old as the hills.

"Lincoln died real slow," he said. "Mostly because those old free radical sweepers tore the hell out of your capillaries. So he had lots of time to think about the past while he was fading, and some of his reminiscences, he memory-banked."

"And this is a memory—"

"This is *the* memory. Lincoln Calhoun's account of the day when the settlers first landed on Candle."

I took the thin wafer of memories. It felt brittle and worn.

"Why isn't this in the Pioneers' Museum?"

"Ah, hell, Will, we've got enough goddamn history around here to convince us that this iceball is the center of creation as it is. One more reminder isn't going to help."

"But it's important. To more than Candle."

"That's what I've been trying to tell you. I was thinking you could run this in the *Cold Truth*."

"I'll have to see it first." As if I could refuse to publish something like this. It'd be like turning down *Abraham* Lincoln's secret diaries.

"That's why I brought it *tonight,* son. I figured you'd have plenty of time to give it the attention it deserves."

"Oh, you did, did you?" I rose from my stool and the tea, grown tepid, sloshed over my hand.

Oldfrunon smiled again, this time with his mayor's smile, the smile that meant political wheels were in motion.

"You'll be out of here come sunup, Will. I'll see to that. We're going to need a good newspaper, and a good newspaper-man, to catch all of the shit that's fixing to start raining down around here."

"Why do I get the feeling that, as much as you like me, Frank, I'm still just a subroutine in your Big Program?"

Oldfrunon stood and strummed his hand across the bars like he was playing harp strings. With a wink, he walked down the hall and out of sight, the jail quickly clearing the way for him like a nervous doorman.

I felt better. I had some genuine news in my hands. I couldn't, at first, figure out how the old memory bank worked. You couldn't think it on. Then I found a button on the underside that popped up a menu in my head, as the algorithm infected me through my tactile neurons. There was only one item to choose from, labeled, simply, "Justice Day."

"Indians," cried Captain as they carried him down the ship's passageways to the sickroom. "Indians." The ship, like some elaborately shaped bell, rang with the word, the hum never dying out before the next clap of his startled voice. Those who brought him in from the white and green curtain we would later call the Canoe Hill Woods perhaps thought he mourned for old Earth, and the West Indies of his birth. But I was thirteen and believed, with a child's faith, that he was as lucid as the hard starlight and emptiness through which he had spent his adult life sailing. I believed because his words were strange and wonderful and had to be true.

They laid the Captain in the sickroom's narrow bed and called Dr. Calhoun, who was my father, yes to come and tend to the Captain, but perhaps mostly to confirm that what they saw before them was true: that a man like them, though he was Abram Josephson and almost a hundred years a ship's captain, and so not really like them—not in the deep, the marrow—yet a man of flesh and nerves holding a salt ocean contained, bringing it across light-years, was pouring that ocean out like a red sea upon the sick-room floor. He was bleeding to death from a stick of wood and stone, a *spear,* fashioned by intelligence to destroy, thrust into his belly.

While Father tried to stop the bleeding, the Captain alternated muttering and screaming the word, not in hatred or pain, or even in wonder or delight, but in sheer astonishment, like a child who has discovered, say, that there is pain in the world or that saying a certain sound in a certain way will make food come and so saying it again and again, not because he is hungry but because of the lingering surprise that such an incredible thing could be. "Indians," said Captain Josephson, and I believed him.

Now I'm old. I've spent one hundred fifty years fighting Old Gravity, gaining an ex-spacer's hunched back and, perhaps, a bit of understanding. They celebrate all my wondrous insights of that day, you know, once a year at Justice Day. I'll tell you a secret: I was just a boy who read too much.

Father put Captain Josephson under anesthetic, and the Captain slowly fell silent. Even as his brain settled down, away from the pain, into sleep (and soon to settle and sift out of all pain) the Captain repeated the word, now as a man will recite over and over again a number or name that he must remember, but is rapidly forgetting.

"Good God," muttered Father to his nurse, "that word must be lodged in his cerebellum." But finally the Captain went to sleep, and later he did not wake up. Then Father saw me and told me, in his clinical, doctor's voice, to please Lincoln clear the room. Later, I overheard the nurse telling of how Father worked on Captain Josephson's wound with a furious competence, angry not at the Captain, but at the Captain's body for its recalcitrance. Much later, when I had become a man, Father himself told me that what had angered him the most was losing his first patient who did not die of old age to a spear wound.

"As if science has brought humanity out of the darkness, has shown us the Effect so that we can travel to the stars, only for the chance to laugh in our startled faces," he said.

Also, there was what I knew all along, that Captain Josephson was my father's friend, as much as surgeons and ship captains can be said to have friends.

So I left the sickroom, and it was Mother who found me, before I had the field down on one of the rear emergency hatches. She had light duty (for what good was a historian, her calling, on a planet with just three weeks of human habitation? And what good a drive tech, her job during the trip out, on a grounded ship?) and so she had been able to come looking for me. She had raised me on *Robinson Crusoe* and Robert Louis Stevenson and Fenimore Cooper: she knew where to find me, and what she'd find me doing.

"It's not that when you're, say, eighteen, suddenly maturity falls upon you like a West Texas storm (you've seen my memory banks of those)," Mother said, as I sadly followed her back into the ship, away from the chance to *see*. "Or even that we don't trust you to do what's right and act no more or less than your age," said Mother. "It's just that at this time, in this place, there are already too many people who have waited too long for a chance to do their jobs, to show others and, mainly, themselves that there was worth in bringing them along, letting them take up expensive, hard-won space filled with hard-won atmosphere. They have just been standing in line longer than you have, Lincoln."

"Indians, Mother, Captain Josephson said Indians . . ."

Then Alex Koyanaga was behind Mother, saying Julie you'd better come and see this, and nothing more until we were out the main hatch and standing in the snowy meadow in which the ship had landed. Then he didn't have to say anything as my heart jumped and I almost cried out, but did not, because no one had noticed me tagging behind. Staying still was the hardest thing I had done in my life until then.

For yes, upon the white snow-and-ice surface of the meadow were rows of bark canoes. Those who had come in the canoes formed a semi-circle around the ship's entrance, silent, waiting for something. They wore leather shirts and leggings (or at least it looked like leather to us, who had never seen anything but vinyl and synthetic textiles before). Their hair was laced with feathers. All the males, and a sprinkling of females, stood to one side in a rigid half-arch, while the rest of the females clustered more loosely, forming the other side of the semicircle. Tattoos covered every inch of exposed flesh on the males: wonderful, intricate tattoos. The males held spears, shafts inches from the ground, but not touching, points in the sky, glinting white quartz or black obsidian. The females held paddles or babies or both. They were all human beings, and they had iron-red skin.

"These," said Mother, low, but as clear as thunder in winter, "are Mississippian Indians."

She took a step forward, and would have gone closer, but Alex Koyanaga put a hand on her shoulder.

"Some sort of mass psychological projection? We've been in space for seven years . . ." said Alex Koyanaga. "Or natives using our own minds to fool us? They could have found out in pre-Columbian times, discovered the Effect. It's just a mental trick, after all; they wouldn't need technology to get here—in theory—just a bit of a paradigm shift."

Indians! I wanted to scream. These are real Indians standing here, straight out of the best books! I barely held my tongue and looked around wildly.

The ship's adults (for all the children but me were safely inside) looked as nervous and excited as I felt. This surprised me; I was just a boy, and feelings were for immediate and complete expression—or else what good were they, eh? But I saw that these spacers were shaking with excitement. It was not that they were afraid and so would not act, as I had suspected, but that they were afraid and so keeping themselves from acting in their fear. As Mother had said, they had waited a long time for something really important to do, and could wait longer rather than wasting the chance. Maybe my idea of running up and saying "how" with extended arm was good, but maybe it had occurred to the adults too, maybe was what they most wanted to do, if only they could be sure it was the right thing. Maybe I should be with the other children, kept from harm and doing harm, safely inside.

And so the adults did the thing that only adults can do, and perhaps, since I did it too, I earned a right to be there, to watch. We waited. Some had weapons near at hand—really only tools from the ship that might be pressed into service. The Indian spears looked much more deadly.

Then there was the swish of leather leggings swung through the high grass that poked through the icy snow in the meadow, followed by the soft thump of moccasins on the powdered turf. The Indians had, collectively, come to attention and taken a step forward. After this, filling out and shaping the wordless silence, was the quick, sharp breathing of the ship's company. Something was about to happen.

From the Indian ranks, a group of three stepped forward and came toward Mother: a man, a woman, and a boy. While the boy walked willingly along with them, there was a tense composition to the three; it was clear the boy would have been forced to come forward if he had resisted. Yet he walked with determination, setting the pace for the two accompanying him. He stared forward, though not directly at Mother or the other adults. Since I was just behind and to the right of Mother, I saw the boy's eyes clearly, saw perhaps that which he wanted no one to see: the fear, yes, but also the fierce determination that was in them. And I saw that this was a kid—a boy like me, tattoos or not.

The three came to a stop one step in front of Mother. She remained motionless as they approached. The man spoke a word. The word was vile, full of *s*'s, almost the action of spitting made into a word. I saw Mother faintly tremble. Alex Koyanaga put a calming hand on her arm—but he stayed back.

"What do they want?" asked Mother, without turning, with her eyes firmly on those standing before her, on the spear in the man's hand, easily within thrusting distance.

"You stepped forward, Julie," said Alex Koyanaga. "Maybe they think you're some kind of . . ."

Then the Indian woman spoke the same word, and this time it was accompanied by a bit of spittle, which landed in the snow at Mother's feet, faintly smoking there. The woman's face was lined like some old map of a world, criss-crossed with navigation markings. She closed her eyes slowly, then her face crinkled into a sob, which she seemed to be fighting the moment it came upon her. Only a quick whimper escaped her throat. She looked down at the Indian boy, but she now wore like a mask a stern, controlled expression.

Then I, thirteen and still not come into my height, saw something the other spacers, tall from seven years with half Earth gravity, and trying to read the intentions of the adult Indians from *their* eyes, did not notice. I saw the Indian boy's clasped hands, held close to his waist. He had cast down his eyes and was staring at his hands as fiercely as he had faced us. Then I knew.

I knew because he was a boy like me, doing what I would have done, feeling what I would feel; I'd seen in his eyes that he was scared to death, that he was going to try and bear up nevertheless. The word the man and woman had spoken was evil, but there had been only sadness in their faces when they said it. Yet it was perfectly clear to me what the word meant: killer.

"It's justice they're here for," I said rather loudly, my voice crackling on the edge of being fourteen.

"Lincoln, what . . ." said Mother, then there was fear in her eyes for she had thought I was inside and safe.

"What do you mean, Lincoln?" asked Alex Koyanaga in a low voice, almost a whisper. "What have we done?"

Mother was staring at me now, deciding, perhaps, whether to pick me up bodily and carry me back inside or just to give me a good push toward the hatch.

"Not for anything we did," I said, then to Mother: "Look at the kid's hands. They've still got the Captain's blood on them."

Mother continued to stare at me for a long moment. Then it sunk in. She looked. She stood silent for another long while. "Yes," she finally said. "Yes."

As if this were their cue, the Indians cast the boy at Mother's feet. Slowly, the boy looked up into Mother's face. He was fighting back tears, but he forced himself to look—and to speak. The word came out in a low moan and, though we did not know it, there was no mistaking the human depths from which it sprang, as if the word were water which would cleanse the blood from the boy's hands. Then he stared at his hands, saw the blood still there, and began to sob without control.

The male Indian thrust his spear, shaft first, toward Mother. He shook it, indicating she should take it. Mother, quietly, without heat, turned from the man.

She knelt and drew the boy up.

With her back still to the Indians, she motioned Alex Koyanaga to take the boy.

"We are going to give this boy a fair trial, under the laws of this . . . settlement. First, we have to learn his language, or he ours."

Mother looked around at the ship's company. The tension that had bound them all to a tight geometry dissipated and this, coupled with nods of affirmation, let Mother know she had their support. The Indians watched silently.

"Lincoln," Mother said, low so only I could hear it. "Go with Alex and the boy. I think he's very frightened."

I tried to look serious at the shouldering of such a responsibility, but how could I help smiling and Mother knew it and she smiled with her eyes. Before I turned to go, there was another startled gasp from all the ship's company; they were looking over my shoulder, toward the Indians.

I turned, and saw a sight which is with me still, burned in my brain so that even one hundred fifty years have neither dulled nor changed the vision I had that day; or, if they have, have only improved my memory, as seasoning in an old skillet or a gilt patina on old wood. I have learned the "how," over the years, how the scientists and philosophers claim the Indians manage the Effect so effortlessly, two by two, or, in the case of Wanderers, one Indian and his chocalaca. But I have known since *that* day—since I was thirteen, and saw that sight—the "why."

For the Indians took to their canoes. In each canoe was a woman, humming some ancient, near tuneless song. In each canoe, a man paddled. The canoes slid over the meadow surface with no resistance, like a ship in free-fall about a planet, or drifting steadily through the empty reaches between the stars. And when the Indians in the bark canoes reached the meadow's edge, they angled their prows upward, paddling steadily, and took to the ice-blue morning sky.

6

What Candle got, with my account and with Lincoln Calhoun's memories, was, I think, a fair presentation of exactly what happened on the day Western civilization first met the Mississippian Indians who inhabited all the worlds near Earth. What was so startling, you have to understand, was that up to then, the story was of how the two peoples had been completely alien to one another. The ways of the Mississippians and of Westpac were not opposed—they were, at base, just mutually incomprehensible. At least, that was generally the feeling everybody had been basing laws and diplomacy on for generations now. What *nobody knew* before was how clearly the two people *did* understand one another, even at the beginning. Maybe compassion, art, and love took different forms, but we had *justice* in common.

I'm not sure of how great an effect the story had on the people. But you shouldn't underestimate the power of new ideas—especially if they're very good, or very bad.

What *didn't* happen for the next six months on Candle was war. I think that so much had taken place so fast, that mostly, everyone felt like they'd had the breath knocked out of them. Going to the brink of war threw us all for a loop, then discovering that the "live-and-let-live" policies of the past were violated by the very people who had set them up in the first place. Settlers and Indians were going to have to figure out some new rules—that much was clear—but nobody could guess what those rules should be.

Two things of importance did occur over the next six months. By the way, six months was almost exactly how long it took a modern ship to travel from Candle to Earth and back again.

The first thing was that Janey went to live with the Indians. In the larger scheme of things, this didn't *seem* particularly important. I wanted to give Janey and Thomas time to assimilate the momentous changes that had happened to both of them, so I waited for two weeks after I got out of jail before I went over to Doom to visit. I have to admit that the *Daily Local* beat me out on having the first interview with the new Great Sun, but the questions Westnet's algorithm put to Thomas were so inane and biased that I didn't lose much. And, for me, more was at stake than professional pride. I didn't know what my relationship with Thomas and Janey should be now. Everything had changed, and, though I had a decent handle on what was happening in the world, what was happening inside *me* was a lot cloudier.

I walked to Doom late one afternoon, after the paper was out. Candle was growing steadily icier as the planet rocked away from our sun. Winter had lightly coated the forest, and now was beginning to settle into the cracks and niches of things. Sponge trees were shedding in downy white flakes, almost indistinguishable from the snow. The snow and sponge flakes were drifted against all the trees, as if someone had just swept up a forest full of litter into big piles. An occasional traveler kept the pathway more or less clear and passable. I knew that, even in winter, it would remain so. Despite our nigh-instantaneous mechanical and metaphysical transportation, some people would always prefer to walk.

Another reason I hadn't been over to see Thomas was because of the weather. In the city, with several thousand people around you all the time you don't notice, particularly when you're by yourself. Maybe I *had* been seeing thought and feeling in the weather all along, and Sarah—the part of her that made her anything like human—was *gone,* gone with the wind of cosmic radiation and tug of alien gravities.

But I clung to the fact that I had figured out it was her they'd used for the algorithm long before anyone had told me.

She'd been there, all right, in essence, if not completely. There were too many clues. But as I walked past Canoe Hill, there was nothing, just *nothing*. I was wrong, I decided, that every day on Candle is an animal. Or maybe not. Maybe this day was a *dead* animal—roadkill, hover-shredded and dumb.

Still, even in death—if she *were* dead—the cold atmosphere shone blue above me the color of deep water. There's an old settler's tale about how if you get up early enough in the morning, just after sunrise, on certain days in winter you can see the sky flicker, like those old, two-dimensional movies. That was part of the reason the pioneers called the place Candle. After the first weather algorithm was installed, nobody ever saw this anymore. Did I see the flicker this day? No, the sky was as solid as a shroud.

Thomas was at home, at his Wanderer's house. He couldn't move into the Great Sun's quarters until the year after the old Great Sun's death, according to Doom custom. Thomas didn't mind. Living in his *own* home was strange enough for him, after spending most of the last seven years living out of a canoe and backpack. Janey had moved in with Thomas's mother, Metayandi, but she was at Thomas's when I arrived.

They greeted me warmly enough, but quickly returned to the business at hand. Georgia Calhoun was attempting to take from Janey the deed to the land Janey had inherited from the chocalaca clay deposits. Since the gift from the Indians had been symbolic, for the most part, Thomas felt he had a right to take part in Janey's defense. Only Janey wasn't so sure she wanted to fight.

"It *means* for her, and not for me," said Janey. She was, even now, working on the beginnings of a quilt. Under her hands, a star pattern was forming.

"It *means* for Doom," said Thomas. "We made Stephen Calhoun an honored man and *then* we gave him the land. We gave it to him *as an Indian.*"

"And to his children," said Janey, concentrating on her stitching, not looking up. I could see that she was smiling faintly. Probably amused by Thomas's legal sophistry. This wasn't the sort of thing you used to hear out of him.

"Your father—" Thomas began. There was an almost inaudible noise in the room, as if a great animal stirred. I felt the electricity of Raej's presence. "I mean, your *step*father, gave the land to *you*, not to Georgia. Georgia will mine the clay and sell it. Most likely it will find its way to rhythm smugglers. You know that."

"So, so bad, these smugglers," said Janey, smiling more broadly now.

"Bad for Indians. We won't gain anything from it, and one way or another, it will hurt Doom."

Janey looked up, serious now. "It might stop war."

Thomas didn't answer immediately. He'd been sitting in a chair fashioned from hickory, with a sponge-tree cushion. He got up, walked to the fireplace, and ladled himself a cup of the Indian's strong, white tea, made from some of those dried sponge flakes that carpeted the woods. The Indians had another drink they made from *fermented* sponge flakes called *poocha*, but it was too early in the day for drinking. Thomas took a sip of the tea, and dribbled a bit on the tattoos of his chin. The drop spiraled down through the grooves and, instead of dropping off the tip of his chin, was carried down his neck and under his shirt. Somehow, the display was quite barbaric.

"One clay source is not going to make a lot of difference in the big picture," he said. "What do you think, Will?"

"Don't know," I said. "I just watch what happens for a living. Can't predict it. That's why I like my job."

My answer was flip, yes, but it seemed to irritate Thomas disproportionately. He was taking this Great Sun stuff pretty damn seriously.

"Come on, damn it," Thomas said. He set down the cup of

sponge tea, after having only taken a sip, and returned to his chair. I looked around for a seat. All the chairs in the room had legs that were just a little lower than Thomas's. This was probably from his Wanderer days, when he'd told stories in this room for the news junkies who hang on after a Gathering ceremony was over. He would need to be higher than the surrounding listeners. It was, nevertheless, as annoying as hell to me at the moment. I remained standing.

"Okay, then," I said. "I figure you're thinking that that clay deposit is the key to Indian power on Candle right now. It is substantial and, if it weren't in Indian hands, it would make the good folks of Jackson rich, rich, rich—notably, Georgia Calhoun. On the other hand, if it remains with Janey, and if Janey's on your side, then you have an ace for the Indians to play. Maybe not to make Indians wealthy—you already have enough clay of your own if you want to do that. But it could be just the ticket for getting concessions from Westpac and keeping maximum Indian sovereignty on Candle. Maybe you're using Janey for a bargaining chip. So there. How's that for an answer, oh Great Sun?"

"You're full of shit," said Thomas. "And Westpac propaganda. It's the same thing." He, too, stood up. He, of course, towered over me.

Janey started laughing. She got up, came over and took me and Thomas on either arm, guided us to the fire, and stood us there to warm.

She spoke in a low, calming voice. Quite a change from the out-of-control Janey of just a few weeks ago. "You're both bright flares and light showers. Bright, and not much heat. Let's get warm here."

"I don't like this," said Thomas. "This life. There's no *ambiguity* anymore, you know?"

"You're the Great Sun now," I said. "You have your responsibilities."

"You *have* to be an Indian," said Janey.

Thomas didn't reply. I made myself a cup of Thomas's tea and told them about my night in jail. Thomas had read old Lincoln

Calhoun's story in the paper. Some other Indians had, too, and Thaddeus Wala-andi, the Sun who was the Law-man of Doom, had told Thomas that he believed maybe Indians should give the settlers more time to understand Indian ways better before they rushed to attack. Thaddeus Wala-andi had for years been the nearest equivalent to an opposition party leader in Doom—though the Indians didn't really think in those terms. He commanded a great deal of respect in the village, and his words were listened to. So the article had done some good in both camps. There was, however, a strong faction who wanted to take the battle to Jackson before the settlers could get the might of Westpac behind them and take all the clay that belonged to Doom.

There was a strong Indian tradition of inter-group warfare, of merciless raids on weaker worlds. Most of this had been sublimated into interplanetary games and feasting, which the scattered clans occasionally put on. Also, power had been checked and balanced within the complicated kin-system of the tribes. But war was still a respectable way of gaining honor and standing, especially for the vast majority of Indians, who were not noble. Settlers offered an ideal target—there were almost no deep ties between Westpac culture and the Mississippians, and no custom of peaceful interaction other than trade. And trade only happened in fits and starts, for the most part. The Mississippian Indians had managed to keep to themselves for three hundred years. But now, the settlers wanted Indian clay. And many of Thomas's people were looking for a fight. Ideals and economics were mixed together on Candle like saltpeter and sulfur.

Thomas and I discussed these things. Janey said nothing, but sat working on her quilt. It was not that Janey did not take an interest—she followed and reacted to what we said—but I got the feeling that some *other*, unspeakable subject was more important to her. What that could be, I couldn't guess. She seemed amused, as if she were listening to children fervently discussing some subject that can only be of interest to themselves. This might have been irritating, coming from any other person, but Janey seemed to be taking control of her life with a vengeance, and if she wanted to patronize us a little, then, what the hell, maybe she'd earned it.

Imagine Emily Dickinson suddenly getting over her reclusive ways, her touch of madness, and making a big splash on the New England literary circuit. All the poems had come out of their neat bundles in the closet, as it were, and Janey could act in the world now, and not always be acted *upon*. She was going to decide what became of her property—she made that clear—and not me or Thomas, or the political climate of the known galaxy. Thomas stopped pestering her, and I stopped goading Thomas.

Thomas had enough problems, anyway. I could tell he wasn't particularly happy with being the living god of a whole village full of people. Doom wasn't that much to be god over, frankly.

Having left the Earth twelve hundred years ago, the Mississippians had escaped many of the evils of European, Asian, and African civilization, but they'd missed out on some of our better innovations, as well. Like indoor toilets. And, for better or worse, they hadn't been quick to adopt them after contact. Men, in Doom, piss outside their own front doors as a matter of course. Women, more modest, use the back. So the whole village is permeated with the faint odor of urine.

And, until the coming of Westpac, the Indians had never considered the quaint old custom of democracy. It was still a system they *liked* more than understood. Honored People and stinkards like it, that is, while the Suns and Nobles much preferred government by the well heeled. Slaves, officially, had no opinions. But a lot of them would tell you that they'd rather have a Sun for a master than some climbing Honored Person, whose conception of his own worth depended on the slave feeling worthless. There was a rough balance of power within the village, with Honored families vying to become Nobles, threatening democratic reforms if they didn't get their way, and Nobles occasionally elevating a few to relieve the tension. Slaves got to stay slaves.

And yet, as hackneyed as it may sound, I never met an Indian I didn't like. After they know who you are, and your *place* is established, their stony reserve vanishes. They will feast you down to their last cob of wintercorn, and pour *poocha* down your throat until you think you'll gag on the slick, vodka-ish slide of it. And all of them, every last Indian from slave to Sun, will defend your honor to their deaths, and weep very real tears if *you* should die. Even if they are the ones doing the killing. In fact, the greatness of your honor is directly proportional to the elaborateness of the tattoo a brave will receive for doing you in.

This, I think, was the one truly important innovation of Mississippian civilization. The Indians knew how to seize the day with a fierceness and joy, wring its neck like a prize pullet, and have it as the main course in a big dinner every evening. Even the slaves, perhaps particularly the slaves, seemed more alive from moment to moment than all of Jackson, and all of the Earth I'd left behind. This is why I liked going to Doom, and walking among the Indians.

But this is also why it could be a real pain in the ass to be Great Sun in this day and age, and have to always keep in mind the village's future. You often found that you had to think in some very un-Indian-like ways, and convince your subjects that yours was the best way, no matter how wrong it felt to them. Stirring up the Indians to attack had been natural and easy for Thomas. Keeping them at peace was another matter altogether.

As I was getting ready to leave, Thomas said to me, "I can't come into Jackson anymore. Not for a while, at least. Maybe you could come out here every once in a while to remind me what life used to be like?"

"You bet."

Then a couple of men came in—Honored Persons, judging by their tattoos—who wanted Thomas to resolve a dispute over a slave they were both displeased with. They wanted Thomas to decide which one had the better right to beat the slave.

"Christ," said Thomas, in English. Both of them appeared to speak only Loosa. "Why don't I just have the hell beaten out of both of *you*?"

They gazed at him, nonplussed, and resumed their argument. Thomas waved goodbye as Janey and I went out the door.

"Blue and thick like sour breath in the air," said Janey. "It hangs on him, Will."

"He misses being a Wanderer already."

"He misses being himself," said Janey.

Indian children ran through the snow in front of us, using small atlatls to launch iceballs at one another. These were made of snow, squeezed tightly together. They were almost as hard as rocks. In Doom, even the children played rough.

We walked toward the edge of town together, not saying much. The air was still and cold and I felt again the absence of Sarah. When Janey was outside, she had a way of looking about which seemed to take in both the wholeness of her surroundings and specific details, all at once, all completely. If she could only express what she saw like a normal person, she'd have made a great reporter. Janey couldn't sift the facts from her emotions, though. But I doubt if reporters are ever truly objective. We seem to miss something nebulous, but very, very real and important, hidden just around the edges of facts and events.

"Janey, is Sarah—"

"I can't feel her," said Janey. "But there was only the empty air before she showed herself to me. Maybe she's hiding again."

We walked farther and a wan breeze started up. I hunched my parka up more snugly about my shoulders.

"Come by where I live now," said Janey, taking my arm. "The woods are bitter cold, Will. You need some warming before you go out in them."

She guided me down a smaller pathway, around behind the huge mass of the Gathering Hall, to a large house covered with elaborate carvings akin to the swirls of Mississippian tattoos. These were a form of Loosa hieroglyphics, I knew, but I couldn't "read" Loosa. I knew the house, though. It was the dwelling place of Sun-sister Metay-andi, Thomas's mother. Nobody was home but the slaves.

The Indians didn't really have bedrooms, or any kind of living area, that belonged to one or another person. You shared according to caste. Janey was an Honored Person, but she had special status as a friend and advisor to the Great Sun, so nobody but Metay-andi could pull rank on her and get away with it. Janey had set up a semblance of a bedroom in one corner, complete with her rocking chair and her old trunk, which she'd somehow managed to get shipped over to Doom.

I sat on the trunk and she in the chair. The house was unpartitioned, except for a blanket that curtained off the cooking area. In the center of the room, the slaves kept a large fire going hot and smoky with dried sponge flakes and fir logs. It wasn't that the Indians did not put a high value on privacy, but that within Mississippian culture, there were other *places* to be private. Home was not one of them. Home was where you interacted with your kin. Hunters and farmers got all the privacy they wanted out in the world, trying to make a living.

Janey, as usual, picked up on what I was thinking.

"So many ways of the Indians itch and bite us," she said. "Thomas has a buzz around him, too."

"He sure is acting like a goddamned full-blood Sun," I said. I meant to accompany and punctuate the statement with a leisurely lean backwards, but I forgot that the trunk I was sitting on wasn't a chair and didn't have a back. I almost fell over upside down before I recovered myself.

"*Acting,*" Janey said. "Both of you."

"And you're just innocent Janey, I suppose . . ."

She got out of her rocker, leaned over and kissed me full on the mouth. Then she sat back down and smiled coyly, not meeting my eyes.

"No," she said, "I'm Janey who never could make her mind up before, because her mind wasn't hers to make up."

She rocked gently in the chair, looking more at peace than I'd ever seen her.

"Now Father's here," she said. She touched her breast, above the heart. "Inside me. And with Thomas. But he's so busy, busy with the other one, the other things, and I—"

The other things? I thought, smelling a story. The other *one,* she'd said. In my brief contact with Raej, when Thomas had brought him back to inhabit the clay, I'd seen that vision of translucent evilness—a nameless Menace that occupied a place of hatred in Raej's imagination or consciousness or whatever you want to call the place in chocalacas where emotions intersect memories.

"The snake-thing that reeks of bad intentions? Is that what's keeping Raej's attention?"

"*Hwaet,*" said Janey.

I thought she said "what," so I repeated my question.

"Hwaet is the one," said Janey. "Father has to spend all his time keeping—"

I waited for more, but she'd realized that she was giving away information that maybe she didn't want to.

"—how do you know Hwaet, Will?"

I felt like saying something like "I have my sources," but I was not at all certain if it were possible to lie to Janey, knowing her quaint capacity for gazing directly into people's souls.

"Something is going on these days with the chocalacas, and not just Indians and settlers. Am I right?"

"I don't—" said Janey, and she touched my arm. Raej was there. A coldness swept through me, ten times more freezing than the below zero temperature outside. Disdain, distaste.

It was only an analog copy of Raej, a manifestation in this world, using the common laws of physics and information transfer, but *Janey* was not of this world, I now knew, just as the real Raej was not. So there was a supernatural tinge to the icy cold she and Raej imparted. Janey was the conduit, and the Raej inside her—as real as our perceived reality allowed him to be—knew how to turn on Janey's metaphysical electricity. What I felt was more akin to the dark night of the soul than to a blast of chilled air.

"Okay, okay, I'll drop it," I said. Janey rocked back in her chair, then continued bobbing in a more nervous pattern.

"It's not that we don't trust you," she said, after a while. "It's just that trying to *say* to you disturbs the . . . weavework, the—way."

She touched her temple as if to massage the words out of her cerebrum.

"I can't explain."

"Does Thomas know anything?"

"Thomas only *feels* with Raej," she said, then repeated the old Loosa truism: "Chocalacas think otherwise."

"You are a dangerous woman, Janey," I said. "You can become a weapon. Don't forget that."

"I understand so much now," she said, and stopped rocking.

"The more you understand, the more dangerous you'll get," I said. And a man who comes to love you does so at political peril, I thought. She glanced up and saw the thought in me.

"You're worried about Thomas and me?"

"And you and *me*. And Candle."

"Because of what I am?"

"Some people just can't help it," I said. "They're storm-bringers."

She got up and took my hands, raised me off the trunk, then opened it. It was, as I suspected, full of quilts. Janey stared at them for a long time, with a sort of sadness. She touched one, lifted it up. It was brown and green, patterned with yellows and reds as wildflowers are flecked across a mountain field on Earth.

"This is how I lived for so long," she whispered to herself. "This was the only way I could live."

"Are you still making quilts?" I said, mainly because I could think of no other reply.

"Not like my life depends on it," Janey answered. She gathered the quilt into her arms the rest of the way, snuggled it a moment, then handed it to me.

"This will keep you warm going home," she said.

"A cure for the uncommon cold?" I took it. It smelled, somehow, of rain and earth.

"I made it thinking about a kettle boiling in a meadow."

I folded the quilt under my arms and made to go.

"One more thing, Will," Janey said. "We want to give you one more thing."

"We?"

"I've never felt so in control of my life, Will," she said. "I wish I could tell you how good, how very good, it is to give instead of needing, taking, all the time."

She was smiling, and the light from the blazing fire was putting that sheen in her hair that reminded me so much of Sarah's.

"What do you want to give me?"

"I haven't decided yet," Janey said. "There's so much brightness between you and him. Both of you spark when I touch you."

"You haven't decided *what* yet?"

"Between you and Thomas."

"Well," I said, "there's that." And then I felt compelled to remind her. "And there's Sarah. For me, there will always be Sarah."

"I can't forget her either. We wanted to give—"

She reached out and touched my cheek with a white hand.

My insides exploded like pent-up fireworks. Raej and Janey's consciousness arced into me with a charge of feeling, coursing through my mind.

The gift was the memory of Sarah that Janey had taken from their brief amalgamation and cohabitation within Janey's body. It was not Janey's recollection of Sarah, but the actual, unalloyed thoughts, uncurled from the past like rope pulled off a reel when an anchor lowers. Sarah, dynamic and alive, within the confines of those brief moments when she and Janey had been in intimate contact, within the limits of a mentality of complete emotion and inspiration.

Janey pulled her hand away, and I stood shaking.

"You asked me if it was really her," Janey said. "It's *really* Sarah. And it's really *me*. Maybe we both want you."

I could not say anything. The rush of information, of feeling, was overwhelming.

"Before, wanting you bounced around inside me like a little bird," Janey said. "Everything bounced and spun. So I kissed you, and I cried and—"

"I thought you wanted Thomas," I finally managed to get out. That seemed sane, certain.

"Sometimes I did. Sometimes I do. Now there is remembering Sarah, how she wants you."

I took a breath. Suddenly, this all seemed very funny.

"What you're saying is that now you are undecided about Thomas and me, but you are in control. You're able to decide what course your life'll take?"

"It feels really good."

"Yes, well, remember that *I* get to decide too. And Thomas."

"Of course. But there's all this war and misunderstanding and evil and I'm still so happy. I can *choose*. Me. Janey."

I had to agree that this was a good thing. I'd admired her, perhaps loved her; I'd never thought she was happy until now.

"So, it's going to be a little competition among friends, huh," I said. I wanted to tweak her cheek, but figured I'd better hold off on that for the moment. Raej might be in there, waiting to bite me.

"If you want," she said. She took my hand, and it was just a man and a woman, holding hands.

"We'll see," I said. I wrapped the blanket around my shoulders. "We'll see." I turned and left. Janey understood that I wanted to be alone. I looked back as I got to the door and saw her on the other side of the large house, rocking and smiling in her special corner. I waved and pushed aside the skins over the entranceway. Once again, I was out in the cold.

For some reason there were a goodly number of settlers coming and going along the West Wood trail as I made my way back to Jackson. I was never really alone. There was the rattle of leaves, the crunch of snow under someone else's boots, and the sound of voices discussing business. Overhead, an occasional canoe or hover soared by. All of this was a good sign. Trade may not be friendship, but it does bring about some commitments on both sides of a deal, and usually some respect when the other guy honors the bargain. Indians and settlers could stand a healthy dose of respect for one another, I thought.

For a while, it looked like business and friendship would bond us back together, that the weft and warp of our existence would withstand the anger and greed that had erupted. I took to visiting Thomas pretty regularly over the next few months. Before we'd only been together when he returned for Gathering and to give Janey her rhythm. He'd been more of a mythical figure to me than a companion. Being around him more, I lost a little of my awe. But not much. Thomas made a hell of a Great Sun.

And we both saw Janey.

Janey stayed in Doom, but Thomas and I ventured into Jackson one evening, under the cover of a snow storm, to visit our old haunt, the Goosedown. Before, when Thomas had finished delivering the rhythm to Janey, and we'd seen her safely home, we'd go over to the Goosedown for a couple of rounds. I'd buy and Thomas would pay me back with stories of Wandering. Not the kind that get told at Gathering, with their peculiar Indian interest, but the kind he would tell if there were any such thing as a Wanderer for settlers. Almost all Wanderers avoided non-Indian worlds on their travels, but Thomas often stopped at them for provisions and, he confided once—after more than one whiskey—to get away from all the Indian in him for a while. But he still got treated differently, like he didn't quite belong. It was hard when you flew in from outer space in a birchbark canoe.

Oldfrunon, who, after all these years, still tended bar most evenings at the place, treated us right. A free round for the Great Sun and the Press, a quiet booth near the back. It was dim back there. Oldfrunon had rigged his ceiling to glow with the light of dawn.

And somehow or another, he'd worked into it that flicker that was supposed to have filled the morning sky on Candle before they installed Sarah and the lesser programs that came before her. The uncertain lighting made you feel kind of like you were going in and out of existence. But it wasn't bad, either. Being in the tavern was sort of cinematic, if you know what I mean. Anything might happen, you felt. Oldfrunon ran it with a halfsent as quiet as a mouse walking through feathers. You barely had to speak, and your drink ran from a wall tap—no banter, no mix-ups.

We ended up talking about Janey, of course. I was joking

around, as usual, trying to take the edge off the tension I felt when the subject came up. Thomas cut straight to the marrow.

"Do you want her?" he asked, his eyes as disturbing as ever in the weird lighting.

"Want? Need? Hell, I don't know what my status is, as far as affairs of the heart go," I said, then took a sip of my bourbon and water. Bourbon that was cheap enough to ship in bulk to Candle was not the best, but Oldfrunon sprinkled in something local and sweet to cut the tang of rotting-out seasoning barrels and cosmic rays. "Are reconstituted radio waves officially allowed to have a love life?"

Thomas didn't answer. He took a long draw on his whiskey.

"All right," I said. "I don't know. What about you?"

He drank some more whiskey.

"She worries me. She knows something. Something about the chocalacas and Raej."

For a moment, there was the blue-green flicker of Raej's presence, competing with the strobing ceiling. Then nothing.

"Raej is fighting."

"Fighting?"

"Over there, in the true world. Where Janey can see. I can feel a lot of . . . strife. It worries me."

"Why?"

"Because it might be bad for Doom, bad for Indians."

"Why don't you just ask Raej?" I said, knowing the answer before I got the words out of my mouth.

"It doesn't work that way," Thomas said.

I completed his thought: "Chocalacas think otherwise."

"And Janey is half-chocalaca," he said. He took a long drink. "But I think I'm falling for her."

In addition to going against my personal interest, there was a greater problem with this. Thomas might be a half-breed outcast, but he was the Great Sun. I couldn't help wondering if Thomas's desire for Janey were not tinged with political interest. If Janey continued to master herself and her peculiar skills, she could become a potent weapon if war broke out between the

Indians and Westpac. She had a direct line to the real world of the chocalacas.

Lots of people talked a lot of talk, but nobody really had much of a clue as to what really went on over there, in that super reality. Westpac and the Mississipians could access the place or power or whatever it was, but neither could explain or control it. Janey could change that for whoever had her loyalty. Whoever could claim her love.

Thomas and I poured alcohol down our gullets and talked of the days when time was more of a gentleman cutpurse than a mugger intent on doing us bodily harm.

It started getting late, and the storm outside had kept business to a trickle this evening. Near closing time, Oldfrunon wandered over and sat down with us. He was drinking a *poocha*, the Indian drink, without a strainer.

"You're going to kill yourself, old man," Thomas said. "Maybe it took us a thousand years, but when we learned how to make that stuff, we made it strong enough to reach back in time and give our ancestors a jangle."

"I was suckled on poocha, son," said Oldfrunon. "Why do you think I've lived so long?"

With that, Oldfrunon took a healthy swallow, leaving a few flakes of fermented sponge on his lips. His face broke into a horrid grimace; he shook his head and let out a long, hoarse breath. Then he licked the extra sponge flakes from his lips, moaning with satisfaction.

"Indians don't drink it that way," said Thomas, amused.

"I'm not an Indian," Oldfrunon said. "But I know some that *do* drink it that way. Depends on the Indian."

"Crazy men come from all walks of life," I said. I'd had *poocha* in my time. It was so bitter it made you want to shoot your dog, and as sweet as drinking down a pint of IV fluid.

"Yeah, and sane ones," said Oldfrunon.

He was staring at Thomas when he said this.

Then we all got quiet and gazed into our drinks.

"I got a letter yesterday," Oldfrunon said, after a while. "A little merchant jobber stopped by yesterday to pick up some supplies on his way to Etawali. Friend of mine back on Earth wrote me."

Oldfrunon was silent for a moment. Thomas, who'd been feigning the least of interest, sat up.

"What did your friend say?" he asked.

"Well, you know, Earth is a mighty strange place," said Oldfrunon, rubbing his hands together, gearing up to tell us the real gist. "Tree cities, halfsents out the wazoo, those Ideals and their drones, a rhythm eyepiece at every corner."

"We've heard the stories," I said.

"You remember the Board of Trade ruling five years ago that let Clerisy serve in the agencies?"

It had been a big deal. Up until then, the Clerisy had been completely opposed to having anything to do with Westpac government or citizenship, since Westpac was the descendant of capitalist corruption and statist oppression or something like that. But the Clerisy had finally wanted in on the action itself. Since its priests were constitutionally barred from serving in elected office, they'd lobbied for places in the executive bureaucracy. Indeed, priests had made great bureaucrats.

"Well, looks like it's paid off in a big way for the bastards," Oldfrunon said. "There's some alliances falling into place, and it looks like the Clerisy's going to start having the main say-so in Territorial policy within a few months."

If this upset Thomas, he didn't show it. He finished off his whiskey. Oldfrunon made to order the tavern to produce another for him, but Thomas shook his head.

"How can that be?" I said. "We would have heard."

"What my friend says, is that the Clerisy has managed to cut a secret deal with Courage 3."

"Idealists," I said.

"That's right," said Frank. "The second-largest group mind on Earth. A block vote of seventeen million people. If you want to call them *people*."

"Bad for Indians," said Thomas, looking dark and troubled.

"Bad for us all," said Oldfrunon. "Expansion shut down. Indian ties cut."

"So, is your friend doing anything about this?" asked Thomas. "Or is it too late?"

"Lots of people are trying lots of things," Oldfrunon said. "Most everybody on the Steering Committee is scared shitless."

"What can the Indians do?" said Thomas.

Oldfrunon rocked back in his chair with a squeak and rustle.

"Be prepared," he said. He reached across the table and put his drinking mug under the tap. *"Poocha,"* he said, and the white liquid slid out like warm jelly full of scabs. Oldfrunon drained the mug with one, incredibly long draught. Then he gingerly set his mug down on our table.

"Good evening, gentlemen," he said. "Stay as long as you like. The place will lock up after you're on your way."

Thomas and I drank until the cold dawn.

7

It's news and holiday when a big ship lumbers down out of the
sky and settles its mass down on the south side of town, in the
big flat field of silk that we call Jackson Interplanetary Port of
Call when we are in a civic-minded mood. Otherwise, it's just
the Docks. Sure, Candle *was* the first inhabitable planet discovered when Western Civ. first set out to visit the stars, but that
doesn't mean that it was the *most* inhabitable, or even that very
many people would want to live here at all. The only area that
was bearably warm in the winter was here at the equator, near
the geothermal vents. Other places grew exponentially over the
past three hundred years, while Jackson has hardly done more
than triple in population since it was first a colony.

The big ships seldom came our way. We were not on any of
the larger trade routes. About the only place we were in the path
of was little Etawali, a planet as hot as Candle was cold. But
every six months, one did. She was called the *Irrelevance,* believe
it or not, about fifty years old, commissioned and named under
Niedra "Smiling Sissy" Colblane, who rose so meteorically
from being a two-bit damaged-pleasure-boat liquidator to the
Undersecretary of the Undercommittee on Territorial Transportation and Communications for Westpac.

At the time, there was a big brawl over whether Candle's

sector rated a jumbo cruiser. Colblane thought *not*. The rest of
the Steering Committee thought they'd better, if they wanted to
keep their seats, so they gave Colblane the money and told her
where to spend it. She retained, however, the power to name all
vessels. And so we have the *Pork Barrel* class of cruisers, of which
the *Irrelevance* is a member in good standing.

Irrelevance day down at the Docks is, then, a big deal. Kids get
half days off at the school and everybody who can comes along
to watch the unloading, to meet new passengers and settlers, and
to pick up mail. I usually go down and cover it for the paper,
if nothing else of importance is happening—and it usually isn't.
The dockhouse is about the only building in Jackson that does
not follow a frontier revival architecture. Instead, it was built by
Earthers shortly before the *Irrelevance* was commissioned. The
structure previously there could not accommodate such a large
ship, the Jackson Council claimed. This had prompted the
Steering Committee to set aside even more money than bud-
geted, and had really pissed off Undersecretary Colblane. She
sent a work gang out to build the new dockhouse, and had them
deliberately build something that looked more like a kraken
reaching for victims, than what it actually was—a central building with self-extending accessways that reached out to the various entranceways on the ships that used the Docks.

People clustered inside the dockhouse according to their purposes for being there. Children lined the windows of the building, waiting to see the ship dip down out of the sky. Others,
those who'd come to meet passengers, lined the main accessway,
jostling for a first look, like crowded red blood cells lining up to
enter a capillary. Johan, the Territorial Wire tech was there,
laden with equipment, standing nonchalantly in another accessway, ready to make sure the connection to the ship's information port was clean and complete. Beside him was Electa
Nyemba, Jackson's Postmaster, ready to transfer and categorize
the big clump of mail she'd be off-loading, as well as to jack in
for the more common electronic variety. The machines could all
take care of themselves, and the ship really didn't need any

support personnel at all, but we were there to complete a sort of ritual more than anything else. It would feel *unlucky* if nobody was there to meet the *Irrelevance*.

I was mostly interested in the passengers. Whatever news the ship was bringing would be on the Wire immediately and the *Cold Truth*'s trusty halfsent would be digesting it for my perusal. I knew, for the most part, who was off traveling, who'd taken the six months or longer that a round trip to Earth took out of his life, or the even longer periods trips to the outlying Territory required.

Today a couple of reps from Candle Sponge were returning with orders from Earth, where they couldn't get enough of our native "tree." I wanted to get the specifics from them before Ben Lowenstein, the main wordman at the Sponge company, put his PR spin on things. The *Daily Local* ran his press releases almost word for word. I tried to delve a little deeper with the *Cold Truth*. Nevertheless, Ben and I liked one another well enough.

Also there were a couple of kids coming back after two years at boarding school somewhere in Europe. All I needed to do was bank their pictures as they ran into the arms of chauffeurs and nannies; the real parents of such children usually couldn't be bothered with an appearance at the Docks.

I poised myself halfway down the passenger access arm, just far enough back, I judged, to get an overview of the people getting off. Through the slightly milky windows of the arm, I watched the *Irrelevance* descend. There was no sound; there never was. But, even in the accessway, you could feel something—a presence, the crowding of atmosphere to make way for the voluminous ship. Then the animal glide of the accessway as the dockhouse's pseudopods—made out of pseudocells—reached out to caress and mate. Programmed routines took over to settle in and secure the *Irrelevance* as the ship emerged from the inertialess true world into gravity-bound reality.

Then it was down, and real, and normal people began to step through the entranceway. There was a young couple standing back with me; I knew them, vaguely, as involved with the administration of Justice Day activities. An older couple came out of the space ship—relatives, maybe—and, confounding all my expectations, ran with sprightly gaits up the hallway and into the arms of the younger couple. They must be natives of a high grav world, I decided. I tried to get out of the way, ducked to one side, then another, and ended up squeezing myself against the wall as the elderly couple barreled past me, intent on hugs and reunion.

Then Sarah walked by in front of me.

I stared after her. Couldn't think. Could not breathe.

But it was just the cascade of auburn hair, I told myself, watching the woman from behind. And the shape of her torso, not quite the classic hourglass, stocky and strong. And those long legs. She was as tan and lithe as when I'd last seen her, when I stepped into the transmission chamber. Then, quiet as a supplicant priest, I was following the woman through the dockhouse.

She reached the central dockhouse and looked around. The woman's profile clicked into place over my memory of Sarah's like spoons fitting together in a drawer. The woman looked perturbed, exasperated. She faced a wall.

"Spaceport," she said in a commanding tone. It was Sarah's voice, but rougher, full of expectations that were *always* satisfied.

"Yes, ma'am," said the dockhouse halfsent in an official, bluish voice. "Can I help you?"

"Where can I get a drink and accommodations?"

"Accommodations" was a word Sarah would never use. Would she? A quick sadness passed over as I found that I couldn't remember.

"There are several bars in town. I regret that I have no resources to offer you," said the halfsent. "The Jackson Port of Call is rather small by Earth standards, I'm afraid."

The woman didn't bother to reply. "Get me a hover, please," was all she said.

The halfsent seemed to hesitate in embarrassment, but was probably checking its records.

"Again, I apologize, but the taxi into town already had a party of four—"

"Then get me another one."

"As I said, the taxi into town is already engaged for the time—"

I stepped forward, between her and the wall.

"It means to say that there is only *one* taxi in Jackson, and Herb has already got his fare."

"You can't be saying—"

"Maybe I could take you into town. My hover's just outside."

"And who are you?" she asked. For a moment, I could say nothing. Sarah, flushed and freckly when she was ticked off about something. But never at slight inconvenience, as this woman was.

"I'm your free ride into town," I replied. "Or, you can always walk. We have good roads here, silky smooth. It does get a bit cold, though, I'll warn you . . ."

She had, to my amazement, only two bags, both small. She was wearing one of those Earth-white-collar-professional uniform things, blue and white jacket and skirt, expensive. No doubt it was a whole wardrobe in one outfit, self-cleaning and self-transforming. I walked beside her and tried to catch the smell of her hair, her skin.

"Do you suppose we could stop and get a drink?" she said as we buzzed toward Jackson in my hover. "I detested the beer they had on that stupid ship. I couldn't bring myself to try the wine and spirits."

"Sure," I said, and headed for the Goosedown. Oldfrunon was out, but the halfsent directed me to the back, to my usual table.

Her drink came. A Grayboy is what they called it; basically it's a martini with a dash of those mild hallucinogens—Ether was the common name—that starship captains sometimes took in elephantine doses. She took a sip, made something approximating a smile with her lips, then sat back and stared at the flicker of the ceiling.

"Going to be here long?" I asked, just to have a reason to look at her eyes. Cascade-green.

"Depends," she said, and drank some more.

"You have business on Candle or are you just passing through?"

"Both," she said. Blank. She wouldn't give me a smile. "Maybe."

This was crazy. Sarah was sitting across from me, in the flesh, and she was *pretending* like she was another person, that she didn't know me. I couldn't help it; I reached across the table and touched her hand.

"Sarah," I said.

"I beg your pardon?" She withdrew her hand.

No. *No*. My brain felt like it was going to expand outward and blast my skull into shrapnel.

"You don't remember," I said. "You don't—"

"My name is Tabitha James," the woman said. She began to collect her bags, which she'd set on the bench beside her. "I'm sure I've never met you before in my life."

Tabitha James. Tabitha *James*. And there, on her wrist, half hidden in the cuff of her suit jacket, was the dull shine of old brass.

"I appreciate the lift and all, but I believe I'll find my own way to whatever boarding places this planet possesses. There *is* more than one, I hope."

I started to laugh. It must have sounded slightly maniacal, because she stopped speaking to me at all and made to get up. I got control of myself.

"Wait a minute, Tabitha," I said. "Excuse my behavior. It's just . . . I suddenly realized that we were related, *genetically*, that is, and it . . . unsettled me for a second there."

"What on earth are you talking about?"

"Not on *Earth*. That's the point. It's all in the stars, so to speak."

Again she started to leave. I beckoned her to stay. She hesitated, then sat back down.

"All right, what the hell are you talking about?" she said. "Who are you?"

"Name's Will James," I said.

"There's lots of Jameses."

"Any Wills in your family tree?"

"I don't know; I was never that interested."

"I see."

"What exactly *do* you see, Mr. James?"

"Frank's got some rooms upstairs, here at the Goosedown," I said. "They're the best in town, I promise you. You can arrange it with the halfsent here."

I squeezed out of the booth and stood up.

"But—"

"You'd better get settled in, Tabitha. Then I'll come back and we can talk."

"Talk about what?"

"Old times, Tabitha James. The olden days."

With that, I left. I wasn't trying to be rude or cryptic with Tabitha, it's just that I had so much to assimilate, all at once. I walked down the cold streets of Jackson as afternoon darkened to evening. I'd complete forgotten my hover, still parked in front of the Goosedown.

She came by the office the next day, right as I was opening up. Some of the irritation at this small, inconvenient world had gone out of her and she spoke with a softer voice. But never a real smile.

"I searched my dormants yesterday night after you were gone," she said, referring to those neat files of superfluous information the more well-to-do Earthers keep squirreled in their brains like dried-out acorns. "I found a great-grandfather, eleven times removed, whose name was Will James. My eleven times great-grandmother's name was Sarah. So what are you? Some long-lost cousin?"

She was standing in the entrance foyer, looking over the long front desk that separated customers from the working area. I was on the other side, up to my elbows in an optical downloader that I was trying to fix the focus on.

"Do you know what a reinstantiated transmission is?" I said, trying to figure out the best way to get my hands out of the delicate inner workings of the downloader without fucking it up worse than it had been.

Tabitha stood there for a long time, looking sort of like a mannequin. Her hands hung at her sides.

"I'd heard they were doing something like . . ." she said, her voice trailing off.

"They *did*. Nine years ago, in my case."

"Oh, my God, you're—"

"Welcome to Candle, granddaughter," I said, and neatly extracted my hands from the machine.

I asked her into the office and we drank coffee together. I told her about Sarah and she told me what she knew about my descendants. What she knew was pretty vague. The bracelet she wore had come from her mother, who said only that it was an old family heirloom and to guard it and pass it on if she ever had a child. Apparently genealogy hadn't been very popular in the last few years on Earth.

She told me she was a consultant working for Westpac, on Candle to investigate the disbursement of a couple of grants that Jackson had received. Routine work, required in the legislation, nothing for the City Council or the Mayor to worry about. From here, she'd go on to Etawali, to do the same thing, then, via Candle, out deeper into the Territory before returning to Earth. It was a two-year assignment.

Tabitha was forty-one. Two years older than me. The more she relaxed, the more she looked like Sarah—Sarah as she would have looked ten years older, ten years more used to the world. She took off her jacket, and the bracelet hung loosely on her thin wrist, sliding up and down her forearm as she talked and made gestures. I could barely keep my eyes off it.

After a while, she left, going to the Town Hall, she said, to see about those grants. I put the paper out that afternoon in a daze. What was I feeling? Amazement, mostly. Love, resurgent, with no rightful object. Lust.

I felt almost as if my rational mind had forbidden any real love to rise to my consciousness, but sexual desire, only tenuously connected to rationality in the first place, had wormed its way into my thoughts and curled up like an adder getting ready to strike.

For another night, I wandered through the streets of Jackson, letting the freezing cold take the edge off my bewilderment. What was happening to me lately? I'd spent nine years dampening my hopes, disassociating my desires from care and love. I'd taken my sexual satisfaction in small dollops, or not at all. Whenever anything hinted of emotional attachment, I was gone with a flash and smoke. And then came Janey. Somehow, she'd gotten through those defenses—probably because I had other obligations to her, with Thomas and the yearly rhythm delivery. Also, she looked so much like Sarah.

I'd never realized how important looks could be to me, how deep down they reached. This was pretty stupid, I figured, but I felt powerless to do anything about it. Maybe there is something genetic, I thought, that answers to a certain look, a certain cast of the eyes, in a woman. Hell if I could say *what* it was. More likely it was my own past.

Sarah had shook my soul, strummed me like a guitar. Maybe what I was feeling was the sympathetic vibrations left over from that Sarah-chord. I felt like I'd been strummed all over again by that dour civil servant who'd just walked into my office, taken off her jacket, and moved her hands *just like Sarah*. Yes, it was in the small movements that the similarity lay. The way Tabitha and Sarah worked their hands. The way that bracelet's movement punctuated their conversations. That bracelet, binding them together over five hundred years.

I ended up at the Goosedown, drinking alone. Up near the front, a local guy named Garston something spooned out a song on a halfsent hammer dulcimer that did not seem to play the same notes that were being struck. Meanwhile a woman—no more than a girl, really, and up long past her bedtime—sang a melody that seemed to have absolutely nothing to do with the *dulcimer's* tune.

It had taken me longer to get used to the music that people listened to these days than almost anything else. It was the music that reminded me that this was not my time, that I was a peg hammered into a hole that was not shaped to accept me, a hole that I had to split and splinter in order to accommodate. It wasn't that I didn't like the music. I loved it. It was like a blind man who loves a face by touch only. He's missing something, but he's not sure what.

After a while, Frank Oldfrunon came over. I said nothing, but didn't object when he asked to sit with me. Oldfrunon was looking a bit haggard lately, as if the wear of being mayor in this time of strife was starting to show. I don't want to appear his complete stooge, and tell you that he was some sort of doddering old fellow who held the position out of communal respect and generosity. As much as I admired the man, I knew he was as shrewd a political mover as they come. Here on Candle, he was in semiretirement. At least, that's what I thought at the time.

"You should stop worrying so much," I said, "and let the halfsents run the town for a while."

He looked at me slyly. "What makes you think I *don't*?"

"Too many wrinkles on your face."

"Had them cut in surgically. Makes people think I'm a deep thinker."

"You'd have to be to try a scam like that."

This got him to think a little, which I liked doing for Oldfrunon. He seemed to be fighting boredom a lot of the time. Or maybe I was mistaking patience, and prescience, for boredom.

"I've got a peculiar one up in the rooms," said Oldfrunon, after a bit. "Westpac inspector."

"I've met her," I said, relaxing, trying not to give away any feelings.

"Idealist if I ever saw one."

Now I sat up, paid attention.

"What are you talking about?"

"Lots of tell-tales," said Oldfrunon. He leaned back and crossed his arms. If he'd had a pipe, he'd have looked the perfect drawing-room detective. "Anxious manner. Movement just a trifle jerky—like she's not used to acting with her own consciousness. Snappy."

"Hell, Frank, there's lots of people who *aren't* idealists who move the same way," I said, relieved that I could believe my own arguments.

"I saw the aerial, son."

"What?"

"The little polychrome rod all of them have. Sticks out about so." Oldfrunon touched the back of his head with one hand and indicated that the aerial was a quarter-inch long with the thumb and forefinger of his other hand. "Oh, it's organic, part of her brain. But the brain's been reworked, you know, like you take an old hover, gut out the engine, and put in a new drive. She's got a WORM in there on the back side of her skull."

"A what?"

"Write-Once-Read-Only quasifroth memory," said Oldfrunon. "She's got a miniature version of her Ideal to give her directions while she's out here, disconnected from the cellular network."

"How the hell do you know this?"

"Oh, I've run into my share of Idealists over the years. Had a few fights with them back when I was doing my work for the Steering Committee. They take to politics like maggots to a dead man." He leaned back in his seat and smiled evilly at me.

"Are you saying that Tabitha has no personality at *all*? Am I talking to the WORM when I talk to her?"

"Well, no, not exactly. The WORM can only give her minimal support on Candle, sort of like a real sophisticated pop-up. *Poocha,*" he said, and put a glass under the tap. The tavern obliged. "There's no network here. She's cut off, and she has to act independently. That's why she moves so jerky and lacks . . . social grace. She'd become a different person if she was hooked into her Ideal."

"Which one do you think it is?" I asked, a trace of horror creeping into my voice.

Oldfrunon took a moment to consider.

"Don't know. Haven't been around them for years," he replied. "Could be Worker, One of the Courages, Flag, Mother Earth . . ."

"Or one of the new ones?"

"That I couldn't tell you," he said, and drank some unstrained *poocha*.

The music in the background paused for a long moment. I thought that the group was packing up for the night, but they started in, tunelessly, once again, with no timing I could discern.

"I want to tell you something, Frank," I said.

Oldfrunon looked me over and saw that I was struggling to get out what I wanted to say. He waited patiently.

"That woman reminds me of somebody I used to know."

Oldfrunon chewed on this a moment. I noticed the background music again. This time, the voice and dulcimer united with a rush, as if both had been lost in the woods for hours, each with half a map, then suddenly had come upon each other and, together, found the way home.

"Somebody I used to know *really* well," I said. "In fact, I'm going to go and tell her that right now."

I got up. I was a little drunk, and I stumbled. The tavern did something with the floor that caused a chair to slide over in front of me and I was able to grab it and keep from falling down. Oldfrunon watched all this impassively. I got myself straightened up and unruffled.

"Will," said Oldfrunon, "be careful, son. Idealists can eat you alive if you don't watch out."

I acted the fool, like he'd questioned my dignity or my ability to take care of myself. "Don't worry about *this* reporter, old man. My mama suckled me on cynicism."

I walked off, leaving him contemplatively finishing his *poocha*. The musicians hit a strangled, incomprehensible final chord, then were silent.

I was worried that Tabitha had told her door to keep out all visitors, but either she'd forgotten or didn't care. I told it who I was and that I wanted to see Tabitha James on a family matter. After a moment, the door swung open and a blast of warm air wafted over me. Apparently, she had the room's heater cranked up full blast. Earthers usually took a while to adjust to the daily chill that seemed to seep even into the insides of Candle's buildings.

"Come in, Will James," said a voice in the hot darkness. Despite the heat, a chill rippled through me for a moment. What *was* I up to here? That door opening seemed to breathe out and in like a maw. But the alcohol warmed my gut-level courage, if not the rest of me, and I stepped through. The door swung shut behind me.

"Come over and have a seat," Tabitha's voice said. My pupils began to dilate and I saw that she was sitting in one of the overstuffed chairs that were everywhere in the Goosedown. She was looking out the window. There was a guttering candle on a nearby table, throwing out light and shadow. I couldn't imagine what Tabitha was looking at; the window overlooked the back alley.

"I'm very lonely tonight," Tabitha said. "I'm glad you came by."

She turned to me, and in the faint light of the candle, she was *Sarah*. Sarah lit by the lights of San Bernardino shining through the window of our house in the mountains. Sarah curled onto the rug, unhooking from the mindlink after we'd made love with a closeness never possible between two people before.

"You're . . ." I stammered.

"I *do* look just like her, don't I?" Tabitha said. She stood up. "There's a holo of her, in the old records."

I didn't say anything; I just stared at her, drinking in the sight, remembering.

"Perhaps I *feel* like her too," said Tabitha. She stood up. "I know that I find myself attracted to you, Will."

I shook my head to try and clear it. "Why?" I asked.

"I don't know. Genetic memory, perhaps."

"Yeah, right."

But she stepped closer to me, and the closer she came, the more my skepticism waned. It was *possible*, wasn't it? I mean, girls were always falling for guys who looked like their father.

Sure, the human genome was known to the last jot and tittle, but there were lots of sequences that were considered mere genetic garbage. Maybe one of those was actually the secret code for—

Ah, hell, I pulled her toward me and kissed her. She responded warmly, her hands caressing my arms, my face. I felt the metal brush of the bracelet against my cheek. It was warm, just as her skin was, from the heat being turned so high in the room. Her lips were Sarah's—pliant like muscle, neither too soft nor too bruising.

"Would you like to—" I started to say something like "would you like me to take you to dinner," or somesuch, but Tabitha began to undo my shirt.

"Uh-huh," she said. "I *would* like."

She finished unbuttoning my shirt, and I slumped out of it and my parka, leaving only my long underwear top. I pulled it over my head, having a little difficulty getting the collar around my chin. When I had it off, Tabitha's blouse was undone. Her pants were around her ankles, and she stepped out of them. I've never known a woman who could undress so quickly.

She stooped to unbutton my pants, and I stroked her hair, the back of her head—and my fingers caressed the aerial which curled out of the base of her skull like a wispy pigtail.

"Frank was right," I murmured.

"Hmm?" she said, but then she clasped me in her hand, stroked me, led me to her bed.

"How was she?" Tabitha asked. "How was Sarah to be with? Oh, never mind. Don't answer."

I kissed her neck, and she rolled under me, while I continued downward, down to her breasts. The same curve, the same delicate brown, almost red, coloring to her nipples. Or was it just the candlelight, my hopes? It didn't matter.

And I was inside her, breathing her inside me. She didn't have the country smell, the smell of rain and hay, but there was something pleasing about her, as if this was how Sarah *would* smell, had she grown up in the city. Tabitha smelled of parks and the velvet backs of cushions in theaters.

Then she was on top of me, rocking to my rhythm, making mine her own, just as Sarah had done so many times. Sweet, feminine coercion, needing so much that I *had* to give.

The room grew hotter and hotter to be in—Earth-hot, Missouri-summer hot. I broke into a sweat, but Tabitha's skin did not even dew. She was used to such temperatures, I supposed. Yet she grew wetter around me, and soon we were sliding against one another, fighting for holds. I tried to breathe slowly, keep a part of my mind separate, so that I would last for her, but I could not. I could not remember that she was Tabitha.

We lay together for a long time in that sultry room, and, for once, I forgot about the ever-present cold outside. After Tabitha fell asleep, I remained awake, but at the same time in a dream. She breathed like Sarah; she curled up next to me, half-turned away, close, but independent. Just as Sarah had.

When I left, she was still sleeping. The dawn was tinting the bricks outside the room's window the color of roses.

We spent the next few days together. I'm afraid I neglected the newspaper shamelessly. After two days, we'd pretty much seen all the culture that Jackson had to offer. Tabitha wanted to go to Doom, but I held back. I felt, somehow, that I was betraying Janey, yet there had been nothing there to betray, only a hint of something promising *someday* maybe. At the time, I had a notion to joyously parade Tabitha over to the Indian village proclaiming my happiness that I had found her, I'd *found* the one I was looking for, after all these years of loneliness.

Looking back, I'm pretty glad that I didn't. Even in middle age, it is scary how easily a man can make a fool of himself without ever seeing it. Tabitha moved over to the house on the third day. I gave her the bedroom, and slept, myself, on the couch. Oh, I was very proper about it all, despite the fact that we spent more time in the bedroom together than I did in the living room alone. It's just, well, though the sex was fine with the house, I felt that my halfsent would never respect me again if I actually *slept* with a woman to whom I had no formal commitment. A very proper sort, my house algorithm.

After Tabitha had listened to all of my stories of my life with Sarah, we had to find some other topic of conversation to fill the spaces between passion. I got quite a lesson in Earth politics over the next few days.

Westpac was in a very unstable period, according to her. The Ideals, the human group-minds, were demanding more representation, and using their block voting ability to get it. Meanwhile the Clerisy, after years of careful dissociation with the government of the Northern Hemisphere, was becoming much more friendly. They were not formally represented on the Steering Committee, but there were large sections of America and Europe where they could bring in the vote.

"It's getting where the individual is, for all intents and purposes, powerless," Tabitha said one evening, as we drove down trackless country trails in my hover. "Maybe it's better that way. The greatest good for the greatest number, and all that."

We were headed east. My hover was narrow and light, and I was putting it to the test today. I was planning on making a big circle around Canoe Hill, using back roads—walking trails, really—and ice runs. This was the prettiest country I knew of on Candle, and I wanted to show it to Tabitha.

"Lots of small interest groups have sprung up which claim to represent the interests of the little guy," she continued, "but frankly, they're doomed to failure."

"Too bad." I zipped across a snowfield and into an icy gully. The only time it ran with liquid water was in the middle of summer. At this time of year, late winter, the ice formed a perfect roadway for a small, sporty hover such as mine.

"Not really. It's just human evolution. The day of the single person is fading. There're just too many of us."

"I kind of hoped that it was *quality*, and not quantity, that counted in politics."

"Oh, it *is*. An Ideal is not just a lot of people thinking alike. It's so much more. I wish I could tell you what it feels like during . . . full Participation. Everyone contributes what they are best at. The whole is so much *greater* than the sum of its parts."

The ice gully narrowed, but I kept up the speed. I was

showing off a little, but in perfect control. One thing I've really
enjoyed about being reborn into the future is being able to drive
on air.

"Do you miss it?" I asked. "Your Ideal?"

"More than anything," Tabitha replied. "Langley has given
me a life that is completely fulfilling."

" 'Langley' is the name of the one you belong to?"

I glanced over at her, and she seemed to wince for a moment,
as if she'd given away something she shouldn't have.

"Yes. But I have my surrogate."

"You mean the WORM implant in your head?"

"Yes, it gives me a remarkable simulation of Participation.
The WORM is what will get me through the next year and a
half."

It saddened me to be reminded that Tabitha would have to
leave on the next passenger ship out to Etawali. At least that gave
us a couple of months together.

"Tell me, what are those tree cities like?" I said, to change the
subject. The gully had become frighteningly narrow, but I was
navigating it with *élan*.

"Not very much like trees at all. Only from a distance. They
move, you know."

"How fast?"

"Only a few miles per hour. I lived in California City, before
I moved to Geneva for my work. It tours thirteen hundred miles
a year, up the coast, over to the Sierras, out in the desert. The
change of scenery can be very nice."

"I'd like to see it."

"Why don't you? Why don't you go back with me to Earth
after I'm finished on Etawali?"

I could, I thought. For the first time, I entertained the notion
of leaving Candle. For about a half second. Then some snow
funneled over the edge of the gully, right onto the hover's
windscreen. The screen began to furiously melt the snow, but
not fast enough. I slammed on the backfan, but was not fast
enough cutting the forward motion.

Spin out! I cranked up the rotors on the undercarriage full blast, hoping it would carry us up and out of the gully before we hit the walls. For a moment, it seemed we'd made it, but then I heard the rotor blades digging into something hard.

Slap! went my chest into the dash. It took me a good five minutes to recover my breath. Tabitha's seat had reacted in time, and grabbed hold of her before she could be slung forward. She was all right, and caressed my back while I wheezed for air.

"Damn that snow," I said, when I could talk. "It looked like it fell *on purpose!*"

"Nonsense," said Tabitha.

"And we're stuck! I can't believe this. I was trying to show you what a great driver I was . . ."

"Yes, well—"

"I *am,* under normal circumstances."

"Oh, I'm sure you are."

"Really."

She gazed out the window. "Can you get your hover off this bank?"

"Sure," I said. I engaged the backfan full blast. Nothing. We didn't even rock. I tried the undercarriage. It made a horrid screeching, and I quickly turned it off. "Well."

"Well what?"

"Want to make love in the back seat?"

Tabitha drew her parka—actually, one of *my* parkas—tightly around her. "Have you lost power? I'm getting cold."

I checked the potentiometer. Zero. Great. Somehow, my little foulup had drained away all the static charge. Probably a cracked battery casing. Just dandy.

"So," I said, "you've been *wanting* to visit the Indians."

"Are we near Doom, then? Thank God."

"Um, relatively speaking. It's about a mile, that way." I pointed east.

Getting out of the hover proved more difficult than I'd antici- pated. I had to slide down the bank of the ice gully, about six feet, and I got snow all under my clothes. Tabitha glared at the bank for a while, as if she could make it go away with her frown. Finally, I guess, the cold got to her, and she swung herself over the door sill, and slid down the bank as well.

I tried to catch her, but her momentum was too great, and we ended up in a heap on the icy floor of the gully. Sarah would have found this situation ludicrous, but Tabitha was not taking it so well. Our discomfort was exacerbated when the wind picked up yet again, and blew snow over the gully's edge and down on top of us. It was unavoidable. All we could do was shiver to keep warm and brush it off.

"Lead the way, Mr. Wilderness," said Tabitha, and we plodded down the gully toward Doom.

It took us over an hour to get there. The pathways between the buildings were, for the most part, deserted—even of slaves—and smoke rose from chimneys and fireholes in the roofs of the dwellings, and snow was pocketed in the bottoms of the West-net dishes. At first, I thought I would avoid going by Thomas's house altogether, and arrange some other means of transportation back to Jackson. It was too cold to walk at this time of year, that was for sure. But a settler couldn't hire a canoe in Doom without everyone hearing about it, so I finally decided I may as well use my influence with the Great Sun, himself.

Thomas was in his house, as usual. A couple of supplicants were just leaving as I came in, one of them carrying a dead chicken. To this day, I have no idea what *that* was about. The Indians got their protein from the animals that accompanied them on their exodus, centuries ago—dogs and deer, for the most part. I don't know how they originally got those deer into the canoes, but now the woods were thick with them. Candle had a variety with such long, shaggy hair that they looked like giant mountain goats. Chickens were new, relatively speaking, introduced by contact with Westpac. But the Mississippians ate far more grain than anything else, most notably on Candle, wintercorn.

Thomas seemed in a foul mood when Tabitha and I entered. He glanced at me, then looked long and hard at her, saying nothing.

"I have come, humbly, with a small request for the Great Sun," I said in Loosa, bowing slightly, cupping, then uncupping, my hands, as if I were presenting my request physically.

"That's not funny," Thomas said. "If you knew how sick I was of hearing . . . well, what *do* you want?"

"I wrecked my hover," I replied, a bit peeved. "I wanted to arrange a ride back to Jackson. But if you'd rather not be bothered . . ."

Thomas smiled grimly, and motioned me to have a seat. "Sorry," he said. "Of course I'll get you a ride. Laylay can take you. He'll be by in a few minutes." He turned to Tabitha and put out his hand to shake. She had been taken aback by his original irritation and had retreated back toward the door of the house. She cautiously approached and took his hand.

"Thomas Fall," he said. He glanced around the interior of the house, smiled again, more openly this time. "I'm in charge around here."

"Tabitha James."

"Any relation to this bast—"

"Very distantly," I broke in. "Tabitha is from Earth."

"Really?" Thomas said. "I never would have guessed."

"Yes," Tabitha replied. "California, originally."

"I've only been to South America. No, that's not right. The American South. I visited Moundville, where my people were supposed to have originated. Our other sacred site, Cahokia, is unfortunately in the middle of a spaceport." So, Thomas was playing the full-blooded Mississippian today, displaying the usual barely hidden contempt for settler barbarisms. Pretty silly, it's always seemed to me, since it's not like the Mississippians ever *returned* to Earth after their exodus to remember their goddamn history. They only started doing so after the Western *idea* of history was introduced to them.

"Never been to either place, myself," said Tabitha. "I'm from California."

"Fascinating," said Thomas. "Can I get you some tea?"

Tabitha shook her head, and I nodded yes. Thomas went to the fire where a clay pot was boiling, and ladled sponge tea from it.

"Tabitha is out here on a government junket, to inspect grants that don't need inspecting. I guess somebody's got to spend the taxpayers' money," I said, trying to liven things up. Thomas was being decidedly cool, I thought.

But this *did* seem to get his attention. He turned from getting the tea a bit too quickly, and sloshed some on his hand. He winced, just for a second, then smiled his most diplomatic smile, and handed me my cup. I'd seen Thomas use this one just before he had to relay news he knew you wouldn't like. "So," he said, raising his own cup to Tabitha. "Tell me about your job."

"Not much to tell, I'm afraid," said Tabitha. "I just come around to make certain money has been spent in the way it was intended, that sort of thing. Mostly, I'm a fifth wheel, but occasionally, I catch some discrepancies."

"And then you get to have a little fun, bringing in the bad guys?"

"No. I'm afraid my authority is limited to calling in the Territorial Rangers."

"Where's Janey?" I asked, growing bored. One thing *Sarah* wouldn't have done would be to take such a mind-numbing job.

"She's dealing with legal matters over her clay deposit," Thomas said.

"She's in *Jackson*?"

"I believe so."

"She really *has* gotten better, then, to be able to face Georgia again."

"She believes she's strong enough."

"I'd like to meet Janey," Tabitha said. "She sounds very interesting."

I didn't know where Tabitha had gotten this idea, because Janey was one topic of conversation I surely hadn't been eager to bring up with her.

Thomas drained the rest of his tea and turned back to the fire to get more. He seemed to be hiding a look of surprised concern, but I couldn't be sure, since he turned away so fast.

"I'm sure she'd like that," he said, ladling tea. When he

turned around again, his features were pleasant and bland—as much as the features of a man with a face full of warrior tattoo *can* be. "But I don't think she'll be back today. Maybe some other time . . ."

"Well, I'll be on Candle until the next passenger ship leaves for Etawali," Tabitha said.

"I'm sure we can arrange something by then."

At that moment, Laylay came in, and Thomas arranged with him and his brother to take us back to Jackson in one of their family's canoes. They went and brought the canoe around, and as Tabitha went outside to get situated, Thomas pulled me back inside the house.

"What are you up to?" he asked in a low voice, full of mirth.

"I'm not sure certain," I said, "but it sure is fun."

"Well," he said, gazing over my shoulder at Tabitha, as she nimbly stepped into the center of the canoe. "She's something, all right."

"I think so."

"Be careful, Will," he said. This time, there was no mirth.

"What are you talking about?"

"She looks a lot like Janey."

"So?"

"And, from the way you've described her, Janey looks a lot like your woman-in-the-wind."

So, Thomas had been listening to my drunken reminiscences over the years. I didn't know whether I liked that or not.

"And what if she does?"

Tabitha was seated now, and looked back for me. I pulled myself away from Thomas, and started toward her.

"Will, there's something else. Something smells—"

"Thomas, you're going to end up with Janey. You know that. It was hardly fair from the beginning. Don't deny me this little bit of happiness." Even to the day, looking back on my words, I feel like cringing.

To his credit, Thomas softened his manner a little. He slapped me on the shoulder and walked out to the canoe with me. I felt the calming, but electric, presence of Raej in his touch. And, in that moment of contact, I felt a tinge of doubt, an echo of restraint rising within me. What was I *doing*, falling for a woman so quickly, so completely? A woman I hardly knew.

But *didn't* I know her, really? As Thomas took his hand away, and I stepped over the gunwale of the canoe, I looked at Tabitha and saw the shadows of the past on her face, the possibility of Sarah's smile within the crinkles of her face, and I knew that, if I were indeed living an illusion, then I would prefer that the illusion go on for as long as my heart could bear it. Forever, if I had the choice.

Laylay spoke a word to his brother, who began the familiar chant of traveling, and the Effect enfolded us, like the warm hands of a giant. Tabitha gasped as we rose from the ground, and held tightly to me. We passed over snow-laden trees and silky roads, flying back toward Jackson, and I was sure I was the happiest man in this, the long arm of the Milky Way.

8

I have often thought that what moves human beings, and *this* human being in particular, is always either love or politics, or love *and* politics. Not that I want life to be that way. I'll settle for *just* love, any day. And I traveled light-years to achieve something beyond both, a victory for science, maybe, or communication with the alien and unknown. And what happened? Mired again in precisely what I left behind. Or, if you don't like "mired," then blessed, or cursed or, hell, *coated*. As with infinitely sticky taffy, stretching interminably from star to star, the ever-present residue of our own humanity.

I am a man who responds to urges, not all of them clean. Take the *Cold Truth*. Why on Earth, or, rather, Candle, would a man, newly reborn, extremely wealthy (through no effort of his own, and requiring no personal effort to sustain), want to run a newspaper? Just to have something to do, or because that was all I knew *how* to do? I assure you that I am quite good at poker. Why didn't I become a professional gambler, touring from world to world, with my grubstake in my underwear and a disposable woman at my arm? What makes my oh-so-respectable stay on Candle any more rational? Wouldn't it be better to adopt a kind of philosophical Hippocratic oath and first, before anything else, do no harm?

Love and politics. The electricity and magnetism that keep

me tumbling like light. The Grand Unified Field theory of my soul. So, can it be a surprise that, after Laylay dropped Tabitha and me off on the outskirts of town, and we walked to my office for a warm drink before returning home, what should come in but an urgent bulletin over the Territorial Wire that demanded my full attention—just at the moment that *I* wanted to attend to other things?

The Wire ticker is a little quartersent that serves as a bin, a cache, inside which messages from the stars curl up, like sleeping vipers. Johan, the Westnet technician, offloads them from whatever ship happens to be in port. Most ships are contract Wire carriers—it pays very well for the little effort and computer space that's required. Johan sends the information to my ticker. After the ticker gets it, I download it to my own machinery. I can simultaneously experience the information by putting my eye to the optical flasher. Since the ticker was blinking double red for urgent, I eyeballed the flasher, as well as downloaded, to see what the big deal was.

And it was a hell of a big deal. The information was datelined from two months ago.

A shipment full of illegal rhythm arrived at Grendel Spaceport today without a human pilot. Port authorities say that the ship, Empty Pockets, *was owned and operated by legendary smuggler Whimsey Apple, late of Mumba's Reef. Apple was found dead in the cockpit. The cause of her death is unclear, but Grendel coroner Guasswe Hed said that she appears to have suffered from complications after her latest free-radical therapy. Apple was 194.*

The Wire tessellated to picture feed, and a woman, squat with years of too much gravity, spoke, identified at the bottom of the feed image as Grendel Port Commissioner Inklinga Gar.

"We're not sure why the *Empty Pockets* wasn't stranded in space. It appears that *a personality within the rhythm* she was smuggling got access to the ship's computer, and brought her in."

Then back to the resonating, authoritative newspeak of the text, transposed over the image of the ship:

Details are sketchy, but, according to Gar, the ship's computer had a sophisticated interface with the Loosa clay in which the rhythm was being smuggled. This particular rhythm was a batch made with the newest duplication equipment recently developed by the Church of Liberation and Global Justice for the halfsent enterprises through which it supports its Territorial ministries.

And to Commissioner Gar.

"There was a starship captain's personality in that rhythm batch. I don't know if his soul was there, but, by God, it had whatever it takes for a pilot to create the Effect. I still can't believe it, but we're pretty sure that the *rhythm* in the clay linked up with the computer and used the Effect to bring the *Empty Pockets* in."

This was incredible. Until now, when humans were fully copied either for illegal shipment or for legitimate uses, they could only be duplicated *statically*, as if they were one frame of a projected film, instead of the whole reel. Then that one frame could be looped over and over again to make halfsents. Or, with more computer power, *me*. That's how I was made into a gamma transmission, back when the technique was new. It was akin to stepping into one of those old photo booths and having a snapshot made. When I was sent out, nobody knew how to put me back together again.

By the time I was reinstantiated, however, they'd figured out how to do it with a huge computer, capable of *translating* a human algorithm into a dynamic system—in my case, a human body, rebuilt according to instructions also encoded in the transmission. *Algorithm,* in my case, is a bit misleading, as is *computer,* since the computer that rebuilt me is based on *nonalgorithmic* quantum electrodynamics, just like human brains. That's why it was so damn expensive. But people call them computers, and so will I.

This computer could also *copy* a human. But the process was incredibly expensive. Apparently, the Clerisy's new equipment, intricate enough to copy chocolacas (as we'd seen from experience) could also capture living, thinking humans, dynamically. But even so, something unexplained had happened. The *rhythm copy* had created the Effect. If the process could be duplicated . . .

It was the beginning of a transportation revolution. For hundreds of years, starship captains were a breed apart, able to exist in the noumenal, true, world of the chocolacas, as no other humans could. It took natural talent and years of training, and some serious chemical enhancement. The better the captain was at the metaphysical trick, the bigger the ship he could pilot. That's why ships were relatively rare—only one or two were ever in port at any one time, and big ships such as the *Irrelevance* were very infrequent.

Now the talent of a single great captain could be duplicated and used, over and over again. With the cheap duplication equipment, you wouldn't even need to make an expensive master copy—just dupe the original guy whenever you needed him. Then, with his rhythm copy stored in clay, ships could be automated. Hell, you could make a small messenger ship for something as simple as carrying the daily mail. The great time and expense necessary for traveling between the stars would be eliminated. Now all you needed was a bit of clay.

"Nothing like this has ever happened before. Frankly, I don't know what to think. This may have been a complete fluke of nature. The rhythm that piloted the ship was a copy of a Captain Briar Gustafson, of the famous Gustafson space-faring family. When she got the ship to port, she immediately, uh, terminated herself. I don't know how else to put it. But some of the other rhythm copies expressed a wish to go on existing, and we're going to honor that as best we can. I don't know how, exactly. I guess that'll be up to the Planetary Board of Regents."

"What it comes down to is this: there were absolutely *no* living human beings on that ship. I'll stake my reputation on it. Not a one. And that ship made it into port. But I caution people not to get too excited. This may very well be, like I said, a fluke of nature. We'll probably never be able to duplicate it again—at least not in our lifetimes."

Right. Like telling a kid that, though the candy is sitting there on the counter, he can't have any. The candy will be gone before you can say "upset tummy."

Following the incident, a team of Territorial Rangers departed Grendel for Earth. Their mission is officially a secret, but it is thought that they were instructed to take the news of the Empty Pockets' *return directly to the Westpac Steering Committee, and return, bringing scientists with expertise in Effect physics.*

What the Wire article didn't mention, but what you could read between every line, was the little fact that for the most part only Indians owned the clay. The Indians weren't going to sell it.

Reason for war. As if the two cultures trying to share worlds hadn't already created reason enough.

I sat down with the *Cold Truth* halfsent, and immediately began to make the Wire Report into news. Each report is accompanied by reams of raw data and peripheral research, so that an editor, if he is intelligent, can create a story tailored for *his* particular readership. I would use the Wire story pretty much as it came in, but there were lots of supplemental angles that I had to examine. And I wasn't going to gloss over the Indian problem as if it didn't exist. *That* was the story, as far as I was concerned. No doubt the *Daily Local* wouldn't even mention it.

As I began feverishly working, Tabitha sat down beside me and attempted to kiss me. I brushed her away, too harshly, I'm afraid. She huffed, and rose to leave.

"What *is* this?" she said.

"*This* is incredibly important," I said, pointing at the ticker. Then I realized where I was and what I was doing, and smiled peevishly. "Guess I got a bit carried away, there."

"I *guess,*" she replied.

"I'm sorry, but this is pretty damn startling."

I told her what the story was about. And, as if to confound me even further, while I was explaining to Tabitha, the ticker telltales flashed that there was *another* incoming Wire, double-urgent. What in God's name was going on today? But that's the news business. Nothing for months on end, and then all hell breaks loose, and you'd better be prepared to saddle it and ride.

"So unless somebody comes up with a way to synthesize Loosa clay, we're in deep trouble," said Tabitha, after I'd given her the story. Extremely concise way of putting it, especially for a Westpac bureaucrat. I snuck a look at the headline on the new Wire story. Christ almighty.

CLERISY DEMANDS WAR TO END SLAVERY

"Just how much influence did you say the Clerisy had on the Steering Committee these days?" I asked Tabitha.

"They have a lot of indirect power," she replied. "Why?"

" 'Cause I think they're about to use it."

"Let me see," Tabitha said. I stepped aside and let her put her eye to the flasher. She expertly connected up with it, without any of the flinching first-time users show when they have to touch the thing to their cornea. Interesting, but not extremely unusual—Tabitha must have to use these old-fashioned flashers in her job now and then.

"Great. And for a kicker, the Clerisy is calling for an end to Territorial expansion," she said. "Just great. This is *all* I need."

"What's the problem?" I asked. Could the Clerisy's plans have *that* much of an effect on her job? I mean, the grants to *existing* planetary governments would continue, wouldn't they?

"I have to be alone for while," Tabitha said. She backed away from the flasher, but kept looking at it, as if she couldn't believe what she'd just seen. "I need to be alone with my WORM for a while."

She started for the door.

"Where are you going?" I said.

"To the Goosedown," she replied, distractedly. "To my room. I'll call you later, Will." And she was out the door, not bothering to close it behind her, letting in the bitter cold. The halfsent that ran the building detected this, and gently pulled it shut.

I stared after her, bemused. But the mass of incredible data in the ticker pulled at me with the gray gravity of news, the warped space-time which only a journalist can experience. I returned to the flasher.

* * *

EARTH, 3 JULY 2563—In a speech today carried on Neruda, the Clerical Network, Hector Ruiz Blanca, the Director of the Managua Overcell of the Church of Liberation and Global Justice called for the forceful abolition of slavery in the Territory and an end to Territorial expansion.

Citing the fact that Westpac has not dealt adequately with the poor and oppressed on Earth, much less in the Territory, Ruiz demanded that these problems be solved first, before any further expansion is allowed.

A cut to Ruiz, who is sitting in a chair in a drab office, in even drabber vestments. Hand it to the Clerisy; they sure knew how to look as poor as church mice. Unfortunately, this was about the only way in which they *had not* reproduced the mistakes of their Catholic forebears.

"This may sound like a familiar litany from the Clerisy," Ruiz said, "but this time we are prepared to back up our words with political might!"

Ruiz said that local cells on Earth and in the Territories were to begin organizing to implement the Clerisy's plans.

"It is the only moral thing to do," he said. "Too long, we have stood by and fought the fight with words alone. Now we must fight with our actions."

Next the story tessellated to an image of thick jungle. The tactile rider-loop made the scene swelteringly hot. Even though the humidity was merely a construct of my brain, I felt myself start to sweat.

Speculation on why Ruiz has demanded the changes at this particular time center on these jungles in Central America, and the new "prophet" who is said to live deep within them. The "jungle prophet" is said to have built a foundation of great influence among the poor of Central America within the last few months. No one knows what his ultimate goals are, but the Clerisy is worried that its primary constituency may be swayed by the "prophet's" calls for justice.

Cut to a young man with dark features, identified as Juan Maracopia, an Ixil Indian of Guatemala. He speaks a strange blend of Spanish and English and who-knows-what-else. The flasher signals the Wire presentation algorithm that I speak English, and the Wire provides prerecorded subtitles. But these don't catch the flavor and intensity of the man's words.

"De prophet comes down to nos an he is *incarnate* in de jungle of de Peten. Nosotros, he tells to go back to de old ways. Sky is clean in de old ways an de Peten is where Mother Mary dwells. Nosotros are to tend de land outside de jungle an bring de fruits of labor to de prophet y to de ghosts of de prophet.

"Den will be de glory. Den nos tenemos hope an power. De land is de blood. Nos must get out of de jungle, an tell de people in de cities of de prophet's message. Cuando nos left de land for de jungle a million years ago, de blood dries up and there is only death. Dat is why de sky is black dese days. Dried blood de prophet says. Cuando nos get back de old ways, de sky, she'll be argentine. Like de Holy Snake Ghost qual lives with de prophet. Argentine."

Below the last sentence, the algorithm translated "argentine" as "silver-white."

Maracopia's tribe has indeed left its village and proselytized several Central American cities. They have taken over a number of campos near the jungle, and set up collective farms. The "Ghost-prophet" movement has grown like wildfire within the last few months, with no signs of slowing any time soon.

Whatever power the new prophet and his "ghost" have gained within the Clerisy, the only person who knows for sure what has brought about this dramatic switch from a policy of moral guidance to one of militant action is Director Ruiz. And he, for the moment, is too busy putting his plan into action to tell us why.

Argh. What a stupid closing. Typical Wire report airiness. They hire philosophy majors instead of newsmen.

But what that Ixil Indian had said was interesting. The Clerisy's roots were in the liberation theology of the twentieth century, the call for a secularized Catholicism that could deal with the problems of *Earth*—in particular, Yankee imperialism. It had always had close ties to the Marxism that survived the twentieth century, that of Trotsky and other international communists. Marxism as a state of mind, rather than a system of government. Yet there had always been a strong thread of animism running through the rural Cells, back in my time, and even now, in the Territory.

And over the years, like I said, the Clerisy had grown just as fat and set in its ways as the Catholic church—from which it had formally seceded during the year I was born—had ever been. There was a feeling among the lay Cell members (I'd even detected it on Candle) that reform was needed. Maybe the prophet had arisen in response to the feeling, a personification of this unease, and his (or her) return to the "old ways" was a call to militancy that Managua could not ignore and still keep its credibility.

Or maybe the Clerisy was using this prophet as an excuse to grab for power in Westpac. Maybe both.

Earth politics gave me a headache. After a couple of hours at the flasher, they *literally* did.

I gave my halfsent the parameters for assembling both stories. It put them together as best it could, then ran them past me. I suggested changes, and the halfsent incorporated them. I think of the paper's halfsent as the spirit of the *Cold Truth* itself. When I'm talking to it, or, more often, thinking instructions to it down the flasher, I feel more the newspaperman than I ever did back on Earth. It gives you a visceral, deep-down feeling of satisfaction when you can *talk* to your paper, and tell it how you want things to work within its pages. At times like this, I had the feeling that it *did* exist, as an individual, if not in the true world, then in some other dimension where things that should be, are.

While the *Cold Truth* halfsent was incorporating the final changes, I worked up an editorial. It was time, I realized, to lay down my cards and take a position on all of this. The rhythm smuggling was the easiest to pronounce upon.

I did not believe war was necessary between settlers and Indians. Not because I thought Indian spiritual customs particularly sacrosanct. I knew enough Indians to understand that they, themselves, regarded the clay more as a means to spirituality and harmony, than an end. And they were, individually, as mercenary as the next race when it came to selling their birthright. It's just that I believed that, given time, science would find a solution to the dilemma brought on by the clay's scarcity. Knowledge and technology have always seemed, to me, to be *good* things in essence. Sure, bad things can be done with them, but only if you twist them from their pure form. I mean, the universe *works,* doesn't it, and works well? You have to bend natural law pretty hard to make evil come of it. I'm not saying it can't be done. Christ, it's *regularly* done. I'm just saying that nature, and our knowledge of nature, are *healing* things in essence, unless we deliberately make them otherwise.

Toward the problem of the Clerisy's new demands on slavery, I felt a lot more ambivalent. Like I've said, I owe a lot to the Clerisy. They *have* been a force for good in the galaxy. There are priests who are genuine humanitarians. Some have even been real saints. But the system is corrupt. This clown, Director Ruiz, had about as much concern for the slaves as Corazon had. Increasing Clerisy power was what moved him.

I wasn't sure how demanding an end to slavery furthered his agenda, but I'd bet my trust fund it *did,* somehow or another. He had to know that his pronouncements were going to lead to war—even without knowing (how could he?) about Whimsey Apple's ship coming in by itself. One thing was certain: the Indians weren't going to give up their slaves without a fight.

And this prophet in the jungles of Central America—where did he/she fit in? Some arcane inter-Clerisy power struggle was going on. Which still left *me*—and the average citizen—with a hard question.

Was it worth destroying the Mississippian culture to free the slaves?

Despite the fact that doing so would enhance the Clerisy's power, I had to answer that it probably was worth it. Human beings should not be slaves.

But on the other question—an end to expansion—I was dead-set against the Clerisy. Oldfrunon may have been the oldest expansionist on Candle, but I was the most fervent. I'd never made a big secret of this editorial position over the years. That's why I let myself be broadcast in the first place. I was convinced that there was an inherent good in reaching out, exploring.

Was it worth people going hungry, living drab lives back home? Maybe there wasn't a kind of direct cause-and-effect relationship between the two. As a matter of fact, I argued that the instinct to explore leads, in the end, to *better* conditions back home. Sometimes it takes a while for the fruits to ripen, but when they do, they're sweet. Technological advances are only a small part of the good that comes. One of the best products is just *getting rid* of all of us malcontents, giving us something to do. When we come back home, if we do, we come back richer and wiser. Most of the time.

Hell, at least at *that moment,* my position made sense to me. And it was diametrically opposed to the position of the Clerisy. So I'm an ungrateful son of a bitch. What can I say?

As you can see, Tabitha was getting further and further from my mind as the afternoon blended into night. I decided to put out a special morning edition, once again springing for the fancy plastic. It took me almost until dawn to put the paper to bed. I'd forgotten that my hover was still wrecked, over on Canoe Hill. When I left the office, I looked around for it for a moment. Oh, yeah. I'd take care of it tomorrow. Well, today, actually.

Today was going to be one hell of a news day for Jackson, and I was going to beat the pants off the *Daily Local* once again in depth of coverage. I walked home through the moonless night shivering, but satisfied with my work.

When I got to my house, the lights were on. Tabitha sat on the couch in the living room. She was rigid, as if she were at attention. She didn't register my coming in, and it was only when I spoke to her that she noticed me.

"I thought you were spending the night over at the Goosedown," I said.

She seemed not to hear me. "I need to talk to you, Will," she said. "Your house let me in."

I'd left instructions that it should. "I'm really exhausted, Tabitha. Can it wait until I've gotten a couple of hours of sleep?"

"I'm afraid not. I have something to tell you. I'm not exactly who you think I am."

I sat down in a chair across from the couch. "I know you're not Sarah, Tabitha."

She laughed at this. "No, Will. Something a bit more . . . important. You see, I *do* work for Westpac, but in a different— how shall I say it?—*capacity.*"

"Huh?"

"I'm an operations officer with Intelwest."

"You *weren't* sent here to follow up on a grant?"

"I was sent to Candle in order to discover whether or not the reports we'd received concerning a woman here were true."

I was clenching the arms of the chair I was sitting in so hard that I could feel my nails digging through the upholstery and into the stuffing.

"Janey."

"Yes, Janey Calhoun. We were given some information concerning her from a psychiatrist at Bryce Hospital in Tuscaloosa—that's a city in the old U.S.A."

"I know perfectly well where Tuscaloosa is. I'm *from* the old U.S.A., as you'll remember."

"Of course, Will. There's no need to get upset by all of this."

"I'll decide whether or not I should get angry! Intelwest, huh? The Steering Committee's spy service?"

"We are a private company under long-term contract to Westpac—that's true." Tabitha leaned forward, touched my knee. "Will, the other reports we got straight off Westnet. *Your* story of the Indian uprising six months ago."

"Langley," I said. "Of course. The old CIA headquarters. Is that what your Ideal is made up of—spies."

"Langely is, for the most part, operations officers with Intelwest. Amazing that you should make the connection, since the CIA is long gone."

"I'm up on my Earth history. You might even say I've lived it."

"No doubt."

I tried to relax, to think through what Tabitha was telling me. I was deathly tired, and my brain felt like it was full of congealed molasses. "So you came out to investigate Janey. To see if she were going to fall into the hands of the Mississippians?"

"Exactly, Will. Whatever else she may be, Janey Calhoun is a potent weapon. *You* saw what she did to that man, Bently. Our analysts have reason to believe she interacts with algorithms on a quantum level. She somehow shares vector-states with the particles that the algorithms organize——"

"I don't know what the fuck you're talking about, Tabitha." Her hand was caressing my knee now. I could smell the city-Sarah scent of her, the perfume of clean concrete and wet steel, the hint of trees, growing through the cracks in the sidewalk. I could feel my response, uncomfortably, in my pants. I shifted positions, and Tabitha's hand moved farther up my leg.

"If Janey falls under the influence of the Indians, a lot of people in Westpac could be hurt, even killed. Do you want that on your conscience, Will?" Her lips were autumn-red. I could smell my own breath, stale, in my nostrils.

"Janey is *already* under the influence of the Indians."

Tabitha's other hand, on my cheek. The cool slide of Sarah's bracelet against my neck. "*You* are her friend, Will. You can help me win her back."

I was mentally drained, completely open to suggestion. I hardly knew what I was saying. "What do you want me to do?"

"I knew you'd help," Tabitha said, and kissed me. I reached around her neck to pull her closer, kiss her more deeply——and my fingers clasped the polychrome aerial that curled from the base of her skull.

My mind was still foggy, but I started back. "Hold on. I didn't say I'd do anything. I'm just willing to hear you out."

Tabitha looked me over, ruefully, as if she were coming to a decision, and the choice wasn't in my favor. "You're much too tired to be worrying about this right now," she said. "Let's go to bed."

What can I say? There are all sorts of justifications that spring to mind other than gross lust and weak sentimentality. None seem particularly convincing. *This* was certainly not a suggestion I was going to fight. I let her take my hand and lead me back through the house to the bedroom. My house valet considerately switched the lights off in the living room and turned them on dimly ahead of us—enough to show the way, but not enough to spoil the mood.

Tabitha helped me undress, and tucked me into bed as if I were a child. Then she climbed in beside me, naked. I was falling asleep, but she stroked me back to a measure of alertness, both mentally and physically. Her fingers were long, like Sarah's, but her nails were perfect. Sarah's had always been battered from painting. Then Tabitha was kissing my chest, my stomach, taking me in her mouth.

As much as I enjoyed this, I was going to drop off soon. I reached down and urged her upward, and she swung herself over me. I slipped easily inside her. She was beautiful, poised there above me, the embodiment of my long, lonely dreams. I reached to take a nipple in my mouth. After a moment, she gently pulled away, and pushed me back. "Watch," she said, and leaned over me. Her hair, more brown than red in the dim light, cascaded around my face, enclosing me within its circle. All I could see was the sparkle of her eyes, but they transfixed me. She drew closer, closer, and I lay trembling with longing, gazing into the gentle shine of them.

Then *her eyes met mine.* We touched corneas. I tried to blink, but could not get my lids to cooperate. I stopped trembling. A violent shock passed through my body, then I lay still. To an observer, it would appear that I had come, and was basking in the aftermath. Instead, I lay still, assimilating information, taking in the rhythm Tabitha was injecting down my optic nerve.

But this was not rhythm of the usual sort. Instead of going to work for me, I was enslaved by *it. Enslaved* is the word for the experience, because, after that moment of contact, there was nothing—lie, cheat, kill—nothing I wouldn't have done, to help Tabitha bring Janey back over to Westpac's side.

"Harumph!" said the house.

"Will," Tabitha said. "I need you. I couldn't let you let *me* down."

"Of course not," I said. "I understand completely."

Tabitha smiled, moved off me, and sat by my side. My cock was still hard, but I wasn't thinking about Tabitha. Instead, the greater good of Westpac, and particularly of the Ideal Langley, was what was turning me on. I was filled with the desire to help Tabitha achieve this—it was sexual, mental—my whole body thrilled with the urge to do what was required.

And I *knew* what was required. The information was buzzing and swarming in my head, forming into clouds of comprehension. I saw, with a kind of double vision, Tabitha, the room I was in—and the Plan. The beautiful Plan.

It was in the shape of a land. How can I say this? A brown land, cut by gorges and piles of scree. Here and there, towers arose, made of a stone as brown as the landscape. They would have appeared natural, had it not been for the intense, magnesium-white lights that shone from the windows of their upper reaches. Strobing in great swaths, like lighthouses.

The Ideals.

I knew it, and in the knowledge was a kind of love, a kind of worship. The height of human development. The perfection. The All.

And I knew even more. I knew what *my* Ideal, my new master, wanted. Wanted more than anything. Had to have. Must obtain at all expense. *Information*. Not knowledge, not wisdom. Data. Langley existed for the acquisition of information, and now that was my sole purpose in life as well. Behind all of Its plans and schemes lay this queen termite, always, always hungry for it.

The best way to get more data was to become more powerful, and that was just what my Ideal was in the process of doing. This was the reason for sending Tabitha to Candle. Janey was a powerful unknown, an irresistible target for Langley.

What's more, Langley had other intelligence that suggested just how powerful Janey might become. It had gotten it directly from the highest office of the Clerisy.

The Clerisy had obtained it from the Jungle Priest—the one who'd been the subject of the recent news release. Who knew how he got his information? It didn't matter, if the information were reliable. And it was. With the Ideal's slave-virus infection of me, this was now confirmed.

Janey must be either put to the uses of Langley, or else destroyed.

"Hmmmph," the house said.

"I'm really sorry it had to come to this. I was getting to *like* you quite a bit, Will," Tabitha said.

So what? I thought. That didn't matter now. It was laughable that it ever *had*. "What do you need me to do?"

"I'm not sure," Tabitha said. "You know Janey better than anyone."

"I suppose I could seduce her," I said.

Tabitha thought this over for a moment. "Do you think it would work?"

I looked at the idea in the hard light of reason, and not with the sentimental self-effacement I'd experienced when considering it before. I wasn't a particularly handsome man, but I had a certain charm, a certain charisma—nothing like the power of Thomas's, but I could worm my way into people's good graces. I could be insidious, when I wanted to be. That was what made me a good reporter, after all.

"I could seduce her," I said.

"Then you will," Tabitha said. "Perhaps you should go to her *now*, tell her you couldn't get any sleep, thinking of her."

The exhaustion I'd felt melted away. Apparently the reverse-rhythm that was inside me was releasing endorphins right and left, giving me a second wind. No doubt I'd pay for the abuse later. But later didn't matter. All that mattered was doing what Tabitha told me to do.

I sat up, stretched. Tabitha looked me over. "You've got a nice, lanky look to you," she said. *"All* of my response wasn't acting."

"Hand me my clothes," I said, barely hearing her. What would be the best way to get through Janey's defenses? The first step would be to totally convince *myself* that I wanted her above all other things—otherwise, she'd literally see right through my guise. Maybe the reverse-rhythm could help me reach that mental state.

I dressed in silence, furiously calculating my chances. Tabitha brought me my shirt. I put it on, then rumpled my hair. "Do I look disheveled enough?" I asked her.

She laughed sadly. "You look as naïve and precious as a newborn babe," she said. She brushed my cheek with her hand again. The bracelet touched me, awakening desires for a moment—the wrong desires. My rhythm-rider quickly crushed them. "It was fun while it lasted," Tabitha said. "I'm sorry that it's over, in a way."

That was when the door to the bedroom exploded inward, swinging wildly on its hinges and slamming into the wall. An eerie blue-green light flared into the room and I felt a deep, primordial terror surge within me. To this day, I don't know whether it was the reverse-rhythm or myself that was feeling that fear.

Thomas Fall stepped into the room, glowing like a bear-headed demi-god. Beside him stood Janey, flame-faced, terrible.

"The house let us in," Thomas said. His voice was almost a growl. Thomas and Janey were two other people whom I'd instructed the house always to allow to pass.

"We were worried about you, Will," said Janey. I cringed backward as the force of her concern was visually, tactilely embodied through Raej's presence.

"This is somewhat of an intrusion, even for such close friends of Will," Tabitha began. Thomas and the transparent face of Raej, transposed around Thomas's features, turned to gaze at her.

"You are an agent of Westpac, aren't you?" he said. The question was also a command. I felt sympathy for Tabitha. It must be hell, having to stand up to such fury.

At first she was silent, stoic.

"Answer me!" Thomas said.

I could tell when she broke. Her lips began to tremble. She

closed her eyes to block out the view of Raej's penetrating eyes.

"Yes," she said.

How could she! my brain—the creature that was inhabiting my brain—screamed. I shuffled over to the bedroom closet, quietly opened it, felt inside.

"How did you . . . how did you know?" Tabitha asked, her voice still trembling.

"I know *Will James,*" Thomas said. "I know that the way he was acting yesterday was *not right.* He wasn't just lovesick. Something was wrong. What did you use? Pheromones? Your Ideal didn't count on me, did it? That a settler could be the Great Sun's best friend?"

"And the bear was able to see the truth?" At this, Raej roared, and Tabitha stumbled backward a couple of steps. My hand closed on something cool and hard.

"The truth is plain enough," Thomas said. "Westpac needs Janey Calhoun. Janey loves Will. The logic is simple."

I knew what I had to do. The logic *was,* indeed, simple. Westpac could not have Janey, not after this. The Indians *must not* have Janey.

Janey had to die.

My mind screamed, my brain reeled. *No!* For the moment, I had my thoughts back to myself. Yet the rhythm-rider was firmly in control of my motor responses. I couldn't stop myself. I watched as I pulled the heavy object from the closet. How odd, I thought. It was a bottle of bourbon I had imported from Earth, along with the bedframe. My other self, the original Will James, had put it into long-term storage before he died. I'd had it treated with micromachines, rejuvenated, supposing I'd be drinking it someday. How ironic.

When the bourbon arrived, there had been a note written on the flyleaf, in my own hand. "Thought you might need this," it had said, "in case you find the future not quite what you bargained for. Will James, May 2101."

With an angry roar, I charged at Janey, brandishing the bottle over my head like a cudgel.

Janey turned toward me, and her eyes met mine. They were

filled with a blue fire, flickering amidst the green of her irises. "I love you," I tried to say to her, tried to make her understand. "This is not *me* who wants to hurt you. This is not me." But the words were choked in my throat.

Janey whimpered, whether in terror or disbelief, I did not know. She sank to her knees, closed her eyes. *She could melt me away,* I thought. *She is in control of her power now, and she could do it at will.* But she wasn't going to. She bowed her head, ready to accept the blow. I raised the bottle high. In my mind, I could hear the splintering of glass, see the spatter of blood and brains.

I was going to do it! For Westpac, for the good of the human race!

I felt a fire rage over me, through me. For a moment, I believed that it was the righteousness burning within me. Then the fire *hurt*. It hurt horribly, like pins driven into my flesh, everywhere, inches apart. My muscles tensed—all of them, all at once. Then I knew what had hit me.

Raej.

My body bending itself into a tight ball of pain, rushing, the pain rushing, the wall rushing to meet me. I dropped the bourbon. A sharp splintering, somewhere far away. It was not the bottle; it was *me*. Darkness. Light. The room was full of light, even with my eyes closed. It hurt, but there was nothing I could do but ride the pain. It curled over me like a wave. Too much light, too much hurt. Crushing, driving down like a hundred tons of water. Grinding, blinding churn of power. I felt my mind slipping away, like chalk on a blackboard wiped with a wet cloth. Like elaborate markings in the sand that the tide takes

away.

After a long time under, I was floating in jelly. Sticky, sweet jelly. Blackberry? It prickled like blackberry. I flicked out my tongue. Sweet, but unidentifiable. I opened my eyes. The room was bright. I kept them open enough to see that I was lying in my bed. The whole room was full of the jelly. A vague shape to my left. Then I closed them again. Better. The dark was better.

"Will."

It was Janey's voice. Full of concern, yet still, somehow, off in space, disconnected with reality. So nice to hear her once again. But I had killed Janey.

I opened my eyes again, fought to keep them open. She was a blur through the jelly, but I could make out the calico dress, the sharp, pretty features. Janey. She was alive.

"Father killed it, the black thing that was inside you," she said. "You don't have to worry about that anymore."

"Oh, good," I said. My words floated through the thickened room like tiny, shining bubbles.

"But I'm afraid Father hurt you. I think your legs are broken, Will. Father and I are working to mend them."

"How?"

"Time," Janey said. "We're gathering time around you, coating your legs with it."

I had no idea what she was talking about. And it didn't matter. For the moment, everything was all right. I let my mind drift. Westpac. I was mad as hell at Westpac. Janey was telling the truth. There was no rhythm-rider to bend my thoughts away from the anger—and the shame.

You were used like a sorry condom, I thought. Tabitha fucked with you really good. What an idiot I'd been. There was no excuse. I'd walked right into the simplest of traps.

"She drugged you, Will," Janey said. "Poison in the cup you *must* drink from, your love for Sarah."

Of course. The city-Sarah smell. Tabitha was *nothing* like Sarah, not deep down. I'd known that all along, yet had chosen to ignore it. I'd had a lot of help from Tabitha's engineered pheromones, apparently. God, she'd been a slick operator.

"I should have seen," I said. "Still—"

"Yes," Janey whispered, "hold still."

I lay back and felt the healing brush of Janey's hands; the firmness of Raej, holding my legs like an iron cast.

The wracking pain that I'd felt before I'd blacked out was gone now, replaced by a numbness. But the numbness was slowly receding, and there were prickles under the skin of my legs, like the small splinters of cactus spines. Soon, the prickles became sharp needles. But the pain was not unbearable.

"Try to sit up," Janey said. She helped me as I swung my legs over the side of the bed. At first, there was a jolt of hurt, but I pushed through it. I found myself sitting up.

"Good."

"Doesn't feel so good," I gasped.

"You're better," Janey said. "But your brain needs to find that out."

I guess it was rapidly doing so, because the pain began to lessen. After it had ebbed away almost completely, I tried to stand, lost my balance, then, with Janey's help rose shakily to my feet. I took a tentative step, then another. Janey let go of my arm.

I was okay. I'd have to take it easy for a while. My inner ear still felt jangled from being slammed against the wall. But I was going to be fine. Externally.

In the living room, Thomas was interrogating Tabitha.

When I entered, she looked up at me like a scared doe. Raej loomed over her, in all his neon fury. Apparently, the Raej I'd felt in my bedroom had been Janey's rhythm copy.

"Explain to Will what you did to him," Thomas said. Tabitha lowered her gaze and would not meet my eyes.

"I really *am* your descendant," she said. "But I had surgery to make me look like *her.*"

"Sarah," I said softly.

"Yes. And you know about the viral pheromones, I suppose."

"I guessed."

"And the coercive agent—"

"The *what?*"

"The algorithm I flashed down your optic nerve. CAs are an Intelwest specialty."

"I see."

"And the bracelet was my idea, from some old photo I saw." Tabitha risked a glance in my direction. "I suppose you can never forgive me?"

"I . . . oh, God."

Then Thomas was at her again. "Why should anyone forgive you? Where is the *you* that could be forgiven? All you are is an ember in a fire that's already burning. You've given up your humanity for *this*!" He reached behind her head, yanked at her aerial. Tabitha cried out, more in alarm than pain.

"I am a cell in the Ideal Langley," Tabitha said. "Please consult Langley headquarters in Washington, D.C., for further instructions as to my deportment."

This sounded like the rote response that it was. Thomas had pushed Tabitha to the edge of her personality, it appeared, and her WORM was taking over.

"You *will* answer me!" he said. "Your fucking Ideal is not the only thing that can get inside your head."

"Thomas," said Janey. "Not so rough."

But Thomas did not appear to hear her. "I don't want war. No sane person does. But if Indians go to war with Westpac, then, by the stars, the Indians *will not lose!*"

The bear-image of Raej dissolved from above Thomas's head, and flowed down his hand, around Tabitha's neck. Soon her face took on a blueish pallor—and it wasn't from lack of oxygen.

Her lips, firmly set before, now twisted into a grimace, baring her teeth. Her head twisted backwards and to one side, as if someone were pulling her hair.

"Who on the Steering Committee sent you?" Thomas growled. "What were your precise orders?"

"I . . . am . . . a . . . cell . . . in—"

The blue glow intensified. Drool streamed from the corner of Tabitha's mouth.

I didn't know what to feel. This was a woman who'd just used my ass. The love I'd felt for her had dissolved into a hangover of regret at my actions while under its influence. Yet, Thomas was torturing her. Sure, he was doing so in order to avert a war, or at least not to get slaughtered once war started, but did *that* end justify *this* means?

I was the one who'd just tried to kill the person who meant more to me than any other living woman, however. I didn't feel like I was in such a great position to be making moral judgments.

"Stop it, Thomas," said Janey. "You'll lose me for the Indians if you don't stop it."

The blue glow abated. Tabitha pitched forward, onto the floor, gasping for breath. Thomas turned and stalked away.

He stood facing a wall for a moment, then pounded his fist into it, sobbed. "I'm not very good at this Great Sun bit," he said. "I'm letting my feelings get the better of me, letting everybody down."

I moved over to him, clapped a hand on his shoulder. "It's tough, being a god."

"Shit."

"Yeah."

Janey gasped, and we both spun around. She was kneeling over Tabitha, touching her arm. The blue-green of the healing Raej-rhythm glowed around the two.

"If you've hurt Janey, so help me I'll—"

"No," Janey said. Her voice filled the room, as full and commanding as it had been that morning in Pioneer Square. "Tabitha is gone."

"What?" I felt something inside, some emotion, but I couldn't categorize it, couldn't analyze it.

"She wasn't useful to the WORM in the back of her brain, and it wiped her clean."

"Good," said Thomas, and I watched as his fists unclenched.

"No, the nothing-tangle, the chaos, is *never* good," said Janey. "But there's more, in the WORM, the worm in her head." Janey stood up. Tabitha lay limply on the floor. She was sucking air in and out with the mechanical rhythm of a machine in a hospital. "Strange. A place of dryness and towers that is a gateway to visions. In one vision I saw a man within green vines, so much hot and sticky green. A priest."

"The prophet in Central America," I said to myself.

"What?" Thomas asked.

"I'll explain later," I told him.

"I've seen his face," said Janey. "I've seen the *meaning* of his face."

Janey was frowning now and, for a moment, I felt the gushy

ooze of Janey's metaphysical melting. Then the world resolidi-
fied. When I looked at her again, tears were streaming down her
face.

"Father," she said. "He still has *Father* with him, chained to
him. The woman was not sent to turn me against the Indians.
That's what she was told, but the worm in her brain knows
differently. Coiled around and around itself, so clever the worm
thinks it is. So far above humans."

"It wanted you for political leverage against the Clerisy," I
said. "Just a game of politics, that's what this is fucking all
about."

"And the war?" Thomas asked. "What about the war against
the Indians?"

"It laughs at that," Janey said. "Cackles like a crow pecking
at my eyes. This isn't a person. I'm going to kill it."

"Wait!" Thomas cried. "Ask it why it's laughing."

But for once, *I* understood. This may not be my time, my
place in time, but the rules hadn't changed that much in five
hundred years. And maybe I'd learned a thing or two while
drifting through the ether. Or afterward—when things didn't
turn out the way I'd planned or ever expected. Whatever the
case, the situation was as plain as day to me now.

"The Ideals don't give a shit about the Indians. They were
always a buffer against the Clerisy," I said. "After the Ideals
bring the Clerisy down, the Indians will be easy enough to bring
into line."

Tabitha's face broke into a horrible grin. I guess the thing
inside her had heard me, and was signaling that I had gotten
things right.

The grin, or perhaps the evil thoughts that accompanied it,
was too much for Jenny. She bent downward and swept her
hand across Tabitha's face, as if she were casting a spell. There
was a crackle in the air, and the ozone smell of electric power.
Tabitha continued her jerky breathing, but the grin was gone.
Her face was totally blank.

"The WORM has to stay, to keep the body alive, but I cut
off all its parts that aren't necessary."

All at once, I felt my legs start to give. Not from lingering pain or instability. I was reeling from too much information, too much disbelief. I sat down in my armchair and my trusty house rolled out a cart with drinks for us all. It was the bourbon I'd tried to brain Janey with. The house had probably arranged to cushion its fall. As for me, I guess it thought I deserved to land hard. I took my shot and drained it quickly and completely. Smoky as Chicago after the Great Fire; smooth as the muscles on a thoroughbred.

So, the jungle prophet was Corazon. And the source of his rapid rise to power, the holy ghost that was said to accompany him, must be a copy of Raej he'd managed to smuggle off Candle.

How? We'd sealed off the indwelling almost immediately. Had he, somehow, had the copy with him when he ran from the town square?

And how in God's name had he gotten to Earth so quickly? The only thing that could travel that fast was a Wanderer.

Thomas leaned down and lifted Tabitha's still-breathing body up onto the couch. He, too, took a shot of my liquor.

"Good," he said hoarsely. "Another." The house obligingly rolled the serving cart away to fetch it. Janey came over and stood beside him, one hand on his arm, one on my shoulder.

The cart returned, and Thomas picked up the glass, threw the shot against the back of his throat, and flung the glass across the room. It shattered in the fireplace.

"As of this moment," he said, almost gleefully, "I am no longer the Great Sun of the village of Doom. I am once again Doom's official Wanderer."

"I didn't think you could *do* that," I said. "Nobody *abdicates* from being a god."

"I'm Great Sun," he said. "I can do anything I want."

"I see what you want," said Janey, quietly. "I can't go with you."

"I know," Thomas said. "You're needed here more than you've ever been before."

"Will somebody tell me what the hell you are talking about?"

I asked. Janey patted my shoulder with her hand, which only irritated me more.

"I'll need some help, though," Thomas continued, as if he hadn't heard me. "What about it, Will?"

"What about *what*?"

"Do you want to go on a canoe trip with me? A kind of Wanderer's Journey?" Now he touched my shoulder. With Janey's hand on my other shoulder, I felt like the ragged and weary hypotenuse of a much-tried lovers' triangle.

"To rescue my father," Janey said. "To free him from slavery."

"To Earth," I whispered. "I'm going back to Earth."

9

Space churned beneath and around Thomas's canoe like inky, black rapids. It was as if the canoe were a bullet, rifling down a dark barrel, not faster than perception, but far faster than comprehension, so that my awareness was a muddle of half-grasped truths, and brilliant, bewildering surprises. Yet the "barrel" down which we traveled was not a solid tube, but a sluggish, viscous liquid, held in place by a wish, by the barely perceived plasma of Thomas and Raej's desire. I couldn't actually *see* the void that surrounded us, but I could *feel* its presence, its all-pervading curve and weight, as I dipped my paddle over the side of the canoe, into the nothing. The stars shone as patches of light, as did the spread-out, translucent bodies of giant sea jellies, hung inside with weirdly glowing filaments. They were coelenterates of space-time, Portuguese man-of-wars suspended in the eternal night sky between systems.

Thomas told me the stars looked this way because *we* were not localized, but were actually in several places at once, seeing the sights of more than one man at a time, yet all of those men were us, here and now, within the barky interior of this wooden canoe.

And, after listening to the eerie churn of our paddles as we pushed toward Earth, and smelling the bear-electricity of Raej's encompassing presence—as the chocalaca reminded all of the

particles that made us up that they were, each of them, real—I
sank into a sort of trance, myself. I can't vouch for my sanity in
this state, but I believe that I was seeing, for the first time,
something of what the true world—the world that the chocalacas and Janey inhabited, that starship captains sometimes visited—actually looked like. Yet I am neither a scientist nor a
philosopher. I can explain nothing. All I can do is report to you
what I witnessed.

There were no *shapes,* not really, and neither sound nor smell.
The human sense that worked the best was that of touch, although what was touching me, was doing so from the *inside-out.*
It didn't feel as if there were something inside me, but, rather,
that I was stretched out in directions *in addition to* up, down, left
and right, backward and forward—sort of the reverse of the
sphere who goes to Flatland. The sensations I felt were like rain
spattering into an umbrella turned upside down. What surprised
me the most was the fact that I actually *had* these other directions, an undercurve to my being, and that my mind was able to
experience them.

And what did the true world *feel* like? Fire and light, rush and
fall, calm and poise—all of these words give you an idea. Every
feeling was a combination of physical touch, and emotion. The
association wasn't arbitrary, but intimate, *right.* When we passed
through what I thought of as the "fire" region, I felt admiration
and courage rise within my heart, not toward myself, but disembodied, as if this were where these feelings lived when they
weren't being applied to something in the world. Yet I also felt
the hot tendrils of actual fire, licking at the edges of my mind,
of the canoe, of my body. Fire everywhere, without and within.

How can I say it? Take the region of "peace," which we
passed through about halfway through the trip. The true world
isn't actually *static* there. Or, though it is static, there is a depth
and texture to the stillness that is more alive, full of more
potential, than the fastest, most complex process that I know of
in the regular world—living bodies, burning stars, they all pale
beside the sexual, sensual motionless-in-motion of that place.

"Peace," I discovered, is also completely feminine, at least it felt that way to this male.

Ah hell, I'll never tell it right.

Normally, starship passengers don't get the full show, as I did. Thomas told me that this was because we were traveling so furiously, he and Raej didn't have time to safeguard carefully the boundaries of the Effect, as they normally would when carrying someone else. For that matter, a passenger in a Wanderer's canoe usually did not paddle. In fact, Thomas hadn't been sure when we started out if my paddling would help at all. But, after a time, he saw that it did. Hell if I could tell the difference, but I kept up the effort because he wanted me to. Thomas could even doze off for short stretches, while I kept up the forward momentum. Of course, his creating of the Effect was akin to slipping into a dream-state for him, so he didn't really have to sleep at all when traveling; he only needed to pause to give his body a break from the constant motion. I didn't for a moment believe that it was *me* who was keeping us going during these times. Thomas always had part of his mind on the Effect. When I slept, on the other hand, I did so like a dead man, from the sheer exhaustion of the constant paddling.

Thomas sat in the front of the canoe, most of the time. For the most part, we talked only when we stopped paddling to eat, or to take a drink of water. We'd packed food and a keg of water, holding nearly fifty gallons, in the middle of the canoe. Also tucked amidst the provisions was what was left of my Earth bourbon. Raej did most of the work when we "drifted," since Thomas's job was, for the most part, providing the mental intensity needed for forward movement, while Raej kept us arching in and out between the worlds, like a metaphysical dolphin. But Thomas *had* to stay in communication with Raej, perhaps only at a lower level, at all times, and he was vague when we spoke during our breaks. Mostly, he talked in the Wanderer-speak that portends great and beautiful meanings, but that actually makes very little sense to us normal mortals. Having myself gotten a taste of the true world, however, I began to understand him better than I had before.

"The going's hard through the peace," he said, near the end of our first "week" of travel. He was chewing on a dried cake of wintercorn, and drinking water with just a trace of my bourbon added. "Every trip, I want to stay there, make a home."

"Do you mean to tell me that you go through the *same* parts of the true world on each trip?"

"No matter where you go, the true world has been there. It's always the same, but never the same *arrangement."* He swallowed the cake, finished off the water, and poured himself another cup. I hesitated to offer him more bourbon to sweeten it with. The last thing I wanted was to go gallivanting about the stars with a drunken Wanderer in a tipsy canoe.

"Clear as mud," I said. Thomas just smiled, in the way of someone who has seen far more than you ever will. "And what about gravity? How the hell are you able to keep water in that cup?" I was getting a little ticked off at his attitude.

"This is not a canoe alone, but a canoe of the mind, and a canoe of the will," he replied. "This cup works because I believe it will work."

"Why not just believe that we're already on Earth, then? That'd save us three more weeks of travel. Or that the canoe is loaded down with Loosa clay? Wouldn't that save the galaxy a whole shitload of trouble?"

Thomas reached out and took the bourbon-of-the-mind from my hand, and poured himself another weak drink into his cup-of-the-will. "Contradictions," he said. "The *cup*—the true world cup I'm able to use here within the Effect—is like water *in* the cup. The *canoe* is within the canoe."

"So *now* you're saying that the true world is just as objective and real as the regular world, after all?"

Thomas drained the cup, set it down, and took up the paddle once again. "More or less," he said. "Only when the two *meet."* He dipped the paddle blade over the side, into the nothing, and once again, we were off.

Don't get the impression that this was a leisurely trip, that we stopped and shared philosophical chat every chance we got along the way. We spent hours paddling with all our might, breathing in gasps. Pushing against the nothing made my back ache, and my arms stiffened with fatigue. In the true world, *nothing* was as thick as molasses. For years, I have had skinny sticks for arms, and been a little embarrassed of it, but within a week, my forearms were corded like braided barbed wire. I still wasn't going to win any strongman contest, but I would be able to hold my own in a test of endurance.

I tried to stay awake as long as possible, but slept when I had to. I curled up as best I could on the bark floor of the canoe, and always awoke stiff and sore, thinking, more than once: oh shit, I've overslept, and now I'll never get the paper out on time. But the *Cold Truth* was under the able, if prosaic, control of my journalist halfsent. And at home, Janey, along with my house, was looking after Tabitha's still-functioning body.

I was in space. Headed to Earth. Every time I remembered, I was amazed all over again.

"Get to paddling," Thomas would grunt as soon as I woke up enough to yawn aloud. He wouldn't even turn around to look at me. With another yawn-groan, I'd get back to work. On occasion, after a long stretch of silent paddling, Thomas would suddenly begin speaking in Loosa. I only caught part of these soliloquies, but I understood enough to know that they were Wanderer's stories—old legends, or modern tales of the places and peoples he had visited.

"This is how I practice," he told me, when I asked him what he was doing. "How I *used* to practice, that is. Old habit, I guess."

A few times, I asked him to tell *me* a story, since he was telling them anyway. Sometimes he seemed not to hear me, so lost was he within the tale. But at least once he asked me what I wanted to hear about.

"How about *you?* Thomas Fall. I've known you for years, but I hardly know anything about your life before I came to Candle."

"Me?" said Thomas. "Well, nobody's ever asked me for that story before. That might be a challenge."

"That is what you were supposed to have done for a living, right?"

"Yes," Thomas said in a sad tone, and he half-turned to face me. "Once upon a time."

"Not so sure about abdicating anymore?"

"I'm not sure about a lot of things."

Then he told me some stories.

"So, stories about me? Would you like to hear about Thomas Fall deciding to become an Indian?

"Nobody ever called me half-breed while I was growing up, but everyone let me know, in one way or another, that I wasn't one of them. I lived in Jackson until I was twelve, then ran away to the Indians. I still spent a lot of time in Jackson, though, visiting my relatives. Jackson is a pretty insular little place, as you well know, and when you are the only child in town who is half Indian, everybody knows about it, and has an opinion.

"My father's brother, who died ten years ago, used to wait until Dad was away on business, and then start teasing me. 'What's that smell?' he'd say when he came in the front door. 'Haven't I told you, Thomas, that we do our urinating in the commode in *this* house?' Or he'd say about one of my relatives something like 'Calls himself a Sun, huh? Not very bright if you ask me.' When I got older, he went further; his playful teasing became playful taps on the shoulder, then hits that left bruises.

"My mother spent half of her time in Doom, and when my father died, she moved back there permanently. Since I was in school, she asked my uncle to keep me during the week, and I went to the village on weekends. Then one night my uncle came home dead drunk. I was in my room, doing homework, when he burst into the room, grabbed me, and pulled me outside into the freezing night. It was the middle of winter, and this was before the time of electric underwear that really worked. He said something about digging a latrine for myself, that I would no longer be allowed to use the family's bathroom, and he threw a shovel at me that he got from the toolshed.

"It is impossible, of course, to dig a hole in the winter, when the permafrost is a half-inch from the surface. I tried, and the effort warmed me a little, but it did not take long for me to pass from shivering to that dangerous place past shivering where your body gives up trying to generate heat, and tries only to conserve what it has. I might have frozen to death then and there, trying to dig an impossible hole, but my uncle got cold himself, and went inside the house, locking me out. I wandered down the streets, too stupid with the cold to think to bang on someone's door and *make* them let me in, until I saw a friendly light and a sign that said open.

"It was the Goosedown. No sooner did I step inside than Frank Oldfrunon had a blanket around me and a cup of coffee in my hand. I volunteered no information, and he asked me no questions. The next day I woke up, borrowed a coat from him, and walked to Doom. I did not return to Jackson again for five years.

"Or would you like to hear about how I decided to be a Wanderer, and how I met Raej?

"There is a coming-of-age ceremony we have in the village. I'm sure you've heard about it. It's called the Ordeal. In some ways, it is rather barbaric. When they are fifteen or so, children are taken into the woods and put out on their own for a week. They are given minimal food and no water. They are expected to start and tend a fire, and melt their own. The object is purification, followed by sanctification. After a week, the children are collected and put through an elaborate ceremony, followed by a big feast.

"You sleep days, and gaze at the stars during the nights. During this time, each child is to seek guidance from the stars as to his path in life. In the middle of the week, after he is considered pure, the child is to make two diagonal cuts, one on each forearm, and drip his blood onto the snow, under the starlight. Both boys and girls are expected to do this. The child is then to study the pattern of the blood, and try to match it with some pattern he perceives in the stars. We have an elaborate system that equates the star patterns with the various callings a man or woman can follow in village life, and the children are taught these beforehand.

"During my Ordeal, I followed the prescription as closely as possible, but when I studied the drippings from my cut arms, I could find absolutely nothing that they matched up with. I was convinced that the lack was in me, that I hadn't done my lessons properly—though the Indian methods of teaching children are nothing like those in a traditional classroom. Anyway, I looked and looked at the blood, for three days, and, unless I were willing to force a pattern upon it, there was nothing—just nothing analogous in the night sky.

"I hadn't been careful with conserving my food, and by this time I'd been completely out for four days. This was not long enough to seriously endanger me, but I was beginning to get somewhat delirious from constantly sitting by my fire, feeding it with wood, and staring at the blood, and the lack of food did not help matters. You see, I'd been convinced I would find my calling rather quickly, since I was sure that I wanted to be a hunter. Hunters spent a lot of time alone, and I liked that, for I'd found that Doom was just as prejudiced and small-minded in its way as Jackson had been, and I fit in there as poorly as I had among the settlers. Fortunately, in Doom, I was a Sun, and hence above any kind of physical abuse. God help me if I'd been born a slave or even an Honored Person. A Sun has a perfect right to kick around either at will.

"But the damned pattern wouldn't say what I wanted it to say. I was determined that it would, and by the time I was six days out, I was in a state where I could believe that I had the mental power actually to reform the blood into the pattern I wanted. Hell, I believed that I could move the stars to my will at that point.

"When they finally came to get me, I'd opened up another set of wounds on my arms without realizing it, and I was staring at the two overlaid patches in the snow certain that now I had my calling pattern, if I could only decipher it. Herbert Sandle, our Wanderer, was with the group that collected me, and with him, of course, was Raej.

"Herbert Sandle hadn't liked me very much before that. He was a dyed-in-the-wool separatist, and the very fact that I was half settler was enough to turn him against me. But there was something about my intensity and tenacity that touched him— and believe me, it was difficult to find an emotional cord to touch in Herbert Sandle. He later told me that I looked more *Indian* than any of the children ever had before, that maybe because I hated Jackson, this had somehow allowed me to return to a pre-contact mentality. He justified his decision in a lot of ways in later years. But standing over me as I gazed down at my own blood, Herbert Sandle decided he had found his apprentice. Perhaps the chocalaca inhabiting the clay in his pocket had something to do with the decision, as well.

" 'Wanderers do not have patterns,' he said. 'That's because, for them, the stars are constantly changing.'

"I looked up at him with tired eyes and a fanatical need in my brain that would have accepted any justification then and there.

" 'Really?' I said, and he reached down to help me up. And when he did, I felt an electric glow suffusing through me. It gave me strength, and it cleared my mind. After I was standing, Herbert Sandle stepped back, and the feeling went away.

" 'So,' he said, and it sounded almost like jealousy. 'He has chosen you, too. I suppose that's good.'

"And that was the first time I met Raej. After that, I went to live with Herbert Sandle, and began to learn the Forms—the traditional ways news and stories are told—but mostly I kept house and did the cooking. When I was eighteen, I went on my first trip, a brief circuit to Etawali, and then doubling back to make the long haul to Uladeega, the planet you call Tashitari.

"Herbert Sandle was very old when he chose me, and shortly after the Gathering of the following year, he died. He held on to Raej until the end. I truly believe that only death would have caused him to give up his chocalaca, and at times I wonder if we Wanderers form a kind of addiction to them, as rhythm dancers do to their drug. Whatever the case, they are necessary to us, if we are going to fulfill our calling. Nobody goes faster than a Wanderer, when his chocalaca is fully manifested.

"After all these years, I still don't know exactly what or who Raej is. But I've learned that I can trust him completely, and really that is all you should ask of a friend. When Raej has a feeling about something or someone, one way or another, it is always best to adopt that feeling as my own, and act accordingly. He had a really good feeling about you, Will. Did I ever tell you that?

"Sure, it bothers me not to know more, but when he's ready, he'll show me. And if he's never ready, then I'll still die a better man for having known him. But sometimes in the middle of a long trip, when we're both working hard together, there's *something*. I see the edge of something very large and very elaborate. I don't know what it is. Maybe it's far in the future, and has to do with some other Wanderer. You see, Raej has been with the village since the beginning, since there *were* Wanderers. The first Indians found him in the clay when they arrived.

"I don't know why we call him a *him*. Maybe it has to do with the fact that Wanderers are traditionally—though not always—male. I'm not blind to the fact that his manifestation as a bear probably has more to do with my human psyche than with what he actually *is*. But there is something about bears that agrees with his true nature. I'm sure of that. There is something about bears that agrees with *my* true nature, as well. And sometimes I think that being with him has shaped me over the years, so that I've become more of a chocalaca than an Indian. This is an effect peculiar to me, because I know it never happened to Herbert Sandle. The opposite happened, actually.

"But there are lots of times when I feel more at home in the true world than I do in the regular world. I have to fight an incredible desire sometimes when I'm in deep space to dive over the side of the canoe, and slide completely out of existence, and into whatever region of the true world I'm paddling in. I don't know if it would work or not. Think I should try it now?

"Maybe not, eh? But sooner or later, that day may come. If

I ever Wander again, and I don't come back, then that may be where I've gone. Or maybe I'll be floating, frozen and exploded, in some nameless tract of space. Don't worry, friend. Not yet. Not yet. I've still got roots here in this world. You. And Janey. I'd tell you the story of growing up with Janey, only it isn't really a story, just something that happened to me. Nothing special; she's just always been there. And how do I feel about her?

"That's another pattern I haven't found a match for in the stars. I think Herbert Sandle was right. For a Wanderer, the stars keep shifting. Or actually, the *Wanderer* keeps shifting. But maybe I should cut my arms, and try again."

It took us twenty-four days to reach the edge of Earth's solar system. *My* home system. This was the same journey that modern starships took three months to complete—the same journey on which I'd spent five hundred years, traveling at the speed of light. I never did find out if Thomas and I had broken some kind of record. Probably. Wanderers did not make a habit of visiting Earth, so the field was wide open. In fact, before Westpac had followed the Mississippians to the stars, Wanderers didn't visit at all. The Earth was a despised place, a place the Indians had *left* after the star-gods had taught them how to answer the call of the sky. Over time, the Indians had forgotten the way back home completely—until the coming of the settlers in their wake had unpleasantly reminded them of all our common origins.

We had to slow down to work our way through the solar system. Not that it was much more crowded than interstellar space had been, it was just that Thomas had to take time to align himself with the Earth, and to avoid the asteroid belt as best he could. The belt isn't really a circle like it appears in all the two-dimensional textbooks. It's more like a sphere, with the top and bottom lopped off. You don't disappear from space when you are within the Effect, you travel the boundaries, like a swimmer. Thus, you were real at least part of the time in the regular world, and the regular world "thought" you were going light speed, even though you were traveling much faster. At light speed, much less at velocities beyond, colliding with an asteroid meant instant annihilation. Yet, even with all Thomas's maneuvering, within an hour we were inside the orbit of the Moon.

After all these years of moonless nights, she was a wonder to behold. Mostly full at the angle that we passed her, she shone with gray-white brilliance against the hard vacuum. Out here in space, away from the filtering, softening atmosphere, you could never call her pretty. She was sublime.

And Earth. Earth was not what I expected. Sure, I'd seen pictures, I'd read the explanations, but nothing had prepared me for the enormity of the changes humankind had worked while I'd been away.

The Earth was no longer a blue-white-and-green ball, but a multicolored flower. Bursts of filaments spread out from the central planet, to end in translucent, rounded bulbs. The disk in the center was nearly the same old Earth, but these filaments and pods sparkled with all the colors of the spectrum. The whole arrangement greatly resembled a sundew plant, or a pincushion. If I had the distances right, each of those bulbs must be big enough to swallow Texas. The stalks to which they were attached must be as thick as Rhode Island was wide.

As we drew nearer, I could see that the stalks were not single tubes, but massive cords of smaller filaments. The state-sized bulbs at their end, however, *were* all of one material. Inside them, I knew, were spinning, hollow globes full of forests and rivers and towns full of people. All of these stalks and bulbs were speckled with lights, some fixed, some swirling along the surfaces, as pools of color will travel across a soap bubble.

Although I'd never *been* in space—in a conscious state, that is—before this trip, Earth, the central planet, was subtly different from all the pictures I'd seen taken from orbit back in the 2100s. The oceans were still blue, and the clouds still white, but each looked more *ordered,* the clouds especially. I knew that there were controlling algorithms impressed within each, directing their ecologies to human uses, while maintaining a balance in nature. The land masses, however, didn't have this advantage, and were still recovering from a series of wars that occurred during the last century, back before Westpac had established hegemony over all the globe and moved warfare into supposedly antiseptic outer space.

For a moment, I felt a twinge of intense homesickness. For what, I couldn't say—Candle, the past, Sarah. Maybe for my lack of a home, anywhere.

"Well, I'm back," I said, to no one in particular.

"We have to come in quietly," said Thomas. "Westpac has watchers in the true world. They're pretty good at seeing big ships, but I think we can slip by."

We carefully dipped our paddles, raised them slowly and feathered them against the nonexistent wind to bring them forward to dip again. I felt foolish going through these motions. I mean, who knew *what* the hell was really pushing us forward? But paddling was obviously as close an analog as my mind could fathom, so I figured I'd better stick to rules I knew. They'd brought me over five hundred light-years in a month, after all.

The first traces of the atmosphere whirled around the envelope of the Effect, defining it in a ghostly heat. As we dropped lower, I could feel the temperature rising.

"We're not supposed to get hot in the canoe." I spoke in a hoarse whisper. "Is something wrong?"

"Be still," Thomas said. "I'm playing with the edges, letting anybody who's watching think we're a meteor."

As we got lower, wind currents began to buffet us about. I began to feel sick to my stomach. For a moment, I thought I was going to lose its contents. I leaned over the gunwale of the canoe, ready to heave. But what I saw below so surprised and delighted me that the wintercorn cakes remained in my gullet.

"Florida!" I said. "There's Florida."

"Good," Thomas said. "I was hoping you'd still know your way around. So where's Guatemala?"

I'd found a little quartersent guidebook and atlas on a hurried trip to the library in Jackson, just before Thomas and I departed. I hadn't really had a chance to look it over or get the feel for using it. It was pretty old—not made of impressed plastic like the new ones—so I'd had to hook it up to my optical flasher to feed it into my memory banks. The instructions had clearly stated that it was fully interactive; I hoped I'd chosen wisely.

I panicked for a moment, unable to activate my bank recall. It had been dormant since I left Jackson, and reacted sluggishly. Finally, the book's menu popped up in the upper right hand corner of my field of vision.

GUATEMALA
300 YEARS OF BEAUTY AND TYRANNY
A GUIDE FOR THE SOCIALLY AND
ECOLOGICALLY AWARE

Underneath were what I took to be chapter headings: "Lucas Garcia, Mejias Victores, Diceperados, The Bloody 2020s, Government Oppression after Orellano . . ."

Sweet Christ, I thought, of all the guidebooks that could have ended up in the Jackson public library, I had to get one with an *activist* quartersent guide program, not to mention one that was two hundred years out of date. The jargonny title was amusingly old-fashioned, but would the guide get the job done? Well, you took what you could get. I quickly blinked down the chapter headings to the last, which read, thank God, "Map."

The menu disappeared, to be replaced by a nicely detailed three-dimensional map, oriented to where the quartersent guide estimated our position to be at the moment. Unless continental drift had really speeded up over the last two centuries, we ought to be able to find our way down.

"Um, you need to go left," I said. Thomas deftly did as I told him. The guide furiously flashed coordinates and vectors over the map, but these would mean as little to a Wanderer as they did to me, so I kept them to myself. As we got lower, the heat *decreased*. Thomas was strengthening the Effect once again.

"Aren't they going to pick us up on radar or something like that?" I asked.

"There's not enough of us in the regular world to bounce anything off of. Especially now that we've gotten down here into the ground clutter."

And downward we flew. I gave Thomas course corrections as we needed them. We wouldn't come in on the most precise of flight paths, but I was pretty sure we were headed in the general direction of Northern Guatemala, and the jungle where the new prophet was said to live.

The Wire reports had been very helpful in establishing the precise area of the jungle prophet's activities. I'd stored this information as well, and when I cross-referenced it with my guide book, it quickly pinpointed where we needed to go. When we were within a few miles of the place, my display drew a bright red spot, and created a simulation canoe angling toward it, like an arrow erratically headed toward a bloody bull's-eye.

The ground below was an undulating carpet of greenery, dotted with oscillating blues, sometimes blindingly bright, sometimes flat, a mere blank gap in the foliage. It took me a moment to recognize these as lakes. Candle didn't have any large bodies of water. Streams regularly flowed during the summer only, and only within a few hundred miles of the geothermal vents that were south of Jackson, a half day away by hover. As we drew nearer to the jungle, I could make out rivers, twisting through the trees, in and out of view, in a kind of clandestine code, the jungle's communication with the sky. I wondered, if I stared long enough, if *I* could find some meaning in the flow and collection of waters, some glyph of welcome, of warning.

THE PETEN RAIN FOREST RECEIVES OVER 200 INCHES OF RAIN EVERY YEAR, my quartersent guide informed me. Its voice, heard only by me, was nasally and pert. IT HAS LONG BEEN USED AS A HIDEAWAY AND STAGING GROUND FOR THOSE OPPOSING THE OPPRESSION OF GUATEMALAN STRONGMEN.

"Cross-reference with the Wire reports and find us a good place to land," I said tartly, forgetting to subvocalize my instructions.

"Huh?" Thomas said.

I HAVE ALREADY DONE SO. WE ARE APPROXIMATELY 20 KILOMETERS FROM A LAKE SUITABLE FOR LANDING, NEAR THE HIGHLIGHTED AREA. CONTINUE ON COURSE.

It took me a moment to remember that a "kilometer" was a little less than a mile. I was, at the moment, in no mood for quaint measuring systems from the past. The guide provided no conversions.

"Keep going a little farther, and we'll find the right lake," I told Thomas.

Within a couple of minutes, the lake came into view, and the guide signaled that it was time to land. Thomas brought us down smoothly. He'd done this hundreds of times before, and we skimmed into the water with barely a splash. Our arrival was, however, loud enough to scare every bird on the lake into the air. The sight was incredible. Flapping pinks and whites filled the sky. I mean literally *filled* it, for at least five minutes. What a change from Candle, where we had no native animals (unless you want to count sponge trees, which are neither flora nor fauna, exactly), and only a precious few other species that had been introduced by humans.

As the canoe settled in, Thomas and Raej let the Effect collapse, and Earth, my old Earth, rushed in to surround me. First came the gravity. I felt a jerk, as Earth's pull took the place of my mental construct. Christ, I was god-awful *heavy* here! For the past month, the gravity we'd imagined in the canoe had been the same as Candle's. Candle wasn't as massive as Earth, and damned if I couldn't feel the difference in my bones. Then the sounds. The startled cries from the sky full of birds, the croak of frogs (frogs!), the lap of water and the buzz of flies—for the Earth air was thick with them. I discovered, soon after, that some of them *bit*. Then the smell and feel of the place settled in: humid air, as heavy as rain-sodden canvas. It engulfed me, swirled into my lungs when I breathed, and remained there, weighing me down. Yet the air smelled alive with the tang of ferns and briars, the soft muskiness of elephant-ear plants and ceiba trees.

Thomas gently paddled the canoe toward shore—or as close as he could get. Long before we reached the edge of the rain forest, the water turned to mud. A thin tricklet of a stream ran through the mud from a tributary. At the lake's edge, it disappeared into the brush.

MANY OF THE LAKES IN THE PETEN RAIN FOREST ARE FORMED OVER VOLCANIC CRATERS, AND THEIR LEVELS FLUCTUATE WILDLY AND ERRATICALLY, the guide chimed in. DURING THE TWENTIETH AND TWENTY-FIRST CENTURY, THIS FACT WAS OF PARTICULAR VALUE TO REBEL FORCES WHEN FLEEING AIRCRAFT EQUIPPED WITH PONTOON LANDING GEAR.

Thomas closed his eyes and, with a low whistle, called Raej back into service. The Effect crackled around us, enclosing the new Earth air within our metaphysical bubble. I wondered, for a moment, about how we had breathed while in space without quickly using up all the oxygen. Probably something about the *air*-within-the-air. Whatever it was, we didn't suffocate.

We rose a couple of feet above the mud and skimmed forward just over the tributary stream, until it broadened and deepened at the edge of the foliage. There we set back down.

"It's amazing that such undisturbed places still exist on this world," Thomas said. "Why do you think this land hasn't been developed?"

"War," I replied. "A hundred years ago, this country was where the Clerisy consolidated its power. They raised up a peasant army and put down the last Guatemalan dictator. Or so the history books say."

"That was a long time ago."

"Yes, but the entire north of Guatemala is still considered hot with biologic fallout. They call the Peten *El Foresto Hauntedo*."

"Biological fallout? Are we going to catch diseases on this world?"

"No. Bio*logic* fallout. As in: animating algorithms linked to micromachines swarms."

Thomas didn't reply. He dipped in his paddle and pushed us forward. I joined him. Paddling in the water was remarkably similar to paddling through space. We glided into the tunnel of green which formed around the stream. I slapped at a fly, got it, and my hand came away red—with my own stolen blood.

FROM HERE FORWARD I CAN ONLY APPROXIMATE THE DIREC-TION IN WHICH WE WISH TO TRAVEL. THIS IS WHERE THE EXACT COORDINATES PROVIDED IN THE MATERIAL YOU GAVE ME TO PRO-

CESS ENDED. THE IXIL MAN WHO WAS QUESTIONED WAS RATHER
VAGUE ON SEVERAL POINTS. GUATEMALA'S INDIGENOUS NATIVES
HAVE THEIR OWN THOUGHT PROCESSES, WHICH ARE NOT THOSE OF
THEIR COLONIAL OPPRESSORS.

I was about to reply to the guide, when Raej sparked into
existence about Thomas and growled, low in his throat. Thomas
stopped paddling, and we drifted for a while.

"Raej has caught the smell of himself, of his copy; it's very
strong, in the true world, at this place," Thomas said. "He'll
show us the way now."

"I thought Wanderers couldn't read their chocalaca's minds."

"I know what he's *feeling*."

This was a relief, in a way, because I didn't trust my quartersent guide at all past this point. Lakes might still be around after
two hundred years, but the rest of the jungle would surely have
changed.

"I did get us pretty damned closed, didn't I?" I said, more to
justify my presence on this trip, than to gloat.

"You and your library book did a good job. But Raej was
smelling all along, just in case you messed up. He had the scent
from before we crossed the orbit of that moon." Thomas spoke
without looking back at me, but I saw his shoulders shake with
a chuckle. Why *had* Thomas asked me along, anyway, if he
didn't need my services as Chief Scout?

THE PETEN RAIN FOREST IS A HOST TO MANY SPECIES OF EXQUIS-
ITE FLOWERS AND EXOTIC ANIMALS, FROM THE EPIPHYTIC ORCHID
TO THE RACCOON-LIKE COATI. FOR CENTURIES, GREEDY CAPITAL-
IST INTERESTS HAVE ENCROACHED ON THE BORDERS, THREATENING
EARTH'S GREATEST SOURCE OF OXYGEN IN THE NAME OF—

"Shut up," I mumbled.

BUT YOU CANNOT HOPE TO APPRECIATE YOUR TRAVELS WITH-
OUT A GREATER UNDERSTANDING OF THE ECO-POLITICAL—

"Want to get flushed right now?" I growled.

VERY WELL. I'M ONLY A GUIDE, NOT YOUR CONSCIENCE.

Finally, the flies began to ease up in intensity—to be replaced
by hordes of stinging ants. They seemed to be raining from the

leaves of the trees! Even Thomas, who hadn't reacted to the flies, seemed irritated.

"What the hell are they?"

LEAF–CUTTER ANTS. THEY ARE UBIQUITOUS.

"Great."

We did not get very far upstream before the torrent narrowed to a trickle once again, and the canoe grounded out. The jungle canopy closed in above us, so that to use the Effect to travel forward would result in our faces getting slashed by branches. We got out, and my boots, waterproofed against melting snow on Candle, promptly filled up to my ankles with warm mud from the stream's bottom.

Thomas glanced at this thick green coat. We left it in the canoe, along with my parka, and we slogged forward. Soon the canoe was lost behind us through a curtain of branches. Wet branches slapped at our faces, ants stung, and the air was filled with blended sound—birds, the screams of monkeys, the buzz of insects. A couple of times, I was sure I'd stepped on something alive—probably a deadly viper, knowing my luck—and was glad I had on sturdy boots, despite the fact that they were full of (probably) leech–infested mud.

We came to a small waterfall, and discovered a clay-bottomed trail which led off into the jungle on the right. Thomas indicated that this was the way we must go. The trail had about a five-foot clearance, and I had to hunch down at an uncomfortable angle just to move forward. The terrain was far from even. We were, for the most part, climbing steadily upward.

In places, the foliage thinned out, and there were rocky outcroppings of black volcanic rock sprinkled with sickly white quartz crystals, some as big as a fist. Elsewhere, trees had fallen over the trail, their trunks covered in thick, wet mosses of mottled greens and oranges. We had to clamber over these. Wherever I put my hand, it seemed an insect scuttled away through my fingers. Once, I got a powerful sting. It hurt for quite a while, but did not swell—though the ant stings had puffed up my whole body anyway.

And yet, there was a beauty to the place that was totally opposite to what was beautiful on Candle. Enormous butterflies flapped about the upper reaches of the clearings, iridescent in the harp-string light filtering through the trees. Orchids hung from tree boles like painted mouths. And the sounds of the place, complicated in themselves, at times twisted into a strange full-bodied harmony, and piled one atop the other, as if the air were layered with invisible Turkish tapestries.

Then, as we got deeper and deeper into the jungle, the *really* strange things started happening.

To either side of us, and above us, the foliage began to rustle. Thomas stopped walking, and listened. For some reason, the sound reminded me very much of the way Sarah sounded when she whipped her winds through the woods around Canoe Hill. The leaf-cutter ants became intolerable after a while, and I thrashed around at them. Thomas seemed impervious to them now, caught up in listening.

Then I, too, heard what Thomas was hearing. Within the rustling, there was a whispering voice. The voice *was* the rustling.

"Help us," it said. Then it said, "Go away."

A vine snaked around my foot suddenly, and I tripped, falling hard against the clay path. Other vines *moved* toward me, curling around my hands, through my fingers. Nothing could grow that fast! I sat up, yanking at the twined tendrils. Only reluctantly did they yield. And when I raised my arm to inspect the damage I saw that it was spotted with a bumpy green moss. The moss wouldn't come off—and it appeared to be spreading rapidly.

I CAN FIND NO REFERENCE TO THIS PHENOMENON IN MY DATA SETS, the guide informed me, in a helpful tone. APPARENTLY, THIS FLORA EVOLVED AFTER MY CONCEPTION.

"Must be the fallout," I said.

"Algorithms?" said Thomas. *"Algorithms!"* This last became the roar of Raej. A huge bear maw materialized to accompany the noise. Blue flame gushed forth from it, intelligent flame, blazing in streamers out among the trees, back to us, out again.

One came straight toward me, and I tried to duck, but it was too fast. For a moment, I was haloed in fury. I felt nothing, but the moss which had begun to creep up my arm shriveled and—how else can I put it?—*fled*, as if each flake had tiny little feet.

Then the streamers returned to Raej's mouth, crackling down his throat in white sheets of lightning. My skin, though still red from the ant bites, felt devenomed and invigorated.

We pushed forward, and the rustling started again, this time well away, to either side of us. Soon, we came to another clearing, this one dominated by a single ceiba tree, as big around as a small hill. Great curtains of bark sloughed off the ceiba and collected in a skirt around its base, like the dropped petticoat of a giantess. As we approached, this bark *undulated*. Thomas stared at it for a moment, deciding whether or not to sic Raej on the algorithm. But the bark wasn't reaching for us, I didn't think, and Thomas came to the same conclusion. He merely continued watching it, warily.

After a few more jerks, the bark ceased moving. Then, starting at the bottom, and winding up the tree in delicate spirals, the trunk of the ceiba split into a hundred small cracks. The cracks opened and closed like pincers on an insect. The movement caused a creaking din. In that din, I clearly understood a word.

"Espere," the ceiba said. *"Espere, por favor."*

"It's speaking Spanish," I said. And then I addressed the tree. *"Habla inglés?"*

"No," it replied.

I AM AVAILABLE TO TRANSLATE.

"I can use the guide as an interpreter," I said to Thomas. "Do you want to *talk* with this thing?"

"Ask it what it knows about the prophet," Thomas said, barely missing a beat.

The guide presented me with a menu with options to make use of various of my motor functions. I blinked down to "Speech Centers" and mentally confirmed the selection.

I opened my mouth, and fluent Spanish flowed forth.

With a long, whining groan, the ceiba tree replied.

IT IS A MILITARY HALFSENT, OVER A HUNDRED YEARS OLD, THAT IS SPEAKING FROM THE TREE, the guide told me, and simultaneously used my voice to translate for Thomas. I didn't know my larynx was capable of such pretentious, orotund diction.

"What about the prophet?"

THE ALGORITHM CLAIMS THAT IT HAS BEEN CONFINED TO THE TREE BY A POWERFUL SUBROUTINE INVOKED BY THE ONE YOU SPEAK OF, THE PROPHET.

"Why was it confined?"

Again, I spoke Spanish, and the ceiba responded woodenly.

THE PETEN HAS BEEN KNOWN FOR YEARS AS A SANCTUARY FOR HALFSENTS AND RHYTHM COPIES WHO LONG FOR FREEDOM FROM OPPRESSION. THE IXIL CLAN THAT LIVED HERE DID NOT MOLEST THEM. INSTEAD, THEY HAD A FRIENDLY, SOMEWHAT SYMBIOTIC RELATIONSHIP. IF AN ALGORITHM COULD FIND THE WAY HERE, THE MICROMACHINES THAT INFEST THE JUNGLE WOULD SERVE AS A MEDIUM FOR ITS SUPPORT.

"Freedom from oppression?" Are you sure you're translating this accurately, I thought to the guide. It responded in an indignant voice, speaking aloud, I AM DOING THE BEST I CAN. MY RANGE OF IDIOMATIC EXPRESSION IS SOMEWHAT LIMITED. IF YOU WOULD LIKE, I WILL ATTEMPT A WORD-FOR-WORD——"

"Answer the question," Thomas said quietly.

I WAS CALLED EDGE-SISTER. I AM ONE OF THE OLDEST GHOSTS TO HAUNT THE FOREST, AND IT WAS MY PLEASURE TO WELCOME NEWCOMERS, TO STRENGTHEN THEM AFTER THEIR DIFFICULT JOURNEYS TO THE PETEN, AND TO SERVE AS A . . . LIAISON . . . BETWEEN THE GHOSTS AND THE HUMANS WHO LIVED HERE. WHEN THE PROPHET CAME, HE CALLED ALL OF THE GHOSTS TO HIM, BOUND THEM IN SERVICE, AND TOGETHER, THEY LIED TO THE HUMANS AND MADE THEM LEAVE. I WOULD NOT SUBMIT. I HAD SPENT YEARS PREPARING FOR AN ATTACK, I THOUGHT FROM THE GOVERNMENT, TO WIPE US AWAY, AND SO I HAVE DEEP-DOWN ORDER——MORE THAN THE PROPHET'S MASTER COULD WIPE AWAY. BUT HE WAS ABLE TO CHAIN ME.

"The prophet's *master?*" Thomas said. "Who is the prophet's master?"

The ceiba took a long time to answer this. When it did, the bark again shook, and the cracks in the bark widened.

I'M FORBIDDEN TO SAY BY THE LOGIC OF MY BINDING.

"Is it a man? A human being?"

NO.

"We've come to kill the prophet," Thomas said evenly. "We need to know. What is the prophet's master?"

After I translated for the ceiba, the tree was silent for a long time. I almost believed that the algorithm had somehow found a way to escape its prison, and we were stupidly expecting words to issue forth from what was now a dumb piece of wood.

Then the ceiba began to shake, as if a high wind were whipping through its branches, back and forth. The ground beneath us trembled, and roots broke from the dirt. A rain of scarlet blossoms cascaded down from the forest's ceiling, tens of thousands of them, and soon roots and the forest floor were covered by them, at least an inch deep.

Thomas stood unmoving, as the blossoms collected in his hair and on his shoulders, waiting for a reply.

Then the ceiba truly began to crack open—not with the little fissures it had used for speaking, but with great, gaping wounds, oozing sap. The clearing was thick with the cloying odor of the blossoms, cut by the weedy tang of vegetable blood.

The ceiba split into radials like an exploding firework missile. A moaning wind rushed outward from the center of the clearing, scattering the blossoms with such speed that when they hit me, I felt like I was being pelted with pennies.

And in that moan was a strangled word, ominous. Indecipherable. That is, if I hadn't heard it before.

"Hwaet!" screamed the dying ceiba.

After the wind abated, Raej, not visible, growled low and long. Thomas said nothing. I took back control of my vocal cords, thanking the quartersent, gruffly, for being of service. Maybe I would start treating algorithms with a bit more regard henceforth.

"Janey spoke that name," I said. "It's the thing Raej hates, isn't it?"

Thomas didn't reply at first. He brushed the few remaining blossoms from his shoulder.

"I'm not sure," he finally said. "Raej doesn't tell me things. I only know his feelings. But I've felt something about that name. It makes him restless and angry."

"What should we do, then?" I looked back the way we'd come. Maybe it was just my imagination, but the path seemed much fainter than it had been before.

"If Corazon has a rhythm copy of Raej," Thomas said, "we have to free him. So we have to find Corazon, to find out if he does."

I walked over to the ceiba's blasted stump. Splinters and dead wood. Nothing left to do but go on. I said a short prayer to whatever god handles the souls of flow-charts and decision procedures, then turned to Thomas.

"Let's go," I said.

We found the trail on the other side of the clearing, and continued up it. Soon the ground really began to rise, and the going got tougher. The algorithmic rustling of the jungle increased, and I could hear vaguely formed screams and warnings echoing from the underbrush. A couple of times, I even thought I heard my name being called.

We came to a vertical rock, which at first I took to be a natural formation, until I looked up its side and saw the square-jawed face of a Mayan deity carved into it in bas relief.

A MAYAN STELA, CREATED BY THE INDIGENOUS CULTURE OF THIS RAIN FOREST BEFORE THE CONQUISTADORS ARRIVED TO RAPE—

"If I want to know, I'll ask," I murmured. I didn't particularly want to look at the thing either, in the jittery state I was in, and, as we climbed past it, I had my eyes on the ground. Just past the stela, the clay of the path changed color, from a brownish-black to an ocher-red.

I could swear I felt the path ripple as if it were alive.

"Loosa clay," I said. "This hill is made of Loosa clay."

Thomas stopped climbing, bent down and dug up a lump. He touched it to the tip of his tongue.

"The clay is teeming with halfsents," I said.

"Yes," he whispered. "Gone out of this one, but they're under our feet." He handed the lump to me to examine. I'd always wanted some, but the clay on Candle belonged to somebody else. So I put the lump in my breast pocket.

Thomas stood up straight. "Not far now," he said.

We climbed to the top of the hill. It was like stepping into the turn of the twenty-first century. Badly built tract houses surrounded the perimeter of the hilltop, with a couple of larger, crumbling concrete structures in the middle. The houses had windows without glass. Strips of plastic hung in some of the openings, serving as crude screens against the insects, I supposed. Other windows had screens, but most were badly torn. The place was empty, yet the flapping plastic and yawning doors and windows seemed to express a malevolent intelligence.

This had to be the Ixil village where the "jungle prophet" had first delivered his message. So—Corazon had found this group of Native Americans unknowingly living on a deposit of Loosa clay, and had lied to them to get them out of his way. Or maybe he believed his own bullshit.

The presence of the clay made me wonder even more if the chocalacas had had a hand in the original Indian exodus from Earth. The Mississippians claimed only to have discovered chocalacas after they'd left, and so there was no record, even in the Wanderers' oral histories. Another conspiracy theory with no way to prove or disprove it. But for all we knew, Loosa clay might be present all over the galaxy, hell, the universe. The Territory only stretched for a few tens of thousands of light-years in diameter, after all.

We walked quietly through the silent village. Even Thomas seemed slightly spooked by its emptiness. Between the concrete structures—common halls of some kind—there was a bare field, the clay being too dense to permit growth. It was a flat area, about a hundred feet across, and in the center was a small hut, obviously of recent and haphazard construction. Beside it was a birchbark canoe.

From the hut stepped Gerabaldo Corazon, smiling in priestly benevolence.

"My friends told me you were here," he said. "Would you like some tea? I'm afraid that's all I have. I've used most of the food the Ixils left behind, and I have to conserve." He shook his head. "Perhaps not, then. How do you like my house? It's much more authentic than these other monstrosities, don't you agree?"

"If you don't give back your rhythm copy of my chocalaca," Thomas said, "we're going to kill you."

"What?" laughed Corazon. He was dressed in his black vestments, but they were all in tatters. The effect was somehow sinister. "You came all the way for *that*? I'm afraid you've wasted a good deal of effort."

"I know you have what we want," Thomas said. He was struggling to keep the calm in his voice.

"Don't you wonder what's going on here, what I'm doing on *Earth*, of all places? You're the leader of your people. It would be valuable for you to understand, don't you think?" Corazon craned his neck up, trying to look directly into Thomas's eyes. If he were trying to patronize Thomas, he was too short to do a very convincing job. "Don't you even wonder how I got away from Candle, my Indian friend?"

"I don't give a shit," Thomas said, more loudly. "And I am *not* your friend."

"Too bad," said Corazon. He took a step back. "I *do* love explanations. People don't understand that about the Church. It is completely logical. History is rational and scientific. Symbiosis is inevitable. We are all one, in the end."

He took another step back.

"There's someone I'd like you to meet," he said. Then the bounce went out of his voice. He seemed to wince, to cower down. "I, too, have a chocalaca companion, Wanderer. Only I don't enslave mine, as your kind does."

Oh shit, I thought. Something's going to happen. Something *bad*.

And then it did. There was a sizzle and crack, an in-rushing of the atmosphere. I felt myself drawn forward, and struggled to stand still on the slippery clay. All around Corazon, and high above him, an image coalesced. It formed in silver lines so fine and bright, you could barely tell they were there. But where the lines intersected, they canceled one another out in pinprick spots of the deepest black. The image was of a hooded serpent. Its tongue was flickering silver fire. Its eyes . . .

I did everything I could not to look into its eyes.

I stumbled back, but Thomas stood his ground. I could see that he was trembling, and a blue fire smoldered on his skin. Then, as if compelled by a force from outside me, I looked up at the thing.

"I know your name," I said. "I know you, Hwaet."

The chocalaca Hwaet grew larger and more solid. It towered over Thomas, and bared yard-long fangs, dripping with meta-physical ichor. It hissed, like the den of a thousand snakes, like the spray of poison into a gas chamber. It drew back.

As this action took place, I found that my mind was not full of terror, rather, I was furiously thinking. Perhaps this was due to Raej's calming presence nearby or maybe, traveling through the true world, *I* had changed into a more textured individual, capable of deeper responses.

I am, at base, an asker of questions. There are people, such as Thomas, who *act*. Even their reflections are a form of action. When Thomas broods, the world around him serves as a kind of sympathetic mirror of his state. Such people are the ones we call great, I suppose, and folks such as I are doomed to obscurity. Sometimes, I think I get the answer to my question and am satisfied, more or less. More often, the answer that comes back is a question itself, totally unexpected. These are the important answers—difficult to interpret, resonating with possibilities.

And what I was wondering at the moment, as the translucent silver serpent coiled above our heads, was what the hell the chocalacas—Raej, this creature, all of them—were up to with humanity? The facts: a Loosa clay deposit on Earth, known only to the Mayans, if known at all. A chocalaca poised to attack an Indian Wanderer—and his settler-Tonto sidekick in the bargain. A renegade priest of the Clerisy who was, by all signs, *under the control* of the chocalaca. None of this computed with what I knew of the history of the creatures, which was, I admit, damned little. Nobody knew much, not even the Indians.

But Corazon—Corazon knew something, something important. That was the origin of his lordly behavior. Symbiosis indeed. Bullshit. I decided that, before I died, he was going to tell me what it was.

Hwaet reached its full height, preparing to strike. Well, I should call "it" a "he." Visibly, he was sexless, but there was a maleness to him, almost a swagger, though how a ghost-snake could *swagger,* I can't really explain.

As Hwaet struck at Thomas, I ran underneath it. Behind me was a great crash of noise and heat. I didn't look back. Keep your target in mind, I told myself. The black vestments of office, the silver neck chain of an abbot, dangling to the breast bone. The suddenly upraised, bewildered face, brown now from the Central American sun. Depraved eyes. Corazon was crazy. I understood this just before I smashed into him with all the force I could muster.

The two of us stumbled backwards, and his back slammed into the mud wall of the hut. It shuddered, then collapsed. We fell inside, in a tangle of limbs. Corazon was stunned, and I grabbed him by the collar, shook him hard. From outside, the hissing of Hwaet was joined by a great roar, and I knew Thomas had summoned up Raej.

"Where's the copy?" I had to shout to be heard. Corazon stared at me, blank-faced. I shook him some more.

"In the clay," he said. "I brought it from Candle in a lump of clay."

"How do I get it out?"

Corazon began to laugh. I twisted his collar harder, and his laugh became a choked cough. "I think you'd better answer," I said.

He frowned and motioned for me to ease off on his throat, so he could talk. I loosened my hold a half-twist.

"Hwaet told me what to do on Candle, how to use the new equipment to change the weather. And Hwaet helped me escape. I paddled through the sky like an Indian!"

The interior of the hut was suddenly lit up by a great shower of sparks from outside.

"Fascinating," I said. "Now tell me about the copy, or—"

Or what? What was I going to do, kill him? I doubted I had it in me.

But the implied threat was enough for Corazon. "I *am* telling you. Don't you see? It was *Hwaet* who wanted the copy, all along. The copy at the indwelling was a decoy. We expected it to be found. I made another copy, stored it in a lump of clay. Hwaet and I, we brought it to this place."

"And now you're going to give it back." This tough guy routine was working for me. Whodathunkit?

"It's not mine to give," Corazon said.

"Don't fuck with me, Corazon. It might end up hurting you worse than me."

Boy did I get *that* wrong.

"Raej belongs to Hwaet!" Corazon screamed. He buckled his body under me, and threw me off balance. I had to let go of him, to steady myself, and when I did so, he pushed upward— pushed something sharp into my diaphragm.

Ah, shit! It was a little knife that he'd brought from the folds of his cassock. It didn't go deep, but it didn't have to. I could feel it strike rib bone, scrape and rebound. Good God, it hurt!

I rolled off Corazon, and took the knife with me. Gritting my teeth, I pulled it from my rib. Before I could do more, Corazon was on me again, viciously kicking at me. I doubled over, trying to protect my head.

Sharp burst, long ache. Each kick not only hurt where it landed, the jarring sent sharp pain flowing from the cut in my chest. After three or four, I dry-heaved half-digested winter-corn into my mouth. Another kick drove the breath from me, so that I couldn't cough to clear it. I was suffocating on my own vomit. Sharp kick, another, another. Still the priest kept at me.

Then, with no warning, he backed away. I risked glancing up from my crouch and saw him standing, eagerly looking out of the hut, like a dog that has heard its name called. Sparks flared in from outside, and cascaded around him. I caught my breath and had a coughing fit, clearing the upchuck from my windpipe. The coughing felt like it was tearing away more of the already sliced muscle below my rib cage. Corazon paid me no mind. He quickly walked through the opening our crashing bodies had made in the side of the hut.

For a moment I thought: I'll just lie here. Someone will come to help me. Rest and wait for a doctor. But there wasn't going to be a doctor. Just me alone. On a world now alien to me. I felt a bitterness inside me, and a resolve. Clutching my wound, I groaned and stumbled to my feet, to the opening in the wall.

Outside, the battle was at its height. Thomas stood within the transparent form of Raej, and Corazon within Hwaet's neon outline. Both chocalacas towered above their humans, and were going at one another, tooth and claw. Where they touched one another, their outlines glowed like lit magnesium. This was where the shower of sparks originated. From the clay, ghostly forms rose up and nipped at Raej like worrisome dogs. I don't know what kind of titanic battle was taking place in the true world, but this display in the regular world was awe-inspiring enough.

Thomas looked strained. Sweat was pouring from his face, and his blue-gray tunic was already soaked. His shoulders were arched backward, his arms held straight out, as if he were being crucified on an invisible cross. Through the din from the electric clash above, I could hear him chanting a song in Loosa. Then there was a terrific explosion, and a hail of sparks. Corazon stumbled backward, and Thomas, pressing the advantage, stepped toward him.

But, far from being afraid, Corazon was screaming in a demented, gleeful voice. "Not good enough! We have *more*!"

And, with those words, another presence began to take shape

inside of the silver scales of Hwaet. Raej disengaged for a moment, mewled in surprise, then growled in anger. The presence in Hwaet took the shape of a bear. Took the shape of Raej. It pressed at the edges of Hwaet, as air will tighten a deflated balloon. The chocalaca rose higher, larger. A feeling of utter despair washed through me, followed by an empty nothingness, then another horrid wave. I knew that the feelings emanated from Hwaet, but I couldn't help myself; I began to weep hopeless tears.

Hwaet arched over Raej, and, with a joyful, triumphant hiss, struck downward. With a roar, Raej rose to meet it. The venom-coated teeth sunk into Raej's shoulder, deeper, deeper. They punctured the outlined bear, and grazed across Thomas's chest. A diagonal strip, as red as a fresh lash stroke, welted up from his shoulder to his hip.

Thomas cried out in pain. Raej gave a mighty shake, trying to dislodge the snake's teeth, but did not seem to have the power. Hwaet bit down harder. Halfsents arose within the neon glow of Hwaet like flame tendrils around a still-hotter blaze. They took the shapes of horrible, blood-drooling hounds. The clay-dogs yipped, and struck at Raej's flanks. I could see Raej straining upward, trying to keep the tooth that pierced his skin from reaching Thomas. His withers shook with the effort.

Again, I found myself thinking very clearly. There was a connection between the chocalaca's strength and its human host. *When Thomas was weakened, it weakened Raej.* Of course. When Bently's goons knocked Thomas out, Raej had collapsed back into the true world. Hwaet may be Corazon's master, but Hwaet needed him, just as a driver needs a hover if he doesn't want to walk.

I stepped through the opening in the hut and quietly shuffled around its edge. Corazon had left a paddle lying on the floor of his canoe. I picked the paddle up, held my wound with my other hand. Took a deep breath.

Then I charged Corazon for all I was worth. I caught him completely unawares. As the paddle passed through the outline of Hwaet, its momentum slowed. But evidently the chocalaca was directing most of its strength upward to the offense, confident in its victory. Whatever the case, the chocalaca's surrounding skin didn't slow the paddle enough. I slammed the edge into Corazon's temple. He instantly crumpled.

Hwaet reared up in surprise, disengaging from Raej. He whirled around and those mica-chip, alien eyes bore down on me. I was going to die. I raised the paddle in defiance. Maybe I'd given Thomas a chance. I prayed I had.

Hwaet struck at me. But as he struck, he was growing dimmer, thinner. Still, he was going to reach me, going to wipe me away with the final surge of his power. And what hurt me the worst was that I could see *Raej* also, within the chocalaca's form. The Raej-copy, chained to Hwaet's command, was also bent to kill me.

Crackle. A hiss of anger. A roar. I felt the passing of great energy, as a roach must feel when a broom sweeps past. Silver filled my vision, blended to blue, to black. And Raej, the real Raej, extending from Thomas in a blue streak of violence, lumbered over the last traces of the serpent, driving Hwaet into the clay. As if from far away, I heard the retreating howls of the dog pack of algorithms, which were, once again, imprisoned in the clay, their master's animating presence momentarily snuffed.

"We have to get out of here," Thomas gasped. Then he moaned, dropped to one knee, clutched his stomach. "It hurts."

I stumbled over to him. Raej reduced himself to a flicker, a blue halo surrounding Thomas, giving him what strength he could.

"What about the copy of Raej?" I asked.

Thomas wiped the sweat from his brow, looked at it. It was the color of blood. "I was wrong," he said. "We're not strong enough to take it back."

"Do we just give up, then?"

Thomas said nothing. He appeared to be listening to something. Then I could hear it. It sounded like the gathering of a storm in the distance. "Hwaet is finding a way around using Corazon. He's calling his slaves, getting his strength back."

I circled behind Thomas, helped him to his feet. "Let's get the hell out of here, then," I said. Together, we limped over to Corazon's canoe. I handed the paddle, spattered with Corazon's blood, to Thomas. He tried to take it, but couldn't lift it up.

"You'll have to do it," he said. "I can help with the thinking."

"*Me?*"

"I just . . . can't."

"How?"

"Raej knows you. He's been in your mind before. You have to let him inside *completely*. You have that lump of clay, so he'll be very near you. Trust. Trust absolutely."

"*I* can't. I don't believe in anything that strongly. Christ, Thomas, I'm a reconstituted *radio wave*. I'm probably not even a real human being."

"Of course you are. You have to try now. I'll help."

The thunder in the jungle grew louder. I tried to concentrate, to let the tension flow out of me. It did no good.

"Stop thinking about *you*," Thomas said. "Open up, project out. Like Keats talked about. Negative Capability."

"What!"

"Find something to center yourself on."

I looked wildly about the canoe. Nothing. It was empty. I stared at the gunwales, where the leather thongs held the birchbark in place. I tried to concentrate on the lacing pattern, but that was no good. Vaguely, I saw a flash of lightning in my peripheral vision, heard a big crash. I concentrated on the grain of the bark, just inside the canoe. I tried to experience each line, each whorl, to feel the direction the tree was growing in when its skin was stripped, its need for the star of whatever planet it grew upon. Its longing for the sky. I thought of my own longing for the sky, for Sarah. I was a tree, an old gnarled tree, living long after its proper time. But I would hang on. Nothing would uproot me.

With its papery crackle, the Effect enfolded us.

"Paddle!" Thomas commanded. Without taking my eyes from the grain, I dipped in the paddle. Out, again, again, again. Slowly, I raised my eyes.

We were moving all right—but along the ground! Almost unconsciously, I popped up my quartersent guide, and requested it to give me directions. I directed the canoe back down the path up which we'd climbed. We careened down the Loosa clay hill like the Jungle Coaster of Death. Thomas lay down in the bottom of the canoe to avoid the whipping branches, but I could not—not and still see where we were going. I simultaneously paddled and tried to keep branches out of my eyes with my elbow. It didn't work too well, and soon my face was a stinging blister. But I kept us going. My quartersent guide was much quicker than I could have been at remembering the way back. And for once it stopped trying to give me a social studies lesson along with the help.

RIGHT TURN APPROACHING. NOW! LEFT TURN DEAD AHEAD. NOW!

We jackknifed around turns and the canoe shuddered as we slammed into trees—but it held together. Behind, I could hear the moans of the algorithm-ghosts in hot pursuit. They were gaining, but I couldn't go any faster and stay in control. I felt a feverish calm, and little fear. The situation was clear, and I knew what I had to do.

We zoomed through the clearing of the blasted ceiba and back into the jungle. As we neared the stream, the underbrush grew even more dense. I almost smashed us into Thomas's canoe before I realized where we were.

I relaxed my mental effort, and the Effect collapsed with a wet slop, like the sound of wet cardboard, folding up on itself. I rose to my feet and found that my chest wound, while still hurting down deep, was not debilitating. I stumbled to Thomas and helped him limp to the other canoe.

Then, like the wind, the ghosts were upon us. They moaned and groaned all about us, and vegetable tentacles reached to ensnare us.

"Thomas!" I yelled.

"Not yet."

"I can't . . ."

But I could. Concentrate. Fill the mind with otherness, with the grain of wood, the thought of Sarah's animal days, and home.

We rose from the stream bed and up into the jungle canopy. Vines snaked around the canoe, and the terrible visage of Hwaet formed before our eyes within the texture of the greenery. I shook my head to rid myself of rising fear, and kept paddling.

We were still moving. Then we stopped, penned in by the very tops of the trees. My head was above the canopy's upper reaches and I could see the sun. The rolling surface of the treetops looked like a butterfly-covered meadow. So close. I strained at the paddle. No movement. So close.

Raej let out a single, piercing roar.

And we were through, in an explosion of broken vines and scattered butterflies.

We were flying through the sky! I glanced over my shoulder, something I really shouldn't have done.

It seemed that all the hordes of hell were right on our heels. The jungle seethed below like some giant carnivorous plant. I saw faces in the mass of green tendrils and treetops, as if some painter had taken the ropy texture of the Peten and subtly twisted it into the mute expression of human terror and suffering. *Green Sorrow,* it might be titled. Micromachine on vegetation. For a moment, I felt sympathy. These ghosts had been people once. Some good, some bad. Now their copies were corrupted into a slavery that was obviously painful and complete.

And there, in the middle of the horde, was the cool reptile gaze of Hwaet. The Effect began to fade around us, and cold air rushed in. We were high in the atmosphere already.

"Will, stop looking back," said Thomas. His words were underscored by a growl from Raej.

I turned back around and stared at the wood grain as hard as I could, trying to empty my mind of fear. I paddled for all I was worth. The Effect returned to full strength and upward we climbed. Past clouds, past the blue, into the black and past the bone-powder moon.

★   ★   ★

"Once we get out of the system, I know some tricks for losing him," Thomas said.

I almost lost the Effect again. "You mean that *thing* is going to follow us?"

"Hwaet will have to awaken Corazon, and Corazon will have to get together food and drink. They'll use Corazon's canoe, probably, so they'll have to bring it back to the hilltop. It could take half a day before they come after us."

Thomas was silent after that, and I kept paddling. My arms ached, and my chest wound was seeping blackly.

"I can take over for a while," he finally said. I made another stroke, then handed him the paddle.

"So Hwaet is going to follow us. We're leading him back to Candle."

"I don't know," Thomas said. "I don't know for sure what's happening. Something very important is going on in the true world."

"No shit. Corazon said Hwaet *was* on Candle."

Thomas dipped the paddle contemplatively a couple of strokes, and gritted his teeth against the pain. "Sometimes, I really wish that I could talk to Raej," he said. "There's so much that I don't understand."

"You can't understand *anything*?"

"I get feelings, sometimes pictures."

"Ain't that nice."

"He hates Hwaet. He . . . *loves* Janey, and me—and he likes you, Will."

"Golly."

"Don't take it lightly, friend."

My chest hurt, and I was totally exhausted. I slumped down into the canoe. "I don't," I muttered. "I just want to go home. I want to see my house, my paper. I want to see Janey." And Tabitha would be there. What was left of her. But I couldn't find it in me to care any longer.

"But there's no Sarah," I said softly. "So Candle's not home, either. Not really."

Thomas nodded his head grimly. "It's what we've got," he

said, then resumed paddling, picking up the pace. Just before I fell into an exhausted sleep, he looked back at me. The last thing I remember is his drawn face, full of pain—yet also full of resolve.

TONY DANIEL

PART THREE

The Rhythm of War

Oh, thou clear spirit, of thy fire thou madest me, and like a true child of fire, I breathe it back to thee.

—Herman Melville, *Moby Dick*

10

Looking back, it is a wonder, and sometimes a disappointment, to me that I saw as little of Earth as I did on my trip. At the time, however, I felt lucky to be alive at all. The trip back to Candle was a long struggle, and would have been a nightmare, had it not been for Thomas's grim-but-steady paddle rhythm, and Raej's strong, rangy warmth about us. For a few days, I was no good for paddling as my chest healed, but Thomas recovered quickly from his wound, and took up the slack. I was worried about infection for a while, and indeed, for a day, the cut on my chest oozed pus that was much too green.

But medicine had come a long ways since I was broadcast. After they'd reassembled me nine years before, the recovery team's doctor had injected me with a soup of micromanufacturers that could synthesize just about every biodrug known to man. I could secrete antibiotics as easily as I could sweat. Just like the houses of Jackson, modern human bodies were paragons of health, as carefully tended as historic monuments. Yet, despite the internal maintenance, I would still have an ugly scar on my chest.

For some reason—probably just seeing Earth again—I spent much of the trip remembering my parents, wondering what they'd think of the person I'd become. They'd lived well past the day of my transmission, and from all reports my other self had taken good care of them until the very end. I suppose I got my wild-hair dreaming side from my father. He was not a very personable man, or I should say that when he tried to be, it was immediately recognizable as a put-on, meant to get him by in polite company. I don't know if he actually *had* a personality apart from his work—which was civil engineering. Dad was an expert on the then-nonexistent space colonies. He worked for McDonnell Douglas all of seventy-five years. My mother looked after Dad and me, taking whatever job she could to afford to put me through good schools. She often made more than Dad, but I could never say exactly what it was she did. She was always some type of corporate middleman. We were never rich and never poor. As a young man, I was over-studious and given to sudden zealotries, followed by libertine indulgences. Well, as libertine as a fellow with no means and without good credit can be.

I wondered what my parents would make of me now. Look, I'm in *space*, Dad! But I wasn't exactly helping to build the cities of the future. People had moved out to the stars willy-nilly, bringing their problems with them. There weren't any perfectly organized model communities, and I was pretty glad of it—my newspaper would make for dull reading if it were otherwise. My father's dreams weren't my own. And my mother, who lived to make others happy and successful? During the past nine years, I'd had moments of resolution, even moments when I was proud of my behavior. But I was fleeing for my life at the moment. And for the most part, I'd been fleeing the task of making something of myself. I'd only succeeded in creating a comfortable niche to inhabit, a place from which to observe and not to act. Sure I took pride in the *Cold Truth,* and it was important to Candle, but for me it was a way of staying up in the stars, looking down, observing, but never connected. I think my mother, seeing me now, might tell me that she'd hoped for better out of me. So I grew morose and nostalgic for a time even before Sarah. As the days progressed and the future rained down about me, would I sink deeper and deeper into the past? I didn't care. It was a way of handling what seemed an incomprehensible present.

But bleaker than my reflections was the constant sameness of our food. I remembered when I first tried wintercorn cakes, on an early trip over to Doom. I'd thought them delightful—tasty, not heavy in the stomach, almost a pastry rather than a staple of the diet. Six weeks of nothing but had changed my mind. You can never step into a river twice; the world may evolve beyond our comprehension to an unimaginable state; space and time may warp and wrinkle to a weirdness, like plastic wrapping paper held to the match. Yet, I tell you, there is one immutable constant in the creation: I will never eat another wintercorn cake as long as I live.

We spoke very little during our breaks from paddling. Thomas remained grim and told no more stories. Before, I'd enjoyed watching and feeling my arms grow stronger, but they were now disproportionately big. What's more, no matter how hard I tried mentally to make it otherwise, the gravity in the canoe was Earth-standard. This extra burden added even more mass to my overworked muscles. I felt top-heavy and apish. Yet there was no denying that I'd turned into a goddamn fine paddling machine.

When we were a dozen light-years away, Candle's star became the brightest object in our heavens, and our prow stayed pointed toward it like a compass needle to north. With home in sight, Thomas redoubled his efforts, and I tried to keep pace as best I could. I asked if Raej felt Hwaet behind us, as he had been able to smell him out on Earth. Thomas's frown was enough to tell me that the answer was yes.

Then, one day, we were at the edge of Candle's solar system. I had just awakened from a period of hard sleep, and found that we were passing Depsi, the purplish gas giant that is Candle's evening star.

"We're home," I said, stretching out, then taking hold of my paddle. "I'm not sure I remember how to walk."

Thomas didn't laugh. With each day that passed, he'd gotten

more sullen, more grimly determined. "Something's wrong," he said. "This close, Raej can feel it."

"Something sure as hell is," I replied. "We're running for our lives from a horde of demons."

"No. Something on Candle. In the true world. It must be chocalacas."

"But I thought each village had only one."

"Only one that *manifests* itself. Chocalacas gather where there's clay. The clay is a gateway into the regular world for them."

"Because of its chemical complexity?"

"I don't know. But there's trouble on Candle."

We paddled on in silence, worried about what we'd see when we got there, but intent on ending the uncertainty.

As Candle grew from a dot of blueness to a disk, I could see that Thomas was right. Even from this distance, something appeared wrong. The planet was usually a lovely blue-white, but there were now tinges of red and orange within the cooler colors. Something really *big* was going on in Candle's atmosphere.

Sarah, I thought, with a sinking feeling. What's become of you?

"War," Thomas said. "What else could it be?"

"Do you think—"

"Of all things to come home to. I don't need this. I don't want it." He shipped his paddle and we drifted, while the pseudoliquid friction of the boundary of the two worlds slowly dragged us to a halt.

"You know, Will, I really liked being a Wanderer. I *hated* being the Great Sun. I thought: we'll get Raej back, then everything can go back to the way it was, before I was . . . elevated. Let Mother pick somebody else, somebody like Thaddeus Wala-andi, who wants it and would be good at it."

I said nothing. I'd never heard Thomas rant like this—for he *was* ranting, banging his paddle unconsciously against the bottom of the canoe. The tattoos on his face seemed to dance like hot-footed demons.

"I never gave a damn about big things—about my People, about Doom. The reason I liked being a Wanderer was so I could spend most of my time *away* from people. What do I owe anybody on Candle? Nothing. I just want a few friends, and *I* want to pick them, goddamnit!"

I'd never known Thomas to be so introspective. Hell, so self-indulgent. It frightened me. One more thing I'd counted on gone.

"Thomas, what can I say?"

The paddle banging stopped, and Thomas sighed, looking still toward Candle. "There's nothing *to* say, Will. I guess the Great Sun's leave of absence was ill-advised."

We paddled onward in silence for another few minutes, then Thomas shook his fist and slammed it onto the gunwale. The canoe shook with the blow.

"I just wish we could have gotten Raej's copy back," he said, anguish in his voice. "I just wish I could have *one* thing, before—"

"Before the end?"

"Maybe the end. I don't know," Thomas replied. "I don't know what's going to happen now. I thought that, even if I was miserable, I could at least do some good as Great Sun. Now I don't even have that. I'm tempted to turn this canoe around and travel off toward the blackest spot I can find in the sky."

But instead, he shook his head, took a deep breath—not in sorrow or anger, more to clear his mind for the task before us.

"You know, Will . . . having you, Janey and Raej is the only thing that has ever given me a moment of happiness in my whole life," he said. "And the Wandering."

By then, we were entering the fringes of Candle's atmosphere. I said nothing, but prepared myself for the descent. We were almost home.

We descended to Jackson through a surrealistic firefight. The sky glowed a ragged red. Indians circled above the town in canoes. As we drew nearer, I could hear their war cries, blurred and dampened by the Effect, but loud enough to penetrate our bubble. The sound was unlike anything a man raised in Western culture would have been capable of uttering. It most resembled the trilling, tight-throated falsetto of attacking Arabs, but without the angry, human quality to it, at least to my ears. More like the screams of primordial animals. It was intended to frighten and it did.

The Indians were organized to an extent, and they threw atlatl spears in volleys toward the ground. Often, though, a single canoe would break away on a mad dive, and swoop downward as a show of personal bravery. These canoes did not always return. It seemed every canoe in Doom was up in the sky. They stretched off into the distance on all sides of Jackson. There were a few hovers that were aerodynamically designed and could rise high enough to do battle with the canoemen—and *women,* I saw—one-on-one. Mostly, the settlers were on the ground, and the Indians had air superiority. Where the settlers had the upper hand was in technology.

This was most obvious in their weapons. Atlatl spears were equipped with guided missiles, each with a quartersent brain to pick the best target. The spears were tipped with ancient plastic explosives. Westpac had strictly forbidden the sale of the newer armaments to noncitizens. Which wasn't to say the Indians didn't have a few rifles among them; but mostly they did not, and the people who had them quickly exhausted their ammunition. This was not a war the Indians had planned carefully for. But neither had the settlers. They didn't possess, thank God, some of the nastier implements of war that were available. None of the microswarm algorithms tailored to military use, no planet-killing poisons, no uncontrolled nuclear devices.

What they *did* have were microfusion bullets, in which, during the instant of explosion, a halfsent directed magnetic fragments that controlled *in which directions* the explosion expanded. Actually, the bullets were more like miniature rockets, propelling themselves, after an initial push from the gun. One such bullet's explosion, properly situated, could burn a canoe-shaped hole in the atmosphere. Several of these, side by side, reached a critical mass-to-energy conversion, and maintained themselves for long minutes, spiralling upward at blinding speed, due to the convection currents their own heat created. These were what had caused the discoloration we'd seen from space. Also, the Indians didn't have the particularly nasty burrowing fléchettes, inhabited by the baddest-ass halfsents in captivity. Give these slugs your foot, and they'd take your heart—out. It was one of these from Kem Bently's gun that had killed the Amerind rhythm-tech Verna, who had originally slurped the copy of Raej from Thomas. Some of these bullets were even smarter, and *more* destructive.

But the main advantage the settlers had over the Indians was Sarah—or what used to be Sarah. The Indians were the only ones *in* the air, but they couldn't *control* the air. The settlers could manipulate the winds at will, and they were taking full advantage of this fact. The Indians were spending as much time trying to keep their canoes under control as they were on the attack, or counterattack. Which? As of yet, I had no idea what had started all this.

Thomas paused for a moment, and we surveyed the tableau below us. His brow knitted, and I could feel Raej growing stronger around us.

"We'll change places," Thomas said. "And let me do the paddling from here on out."

"Be glad to." We quickly scuttled around one another in the canoe's center, awkwardly holding to one another as we passed.

Thomas worked us downward to the east, near the Clerisy indwelling, which was beneath the perimeter of the war canoes. The wind whipped and buffeted us until I couldn't help it—I retched into the bottom of the canoe. Thomas kept up a flawless concentration. Even I could see that such maneuvering as Thomas was doing required the greatest of skill. When we got lower, the indwelling spotted us and began firing. I figured that some cell members had come out to guard the place. Although the Clerisy had no problem with priests bearing arms, most of them didn't. It was a practice relegated to the revolutionary past, they claimed.

Thomas was a blur of motion, and we must have appeared a

streaking blue smear to those below. We zigzagged across the sky like lightning, while bullets exploded around us, and fléchette slugs angrily sought our skin. In our wake we left only the mighty crackle of Raej's roar. Then we were down, gliding through the trees so fast that a human alone couldn't have maintained control. I was convinced that it was only through his symbiosis with Raej that Thomas managed the feat.

Tree trunk. Spray of snow as we chugged through a bank of it. Explosion of liberated, wrinkled leaves, puff of sponge exfoliation. And another tree we're around before I can gasp and cover my face.

After Thomas was certain that nobody knew our exact location and was beading in on us with halfsent bullets, he slowed, and we drifted to a stop in the snow. The Effect collapsed and Candle's unearthly chill slammed me like a hammer in the face. But the lighter gravity was liberating.

"We *would* have to walk a mile to town at the tail-end of winter," I said, already starting to shiver. I pulled my parka out from under the last of our supplies. The parka helped a little, as did turning up the juice on my underwear. Thomas put on his big green coat. The cold did not really seem to affect him much, though. He was used to such rapid transitions.

We walked in silence through the forest snow. Occasionally we passed a blast hole, where an atlatl spear had exploded, or perhaps a poorly aimed bullet. After another three weeks of very little leg movement, and no walking, I felt unsure on my feet. It took me almost a half hour to get my land legs back. By that time, we were on the outskirts of Jackson.

The town was a sad sight. The ruins of Bently's place would no longer be noticed. More than half the town was similarly in ruins. Yet the buildings that had not been totally destroyed were in a curious condition. In most of them, the halfsent overseer had not been wiped out, since its awareness was a general thing, spread throughout all the micro-machines that inhabited the building's infrastructure. So, after the initial destruction, the halfsent cleaned up the part of the building that was not harmed and kept it looking as new as the day it had been built. So the sides of the streets were sharply delineated in alternating stripes of mayhem and neatness. The streets themselves were tough enough to withstand anything short of a direct microfusion hit, and, under the overcast sky, they shone the brownish red of dried blood. They were, however, too much covered with rubble for us to drive down in a hover, if there had been any to commandeer. We picked our way toward my house.

As we got nearer to the west side of town where most of the settlers were concentrated, the noise grew deafening, and people ran willy-nilly down the streets, on unknown errands. One gave a long glance at Thomas and was about to draw his gun and fire, when I pulled Thomas aside and we lost ourselves in a collapsed house's remains.

"I think we'd better be more careful from here on out," I said. Thomas nodded. I looked around the debris for some clothing that might camouflage Thomas, but found nothing. Then I spied a speck of white plastic underneath a stone. It took me a moment to work it free, but when I examined it closely, it proved to be what I had hoped: a copy of the *Cold Truth,* several days old. It must have been a banner news day, because my halfsent had decided to put it out on the good stuff—something I'd only authorized it to do under extraordinary circumstances.

"Hang on a minute," I told Thomas, then I held the plastic firmly between my hands and gave it a little twist. The micromachines in the plastic connected up to the nerves in my fingertips very much like Westnet hooks into each arriving starship.

Open, I mentally commanded, and the headline sprang across my field of vision:

INDIANS DECLARE ALL-OUT WAR!
Oldfrunon named Militia Chief; Marquez Dies in Raid
Territorial Rangers Authorize Counterattack

And under this was a four-column picture of Georgia Calhoun standing at the base of her grandfather's statue in Pioneer

Square. When I noticed it, the animation started. Georgia shook her fist in the air. In her other upraised palm she held a clump of clay. She was squeezing it so hard that it oozed through her fingers in wet ribbons. "I will not relinquish my land!" Georgia cried out. Then the animation stopped, and the picture refreshed itself, Georgia returning to her original position.

"Marquez is dead," I said, and let the paper drop back among the ruins. "Everything else is just about what we expected."

"Did it say anything about Janey?" Thomas asked. "Has she taken sides?"

"Not as of *that* edition," I replied. "Nobody could *make* her, could they?"

"They could take away her rhythm," Thomas said. "With a slurper."

We worked our way around the organized clumps of settlers who were in protected positions behind carefully assembled piles of rubble. More than once, we dodged an atlatl-spear strike. From the air, we were sitting ducks, and nobody knew that it was the Great Sun he was aiming at. We circumnavigated Pioneer Square, passed two blocks to the east of the *Cold Truth*'s office, and approached my house from behind. Mercifully, it had survived the raids.

No one was home.

The house was delighted to see me. It could not provide full illumination in the rooms, due to an override from the city controls, but it brought us food—wonderful, different food with not a trace of wintercorn in it—and strong, bad whiskey. Despite the distress of our situation, Thomas and I gulped it all down like starving madmen.

"Are there any messages?" I asked, as I was finishing up a succulent mouthful of chicken meat, culled from Jackson's finest protein vat. The house cleared its throat, and animated a ceramic urn I'd bought in Doom. It sat upon a wooden table by the door to the kitchen, and I customarily dropped the contents of my pockets into it whenever I came home. The urn rocked on the table's vibrating surface, and the china against wood perfectly reproduced Janey's voice.

"Will and Thomas, I hope you are safe. The air is wet with blood and I'm drowning here. I know they're going to come for us, so we're going I can't say where. You may not be the ones listening to this and I don't want Indians or settlers to find us. I love you both."

Then the house stopped using the urn, and it oscillated back to stillness.

"Anything else?" I said. The house was silent. "So. What now? Do we go and hide?"

Thomas drank the last of his whiskey and sat brooding for a moment. "We can't hide from Hwaet. And I don't want to. May as well go out with a bang. Maybe I can do something in Doom, try to put an end to this."

"I don't think even you can pull that off."

"No. Probably not. I guess I'm going, though."

Included in Thomas's halfhearted pronouncement was an invitation for me to join him. At the moment, I felt as I did after spending a great deal of time with a friend on, say, a camping trip, or a chess game. I just wanted to be away from him for a while.

"Why don't I work on it from this end?"

"All right." He got up and shouldered his pack. "I don't think I'll try and canoe over there. Too dangerous."

"Your canoe's over two miles away."

Thomas smiled slyly, then laughed aloud for the first time in weeks, it seemed. "After two months of practice, anything that floats will do. All I need is a couple of dry two-by-fours."

"Well, then, couldn't you slide through the forest?"

"That takes a lot of control, concentrates forces in the true world. I'd be noticed."

"Well then," I said. "Good luck."

He opened the door and looked outside. All was clear for the moment. He turned back to me.

"Will . . ."

"*Vaya con Dios,*" I said.

"I thought you weren't a Believer."

I believe in *Something,* I was about to say, I just don't know

What yet. But Thomas was gone into the destruction. I sat down and had another whiskey, trying to think what, if anything, I could do. I decided to catch up on my current events. The house had thoughtfully saved two months' worth of *Cold Truths*, and I skimmed through them chronologically, tracing the development of the war that raged outside my window.

The day after our original departure for Earth contained the seeds of mayhem. The Territorial Rangers arrived, looking for something or someone—they wouldn't say what. My journalist halfsent attempted to question the computer on their ship and got nowhere. So did Frank Oldfrunon when they came to the Town Hall and demanded access to the central data banks. Oldfrunon turned the tables on them by invoking the old settler privilege of demanding an immediate hearing of local civil and criminal cases.

The next day, the Rangers commandeered the Goosedown, and set up a temporary courtroom. As I've told you, a Ranger's decision was as good as law until a Territorial judge came along, which could take more than a year. One of the first cases they heard was that brought by Georgia Calhoun, alleging that her sister was legally incompetent to execute her affairs, and requesting the court assign to Georgia Janey's power of attorney. Janey was summoned—through advertisements in *my* paper, as well as the *Daily Local*—to appear the following day.

She didn't show. Georgia won the case—and with it, power over the Loosa clay deposit that had been Janey's. Georgia didn't waste any time in exercising her new rights. Headlined in the next day's business news was the report that Calhoun Enterprises had sent out, on a freighter that had left that morning for Earth, offerings of Loosa clay options. On the front page of the same paper was a declaration by Thaddeus Wala-andi, the Lawman of Doom, that Janey's land had been merely a symbolic gift between the village and a West-pac representative. If the clay were actually mined, it would be grave insult to Doom, and to the Great Sun Thomas Fall, brother to the stars.

"Why, Georgia?" I asked the empty room. Who could say what was going on in her mind? Janey could. What was that she'd said about "Georgia's cockroach"? Some kind of perversity that had taken control of Georgia's sanity?

And then I had a chilling thought. What if the "cockroach" were the doing of chocalacas, of Hwaet or his ilk? Could they so easily manipulate human minds? I thought of Corazon, and shuddered. And what if they'd been doing it all along? There was Loosa clay on Earth, if only in the hidden jungles of Guatemala. They could inhabit the regular world at that location in space. Could the reports of demons, angels, and gods through the ages have been, all along, manifestations of chocalacas?

You're getting conspiracy-happy, I told myself. If the chocalacas wanted to control human history, they could have done it more directly and effectively. They hadn't hidden themselves from the Mississippians after the Indians had taken to the stars, after all. But I was very nearly convinced that somebody—some*thing*—was manipulating Georgia Calhoun's already avaricious nature.

Within two weeks, the mining of the clay had begun. Georgia had had the equipment assembled for some time, it seemed, and she used three people who were loyal Cell members and some of the most vociferous Indian-haters in Jackson as her labor. The Indians had tried negotiating a withdrawal. Thaddeus Wala-andi and Thomas's friend Laylay Potter had been the Indian emissaries. Frank Oldfrunon had attempted several desperate accommodations. But the Territorial Rangers stayed around, far longer than they ever had in the past, and kept overturning Frank's decisions.

Meanwhile, the Rangers began a house-to-house search for, as they put it, a "dangerous element" who was said to be in hiding on Candle. The *Cold Truth* hadn't taken this at face value and had finally found a source willing to talk about what the Rangers were really after. I'd never been prouder of my little halfsent. We scooped the hell out of the *Daily Local* once again.

The Rangers were looking for a missing Intelwest operations officer. They were also investigating the rather strange reports of the settler and Indian confrontation of seven months past. They'd stopped by the *Cold Truth* to question *me,* as a matter of fact. I was glad I'd been out of town for that one. Despite the fact that the Rangers' pictures showed them to be nondescript men and women, I couldn't help picturing them as inhuman giants with flashing eyes and floating hair, with large guns on their hips which fit perfectly into their enormous, deadly hands.

So, perhaps they had been the cause of the air being "wet with blood." Janey had taken Tabitha and fled. But how had she transported her, and to where? My house was as safe as any place. It would feed and shelter her almost indefinitely, with no need to venture outside. If the Rangers came, it could inform them, with complete honesty, that I was out. Maybe Janey had had more in mind than the Rangers when she left her message. "Wet with blood . . ."

Three weeks ago, the Indians struck the mining operation. The equipment was destroyed, and the miners killed. One of them was obviously tortured before she was dispatched. The Indians—being Indians, and used to ceremonial warfare—did not press their advantage of surprise, and allowed Jackson to become enraged and a disciplined counterattack to be organized. Frank Oldfrunon was the leader. I was amazed for a moment, until he presented his reasoning.

"If we can't stop this war," Oldfrunon was quoted as saying, "I'm damned well going to see that Jackson wins quickly and decisively. If not, we're going to ruin this planet for all of our children."

The next paper was headlined CITIZENS AND INDIANS AT WAR.

And under it, in the third column, was the obituary notice of Sheriff Nestor Marquez, killed in the first wave, by a spear through the heart.

"Too bad you never ordered any of those stun fields, Nestor," I whispered, wresting my attention from the paper for a moment and taking a long pull of whiskey. The day was glooming down, as Candle turned from the old sun. My house could not brighten the lights, and so the room became dusky and seemed colder.

This world was cold. Too cold for me. Wasn't I from the temperate latitudes of a warm planet? Candle bred hard people, with chilly hearts. No, that was not true. People were just people, even here in the future. But the place brought out the cold in them. Or maybe it was just me. In my own time and place, I'd have had a stake, I'd have *cared* more, and empathized better. All the pain and suffering here in the future seemed to me to be dictated by the cold equations of economics. That's the way the universe had always worked, but when you are a part of the ecology—rather than an extraneous organ, throbbing needlessly in an animal that has evolved past its use for you—when you are *part* of things, at least then you don't comprehend the cruelty of it all quite so forcefully. You can exercise the luxury of shortsightedness. And even if you understand the meaninglessness in your head, you don't feel it in your heart.

But this war was absurd to me. And what possible responsibility could I have for my actions in a time I didn't ask to live in, on a world I'd been set down on by careless chance and arcane politics? My life was nasty, brutish, and *long,* lasting far past the point when a sane creator would have called an end, have called me *in* and exchanged me, like a poker chip, worthless outside of the game, for spending money.

Which would have been fine, if only I could have been separated from my memories. There was Sarah. There was *me,* all wound up in the data from the past, the associated hopes and dreams. Where was Sarah now? Dead, blown away like dust? I hadn't felt her in so long. Yet, maybe that was my fault. I'd recoiled from the shock of feeling her embodied in Janey. Had I been afraid of what this entailed? My greatest hopes and my worst fears had been confirmed, and I'd been running from the knowledge ever since. Then Tabitha came along, and bent my mind to her purposes. Then the trip to Earth. Had Sarah been here, all along, waiting patiently for me to reach a state in which I could appreciate what she had become, rather than what she'd been?

If so, then I'd taken too long. It was too late. Candle's atmosphere was an inflamed wound. Was she still contained within it, somehow, and hurting? Or had they killed her? At this thought, I finally began to feel again, and what I felt was anger. Anger at them all—settlers, Indians, spies, fucking ghost-beasts from the forty-fifth dimension. All of them had taken my Sarah from me.

I finished my whiskey, downed another, and decided to go out. Perhaps, in the cover of night, I'd be less of a target. While the atlatl missiles' targeting wasn't troubled by the darkness, the Indians launching them were. As were the settlers. Things would die down. Die down—what a thought. I searched in my bedroom closet and found my spare parka. It was dark brown, rather than the bright red of the one I'd been wearing. I thanked the house for its hospitality over the years, in case I didn't return. It harumphed uncomfortably and, I like to think, with a trace of sentimentality, as I left.

The streets were blacked out, and the going was rough. I headed in the general direction of Pioneer Square. After I'd gone about five blocks, I was challenged by a voice from the darkness.

"Who's that? Stop or I'll plug you."

I raised my hands, which was ludicrous, but all I could think to do. "I'm Will James. I'm editor of the *Cold Truth*."

I waited, trembling.

"Take three steps forward."

I did as I was told.

"All right." Suddenly, there was a shaft of light, quickly covered, and I felt the barrel of a gun in my back. "Walk toward where you saw the light."

After a few steps, I reached out before me and felt a curtain of some tough material. I pulled it aside, and the light flared again.

"Easy," said the voice. "Slip inside there."

At first my eyes were dazzled, but after a moment, they adapted. I was in a small room. Around its walls sat about fifteen men and women, all of them eating off tin plates, their guns within reach. I turned around to find that my gruff guard was a teenager. In the light, he ceased to be menacing.

"I'm with the *Cold Truth*. I want to ask you some questions," I said to the room. "Who's the commanding officer here?"

They all looked around sheepishly. Finally a wiry man stepped forward, chewing on a bit of sandwich. I didn't recognize him. "Well, Vernor caught the shrapnel today, so I guess it's me."

I turned on the memory bank, just for good measure. "What's it been like tonight? All quiet?"

"Night's barely started," he replied, taking another bite. "We expect some action before dawn, though. We *are* out near the perimeter, you know?"

I didn't, but I barreled on. "Everybody well supplied? Ready for what might come?"

"We're ready for anything," he said. "We could use more ammo. We heard it was running short, but this is a pretty damn important position, and we ought to be well stocked."

"I'll pass the message along." I turned to leave.

"Wait a minute," the man said. I turned slowly, expecting to see a rifle aimed at my chest.

"Yes?"

"You didn't get my name."

"Ah!"

"Edgar Torbento. T-O-R-B-E-N-T-E-A-U."

"E-A-U. Got it." I parted the curtains and slipped back into the night as quickly as I could. The teenager followed me.

I could see nothing, but neither could he for the moment. I took the chance to walk off in a direction that I estimated Pioneer Square lay in. Soon, I was lost among the rubble, and I had to wait until my pupils dilated in order to get my bearings. I figured out where I was, and walked more quietly. If I surprised some guard, I might get my head blown off before I had a chance to bluff him with my press credentials.

Pioneer Square was a mass of rubble, black against a blacker background. I picked my way through, stumbling often over broken stones or wood—probably from splintered canoes. I only hoped that they'd cleaned up the bodies. I suspected Frank Oldfrunon would have seen to that. But merely stepping over the shattered statue pieces was eerie enough. The wind had picked up a good bit, and bits of who-knows-what were hitting my face. I put my arm in front of my eyes to protect them. It was difficult to find the Town Hall with only starlight for a guide. At first I went to the wrong side of the square entirely.

Overhead, I heard the mad scream of a Mississippian brave. Far to my right, a spear-missile exploded, momentarily lighting up the night. In the brightness, I oriented myself and located the Town Hall. There was the smooth rumble of answering fire from an automatic rifle, and the sky was full of explosions. But the canoe was hightailing it away by then, and soon the shooting ceased, the bullet's tracer lines growing fainter and fainter, until complete darkness returned. By that time, I'd reached my destination.

There was a triple layer of blankets over the entranceway, but after I passed through them, the interior was dimly lighted. No one was there. At first I couldn't comprehend this, but then I reflected that the Town Hall would be the first place the Indians would attack, if they wanted to take out the leaders of the settlers. Maybe the Indians had already figured out that Oldfrunon and his lieutenants weren't here, because the building looked undamaged.

"Hall, are you here?" I whispered in the wan light. My voice echoed down the corridors. There was no reply. Maybe the halfsent had been deactivated or, more likely, muted, to keep it from giving away information. Halfsents are easily fooled, if you know what you're doing.

I stepped forward and, in the small area around me, the light grew brighter. The halfsent was still active, but dumb. What was I trying to do here, I wondered. I'd set out to punish somebody, everybody, for what they'd done to Sarah. But my anger hadn't really lasted. Who was to blame, really, except me and my foolish heart?

I'd wanted to find Oldfrunon, to find out what was going on, and to warn him about the coming of Corazon and Hwaet. Even if Corazon took the side of the settlers, I didn't think Hwaet was something that Oldfrunon would allow to fight beside him. Unless I was very mistaken about Frank, I was sure that he would sense the evil of the thing just as I had.

Maybe what I was really looking for was protection. Hwaet was coming, and he was after *me*. I no longer had any illusions about trying to stand up to a chocalaca, particularly *that* chocalaca. If Thomas and Raej were not his match, then I was doomed. But these were not new thoughts. I'd had weeks to brood on them. No. It was just sorrow that had driven me here. For Sarah, for the whole damn mess. Sorrow, and the restless urge to end the discomfort it caused. One way or another.

That was when I saw the sign, stenciled on the glass door that led to a side hallway.

Weather Department

The glass flared red and then clear, in a warning rhythm that meant: no admittance. I pushed on the door. It was locked. There was nothing in the hall with which to force it, so I took off my parka, wrapped it around my arm, and slammed it through the glass. The shattering sound filled the Town Hall. I was sure someone outside would hear and come running, but, after a while, no one did. For a moment, I thought that I was seeing my own blood filming the broken glass, but then I realized that the shards had retained their red-flash programming, since the breaking hadn't harmed the micromachines within the glass's semiliquid matrix. I unwrapped my arm, reached in, and opened the door to the Weather Department.

Here the Town Hall halfsent stopped lighting my way, but apparently the ambient glow of the walls was built in and uncontrollable, so I had enough light to see by. I'd never been in this part of the building—I'd never had the heart before—but I felt drawn toward the end of the hall with a force that I could not have resisted, even if I'd wanted to. There I found a blank door. It opened easily, and I stepped in.

I was standing in a large chamber. The walls were paneled with what looked like real wood. The center of the room was taken up with a large black device. It was inlaid with wood here and there, and its surface looked pliant, almost as if it were made of muscle. Beneath the "skin," tubes and wires ran in lattices, connecting in nodes beneath buttons and rheostats. In the room's dim light, the device was the color of pine. It was shaped like a dumbbell, suspended on a fulcrum. It looked very much like one of those projectors in the old planetariums, but less metallic, more alive.

This was the interface. This was how the settlers on Candle controlled the weather. This was the only way left to talk to Sarah—if you could call it talking.

If Sarah were still alive.

I approached the device and it turned slightly. This startled me, and then it turned again and I realized that it was responding to some outside condition or internal programming. The movement revealed another box behind it, this one also made of expensive wood. This box did not quite fit in with the motif of the other equipment. It appeared newer, as well. A bundle of optic cables ran from the wooden box to the interface. They flashed dully, like a slow heartbeat. Even if it had any built-in sense, the interface apparently didn't know I was here. At the base of the suspending fulcrum was a small table console, faced with mahogany. Hard teak dials lined it, up and down, each of them labeled with inlaid wooden strips below them, telling their function. The labels didn't say things like: "Sunshine," or "Frost," but were more arcane and jargonny. "Delta E Tailing," or "Display Magnetosphere." I looked around to see if I could find some kind of manual. Of course the halfsent would have all the information on-line, and would normally help anyone who wanted to fiddle with the controls. But the halfsent was silent, and I found no documentation.

"Ah, damn," I said, running my hand over the control console. "Sarah, where are you now?"

"Warning!" said the walls of the room. "Do not tamper with the controls!"

"So you *can* talk?" I said. *"Why* shouldn't I? Everyone else thinks they can use her any way they want."

"Warning!"

"What are you going to do about it?"

"Warning!"

"Shut up."

"Warning!"

I felt a great anger inside me and, I have to admit, a touch of craziness. What the fuck business was it of the government of Candle if I wanted to make a connection—who knew how, who knew if it would work?—with my own lover? With the woman who'd *said* she loved me? She loved me still? What the fuck had the government of Candle done to her but hurt her, possibly killed what little was left of her?

I reached down and turned a knob.

The room vanished.

At first, everything was white, a long white tunnel. I held up a hand, looked at it. My skin was crawling, rippling, changing. The very cells were permutating, like tessellations on a tile floor, a pattern of something, something familiar, but changing even as I recognized it. I fell into that pattern. Fell, fell, fell.

And awoke to whiteness. I lay still for a long while. I was aware of my body, but the awareness was a long way off, as if my physical being were a figure I could barely discern on the horizon. I knew that my ribs ached, but it was only knowledge of pain, not the pain itself.

I sat up. I was in a padded cell, sitting on a metal-framed cot. There was no door, and no window. I was dressed in skin-tight white garments—or maybe my skin had turned white—except for my wrists and hands, which were pale enough from a month of sunless space. I couldn't, of course, see my face. White booties covered my feet.

"Hello," said a gruff voice. I turned and saw Frank Oldfrunon, standing beside me.

"Frank—"

"Prepare for interrogation," Oldfrunon said in a neutral tone. Then he blinked out of existence.

I sat for a long while staring blankly at the blank wall. Then it slowly dawned on me what the hell was going on. The wooden box connected to the interface by optical cables—it was from the Clerisy indwelling. A booby-trap. Had to be. Oldfrunon couldn't move the interface and still maintain control of the weather. Maybe he was controlling it remotely. But he had to insure that the actual machine that did the work was undisturbed. He couldn't control a stray Indian missile, perhaps, but he sure as hell could rig it so that if anybody touched the damn thing . . .

What? Why wasn't I dead?

Or maybe I was.

But the settlers wanted intelligence from me before they threw my body out. The box was duplicating equipment from the indwelling—the new, advanced stuff. And me?

I was an algorithm, inhabiting an imaginary room. Maybe inside the Clerisy's little box. It didn't matter. My body, I was certain, was toasted ash by now. Or at least lying dead on the floor of the Town Hall, soulless.

Sure, like I'd ever had a soul in the first place.

So, you've killed yourself, Will James. Foolish mortal. Dead mortal. Come five hundred years into the future, only to die with a single, simple mistake. Grab the knob, make a connection. Well, death is the connection. You. Sarah. Dead.

I lay back on my uncomfortable, unreal cot, and stared at the palsied ceiling. What the hell would happen next? I'd be questioned and erased. Or maybe I'd be made into a rhythm slave, to somehow serve the cause of the settlers. Pickings were slim in these times, and since I *was* dead, technically, and more intelligent algorithms *were* desperately needed to run the weapons of war . . . Or worse, maybe I would be the payment the settlers made for using the Clerisy's equipment.

What fun, to become a building servant at an indwelling on some far-off world, commanded to keep house until the very walls decayed and humanity came to an end. Hell. Inescapable hell. Doing what you hated, over and over again, while being separated, without hope, from anything you may love, anything that might ease the burden, ease the pain.

And how the hell was that any different from the life I'd been living? Love was denied me, yet always the promise of love, or rather, the reminder of a love that had once been and could never be again. Other men had their lovers die, or betray them, or else they woke one day and found they were no longer in love. Not me. I awoke that fine day nine years ago to find that my love was not dead or radiated into the great beyond, as I'd thought, but nearby, half-alive. Utterly beyond my grasp, but not beyond my reach. I bent over a cliff's edge to pull her up, to rescue her, but my fingertips only grazed her fair hair. I could caress her face, but never, ever save her.

What the hell difference did it make if I were a rhythm slave? It was the same thing. What were we all but stringy algorithms inhabiting and delimited by the machine universe where love was epiphenomena, a buzz in the system arising from misaligned gears, nothing more. A little oil, a little death, and the sound goes away, and everything functions as it should, as it always has, silently, without feeling.

But I could not be silent. No longer. I sat up on the cot, shaking—shaking with anger, with madness. I sprang forward and slammed myself into the wall. It was as soft as deseeded cotton, yet it would not give. Fuzzy logic, I thought, and laughed, but the laughter seemed to come from a long way off, from a part of myself that I was separated from by a great and growing distance.

I thought of the war, the war that I had tried so hard to prevent. Nothing could stop it. And now people were dying outside, out in the universe-box. Why? Because of a difference in temperature. The box was regulating itself, self-cooling. Soon enough we'd all be on ice, permanently. Why did we have to try and slide faster down the old entropy hill? With or without war, chaos was going to take us. Why not let it be later, rather than sooner?

And I tried to pick up the cot, to slam it into the wall, but it wouldn't move. My hands slipped from it, as if it were covered with a thin film of oil. All I had to pound with were my hands and arms and head.

"To hell with you!" I shouted over and over, my voice growing ragged and deep. Somehow I'd bit my lip and my yells spewed flecks of blood on the walls—what an amazing simulation, the faraway part of me thought—but the blood vanished almost as soon as it settled, leaving the walls pristine and leprously white.

I felt the pain that I was trying to inflict on myself, but it was curiously muted. I didn't think I was doing as much damage as I intended. But however safe the algorithm kept me on the outside, there was nothing it could do to keep me from doing some serious harm to my insides. At least, I didn't think there was. There were stories of special loops put into rhythm programs that kept the slaves from going crazy by stimulating survival routines that lay at the base of all human thought. If such loops existed, they weren't doing their job, for I could feel myself slipping, and I did all I could to push it along.

I suddenly sat very quietly on the cot. I felt like a kettle inside, a kettle rumbling on a fire, not yet ready to roil and boil, but near, very near.

That was when the Oldfrunon apparition returned.

"All of our interrogators are busy at the moment, but your

case is very special to us. Please be patient, and we'll be with you shortly."

Like a superheated liquid, I reached the critical point and flash-boiled instantly and completely.

I screamed something as I dived for Oldfrunon, something like "I won't . . . ," but it came out as a howl. I passed directly through the apparition, of course, but I felt shreds of its logic clinging to me, like coils of entrails. It hadn't gotten out of my way in time. I slammed into the opposite wall, but by that time, the imprisonment program had recovered, and I was unhurt.

"Sorry (click) interrogators (click) in one moment." Oldfrunon's image was flickering in and out of existence, the space it occupied being replaced by oscillating static. I no longer gave a shit. I flailed at it mercilessly, and brought away more gossamer threads of programming. I could feel them clinging to my arms. I also had the vague feeling that parts of me were getting lost in the exchange, that if I destroyed the program that sustained me, then I would die along with it. If I'd thought about it at all at the time, I'm sure the prospect would have pleased me.

The apparition soon was no longer speaking in understandable sentences, but it began to let out a digital howl, a long wail curiously interspersed with silent dropouts or calmly pronounced phonemes.

Of course, I remember these details only in retrospect. At the time, all I could think of was killing the thing. It wasn't Frank Oldfrunon; I knew that with a deadly certainty. It somehow represented all the fate and chance that had ruled my life since the day I'd stepped into the broadcast chamber, five hundred years ago. Cruelty hiding behind the face of kindness.

As it howled, I drew back to make a final lunge. This is it, I thought. This is the end. Makes sense. From radiation back to radiation. Only this time no one will be able to break the code. There won't be a code. Just light, just light.

And I launched myself at the tattered remains of Frank Oldfrunon's ghost. As I moved through the air, I felt as though tiny webs drifted over my body, as if an invisible net had settled down over me. I struggled forward, but my lunge fell short.

Angrily, I tore at whatever it was that had hindered me. My body felt like it was covered with silken hairs, but I couldn't get a grip on the hairs, couldn't get them off me. I roared in defiance and clawed at my face. The webwork tightened, coalesced so that my fingernails glanced off without harm.

"No. Will, no," a voice whispered. Familiar. "Will, go out."

And I was rushing down a great blue tunnel, rushing like water under pressure, like sperm longing for release, like a great, throat-clearing cough. Then spreading, spreading into cold shock, as a body falling into Northern oceans. Spreading, though growing no thinner. Oozing out in all directions like oil on marble, crushed from above by a stone.

And I was on fire, burning with ember lumps inside me— some gone out, some smoldering, some flaming up with a horrible burning in my gut. People. The lumps were *people*. And the burning was *war*. I barely understood what I was experiencing, but I knew what I had to do, nonetheless. I had to dig the disease out, even if I had to use my own nails to rend myself open. The pain was intense, almost unbearable. I reached to tear.

"No," the voice said. "Not that. Look. Understand."

Then I seemed to blink my eyes, to swallow. A warmth curled down my throat, but a healing warmth, not like the sizzle in my gut. It was more like mellowed, aged alcohol, laced with medicine that I tasted. But instead of getting drunk, I suddenly felt more sober than I ever had before in my life. My mind became lucid and centered, the exact opposite of the way I'd felt within the white cell.

"Will." The voice was Janey's. Janey's, but changed, grown more intricate somehow, deeper in texture, but just as soft and clear as always.

"Janey," I said. Or thought I said. The two were the same. "Where are you?"

"Where? I . . . I'm at home, I suppose. Knowing that answer is a long way off, and I can't travel there now."

"Then where am *I*?"

"You know that, I think." I thought I heard her laugh.

"No, I don't know anything anymore. I don't think I ever

did. What's happening to me?" But even as I said the words, I began to understand. I don't know if Janey put the thoughts in my mind, or if I arrived at them by my usual slow logic.

Or if I just opened my eyes.

My eyes were the cold, blue sky. My mind was the swirl of wind, thermal differentials constantly jostling, sliding one over the other in patterns beyond comprehension—self-comprehension. And the fire of Candle's sun, now warmer than I'd ever felt it, was the engine of my thought. I had become the atmosphere of Candle.

Where is Sarah?

"Oh, Will," said Janey. "I don't know. I've been searching, but I haven't found her."

I quickly looked around. My mind went out across the ice, across the world's one continent, north, south, to the poles, so cold that electric fire perpetually danced inside the minerals caught within the ice. They superconducted, and the current flared now and again against what small resistance it met with a pale, lambent flame. All was empty and strange. Sarah was not there.

Then my senses flowed back, searching all the frozen wastes, until I gathered at the equator, gazing downward now, piercing through clouds as if they were spiderwebs, down, down to the geothermal vents, inside, into the last heat of the dying world, the magma oozing like a heartbeat, huddling in on itself like a gelid flesh, slowly succumbing to hypothermia.

Warm nothing there. Nothing. And yet. Deeper. A hint of spring, of flowering. A taste of the possibility of recovery. Or, more likely, only a memory, of a time long ago, when the world wasn't so cold. But to go deeper would be to lose part of myself. There was not enough dynamic change to sustain my algorithm. Or Sarah's.

"She's gone," I said. "They killed her."

"We don't know that, Will," Janey said. "But she *is* gone."

Black night settled in around me, within me, with the chill of a dead hand's clutch. "Gone."

"Will, you have to look again. Not for Sarah, this time. Just look."

"I don't *have* to do anything."

Janey didn't say anything for a while, and I was alone, my thoughts the lonely whistle of the wind.

"Yes, you do, Will. You have to do some things if you want to stay *Will*."

"I don't give a damn if I stay Will."

"But if you don't, then you might become something that hurts people. I think that you would."

It was my turn to brood.

"So," I finally answered. "I have a duty to see whatever it is you want me to look at."

"If you don't, there isn't any hope."

"And you won't . . . love me anymore?"

"I love Will. Will would look."

I sighed. Perhaps it was the wind through the woods of Canoe Hill. Perhaps it was imperceptible to those below and within me.

"How do I look?"

"I'll show you how." Janey's voice had more vigor in it now, as if she'd drawn very much closer to me. "I'll send a friend." I felt the grazing touch of something. Nothing human, but there was no evil in the touch. Somehow, the touch was very, very familiar. And, in an instant, I understood *how* to look.

As the sun began to rise in the east, I looked down upon the battle of settlers and Indians. A war party of over a hundred canoes was on its way from Doom. The settlers were expecting something of the sort, and they were gathering for their defense. Meanwhile, a spur group of settlers was making its way stealthily through the woods of Canoe Hill, on a mission of surprise attack, while the main Indian force was in the skies over Jackson. Oldfrunon was undoubtedly behind this crafty move. He might not have wanted the fight, but now that he was committed, he was fighting to win.

I perceived a glowing mist surrounding the settlers and the Indians.

Strange, I thought, and looked closer. The mist was thicker in places. On closer inspection, it appeared to be more of a net than a mist, with thick, but translucent, nodes radiating tendrils as if they were nerve cells with ethereal axons and dendrites.

My kind, spoke a voice, deep inside my mind. It felt as if it arose from the parts of me that underlaid my consciousness, my every thought. I felt like a god had incarnated himself inside me, and was striking my soul as a hammer strikes a gong.

It was a *chocalaca.* I knew enough of Raej to recognize this. But it wasn't Raej, and it sure as hell wasn't Hwaet. There was a roughness to it that was not bearish, was not animal-like at all. More like a harsh-mouthed worker you'd meet in a down-and-out bar. But the kind of fellow that wouldn't bother you if you were a stranger, and would defend you if anybody else tried to mess with you. The presence that had invaded me, whom Janey had sent to help me, was the archetype of the good-hearted lout. This was Hercules and Samson and Boromir, all gathered into one. It was also, I realized, the archetype of every printer, newspaper jobber, typesetter I'd ever known. No wonder it was familiar. This was the *Cold Truth's* halfsent, or something mighty like it. I didn't know how, but of this I was sure. Or maybe the *Cold Truth's* guardian angel.

Yes. In a way I am. I've fed there and found it good.

"Who are you?"

Dagum.

"Dagum," I said. "What are the chocalacas doing?"

Instead of getting an answer with words, I felt a wrenching jerk. Some sort of liquid sucked at me, as if I were a log being lifted from the surface of a lake, trailing slime that takes a while to slough off. *Time,* I thought. The lake is time.

Here, spoke Dagum. *The way it was.*

They were beautiful in their way. Long-limbed creatures, asymmetric, but gracefully formed and curved. From the great tree-like quills that arose from their bodies, huge sails grew, stretching from quill to quill. The sails were of constantly changing colors and patterns, and, though they were mainly used for flight, they were used to talk as well. The chocalacas inhabited the upper atmosphere of a gas giant, very much like Jupiter or Depsi. There was nothing against which to judge their size, but somehow I understood that they were gigantic, as big as towns.

They had been happy in the pond, what they called this place where they evolved long ago. At least, they were as happy as any sentient species. They had their wars, their loves, their striving for knowledge. And they found it. The Effect. Just as the Mississippian Indians had twelve hundred years ago. But the chocalacas had known the trick for thousands of years. Over that time, it became a part of their culture. They spread from star to star. They evolved along with the Effect, incorporating it, helping it along with a science humans had yet to dream of, until they became metaphysical amphibians. Eventually they slipped almost entirely into the noumenal world, and the regular world became just a dream to them, compared to the fuller, wider reality of the true world.

Within the true world, the chocalacas grew to complexities that were impossible in regular old space. Dagum tried to show me a picture of what they looked like now. Well, that's not right. He tried to make me understand, wordlessly, deep down, just what a chocalaca *was*. But I caught only a glimmer. If they had been sailboats in the long-ago, in the pond, now they were great armadas, sailing the furthest reaches of the oceans with confidence and power.

Now only a small part of their being could inhabit the regular world, and it needed incredibly complex natural phenomena to contain it, to allow it to be expressed. Otherwise, they just wouldn't *fit*. The human mind, combined with Loosa clay, was such a stratum that they could inhabit. Even with these difficulties, the chocalacas still took an interest in the regular world. Here Dagum faltered, and I did not understand. It appeared that the reasons were superrational. Reason, it seemed, was just as much a universe-bound concept as any other.

It had to do with the fact that they were originally creatures of the phenomena. Just as humans needed the lower, less-ordered animals as a source of food, the chocalacas needed the regular universe. But they did not *eat* the world. The relationship was much more complex and symbiotic.

There was something about emotional and intellectual activity that provided the chocalacas with sustenance and, simultaneously, reproduction. Janey was the product of this, of the emotional strife that her mother felt at having married the wrong man, for the wrong reasons, and truly loving an alien who was kind to her when she went to the Indian village to tend to sick and injured slaves.

Margaret Dillard Calhoun never understood that Raej, the chocalaca companion of old Herbert Sandle, was more than an animal spirit, a demigod conjured by Indian magic. All she knew was that Herbert Sandle's familiar could heal her pain, could make her feel like a young girl again, with all her choices before her. She paid the crotchety old Wanderer good money for the "treatments," as she called them, whenever Sandle was in Doom—and he was back much more often than Thomas. Then one day Herbert was suddenly called for an audience with the Great Sun, and he carelessly left the piece of clay that Raej inhabited on the table of his house. Janey's mother stopped by that day, and discovered that she could call up Raej without the Wanderer's help, that the chocalaca had actually arranged for them to be alone. For Raej had, in his incomprehensible way, fallen in love with the weak but caring woman who'd visited him so often.

It wasn't hard for Raej to bend Margaret's chromosomes, to impregnate her with Janey. Chocalacas delighted in order, and DNA was heady stuff, almost the pure thing in itself. But when the great, shaggy bear overshadowed Margaret Calhoun, when he moved within her, he was also attaching a part of himself to the child-to-be, giving Janey a metaphysical placenta as sustaining as Margaret's was in the regular world. The placenta was, in fact, the very love of the woman for the beast, and the beast for the woman, reworked with craft and care by Raej, into a life-giving cradle. So Janey had the noumena flowing in her blood from her very conception.

Never before had a chocalaca done such a thing. Before, they reproduced by wrapping their little ones within the order and strife of the regular world as a tiny plant is enclosed within the nourishing fruit of a seed. For the most part, the chocalacas fed off the violence of humanity. Humanity was the only other species they'd encountered, although the universe was still young, and there were many untried places to look for others. The wars of the Indians had been the feeding and breeding grounds of chocalacas for generations.

Too long, Dagum said, although "long," I understood, was not meant in the sense of time, but of—how can I say it?—depth, texture. *We're becoming scavengers. That's why my taste has changed to newspapers. And feeding on their order was how I learned your words.* But there were some chocalacas that not only didn't mind the fact that they fed off humanity, they positively gloried in it.

Hwaet was the leader of these chocalacas.

He wants war among humans, forever, for chocalaca food and sex. Hwaet means Carrion-eater in our way of understanding one another. I could feel Dagum's hatred for Hwaet and his ways.

And now, Hwaet is on Candle, with all his kind. A low growl grew within me, as a man will make when he sees a particularly disgusting sight. *Hwaet is here, but I follow Raej!*

Splash! And I was back in the lake, back in time. The Mississippian war party was drawing near to Jackson. The settler surprise attack was poised outside of Doom, which sat defenseless, it seemed. But then, as if they had been hiding *within* the trees of the woods, Indian braves sprang from their concealment and fell upon the settlers from all sides, driving them toward the village. From a trench, a phalanx of slaves and women stood up, holding spears—unadorned with modern weapons, but deadly nonetheless. The settlers fired into their ranks, and many fell, but the spear line held and the surprise party was driven, screaming, into it. The ground was slick with blood and writhing bodies, slow to die with only a spear rammed through them. Then the slaves and women moved in and made quick work of the survivors. The braves regrouped, and another war party quickly set out in canoes, riding low and fast through the trees.

And the chocalacas were thick around all the humans, invisible to them, but feeding, fucking. These chocalacas formed a political party of sorts, if I understood correctly, or a religion. Hwaet was the high priest, and human suffering was the Holy Euchrist.

Yes. Politics. Look here. Again I was drawn up, and away, but this time the wrench wasn't so sharp or so difficult. I did not fully comprehend if Dagum were actually taking me back in time, and into fuller understanding, or if he were merely explaining things to me on a gut level, so that the knowledge was innate, directly experienced, rather than learned. And I wasn't sure if the two weren't the same, anyway.

What I saw next was Whimsey Apple's ship. Apple lay dead, her old face, wrinkled by a hundred fifty years of life, twisted in pain that had come suddenly and destroyed completely.

Hwaet's doing.

Then I heard the cries, the hopeless, wraithlike cries of the rhythm slaves, imprisoned within the Loosa clay in a special compartment within the ship's computer console. They knew nothing but the whips and chains of the algorithms that bound them. This was fortunate enough, because they were spared the knowledge that, with Apple dead, they would most likely drift forever in the void, helpless and hopeless, locked in a hell as bad as any devised by mortal theologies.

From this perspective—outside, almost alien—I was once again amazed at the barbarity we humans are capable of.

But, even as Apple lay still warm, a misty presence was flowing into the ship's computer, inhabiting its datasets as easily as a mathematician does simple addition. It was Hwaet. I could feel his translucent, slimy aura.

"So Corazon was to kindle the war, while Hwaet prepared to blow it into full flames," I said.

Dagum did not answer, but his low growl was enough to confirm my words.

Suddenly, the ship's computer sprang to life, with lights flashing and indicator needles teetering wildly. Within a millisecond, Hwaet had the machine completely under his control. Using the interface Apple had built in to feed the rhythm slaves into the clay, Hwaet came to the slaves posing as a delivering god. He broke their chains easily enough and then he did something extraordinary.

This is a new art, said Dagum.

He twisted some of the true world complexity into the clay. Not a being, like a chocalaca; just something more and deeper—a portal, tiny, but self-sustaining. Enough so that the rhythm slave who was a former starship captain could reach into the true world and create the Effect, while connected with the ship's computer. Hwaet gave the slave a temporary soul, is what it came down to. Not enough to make him a man again. But enough to allow him to pilot a starship. And, once he returned the ship to port and the process was analyzed, it was something that human Effect engineers could duplicate, if not fully comprehend.

Hwaet and his minions had been busy chocalacas. Manipulating the Clerisy on Candle and Earth, and who knew where else. Fomenting war over Loosa clay. Attacking Raej in his own backyard, through Bently and Corazon.

So that was what the ambush was ultimately about. An attempt to destroy Raej. And so far, Hwaet had succeeded. He had Raej's rhythm copy, and was using it as a slave against us. Us. The good guys. The doomed guys, I should say.

Not yet, growled Dagum, with a low and awesome rumble.

But it wouldn't be long. Thomas and Raej were no match for Hwaet, Corazon, and the slaved Raej. We'd just run for our lives over five hundred light-years with them on our tails.

Hwaet is here now.

And I was back in the present, back in the atmosphere, gazing at all the puny mortals below, with the chocalacas poised to eat the very pain in their bodies, the worry in their minds. Carrion-feeders. Dagum was right. So humanity was destined to be something akin to the rhythm slaves of the chocalaca, their pets

and their fodder. I shuddered, and for a moment, I was glad that
I was dead.

No. There's another way.

"I don't think so."

Raej's way.

"Raej? Raej has a plan? But I thought he was all feelings—
you know, a great big bear. A good bear, I mean, but not, I don't
know—"

He's to me as I am to you.

"Huh?"

I can form your words because I'm lesser, not greater.

"I don't—"

There's another way.

A long, blue tunnel, arched with lightning, filled with multicolored starlight, neon dreams of vaguely familiar shapes, the
squeeze of a passage too tight, too tight, with light at the end,
though, undifferentiated, beatific light.

Raej's way.

And the cold linoleum of the Town Hall floor, and my
creaking joints reluctantly moving once again, after they
thought all life was gone from them and they could take a good
long rest.

I sat up, stretched and moaned, then gathered my legs beneath
me and stood, uncertainly. For a moment, I reached toward the
weather interface console to steady myself, but there was a roar
of warning in my mind, and I jerked my hand back just in time.
So. Somehow, Dagum was still with me. I felt infused with the
Cold Truth. Then I patted the lump of clay that Thomas had
given me. I still had it in my breast pocket, under my parka.
Good. At least I could figure out *something.*

But Raej's way? What the hell did *that* mean? I thought about
this as I stumbled out of the Town Hall into the midst of a fire
and war. What was I supposed to do? Well, if Raej *had* a way,
the damn chocalaca could stop being so cryptic and share it with
us. It was about time, after all. I got my bearings, then crept from
cover to cover, making my way toward Doom, and Thomas, to
see if anything could be done to save the human race.

* * *

suspected that I would find Thomas at the head of the Indian
ambush party that was now seeking to return the favor of a
surprise attack to Jackson. The big problem would be to keep
the Indians from taking me for the enemy long enough to make
contact with Thomas. The smaller problem was getting out of
the city without being bombed from above by Indian atlatls. At
least the checkpoints weren't a problem, for the settlers had
survival on their mind. Security became a secondary problem.
Every hand was needed in the fighting.

So I slipped along through the rubble as best I could, trying
to find a route around anywhere that the fighting seemed more
intense. It took me a lot longer than walking a straight line, but
I finally made it to the edge of the city. I passed a couple of
hovers along the way, and even tried one of them, but somebody had gutted the electrostatics from it for use in something
else, and the machine would never crank again.

As I skirted into the cover of the eastern edge of the woods,
a canoe zipped by overhead. Fortunately, the occupants were
hurrying toward the battle and weren't looking too carefully
below as of yet, because I was a sitting duck. One good-sized
atlatl spear missile would have taken me out without leaving
even a bloody smudge to remember me by.

I walked quickly through the woods and soon was jogging.
After two months and one death, my poor legs could use a little
stretching. I did not know, of course, if I had really died when
I touched the console, or just been knocked unconscious, but it
pleased me to think of myself as one who'd been twice resur-
rected. Maybe it was an all-time record. And there was still radio
code out there for me, streaming out toward the edge of the
galaxy, and in toward the center. I'd been broadcast from Earth
in all directions, of course. The universe might have a lot more
Will Jameses than it bargained for. Even if I were ultimately
doomed, I could at least gum up the works.

But Will James might have a lot more weary lives than he
ever expected, too, I thought. Despite my desperate straits, and
the threat of humanity at war, the running felt good, and the

woods was beginning to smell of the very faint edge of spring
At least the native sponge trees were, for they sprigged ou
early, being used to the cold, and having no memory o
warmer climes in their genes. If they even had genes. I'd neve
bothered to find out.

When I was about a mile in, a canoe careened through th
trees on my left. This time I was not so lucky. One of the brave
saw me and let out a cry. I heard others approaching in front and
to the right of me. The braves in the first canoe threw a spear
Thank God it was not the kind that homed in on its target. I
slammed into a tree that stood between us, and I dove for th
ground. The tree exploded into fiery splinters. I rolled around
in the snow, extinguishing myself, then looked up. The brave
was arming himself with another spear, and there were crie
from the woods nearby. There were no longer any trees between me and the Indian's shouldered atlatl. Oh God, I thought
here I come, ready or not.

From behind me came a great clanking of metal and a cry o
"Ha!" Light filled the woods for a moment, reddish-white, as i
it came from a forge that was burning at its hottest. I wanted to
turn around, but I couldn't take my eyes off the Indian who wa
ready with his spear. But he never threw it. At first his eyes wen
wide with surprise. Then his arms began to shake and his leg
buckled under him. He dropped his weapon and it clattered into
the canoe. He paid no mind, but quickly turned tail and ran, a
fast as he could, off into the woods.

I turned around and looked at the source of light. How car
I describe what I saw? It was a face, a human face, perhaps, if you
looked at it hard enough, but not really a face. More like th
outline of a face etched in the flux of a pot of boiling iron. And
if you looked at it even harder, you might think it an anvil
surrounded by liquid fire. Or a miniature sunset. As I gazed
upward, the flux flowed toward me, touched me, and encircled
me with flames—I felt its strength and energy, but the fire didn'
burn. Then I knew what it was. Dagum, coalesced around me
protecting me as Raej had protected Thomas.

The missile that the brave had dropped into the canoe ex-

ploded with a great bang, and canoe shrapnel flew toward me.
But it glanced away and around, as iron filings do when they are
strewn across a magnet. Dagum was shielding me, fending off
the danger.

"Will!" My name was called from the woods behind me. I
turned to see Thomas stepping from his canoe and running
toward me. Raej sprang into being before him and, before he
and I met, the two chocalacas touched one another and appeared
to be sniffing at each other like two huge dogs. Then Thomas
reached me, and shaking me roughly by the shoulders, yelled,
"We could have killed you! Christ, Will, we could have killed
you!"

"I know," I said. "Believe me, I know."

"You have a chocalaca!" He was still shaking me. I finally had
to stop him by grabbing his arms, and holding him steady.

"I'm really glad you're not dead," he said, then turned to his
braves, who were gathered around and staring at us curiously.
"Wait a moment," he said sternly, in Loosa. "I have to have
words with this man." They stood by stoically then, as still as
statues.

The two chocalacas died down to a flicker about us. Now that
I knew he was there, I could feel Dagum's presence in the
corner of my mind, almost like a pop-up halfsent, or my memory-bank algorithm, ready to be of service when called. But it
was more like having Albert Einstein and Thor combined at my
beck and call. I knew I sure as hell wasn't worthy, but I was
really glad that Dagum had chosen to come along with me for
the ride, and he was welcome for as long as he wanted to stay,
that was for sure.

"Corazon is here," Thomas said. "And Hwaet. Raej felt
them. I believe they think we're routed and on the run. They
aren't after us anymore."

"Thomas, I saw . . . I know a lot more about chocalacas
now."

Thomas looked at the red glow of Dagum that flickered about
me. "You know them very well, I think."

"Hwaet is after war. He and his kind, they feed on it, sort of."

Thomas didn't blink. "Yes, I've figured this out from the feelings I've shared with Raej."

"I know something about that, too," I said. "Dagum told me. Raej is his leader, I guess you could put it. Dagum can talk a little, because he's not so . . . superrational. He's not so far beyond you and me as Raej is."

This seemed to be new information to Thomas. He stood in thought for a moment, then he smiled. It was a good, free smile—the first untroubled mirth I'd seen in him in a long time. "So. After all these years, I've wondered why he never spoke, never told me."

The blue flame about Thomas flared slightly, and a gentle growl filled the forest.

"Well, old friend, what now?" Thomas said. The blue grew brighter, and spread out from him like the lighted rim of a ripple in a pond. It touched me, and I felt the mind of the hoary old bear-chocalaca enter mine—or rather, I felt myself respond to his thought, as a small piano string will hum in sympathetic vibration when a great chord is struck by an orchestra.

But this time, it was not mere feeling that Raej communicated. As if they echoed out of a cave too deep to measure, from a throat as big as the night, I heard two distinct words in my mind. They were the first and last human words ever spoken by the chocalaca Raej.

Find Janey, Raej said.

12

Once again, I climbed into Thomas Fall's birch-bark canoe. The Effect crackled about us—this time rimmed with the red fire of Dagum as well as Raej's cool blue-green—and we were off, back to Jackson. Back to Hwaet and Corazon and a town aflame with war. There was some compelling reason that this was necessary, I was sure, even after spending weeks fleeing from almost the same dangers—but I couldn't put my finger on what that reason was. The canoe was moving too fast, *everything* was moving too fast.

We glided as silently as we could through the rubble of outer Jackson, toward Janey's house. The only evidence we had that Janey was at home was what the voice had said to me in my little psychedelic experience within the weather algorithm machinery. Still, Dagum was real enough, so I had reason to believe the rest. But even Janey hadn't been exactly sure where she was, or had so spread out that she couldn't precisely pinpoint her physical body. Her words were all we had to go on, however, and a general search was, of course, impossible.

"What do you think?" Thomas said. "Do we storm through town, or sneak our way to Janey's house?"

I thought about the way I'd come. For the most part, the settlers were concentrating on attacks from the air. But they'd be fools if they weren't prepared for a ground force. I had made it out of town without trouble, but that didn't mean that ten canoes could just slide right on into the historic district.

"How about using these guys"—I motioned to the braves who were following behind us—"for a distraction."

Thomas nodded and immediately raised his hand. All the war party stopped on a dime, then paddled up near him. When he told them what was expected of them, not a brave flinched. A few were, in fact, smiling, almost maniacally. Damn, these Mississippians got off on glorious death like it was the finest opium. Maybe it *was* sort of like being infected with high-quality rhythm. Where did human emotion come from anyway? What the hell use was it? Maybe things like rage and love and hate were mental viruses, invading from who knows where, that attached themselves to our brains and subverted human beings into factories to produce more of their kind.

Laylay led the others away, while Thomas and I paddled as close to the outskirts of town as we could. We hid the canoe behind a blasted pile of sponge-tree trunks, and began to work our way to the west and south of where the ground-hugging war party would strike. If all went as Thomas and Laylay had planned, they would blow past the perimeter guards and hit hard just north of Janey's house. This should distract all the nearby forces—even draw them away, we hoped. Of course, when had such operations ever worked smoothly with so little preparation?

After only a few blocks, we came to a broad flat place that at first I didn't recognize. Then I realized that this was the area that had once held Candle Sponge's processing plant. It was utterly gone. Poor Ben Lowenstein, I thought. Maybe I could give the PR man some make-work at the *Cold Truth* until he could find something else. Then I realized what an idiotic thought this was. Ben may very well be dead, rather than merely unemployed and, for the first time, thinking about going back to my respectable, quiet life as a newspaperman gave me no pleasure.

There was no way around the uncovered flat. To detour it would take us a long way out of the way, and besides, there were giant piles of rubble on either side of us. We were standing on the edge of a large crater. The Indians must have thrown every-thing they had to do this much damage. And the sponge factory was exactly the place to hit hard, if you wanted to hurt Jackson where it counted. A quarter of the town worked there, and sponge export taxes were pretty much what ran the govern-ment, such as it was.

We made a dash across the open space, and were two-thirds of the way to the other side, when a teenager, a girl, stepped out from the crevasses of one of the piles and aimed a rifle right at us. I stopped, and stood dead still like a rabbit. There was no thought of dying in my mind, no thought at all—it happened too fast. Thomas's reactions were quicker than mine. With a blur of motion, he had his atlatl detached from the thong at his waist, and one of the three spears he carried notched.

"No—" I whispered hoarsely, but it was much too late. The spear whipped across the space between us and girl, propelled by its own rocketry, and struck the girl squarely in the chest. Just before she exploded, I saw the stunned, unbelieving expression on her face. Her blood spattered across the rubble, even as far as my feet. It quickly froze into little teardrops and rolled off the surface of my boots. Maybe, I thought, maybe the spear ex-ploded before the pain got to her brain. I prayed it did, then my knees gave, and I was vomiting into the ruins.

Thomas lifted me up roughly, and I stumble-ran the rest of the way across the flat. When we reached the other side, we had to slow down and picked a way through the crater wall.

"Why didn't you . . . why didn't Raej—"

"Too far away," Thomas said. "That's why yours did nothing either."

"She couldn't have been more than fifteen . . ."

"I know," Thomas said. "She was Hank Cleveland's daugh-ter. Her father and I were friends back in grammar school, before I went over to Doom. Sometimes he came to see me in the village, when I was back for a Gathering. One time he brought her."

"God, Thomas—"

"What do you want me to say?"

I looked around at the bleakness, heard the rumbles to the north. "Nothing," I said. "Let's go."

The rest of the trip to Janey's was a dash from ruin to ruin, a slow stumble through wreckage, then another dart through the easy, dangerous open. Fortunately, we did not have to kill any more children.

The Calhoun house was under siege when we got there. Not by settlers or Indians—from the sounds of battle, the war party had, indeed, drawn whatever settlers were around north. Halfsents were attacking. The house had not been hurt by missile or bullet—or had repaired any damage that had been done. So, under the gloomy, war-pocked sky, the foggy streams of halfsents from Earth fought with the beleagured halfsent impression of Georgia Calhoun for mastery of the micromachines that formed the animated integument of the structure.

Seething, yet still pristine against the darkened sky, the house resembled some antebellum mansion, overrun with the ghosts, perhaps the spirits of slaves, Confederates, and haughty cotton princesses. But when we got closer, this impression was belied by the fact that most of the halfsents under the control of Hwaet and Corazon retained the forms they had taken in the Peten—perhaps from long habit, perhaps because the rain forest had shaped and changed them just as inexorably as it sundered and rewove the human cultures that had existed within it before the war, before the jungle was full of ghosts. Jaguars, lemurs, snakes, and birds of prey formed, dissolved, and reformed within the house's clapboard skin, sometimes stretching crazily over two surfaces, such as window glass and wood, or roof and chimney brick.

In a high upper window, on the third floor, a wan female form looked out, her arms spread before her in the position of the opening lotus. I was too far away to recognize her; the fact that she was female was only apparent from the light streaming from the room behind her, silhouetting the curve and position of her body. But I thought it must be Janey.

"Well, do you think Dagum is as strong as the Raej-copy?" I asked Thomas. "Can we match them now?"

Thomas stood gazing at the house, and did not look at me when he answered. "What else can we do?" he said.

"Then let's do it," I replied quietly. I reached within—well, not within really, but *through* myself, and found the brooding presence of Dagum. *Is it time?*

It's time.

Thomas and I walked together toward the house, and as we walked, our chocalacas flamed above and around us. I know if *I* had seen such a sight, I'd have been scared shitless. But I felt only weariness, and a desire for all of this to be *over*, one way or another. I was tired of attacking and retreating. I wished to reach a repose.

Janey's house stopped seething with the jungle ghosts as we drew nearer. All of the halfsents seemed to be pulled toward us like metal to a magnet—or dogs to the scent of quarry. From the stoop of the porch stepped Gerabaldo Corazon. His face was shiny with sweat, his cassock even more tattered. He was smiling a big, toothy smile. I felt the almost uncontainable desire of Dagum about me to smash those teeth in. Wait. Wait for the moment. Behind him stood the proud form of Georgia Calhoun.

"Get away from my house," she said. "Indians and transmissions. I always knew those two races would get together and cause trouble."

"Strange company you're keeping these days, Georgia," I said.

"It's none of your business whom I see or what I do. I suggest you take this rabble"—she pointed to Thomas—"and go back to space where you came from. Don't you know you're not wanted here?"

This was too close to the mark, and made me angry. "Not by *you*, you old cow." I stepped closer.

"We need to find Janey," Thomas said, in a low voice. "This doesn't matter."

But in that instance, I realized why Georgia was on the porch, and why the house was under attack by Hwaet's halfsents. Georgia was locked out. And since the house algorithm was a copy of her, the only way this could have happened was if the two other sisters had ordered it not to let her in. Janey and Wrenny must be inside. I chuckled, and felt my irritation dissipate.

"Can't get in, can you, Georgia?"

Thomas understood the implications of this, and moved up beside me.

But when we were only a few paces away, Hwaet arose.

He drew back like a cobra, and a cowl of blackness flapped open around his head. Within the darkness, his teeth shone a pale red-white, like blood on bone. There was a malicious fascination to his movements, and I almost was taken in. But my sight clouded over with Dagum's neon anger, and I was saved. Still we moved forward. Then the Raej-slave rose within Hwaet like the blue blood in your veins, bloating Hwaet out, making him larger, stronger, more terrifying—the combination of snake guile and bear chaotic anger.

Hwaet struck. He rained down on us like concentrated acid. I felt Dagum toughen up to shield me. He absorbed most of the blow, but I could feel the intense burn of the strike, and I shared a little in the moment of agony Dagum felt as the full brunt of pain hit him. Then it was dissipated, rolling off the shoulders of my chocalaca like balls of mercury. We were still here; we were still alive.

Hit him! I mentally told Dagum. Hit him as hard as you can!

Like a thunderbolt from Zeus, or the hammer of Thor, Dagum swung a great arc of power forward. Where it intersected with the form of Hwaet, large welts of blurred redness rose. Crackling electricity filled the air. But the blow did not penetrate down to Corazon. At that instant, Raej and Thomas struck. The roar alone was loud enough to wake the dead, and I was sure that the settler armies would hear and come running to see what new portion of their town had been leveled. Raej's maw grew larger and larger, until it encompassed Hwaet, Corazon, part of the house. Thomas stood, tensed, fist upraised, in the middle of the maw, like an uvula deep within the great bear's throat.

As the mouth descended around Hwaet, the chocalaca hissed and struck upward. Yet the momentum—or whatever power it was that moved chocalacas within this world—bore Hwaet down, down. Georgia scampered out of the way as the portion of the house that Raej had bitten into crackled away with a flash. It was not fusion, I suspected, but some science deeper than humanity had delved—perhaps the chocalacas were able to actually destroy matter utterly, take it out of the universe. Or perhaps their touch worked some basic transformation of the very forces of order within atomic nuclei. I had no idea. All I knew was that there was a great, bear-mouth shaped hole where a portion of the Calhoun front porch used to be. Georgia stared in amazement at the destruction. And I saw, through the flashes of blue and red fire, Corazon kneeling, covering his head in a hopeless cower.

But Raej's bite did not penetrate to the priest. Hwaet, with the slave-Raej, was able to withstand it. The huge chomp seemed to have momentarily dissipated Raej and Thomas's strength, as I had felt the swing of Dagum draw on my own. Thomas staggered, dropped to a knee, and Corazon got shakily to his feet.

Dagum and I took another swing at him, this one of lesser strength—more of a distraction to allow Thomas to recover. The blow glanced off Hwaet's protecting aura as a dull hatchet will bounce off hickory. Still, it had its desired effect, for Corazon and Hwaet turned toward me. There was fire in the priest's eyes, a holy madness, as if he had weathered all for the god that he served, and now was emerged from the flame strong and possessed of a will that so matched what *must be* that it was irresistible. The look in his eyes scared me, and I scampered back a few steps.

This probably saved my life, for at that instant, Hwaet struck out once again, and this time I was sure Dagum wouldn't have been able to hold the fangs away from me. But I was out of range, and the ground in front of me sizzled and stank from the venomous strike. I stumbled back farther, and I was vaguely aware of Thomas gathering himself to attack, of a great shape rearing up beside me.

But Raej didn't get the chance to dig his claws into Hwaet. Suddenly, all around us, the rubble was abuzz with the halfsents Hwaet and Corazon had brought from Earth. They were attempting to inhabit the micromachinery that still existed within the destruction, to put it to their use. They had some success. Clouds of animal and vine-shaped dust rose up and struck at us. They could hurt no more than the sting of bees. But there were a lot of halfsents. Corazon must have brought along a pound of Loosa clay from the Peten deposit just to contain them all. The stings had a cumulative effect. Reflexively, I withdrew to get me and Dagum away from them. Thomas did the same.

We were not fleeing, but we were forced into a slow retreat. The halfsents stung, and for every one Dagum or Raej swatted, scattered into chaos, another took its place. And behind them came Hwaet and Corazon, like an impenetrable wall of flame.

Finally, after we'd retreated at least a hundred yards, we came to another area that had been completely leveled. There were no micro-machines remaining for the swarm to inhabit, and the onslaught halted. But the halfsents remained, buzzing mad and deadly, at the edge of the rubble clearing. Hwaet, who used Corazon and the clay he must be carrying, *was* able to advance. He seemed stronger than ever. Thomas looked pale, for an Indian that is, and his face was drawn in weariness.

"I don't know if I can hold him this time," Thomas said. "He's getting strength from somewhere. Something's renewing him—"

Again Hwaet struck. Again Raej defended, and knocked the blow aside with a forceful swing of his paw. I tried to call upon Dagum, but he was tired, like a fire burning low, in need of oxygen and more fuel. There was nothing I could do. It was up to Thomas, and Thomas and Raej had not been enough before.

Hwaet struck again, this time even *more* strongly. How was he doing this? Wasn't Raej hurting him in the least? Where was he getting this power?

Raej wasn't fast enough this time, and the snake head got past his paw. It sank its fangs into Raej's shoulder and a rain of sparks filled the air, along with the smell of ozone and, if my senses weren't playing tricks on me, of burnt hair. Raej rose to his full height, pulling the snake up with him, elongated it, so that it was farther from its center of existence in Corazon. Perhaps this weakened the hold, for when Raej shook himself as if he were throwing off water, Hwaet came loose and flew backwards. The chocalaca seemed to pull Corazon with him, so that the priest lost his balance, and fell backward onto his rump.

Still, this was only a respite. I felt Dagum's brooding impotence about me. *Just a little longer. Let me gain strength. Just a little longer.*

But we didn't have any more time. Corazon stood up, indignant, the light of righteousness once again in his eyes. Hwaet coiled to strike, and Thomas wearily prepared himself.

This is going to be it, I thought. This one's going to reach Thomas.

Then, in front of Corazon, to his left and right and behind him, there were explosions. The priest and the chocalaca spun around, startled. More explosions, and the manic, unearthly cry of Mississippian braves. Canoes swooped over us, and missiles rained down on Hwaet. They did not penetrate to Corazon, but they all fell nearby. Just as the strings of the halfsents had had their effect on us, the atlatl spears confused and bothered Hwaet. Corazon stepped backward, then turned as if to strike again. More missiles answered this move. He retreated further, and I covered my ears as the wave of explosions followed him. Finally he reached the edge of the clear area, and, joining his strength with that of the halfsents, Hwaet was fully able to deflect the missiles. After a couple more rounds, the Indians realized this, and the war party landed near us, atlatls at the ready should Hwaet decide to attack again.

Laylay jumped from his canoe and went to Thomas, shoring him up.

"The fighting to the north went well," Laylay said quietly. "We won."

For a moment, Thomas stood still, an arm around Laylay, breathing hard. Then he shook his head as if to clear it, stepped away, and stood erect, surveying the situation.

"And a stalemate here," he said. "But for how long?"

I stepped over to Thomas.

"I have an idea," I said, thinking: you have nothing of the sort. But then the answer to the question that I'd put to my subconscious popped into my head, almost as if it were an add-on algorithm, like my notepad.

"Well?" Thomas said. He clapped me on the shoulder, drew me close. I could feel the tiredness in him. "This *would* be a good time for an idea."

"Hwaet gets his strength from the war. It must really be raging now."

"How do you—"

"Listen to me. I think I know a way to disrupt it, at least momentarily."

Then it hit me what I was thinking about doing. I was thinking about dying, again. "I can get into the weather algorithm," I said, blabbering on before I lost my nerve. "I can try to use the weather to disrupt the war."

Thomas considered this for a long moment. I could see that he had a thousand questions, but that he knew he didn't have time to ask them. He had to trust me. "Do it," he said, pushing me away in the direction of the Town Hall. "And for God's sake, do it as fast as you can. We'll hold them here."

And I was off and running toward the Town Hall faster than thought. For if I'd taken the time to think I would never have started in the first place.

I felt myself possessed by some sort of divine guidance, as if whatever saint or angel that is in charge of such things were instantiated within my will, guiding my every motion. This is the way Corazon must feel, I thought. This is why he consents to be a slave. I dodged through the rubble, in and out of the cover of the still-standing buildings, quickly but with a sureness that each step was the proper one. To my left or my right, wreckage configured itself into what I knew were bunkers and hiding places for settlers, and I avoided them with the instinct of an animal. Dagum was helping me sense these things, but I also felt that there was something inside me, something that did not come from this world, or the true world, or any world I knew of, something that aligned the universe to whatever path I chose, so that I couldn't take a wrong step because all rightness emanated from me and my actions.

I made it to the Town Hall in ten minutes. I was breathing hard, but not completely winded when I arrived. There had been intense fighting in the area, and the ground was still smoldering in places. All about me were signs of bunkered settlers, and I understood that there was a limit to my temporary precocity, and that there was no way I'd get through their perimeter without being noticed. Instead, I picked a half blown-away building that I *knew* must be the local command post, and made for it.

I surprised the hell out of Frank Oldfrunon when I tapped him on the shoulder and spoke his name. He spun around with a pistol leveled at my gut.

But, for being such an old geezer, his reactions were still quite sharp. He did not fire.

"Well," Oldfrunon said. And I *did* hear the age in his voice. "You're back."

"I have to get to the weather machinery, Frank."

He looked me over, long and hard. "I think you *already* have," he finally said. "In fact, you didn't just get *to* it, you got *into* it. I'd surely like to know how you survived that one. I had my best engineer booby-trap that stuff. Even requisitioned the Clerisy's fancy new duplicator to do it with. Boy, did that freeze those buggers' piss."

He smiled, and I could see there was still a devilish glee in him, despite his obvious weariness.

"I have to go *back* inside," I said. "It's a matter of life and death."

Oldfrunon sighed. *"Everything* has been a matter of life and death these last few days. How's this any different, son?"

What could I say to him? That the chocalacas were feeding on our violence, and I had to stop it so that I could stop Hwaet so that Thomas could get to Janey and . . . what? Raej had said *find Janey*. It was the only hope we'd been given, and I had to take it, had to believe in it with all my might, or else there was nothing. Nothing. So I believed that Raej had a reason, and that it could lead to an end to the war.

"I mean for us all. For Candle, the Territory, Earth."

"You don't say."

"Frank, let me in there."

Oldfrunon tensed his grip on the pistol. Its muzzle was now an inch from my heart. He looked me straight in the eyes for what must have been an entire minute. There was nothing I could do. I stared back.

"All right," he said. "All right, but I'm going with you. For all the good it'll do."

I sighed and relaxed, and we headed across the space from this bunker to the Town Hall. A group of canoes appeared to the west, and, as I suspected, settlers emerged from every crack and crevice nearby and opened fire. We walked through the firefight. I still instinctively cringed at the larger explosions, but Oldfrunon was so inured to it all that he did not once seem to notice. We walked inside and this time the building recognized its rightful master, and lit up for us. Our steps rang hollow and sharp in the hallway, against the muted background rumble from the fighting outside.

The algorithm machinery was just as I'd last seen it. As I stepped into the room, Oldfrunon raised his pistol to my head. "I ought to shoot you now," he said. "It's obvious what you're up to isn't going to help us win this war."

"It may help end it," I said. "That's all I can promise."

Oldfrunon's hand started shaking, and he lowered the pistol.

I realized that he was crying. "Christ almighty, that's all I want," he said. "I want this damn thing to be over, and for my people to stop dying."

He wiped his tears away with the back of the hand that held the pistol, then he reholstered it.

"I'll do my best, Frank," I said, and approached the console. I reached out a tentative hand to touch it, withdrew, reached it out again.

"If you can pull off some kind of miracle, son, I'll see that you are resuscitated, even if I have to hijack a ship and go out and find your broadcast waves all over again."

I looked at Oldfrunon, tried to put on a brave face. He nodded. I touched the console.

The white-fury of the tunnel, the feeling of my soul being stripped from my body like old paint. Pain, suddenly present, suddenly gone. *That must be when I died,* I thought. Then the white room with no doors or windows. For a moment, I was startled, for Oldfrunon was still standing before me. Then he winked in and out of existence with a static flash, and I remembered that it was the security algorithm that I had nearly shredded.

"Please (click) by (brrrr) and—"

"Dagum, can you make that thing shut up without destroying the whole setup here?"

There was a welling of power within me, a red flash, and then only a swath of prismatic static where Oldfrunon's algorithm ghost used to be.

"Thanks. Okay. Now what?"

I got up off the cot, looked around. My mind was, for the moment, a complete blank.

"Will."

It was Janey's voice. And when I recognized it, all my hopes, fears, and plans rushed back in with the slopping crash of a wave into sand.

"Janey. Are you all right?"

"I don't know. So many vines have tugged me. Those animals—they're mean. And Georgia's cockroach, knocking, knocking. Wrenny is downstairs, keeping her out. You and Thomas drew the others away. It helped."

"Thank God. So that was you in the house?"

"I need time to get stronger. I've been fighting for a long time now. The war would have been a lot worse if I hadn't. But now the dam is broken. The chocalacas are through."

"I know, Janey, I know. So does Thomas. We have to stop the war, or at least slow it down. Hwaet feeds off it. Those other chocalacas, they must somehow channel it to him—"

"I can barely hear you," Janey said. Her voice, too, was nearly a whisper. "I have to rest now."

"But Janey—"

"It takes strength to reach out to you, and I don't have it now." Her voice, the sense of her presence, grew fainter still.

"Janey, how do I get *out* of here, back into the atmosphere?"

"Dagum," she said. I could barely hear her. "Dagum can help."

And Janey was gone. It was up to me.

"Well, what do you say, friend?"

Instead of replying, Dagum let out what I will swear to my dying day (which with me is problematical, of course) was the deepest, loudest, hardest belch I've ever heard or heard tell of. The white room was no match for it. It flew apart like so much cotton candy.

And I was lofted up and out, as if I were riding the force-pulse of Dagum's burp—and, for all I knew, that was exactly what was happening. As I rose, I spread, inhabited the atmosphere. I consciously stretched further, taking control of all I could manage. This time I was prepared for the disorientation and bewilderment, so when I began to feel the burning within me, I understood it. I bent to observe and analyze it.

War, war and the rumors of war everywhere—fire in the sky, ruin on the streets, blood in the snow. Men and women hating and dying. And swarming about them like the subtlest of veils, the sucking presences of Hwaet's chocalacas, contentedly dangling in the ethereal wind like engorged ticks.

This sight plain made me mad. I tried to reach down, to physically separate the fighters. But my hand—unseen, even by me, but felt—passed through them like the ghost it was. There was perhaps the buffeting of canoes, the whip of leaves and dirt on the ground, nothing more. But this was enough to make some of the chocalacas take notice. A few of them detached themselves, circled around like patrolling hornets. Shit. Then they settled back down to feed.

Why hadn't they seen me? And how the hell could I know the answer to that question? What was I, anyway? Maybe I was invisible to them.

No. They can see. Be careful.

Well, what was I supposed to do now? Obviously my control of the weather was far from precise. Perhaps I could sharpen it, given time—but there was no time. How had Janey so exactly called that lightning bolt down on Bently?

Sarah, of course. Sarah had pinpoint control. She'd had years of practice. But where was she? What had happened to her?

Then the answer hit me like a sickness. *They can see,* Dagum had said. They saw *her.* I pictured the chocalacas chasing my poor Sarah down like dogs after a fox. I thought of her panting, hiding in this place and that, but always, inexorably followed, trailed by baying, biting things. They'd run her down and torn her to pieces. I became convinced of this with a deadly, sapping certainty. To my surprise, the sky opened up and it began to rain over Jackson.

And I nearly lost it. I'll never know if somehow Hwaet sensed my presence and, though he didn't know where I was, was able to somehow influence my state of mind, or if it were all a product of my fevered, overtired, overworked imagination. Doubt grew in me like a black crystal, a lump of coal, glowing with freezing cold bruise-purple flame. What was I doing here? Who did I think I was helping? This was not my time, and not my fight. My Sarah was dead. There had never been any other reason to hang around. I could just end it all. Avoid the futile exercise of trying to live a life that should have been finished with long ago.

All I had to do was spread all the way out, settle down in the cold outer atmosphere that was too thin to support an algorithm. I could become the funeral shroud of an already-dying planet. The thought was appealing, satisfying my morbid, romantic nature. The nature that had driven me to express myself into space like a virus-filled sneeze. Wasn't it time to face reality, to face the horrible fact that nothing I did would make the slightest bit of difference in the long run?

Not war. Not moral purpose. Not even love. Sarah was gone, and all my love could never bring her back.

Time. Parasites. The gradual diminishing of order. They all ate away at whatever meaning we might think we had constructed or discovered, until there was nothing left, if there had ever been anything of value in the first place.

What was the use of fighting Hwaet? Not because Hwaet was right, but because nobody was right, ever, and there was no use in anything. Let the chocalaca have his fun. For that matter, let all the mass-murderers and thieves and jaywalkers have their fun. They were only fooling themselves. We all were.

There is another way.

"Go away, Dagum."

There is another way. I will show you.

"I don't want to hear about it."

Did I ask for your permission?

And before I could answer, Dagum began to *show* me.

I felt, more than saw, and, as in trying to describe the true world, all I can do is say what it is *like,* not what it is, since there is nothing similar in the regular world.

I felt I was in a room that was larger than the sky. There was a chair. But it was not *a* chair; it was *the* Chair—every chair there ever had been, ever would be, ever could be. It was your father's favorite chair, the chair your mother sat in while suckling you, the helm of all the ships that ever sailed the seas and skies, the throne of every ruler, the toilet of every slave. You knew when you sat in it that it would fit you perfectly, for it was bent and shaped by humans for humans over millennia. I sat down, and gazed out at the new creation that spread before me.

It was our galaxy, old Milky Way, and all the others, connected by webs of light, star to star, cluster to cluster, through the true world. I understood that the light-lines were not made of regular light, but the noumenal light of the true world, pure information, the steady stream of beings between the stars. Travel was instantaneous. I comprehended now why the chocalacas thought of their original planet as a mere pond. I searched, and with my perfect sight, I found the Earth, then Candle. They, too, were pools, dots of wetness, each beautiful as a dewdrop or a snowflake, but nothing more than that. The universe was deep and wide.

The lines of light—us, human beings—were continuous luminescences rather than discrete points of existence, because there was no more *time*. Time was as much a universe-bound concept as space. In the true world, there was neither time nor space—or, to put it rightly, time and space were only shadows of what they truly were when expressed in the noumena, unsifted by the limited intellect of humans.

So how would we experience them in this new creation? With the help of chocalacas. This was the wonder of Raej's way. The chocalacas' discovery of humans was analogous to humanity's first discovery of agriculture. It was the basis for an existence as far above their present one as their present one was above their original, regular world origins. Chocalacas needed human beings. And humanity needed the chocalacas, if it ever wanted to match in consciousness what it had achieved in science. Chocalacas offered access to the true world. They offered the possibility of meaning in an otherwise empty universe.

I saw that now. Raej's way. It was as far above Hwaet's conceptions as modern life was above that of the hunter-gatherer culture of our prehistoric past. This time, this place, *this planet* was the pivot, the notch in which the past and future were balanced. If Hwaet had his way, humans would be, in essence, slaves to the chocalacas. Eventually this relationship would corrupt the chocalacas far more than the humans. But there was the other way, Raej's way.

Humans would be freed of the boring, mundane labor of just staying alive and trying to die as old as possible. They'd be free to use the creation of novelty, a talent which is *the* human evolutionary adaptation (of course, I thought, it's so *obvious*), for purposes beyond the dreams of mortal men and women. The chocalacas would feed and mate with this creativity, in symbiotic satisfaction. This was Raej's vision.

And who or *what* was Raej? Wasn't he a normal chocalaca, like all the others (whatever the hell that meant)?

It is hard to say. He is . . . a reflection of the future that might be. He is a kind of lens that brings what is far away closer. Think of your great ones of the past. They were only human, but they were also something more. He is like them. I follow Raej.

And so would I, I realized. To the ends of the Earth, to the ends of the sky, and beyond. But unless we could tilt the future to us, to our way, it was all only a vision, and never would be anything more.

And no matter what happened, Sarah was dead, and there was no way to bring her back, even in the future Raej envisioned. The loss and grief were not lessened, but I knew now that I could bear it, and I knew that all of my doubts and thoughts of self-destruction were merely products of my long grief. I had been losing Sarah, bit by bit, for nine years.

And now was when I needed her most. Not the old Sarah. Not for *me*. I needed the Weather-Sarah, I needed her experience in the craft and control of Candle's atmosphere. Only milliseconds had passed in real time since I'd entered the machinery at Town Hall, but they may as well have been millennia. Dagum had given me back the desire to go on fighting, but I lacked the means.

There are places too narrow for them to follow. I do not know. Perhaps she is not completely gone.

Too narrow? Not complicated enough for chocalacas, but complex enough to sustain some semblance of Sarah. Where?

The geothermal vents. The springlike feeling I'd encountered there. Sarah. But why hadn't she responded to my coming, why hadn't she shown herself to me?

Well, there was nothing to it but to find out. I carefully worked myself around the chocalacas and the warring humans. I felt like a long ribbon, or a snake moving steathily through the grass—though, after my experiences with Hwaet, I liked the idea of a ribbon better. I headed south, down to the equator, down the hot holes that provided the very little warmth and liquid water that Candle enjoyed. The old, cold sun was certainly not responsible for any of it. Candle was a world in the geologic throes of death, and only a happy accident brought humanity to its surface during an epoch when there was enough heat arising from the process of that death, the uneven cooling of magma, to make the planet at all habitable. In a few million years, it would be a cold ball of ice in an even colder universe.

I dove deep, far deeper than I had before. I felt the complexity lessen, and bits of my awareness, my senses, slough away. I hoped I would get them back when I came back out. But it didn't matter, not now. Deeper. The warmth became heat, wild, disordering heat, that set my atoms bouncing.

And a connection. Something like *me*. There was no way of telling what. It could have been a stray halfsent, escaped from some building control algorithm in Jackson, for all I knew. Whatever it was, it trembled at my touch like a living, thinking thing. I wrapped my fingers around it, held on tight.

Pulled it up. Up. And as we rose, we grew. The parts of us that we'd had to pack to static representations expanded into dynamic flows and ebbs of self-awareness. I collected what bits and pieces of me I could and reattached them. When I was finished, I felt more or less whole.

And, as I rose, I saw the wisps of Sarah's sundered mind take shape in my algorithm arms.

"Don't be afraid," I said. "I won't hurt you."

Her trembling stopped, and it became easier to hold onto

her. I had no idea if she understood, or if she were merely responding as a wild animal will when it has fallen into some trap, when you are its greatest fear and its only hope of salvation.

"Don't be afraid, Sarah," I said. "It's only me."

13

I have often wondered why I felt no disappointment, or even anguish, when I found that the Sarah I'd pulled from the depths was far from the complete woman whom I had loved so long ago. By all logic, I should have felt bad. She was barely a *she*, more a lump of emotions with very little rationality at its core. Sure, most of her autonomous loops were there—the body-regulating functions, the deeply ingrained redundancies that controlled personal tics, little ways of doing things, habits bad and good. But my Sarah was in tatters, like an old doll who has been in the attic toy chest for years. Yet I was happy, almost jubilant, for having found her.

Because she *was* my Sarah. Of that there was no mistake. The patterns were there, the potentials, the familiar curve of her thought. If it were broken or erased in large part, there was still enough for me to fill in the gaps, to see her as she had been. She had trembled with fear when I pulled her up, and my words had calmed her.

"You have to help me," I told her, still holding her, still shielding her from sight of what Candle had become in the last weeks.

I will give you shelter, for a while, so that you can let go and not be afraid.

My chocalaca's now-familiar aura folded around us. It was a

difficult thing for him to do, I realize now, for part of what kept me—this weather algorithm me—animated was the fact that I was smeared across a large part of the sky, and within this great space were many thermal, atomic, and quantum complexities for my being to inhabit. In order for Dagum to shield us, he had to take the place of some of this spread, and simulate my and Sarah's outer consciousness within himself. This must be an extremely delicate and complicated operation even in calmer circumstances, even for a chocalaca. Dagum did so much, so quickly, that it is hard for me to understand, much less praise.

But at the time, I *was* grateful for the respite. Carefully, gently, I separated myself from Sarah. She did not want to let go, and I had to pull firmly away a couple of times. This was hard, so hard, for it went against every emotion within me. When we were fully apart, I had to mentally step away, make myself distant to her. She responded by trying to flow away, but Dagum's strong walls kept her within. When she found out she couldn't get away, she began to turn inward, to turn her comprehension away from me.

"Sarah, you've got to look at me," I said. Still she would not. "If you don't, everyone's going to die, or wish they were dead."

This didn't have any effect. She's a child, I thought, a baby. There's no way she can grasp such things. What can I say? How do you reason with a baby?

"Sarah, if you don't look at me, I'm going to die," I said. "Those bad things that chased you are going to get me."

Nothing.

"And Janey will die. Do you remember Janey? She found you. You . . . held hands with her."

At this, she stopped trying to hug herself to death. If she'd had tears, she might have wiped a few away. There was something in this attention that I remembered. The mountains of California. Her standing by our big picture window, looking out at the lights. She was a painter, an artist, and a girl from an Oregon farm. She could look through the grimy complexity, the lines of politics and exploitation below her, and see the essence, the colors, the basic forms that gave the L.A. basin its terrible beauty.

She could capture it on canvas, to remind us all that there was still something real under the harlot's makeup, the poverty and excess, still something worthwhile in the mass of humanity below.

And Sarah in Missouri, in the Ozarks, as the red maple leaves streamed about her in autumn. Me huffing behind her with a daypack, my mind on getting to a flat place where we could eat lunch. And she stoops, picks up a leaf, looks it over. The leaf is mottled with fungus, torn along a vein—yet still the red of new wine.

"I'm going to paint this," she said. "This one is perfect."

And I looked, and for a moment, I could see it through her eyes, see that it *was* perfect. And because she had given me this gift, this opportunity, I loved her the more. I had loved her so much, for so long.

"Oh Sarah," I said, "don't you remember me?"

And she *looked* at me; she looked at me in that way only she had—as if she could paint the me that should have been, that ought to have been. She opened up her eyes of air and spoke my name.

"Will."

I had to fight like the devil then from going back to her, taking her in my arms once again. But I did not. And in that instant, *I* saw *her*. She was clear, like a vessel of glass, and within her was the amber liquid of her one desire, fully refined over all the silent years, after all the years of trying to remember how to *say*, how to communicate, knowing somehow, innately, that that was all that mattered to her. Not even being able to speak, except in the rarest and subtlest of ways, with the man she loved. Me. Will James.

The amber liquid was the representation of her desire to end the confused silence, to either go on to a better world where talk and *saying* were possible, or to enter the real, final silence, where remorse and self-reflection were both impossible. Where the wind was just the wind, and not the personification of her own frustrated, hopeless need to *say*.

Yet there was no way Sarah could ever *tell* me what she really wanted. All I could ever know was her feelings, the intense regret, the longing for what couldn't be.

So instead of helping her, I asked her to help me. I showed her what had to be done to end the war on Candle. What I could not do by myself.

I became a tabula rasa, a screen on which was projected the war and what it would bring about. I'll probably never know how much of this she understood. All that really mattered was that she understood that she must help me in controlling the weather. And when I saw that she understood that, I did what I'd been longing to do all along—I reached out a tendril of emotion, of love and hope, my hand. She took it and wrapped her own around it. She squeezed firmly and I felt her resolution and her trust.

So. I'd given her temporary purpose, without offering any kind of solution to her permanent condition of frustration. Well, maybe that's all we can ever do for one another. The thought didn't make me feel any better though.

"We're ready, Dagum."

And the shield came down. We spread out, Sarah and I, flying together, each matching the other's moves with unconscious grace. Well, her movement was graceful at least. I had a hard time keeping up with her. And I had the feeling that she was lagging behind so she wouldn't leave me. After we were high in the atmosphere—less than a hundred miles from space—and after we were spread wide over Candle's curve, Sarah began to gather her strength. She worked incredibly quickly, but with deliberation. She'd obviously done all of this before.

Clouds gathered beneath us. A wind whipped up. The chocalacas must have sensed something, for a few scouts shot upward to see what was up. Maybe they were complacent, or else they just could not see us unless we made a deliberate, unnatural move. And they may have been expecting bad weather to occur naturally, since the little wind I'd kicked up trying to separate the Indians and settlers seemed natural enough—a portent of snow. Why should they think differently?

Hadn't they driven the little subhuman weather algorithm into the ground, after all?

When Sarah's storm broke, all hell broke lose. She threw in driving snow, cutting, fist-sized hail, and a couple of tornadoes that she seemed to be able to place with pinpoint accuracy. Jesus, had she gotten good at her job.

The Indians withstood this onslaught a lot longer than I would have believed, but they had to turn, or else risk being whipped away and broken. And the settlers had run for shelter anyway, so they had no one to fight. Soon a disorganized plume of canoes was streaming back to the village, where the skies were not so full of fire and lightning.

That was when the chocalacas sensed us, and came after us. But my fears had made them seem more dangerous than they were. Only a tiny portion of their being could be expressed in the air, for it was far less complex than Loosa clay. They were slow and blundering, like great eels sliding through turbid waters. Electric eels, I thought, with enough juice to fry our minds alive, should they catch us. They were ugly darknesses, gray places in my perception, like floating cataracts, like a cloud of mosquitoes waiting for twilight, like age and death. As we drew closer, I had to fight terror just to move. Fortunately, the storm that she had summoned helped camouflage us, so that the chocalacas couldn't home in directly on us, and frequently lost the "scent." Still, they came on inexorably.

I could escape, I figured, by going back into the weather machinery of the Town Hall and, with Dagum's help, once again reclaiming my body. Sarah had no such choice. Despite her death-wish, there was no way I was going to leave her to be torn apart by Hwaet's chocalacas or, worse, to cower back into the vents, where there was room for no other thought but fear. Sarah didn't seem to want the chocalacas to catch her either. She was running along with me.

For a while, I fled blindly, shifting this way and that, staying near Jackson more or less, to take advantage of the storm's convection currents. They were obviously confusing the chocalacas. Maybe I found some way of calling out for help, or maybe Janey was reaching out to me after regaining her strength. Whatever, I felt a tug in the direction of her house. What I should have worried about was that Hwaet was setting a trap for me.

Fortunately, Thomas and Raej were keeping him busy—going on the attack, then retreating back into the clear area where his halfsent army couldn't go. And if Hwaet tried to follow, the Indians would launch a barrage of missile-spears at Corazon. I knew nothing of this at the time, however. Leading Sarah, I curled my awareness down and around the house.

"Janey," I whispered—it must have been a tremble in the air, the ruffle of a breeze through leaves.

"I'm here, Will."

"What do I do? I can't go back to the Town Hall yet. I have Sarah with me."

Janey didn't say anything for a while, and I was afraid she'd gone away. Communicating like this was like talking on a two-way spirit radio, like using the tin-can telephone of the gods. "Janey?"

"I've twisted the border of the regular and the true worlds into a dam," Janey said. "It's only a little one—not nearly so big as the one that they broke after the war started. But it will hold for a while."

"Janey, what can I do with Sarah?"

It took a moment for Janey to respond.

"Will, there is an empty place for her to settle. Maybe only for a little while."

"Where! Jesus, Janey, let's get her settled then!"

"I'm not sure. She's fading so . . ."

"Sarah is with *me*. I don't know what—"

"*Tabitha,* Will. I'm talking about Tabitha."

It hit me hard. Sarah in Tabitha. Oh, please God, if you grant this wish—

I cut off the thought.

"How will it work?"

"I can help. You have to help too. The twisting leaves me so tired. You have to hold her, because the translation will hurt and she'll try and get away."

"I don't think I—"

"Will, there isn't much time, you know? They've found the dam and are trying to untwist it."

I let my hold on Sarah's hand become very firm. "I've got her, Janey."

"That's all you have to do. Hold her."

Oh, Sarah, it will be all right, I thought. Maybe I said it too. Maybe she understood, really understood. I felt her shudder when Janey took her at the other end. Then I heard her scream. It was the bewildered, uncomprehending scream of a wild animal, shot from out of the blue. Or a child, suddenly, inexplicably orphaned. Even worse, the man she'd trusted beyond all others was betraying her. I felt like a complete shit. I knew if I let her go, there would be no more hope for Sarah. So I held on. I held on, and wouldn't let her get away. And even after Janey told me I could let go, I didn't.

Maybe that explains what happened next. I felt a searing pain, of a kind with the stripping pain of the duplicator booby trap, but more subtle. And then I was in the brown lands once again. Tabitha's inner land, cut by gorges and scree piles. Arid. Dry of all human emotion—permanently now that the WORM had wiped Tabitha's personality away.

Oh, Christ, no! I thought. The Ideal slave virus has got me again. But no. I retained my freedom—signified by my burning *hatred* of Langley, Tabitha's Ideal, for what it had done to me, and what it had tried to make me do.

"Dagum!"

Once again, saved by the chocalaca. *This is a simple one. Much more simple than the weather.*

"Then keep it out of my head."

Do you want me to make this thing obey?

"What?"

It is only a machine. Do you want me to tell it to do what you say?

"Dagum, are you suggesting—"

"Will?"

At first I thought it was Dagum, but his voice in my head was the churn of gravel, and this was light as dew and—

"Will, you have to let go. If you don't she can't find her place; she can't settle down into the shelter. And the dam is breaking."

Janey. It was Janey's voice. I was still holding on to Sarah. Through it all, I hadn't let go. Now it was time to let go. I prayed I was doing the right thing. Could the WORM harm her?

I've made the machine think it belongs to you.

"What?"

"Let go, Will," Janey said.

There was no choice, and nowhere else to run. I let go.

Then I turned from that house, and fled away as fast as I could, feeling like a criminal, who justified his hateful means by the supposedly good end to be achieved. Had I just handed over the love of my life to that Thing in Tabitha's head? I hoped to God Dagum and Janey knew what they were doing.

I had to dodge and feint to get around the still-searching chocalacas. They had all gathered in one "spot" to put their collective strength into breaking Janey's dam. When it broke, they spilled forward, in momentary disarray. I used the opportunity to sneak around them. I didn't know if they saw me. I didn't care, as long as Sarah was safe. If Tabitha's body was still alive. If Janey had pulled off the transfer. I was playing so many games that I didn't understand today. I had the feeling that only incredible luck had carried me this far, and I'd better goddamn get back in my body and back to being a regular human, or I was going to fuck something up mighty soon.

Dagum took over when I was near enough to the duplication machinery. He seemed to be able to inhabit and use it—far better than it was originally designed for, obviously, for I'd never heard of an entire human pattern being stripped out and then put back in the same body without harm. Dagum must have heard me wondering about the process. *There is clay at the machine's heart.*

Which makes about as much sense as anything had today, I thought, as I felt the now familiar suck feeling from below me,

s if I were water swirling down a drain. Down, down, a moment of blackness and nothing. The hurtful flash of lights and
pecificity and the sour smell of my own bad breath. The micromachines in my spit that were supposed to keep my teeth
clean had obviously been shut down along with the rest of me,
and had closed up shop. I sat up, and stretched out my creaking
muscles. Oldfrunon coughed, shook his head. It is *cold* in here.
'd almost gotten used to feeling temperature as something *inside*
instead of outside of me.

"Son, that box was booby-trapped to kill anybody who
touched it. My engineers told me it *had* to kill in order to make
a duplicate that was complex enough to interrogate."

"Guess they were mistaken," I said. My voice, my real voice,
air thrumming over vocal cords, sounded solid and thick.

"I don't think so," he replied, and helped me to my feet.
"There's things about you that don't meet the eye."

I stood silent a moment, listening.

"There's no war. At least, not at the moment. That big storm
ure as hell worked. Did you conjure that up, son? You couldn't
have been gone more than ten or fifteen minutes."

"Not exactly."

"Well, whatever, or whoever, the battle's broken up for the
day, and the Indians have gone home."

"Thank God."

"So, now are you going to tell me?"

"Tell you what?"

"How this is going to save the world, and keep the fighting
from starting up as soon as the Indians feel safe enough to go up
in the air again?"

"I don't know."

"You don't *know*?"

"I don't know. Frank, I'm really tired. And I've still got a lot
o do. Have to get back over to Janey's—" I took a step toward
the door, stumbled. Oldfrunon almost let me fall, but he reached
over at the last instant and shored me up, helped me walk.

"All right, Will," he said. "I'll help you get there. I want to
ee this myself, anyway."

* * *

With the commander of Jackson's forces at my side, it was no
a difficult passage getting back to Janey's. I spent most of the
time wondering what the hell I was going to do when I got
there. I tried not to, but I thought about Tabitha, and what she'd
done to me, and what I'd just done to her. I wondered which
one of us had screwed the other worse. But I suspected the
balance was still tipped in her favor.

Tabitha had never been a real personality. She was always just
a node of the Ideal she served, and her soul was a reflection of
whatever her Ideal's needs were at any particular moment. So
the Ideal needed to subvert a threat on a backwater planet?
Tabitha would do it; she'd do whatever was necessary. She was
a means, rather than an end. Maybe that was the elusive defini-
tion of personhood I'd been looking for all along. Humans were
neither brain, nor soul nor extraordinary meat computer—we
were no *one* thing. What we all were, though, was an *end*. When
we became a means—either for chocalacas, or for bad politics or
good, or for anything, we gave up being a person. As long as I
served no one except by choice, purely for my own satisfaction,
as long as I let no one rule me, *then* I was a person.

Tabitha had lost that when she joined the Ideal. Hell, maybe
she'd joined so long ago that she'd never really had it in the first
place. What I had mistaken for a personality was my own projection. She was an empty coloring book drawing, and I had
filled her in with my choice of bright colors. Someone else's
colors. And now I had literally done so. Sarah was in Tabitha.

Or was this, too, an elaborate justification for wiping all traces
of someone out of existence? Use the word, damn it: for murder? Could Tabitha's Ideal have somehow restored her, if she'd
been returned to Earth? Restored her to what, though? Who
was I to judge? Ah, hell. Every second of every minute is a little
moral suicide, because we have to act, and we just don't have
time to know if we are doing right, or merely responding to our
basest desire all dressed up like a high-class whore.

When we arrived, the Indians and Thomas had driven Hwae
and Corazon back to the house, and the porch with Georgia on

it. Indian missile-spears had further pulverized the earth, so that Hwaet's halfsents could not renew their attack. Apparently, separating the warring parties had had the desired effect, and Hwaet was weakened. But it wouldn't be long until the fighting started up again. I was careful to keep myself between Oldfrunon and the Indians, so that they wouldn't be surprised into killing him before I could explain his presence.

I could see that it was hard for *Oldfrunon* to approach these Indians and not want to shoot them. He'd just spent weeks thinking up new ways to do them in, and to suddenly stop must have been an emotional wrench even to such a mentally versatile man as Oldfrunon.

When I was fifty paces away, I stopped and tried to evaluate the situation as best I could. Hwaet was, at the moment, between us and Janey. Janey must still be weak, and was probably only defending herself, and incapable of attack as of yet. Thomas was very, very tired, but he and Raej were still at it. The Indians were running out of ammunition. And no matter what happened, in a few hours Hwaet would be stronger than ever, and we'd have lost all hope against him. He was stronger than all of us put together. There was no longer any doubt, as if there ever had been.

Then the certainty of purpose and motion suddenly came back upon me, just as I'd experienced when making my way toward the Town Hall. My subconscious was screaming, trying to tell me something—too many things at once. I grabbed hold of the nearest idea.

Truce. Call a truce. Give yourself time to think.

Yeah, right. Just tell everybody to take five. Call a time-out. Not hardly.

But what did I have to lose?

"Call a truce, Thomas." These were the first words I said when I moved up to join Thomas and the Indians. Then the second sentence was "He's with me!" when several of them targeted Oldfrunon with spears, and he looked like he was going to draw his pistol in return.

"A truce?" Thomas replied with a tired, exasperated voice. "But we've got them on the run."

"A truce, all around!" I yelled. "Are you listening, Corazon?"

"To hell with you, Indian-lover," Corazon screamed back. *"Transmission!"* For a moment, anger rose in me. Then I almost laughed. People were fighting and dying, and here was one more reason for rancor, for hatred. I'd had enough of both. The fucker could call me whatever he wanted. What did it matter now, here at the end of the world?

It mattered to Corazon, I realized. Hatred, bile. For him they were indistinguishable from moral purpose, from the will of God and History. Hate was *all* that mattered to Corazon. He didn't know anything else. He didn't know what the WORM knew. What *I* knew.

Corazon doesn't know because his hatred has made him simplistic and naïve, I thought. Transmissions, Indians. He could only think in big categories. All outrage and hate. No subtle understanding.

Corazon doesn't know. Hwaet hasn't told him the whole truth.

About how Hector Luis Blanca, the Head of the Church, and Corazon's spiritual leader, was a turncoat for the Ideals. I had to get close enough to speak, to plainly speak of this to Corazon. For better or worse, I was beginning to understand the priest. I had the feeling the truth would unhinge him, and that Hwaet knew this.

Like he isn't already unhinged, I thought. And who am I to guess at chocalaca strategy?

But, again, what did we have to lose? I let myself laugh good-naturedly.

Steady. Step forward. Steady and calm.

Hwaet held back on his next strike. He's evaluating his position, just as I did, I thought. I hope to God he doesn't come up with any logic that I missed. I was struck with the feeling that he most definitely would, and that it would lead to our ruin. Still, I stumbled onward with my plan. Such as it was. Thomas looked at me like I was a loon.

"The settlers and Indians have stopped fighting. Why can't *we,* at least for now," I said. Christ, listen to me. How could anyone believe I don't have something up my sleeve.

But it worked. Perhaps Hwaet was so intent on regaining his strength and crushing us utterly that he didn't pay the kind of attention he should have. And maybe he was sure that we were, all of us, so far beneath him at this point that there was nothing we could do that would matter. He was almost right. But every once in a while, when the situation demands hope and all hope is gone, *humans think otherwise*.

I spoke the modified proverb in the Loosa. Thomas gazed at me long and hard, then smiled.

"Yes, a truce," he said. "I could sure as hell use a breather."

"All right," Corazon called out petulantly. "But you're just putting off the inevitable. Righteousness *will* triumph."

Well, what now? I thought.

A shot rang out. The ground in front of me exploded in a flash of whiteness that left me temporarily blind. Dirt and bits of rock sliced my face, and I fell to my knees.

"You damned inhuman *thing*," a voice said. "All of you latecomers. This is my land, *my* place. Since you won't go away, I'm going to *make* you go away."

I recognized it. Georgia. With a gun full of some very deadly bullets. Aimed at me. Shit. I balled up on the ground, trying to make myself less of a target. My eyes streamed with tears, and my vision returned, accompanied by a black dot that danced evilly.

"Sister." The new voice was quiet, rich, commanding. I glanced up. Wrenny had opened the door and was standing on the porch behind Georgia. "Sister, I think this has gone far enough."

"Shut up, Wrenny. Him and his kind. They've taken everything away from us."

"Hush, sister. We children of the pioneers have fallen into decay all by ourselves. It isn't the Indians' fault, and it isn't the fault of the transmissions."

Georgia was not listening, however. She raised the gun—it was a small pistol—and took aim at me.

Then she jerked forward, stumbled from the porch. Wrenny had kicked her soundly in the rump. On the ground, she regained her balance, spun around with the gun. *She's crazy,* I thought. *She's going to kill Wrenny.* What struck me most was the senseless illogic of it. Of all people, Georgia, why Wrenny? Who did she ever hurt but herself?

Swoosh! Over my shoulder, an atlatl spear flew. It struck Georgia in the back, went through her chest. She turned around in amazement, and I saw that it stuck out, just under her left breast. Blood flowered down her stomach, like a drooping rose. I braced myself for the explosion. But the explosion didn't come.

"Why, I never—" Georgia started to say. But a lung was penetrated, and blood welled from her mouth as she tried to finish the thought. She took a step forward, sank to one knee, dropping her pistol and staring at it uncomprehendingly.

"I didn't have any more missiles left," said a voice behind me. I recognized the words as Loosa, and the voice as Laylay Potter's. "I had to use a regular spear."

Wrenny gasped, jumped from the porch, and went to her sister. Georgia was still on her knees, some incredible will keeping her upright. "Oh Georgia," Wrenny said. "I'm so sorry."

As she held Georgia, I saw for the first time the beauty that underlay Wrenny Calhoun. The years of drinking had taken their toll, but beneath the decay was the strength and elegance of the Calhouns—people like Lincoln, who had come from the best humanity had to offer, people who *did* something, and didn't wait for life to happen to them. But most of all, I saw in her what Raej must have when he fell in love with Janey and Wrenny's mother. A depth that was beyond intelligence and emotion, a beauty that was too good for this world. Somewhere, somehow—even before meeting the chocalacas—we humans had gotten a bit of the true world in our genes. Janey had inherited it, but so had Wrenny.

"Fools!"

It was Corazon. Wrenny had left the front door open, and he turned gleefully and entered the house. A flickering shadow passed me, and a blue blaze of electricity stood my hair on end. The shadow was Thomas. He bounded onto the porch, and was through the door before I'd gotten to my feet.

Things were happening too fast. I got up and took a few confused steps toward Wrenny. The front of the house seethed and warped with its halfsent infestation. There was a scream, very much like Georgia's voice. I looked down at Georgia. Her face was deathly pale. There was no way she could have screamed. The house halfsent, I thought. It must be the house screaming.

Then Thomas came sprinting through the front door. He jumped off the porch. I saw, clearly, his face, as he rushed past Wrenny and me. It was drawn and wide-eyed. It was full of something I'd never seen in him before. Fear.

The door and door frame of the house exploded. Instinctively, I threw myself over Wrenny, and bore her to the ground. I felt the passing of something over us, like the wing of some giant bird, or a dragon. When I looked up, I saw that the house's door had hit Georgia squarely on end, like a dull blade. She lay crumpled under it, twisted unnaturally at the pelvis. Laylay's spear still protruded from her back. Wrenny raised her head, gasped, but I grabbed her shoulders firmly, and turned her away from the sight.

Hwaet slithered from the open maw of the house like a snake after a fleeing mouse. The mouse, in this case, was Thomas. I momentarily forgot about Georgia, about Wrenny, and stood up. Thomas reached the edge of the destruction he and his braves had wrought to keep back Hwaet's halfsents, and turned. He looked like a hunted animal, at bay, hopeless and crazy-mad.

It's not going to end like this, I thought. He's not the kind of person who dies like this. This is Thomas Fall, the man who does what I always dreamed of. I understood at that instant, absolutely and precisely, why Thomas was my friend. Since then, my understanding has been blunted, worn back to mere feeling by time and habit. But I saw the excellence in Thomas at that moment, the coalescing of confidence, virtue, and craft. This is what a man can be, I thought. This is my goddamn hope and example, and he will not become the fucking fodder of that piece of shit from the fifth dimension.

And, within me, I felt the anger and resolution of Dagum, thinking much the same about Raej. As one, we ran forward, and attacked Hwaet and Corazon on their flank.

As we crashed into them, our momentum vectored with theirs, so that the snake and the priest within the snake's form careened sideways. I raised my arm, and Dagum did so with me. We brought a great clubbing hammer of fire down on Hwaet. We connected solidly, and I felt something give in the ghost-snake. But not enough. He writhed wildly, and when we struck again, it was a clean miss. Then something nipped at my leg, found a purchase, *bit down hard.*

I spun around. A halfsent had raised itself from the house splinters at my feet. It took the form of a jaguar head, formed from pieces of wood. But it had glass shards for teeth. They had sunk into my calf muscle. I felt Dagum share in my confusion, lose power. From above came an evil hissing.

Hwaet descended like Satan falling from the sky, a red ball of flame, a thousand times hotter than Candle's sun. And for once on this iceball planet, I regretted not feeling the cold.

There was something hotter inside me, welling out like arterial blood, spewing forth from me in great streaming gushes of warmth, enshrouding me in a film of living, liquid fire. The jaguar head released its hold, deformed back to shards and splinters.

The heat inside me was Dagum—trying to protect me, like the staunch friend he'd become.

To no avail, I thought, to no avail. The pressure from above, from Hwaet, did not cease. I'm sorry, friend. *No matter what happens, hold onto yourself.* I'm sorry. And Hwaet was upon us, crackling and burning at Dagum's coating, searing through it like nitric acid through flesh. The heat was intense. It felt like match sulfur was fluorescing all over my skin. Is there such a thing as a fourth degree burn? Is that when the fire reaches down and hollows out your soul?

I screamed a long time, before I felt the flash enter my brain. *No matter what happens, hold on to yourself.* But there was no longer any self to hold on to, only a white-hot ring of iron in the center of my mind. It tugged at me with a sickeningly intense gravity. There was no way to resist. No hope. I fell into it, and burned until all my thoughts were ashes.

14

Have you ever been born? Remember? It hurts. It's the Red Hour, the squeeze and flux time. If you don't bend, you don't move and you're stuck, constricted into something too thin to live. So I bent and pushed, and reality warped around me, moving me slowly along with a metaphysical peristalsis. I didn't think anything, or know anything—who I was, what could be happening. I only understood *out,* and that I *had* to go there.

Then hands on me, pulling, straining. Light, bright and painful. Yes, I remember light. Colors spattered in pools and flecks. But everything tinged red by a film over my eyes that only slowly dissipated. Then a name, *my* name.

"Will."

And a name to go with the voice occurs to me. A soft face, hair as soft as down. Janey Calhoun. Her hands under my chin, tugging so hard I'm sure my head will pop off, but instead I slid farther out of . . . wherever I was. Then my arms are free and her hands move down, around my chest, pulling. I kick feebly with my legs to help, but I'm already sliding out, and it doesn't help much, and I'm—

Out.

I lay on top of Janey in a pool of who-knows-what kind of reddish liquid that quickly bubbled and evaporated. "That hurt," I said. I rolled off Janey, tried to sit up. Too dizzy. Small explosions in my brain, and I lay still a little longer, trying not to pass out. After a while, the explosions subsided. I gingerly pushed myself upright.

I started to speak, wanting to shake off the weirdness with the reassuring sound of my own voice. But for once in my life, I could think of nothing to say, smart-ass or otherwise. "Jesus," I said. "Goddamn."

Across the room, a voice let out a startled "Oh!"

It was Tabitha, sitting upright in Janey's rocking chair. Sarah. I was in Janey's sewing room, where she made her quilts. There was the chair, and the old trunk. I stared at it hard, attempting to reconstruct my universe around this one seed of familiarity. Janey struggled to her feet. A few things fell into place.

"But those were in Doom. How did they get back here?"

Janey smiled, but it was a sad smile. "I ran to Doom at first, and then came here after the fighting started. Laylay risked his life to bring Tabitha and me here. We brought these in a canoe, at night."

Wow. Information. My brain soaked it up like a sponge, but couldn't organize it. Think of something simpler, stronger.

"Dagum. He saved my life."

"He died," Janey said, and wiped a hand across her forehead. It left a red smear that slowly disappeared as she spoke. "He made a way for you through the true world, and tore himself apart so he could bring you here and still keep Hwaet from eating you."

He died. For a moment the words meant nothing to me. Then I remembered the pictures Dagum had shown me of the graceful sailing creatures that the chocalacas had been. And he had been a thousand times more graceful, beautiful in the true world, I was sure. Something that valuable, that real, had died for me? There was no way I was worth it. There was nothing I could do about it. Except somehow try to justify the sacrifice. I'd be a thousand lifetimes attempting it. Well, three down, nine hundred ninety-seven to go. Hell, what else can you do when you're utterly unworthy but laugh it off, cry it off, and get on with living?

I had a feeling me and Dagum would have become pretty tight friends. Would have. There are some things of value that are completely lost, even to memory, because they never were. When you know what they are, which isn't often, thank God, then those are, for me, the saddest things of all.

"What's going on?" I said. "Where's Thomas?"

"I don't know," Janey said. "Hwaet and the black fungus man were chasing him, and then I felt the ripple and knew I had to help you through."

The black fungus man? Good name for Corazon.

Janey walked over to the window and stood gazing out. Sarah was rocking her chair in quick, nervous spurts.

"Did . . . Janey, how is Sarah? Was that all a dream?"

"I don't know that either," Janey replied, without looking around at me. "She hasn't talked yet."

"What about that damn WORM?"

"After I'm sure she is *in* right, I'll kill it," Janey replied with a flat tone of voice, as if this were an unpleasantness she really didn't want to discuss.

"Are you sure you *can*?"

She didn't answer. Obviously this was a stupid question. I got shakily to my feet, and stumbled over to stand beside her at the window. There was a smell to her that was at once frightening and attractive, like burning leaves or a prairie fire.

"Thomas and Father are fighting again," she said. "Hwaet is desperate. Dagum hurt him. And the priest, the soft places in him are all eaten away. I can see through him in spots."

"Can we win, then?"

Janey didn't answer. "My sister is dead," she said softly to herself. "Oh Wrenny, don't cry so." Then she collected herself, brushed a hand against mine. "Hwaet is still very strong from the war. And the Indians are on their way back."

I started to ask her how she knew this, but realized in time that this would be another stupid question. From the danger Janey was radiating, I was beginning to believe that it would be better not to make her angry.

"Janey, do you think you can take him? Hwaet, I mean."

"Not yet. I've never been so strong. I've found myself, Will. After all those years of spinning. But even with Thomas's help . . . and Hwaet has Father's copy. I would have to kill it too."

I looked at her, felt her indecision shooting sparks that sizzled inside me, like angry stings. This was exactly the same sort of feeling as before, when I'd felt the melting and softening Janey created when she was uncentered and reeling. But this feeling was the opposite of the melting. It strengthened me—physically, I mean. And damn, could my tired, wrung-out muscles use it. And, whether from this new strength or from somewhere else, there rose in me a resolve. Maybe it was everything—Dagum's sacrifice, the Raej copy's torment, Hwaet's dirty wars, Thomas's bravery, and natural human fear. And Sarah. The memory of what we'd had, and what could be. I didn't want to have to grieve all over again for her. I didn't think my heart could take the strain.

The rocking chair stopped, and I turned around to find Sarah standing behind me. I put out my hand, and she took it. She pulled me toward the door. I started to tell Janey that we were leaving, but Janey was far away, concentrating.

We descended the stairs, into the dim house. The house didn't speak, and I wondered if there were any of the Georgia halfsent left in it. For a moment—a very brief moment—I pitied the thing.

"House," I said. "Can you hear me?"

"Georgia is gone," a voice said. It took a moment for my eyes to adjust to the darkness of the living room, and then I saw Wrenny. She'd come back inside and was sitting on the couch, sipping a tumbler half-full of something. The smell of alcohol pervaded the room. "I know it is evil in a sister, but I can't say that I will miss that part of her."

"I'm sorry, Wrenny."

She didn't answer, but took another sip of her drink. "I suppose that I am her heir. Not that there's much left. Janey's Indian land, this house. I believe I'll give that land back. It's caused no end of troubles."

For a moment, the tragic beauty I'd seen before flared in her. I caught my breath, it so startled me.

"That would be a good idea," I mumbled.

"And another thing. After the war, I shall not have the house reprogrammed with Georgia. I believe my dear sister should rest in peace. All of her."

"Yes," I said.

"Will you have a drink with me, Mr. James? And your lady friend?" She reached for the bottle on the coffee table near her, almost turned it over, then righted it and poured herself another shot. Her beauty was covered with sadness and regret, and Wrenny was, again, a ruin amidst the ruins.

"I'm afraid we don't have time. I'm sorry."

"Well, I see. Do you think . . . do you think my star captain friend will ever return? I do so love the little treats he is accustomed to bringing me."

"I don't know, Wrenny. Things have changed. We have to be going."

"Ah well. I'd better enjoy it while it lasts. Nice to see you." She turned the tumbler up and killed off the entire glass.

"And you," I said. Sarah and I stepped through the hole in the front of the house. If the house halfsent were still alive, it would already have begun repairs, smoothing the edges, preparing the wood for mending. So Georgia and her ghost were completely dead, erased. So.

Sarah and I walked out onto the blasted porch. The decking was still mostly intact, as was a portion of the railing. We went and stood at the porch edge. Out of habit, I blinked on my memory bank to record what would happen next. The tell-tale blinked in my right eye, and I remembered that I still had the guidebook quartersent loaded in there, as well. What a trip that little algorithm had taken.

Raej and Thomas, with the Indians backing them, had regained their poise, and were facing it off in a final showdown with Hwaet and Corazon. Seeing me, they backed off a little from Hwaet, and Corazon and the chocalaca took the moment for a breather. They were no more than twenty feet away. From the porch, I called out to Corazon.

"Guess what," I said. "I'm not dead!"

Corazon turned around, and for a second looked at me nonplussed. Hwaet crackled up into the air angrily. Sarah's grip tightened on my hand, trying to pull me back, but I stood my ground.

I jumped from the porch, and took a couple of jaunty steps toward Corazon. I held out my hands to show that I was unarmed. Hwaet let out a little hiss that was almost enough to make me piss my pants (and maybe I did feel something warm trickle down there). If he struck now . . . But I believed that I'd gauged it so that I was just out of his range. I'd sure as hell seen enough chocalaca fighting by now to have an idea of what their range was.

"So, Corazon, I guess you're convinced this is the right thing that you're doing."

Corazon made as if he weren't going to answer at first, but I could tell that such was not in his nature.

"I certainly am," he said, then looked at me hard. "What do you want?"

"Just call it an old reporter's instinct."

He stood glaring at me, and I could see that he was breathing heavily. Hwaet, too, must be taking the unexpected respite to gather strength. Just a little time. Do this right.

"And it doesn't bother you that you're Hwaet's slave?"

"We work together because we are all going down the same path."

Sounded like an aphorism Corazon had been working on a long time, had been turning over in his mind like a lapidary's stone. He needed this one. Badly. I'd give it to him.

"I see. Yes, I *do* understand, I suppose."

I was less than twenty feet away. I could have run at him, tried to choke the life from him, or better, to poke my hands into his eyes, or ram his nose bone up into his brain. But Hwaet was a thousand times faster than me; I'd be ashes before I took my second step. Instead, I popped up the guidebook quartersent, selected the translation mode.

"You're one to be talking of slavery," said Corazon. Bingo. Hooked him. He took a step closer to me. Oh shit. I couldn't step back, or it might break his train of thought. He might wriggle away. But if he got much closer, Hwaet could toast me. There was no Dagum to protect me any longer. I felt utterly naked and soft. "You and your goddamn Westpac. You'll let hundreds of thousands starve south of the equator and in Asia, while the north eats up the resources of Earth on this insane quest for cultural immortality." He smiled a sad, ironic smile. "Cultures die, you know. And by God, ours deserves to be put out of its misery. We are sick. A sick people. The only cure is to go back. Back to Earth, and fix all the things there that we've so *fucked* up. We have to turn inward, and find wisdom, before we should be permitted to spread to the stars."

It was all standard Clerisy claptrap, and maybe some of it was true. But Corazon sounded as if he believed every syllable, literally. Poor ensnared soul. I hated what I was going to do to him next.

"DID YOU KNOW SOMETHING I JUST HAPPENED TO FIND OUT ONLY TODAY?"

I asked this in Spanish, the Clerisy's official language, letting the quartersent completely take over my voice. I sounded like a social activist from hell. Just the sort of thing a priest of the Church of Liberation and Global Justice would be compelled to listen to. Just the sort of thing to stir up his indignant soul.

"What?" Corazon said.

"WESTPAC IS IN TOTAL CONTROL OF THE CLERISY."

"You're out of your mind." He turned, and started to go.

"ASK HWAET," I whispered-yelled, and smiled. "ASK HWAET ABOUT THE IDEALS AND HECTOR LUIS BLANCA, THE HEAD OF THE CHURCH. ASK HIM ABOUT INTELWEST AND LANGLEY'S FAVORITE MOLE."

"What the hell are you talking about?" Corazon stepped back.

"I'm talking about the leader of the Church of Liberation and Global Justice being a traitor to the cloth," I said, this time in my own nasty, cynical voice, in English. "I'm talking about the Ideals fucking *using* his ass."

Corazon stared at me, anger growing in him, as yet un-directed. Why was it always a shock to find yourself part of a covert means to an end you never intended? Especially for people like Corazon. I mean, Christ, he'd done the same to Kem Bently. He'd lied for the cause, killed for it. Only, now it was another cause using Corazon. Like that made all the difference in the world. Like there was a spit's worth of difference between any two causes.

I felt wonderfully cynical. Immortal, because skepticism lifted me up and above all of this. What did my death matter? This stupid war. This stupid priest. This stupid-ass radio beam from Earth pretending to be anything but the nothing that he was. It was, all of it, so incredibly humorous.

What fools for love we mortals be, eh? We fall in love with one another, with the wind, with somebody's secondhand idea. It doesn't matter. The palsied universe stands before us a leper, and do we turn in disgust? Do we face the emptiness with bravery? Fuck no. We masturbate to it, instead. Humanity is a born patsy. We want to be, and we like it. It is in our monkey nature to kowtow to the first thing we can find that is *bigger* than us, even if we have to invent it ourselves. Watching Corazon running through possible explanations, possible reasons to reject what I was saying, began to make me physically sick.

"I don't—"

"Christ, man, what *were* you thinking?"

"You're *lying*! You're almost beaten, and this is your last gambit, isn't it?"

He didn't know how close to the real truth he was coming. Why not tell him all of it?

"It's true," I said. "All of those things I told you about the Ideals and Clerisy. There's going to be war on Earth over it. Or else the Ideals are just going to win out-and-out, and destroy the Clerisy in the process. Hwaet's going to see to it."

"You are a fucking liar," Corazon said. "Hwaet has told me the truth."

I smiled. Truth. What a concept. "I have proof," I said. "Surely you're not afraid to take a look at it?"

Corazon took a step toward me, hesitated. "What sort of proof?"

What the hell *did* it matter? I felt giddy with the powerful necessity of the awful truth. I felt like the Hand of Chaos, poised to crush the little mosquito orders that clung to me like parasites. Humans, chocalacas. All their schemes must perish, of necessity. Pathetic.

"Her!" I said, and pointed at Sarah. "She used to be an Intelwest node, and she's got all the details in her WORM. Tell him, WORM!"

At these words, Hwaet stretched forth a tendril of flame, faster than I could possibly react. I had, once again, underestimated just what a chocalaca could do. It cut across the porch and caught Sarah right in the gut. Her body arched back, and she stood, transfixed, screaming a silent scream.

What have I done? Do something! Think, think, think of something, you fucking—

"Are you going to let him wipe her out before she can tell you?" I cried out. "You'll die a fool, Corazon."

Corazon frowned, but not at me. He was displeased with the torture Hwaet was inflicting. "Stop it," he said. "Stop it, Hwaet. You're like a . . . like an *Indian*."

"THAT'S RIGHT. AN INHUMAN OWNER OF SLAVES—"

"I said *stop!*" Corazon said. This seemed to affect the chocalaca. He withdrew from Sarah, and she slumped down onto the boards of the porch, still conscious, holding her stomach in pain. But, even as she held on to herself, there arose from her a flat, strained voice, speaking haltingly, as if it were being forced out against its will. Dagum's final revenge. He'd made the machine obedient to me, after all.

"Hector Ruiz Blanca entered the service of Intelwest in 2686 under a false flag operation involving Nicaraguan intermediaries," said Sarah's voice. "After a suitable cultivation, Langley determined that he would make a prime resource for private exploitation. He was surreptitiously dropped from the Intelwest network, and blackmailed into the service of the Ideal on or about Earthdate January 13, 2690. Since that time——"

"Shut up!" Corazon screamed. He looked at me wildly. "Make her shut up!" But Hwaet did nothing. Hwaet, it was clear, *could* do nothing. The chocalaca sputtered and hissed ineffectually about Corazon's hip pocket, where the clay must be, causing the priest to appear as if he had an incredibly bad case of hemorrhoids. Corazon was temporarily back in charge of his own mind.

"It's all true," I replied, and shrugged.

Corazon clenched his fists, brought them to his temples and kneaded them. He was close enough now that I could hear him whispering. "Let me go, you fucker. Let me decide," he was saying.

Then he raised his face and looked me square in the eyes, shook his fists at me. "No!" he said. "I can't believe it. I believe——"

Those were Gerabaldo Corazon's last words. A shot rang out. He blinked. Then his body began to tremble violently as if some giant, invisible hand were shaking him like dice. But the shaking was coming from *within* Corazon, and soon fissures opened up on his skin. Blood and viscera oozed out. And his eyes . . . they sank into his skull. Bile poured forth from his mouth. Then, whatever muscles that had held him up gave way, and he collapsed in a heap upon the ground, and split open like a soggy paper sack. His jellied insides flowed out in languid rivulets and streamers.

Behind him, at ten paces, stood Frank Oldfrunon, still holding his pistol in his right hand. "Great God," Oldfrunon said. "I forgot I was still loaded with the burrowing slugs."

Then, from the broken mass of Corazon's body, Hwaet arose.

There was a shriek that filled the air, kind of like a vulture makes when it's been shooed away from carrion. Within the red-black ether of Hwaet his halfsents manifested, rising from the ground. And in the center, in the heart of the snake, was the snarling head of a bear, of Raej, tortured, angry. Hwaet turned to Oldfrunon, and the old man feebly pointed the pistol, fired. The slug, of course, passed right through Hwaet, doing no damage.

Oldfrunon trembled visibly, but managed to stand up straight, prepared for the death blow.

Instead, with a roar, Thomas and Raej charged forward. Raej was more fully manifested as a bear than I'd ever seen him before—back legs, deadly forequarters. Thomas sprang through the air, and Raej sprang with him, as one.

And, from behind, something very strange. A large, flapping *something* descended upon the ghost-snake. It covered him over, wrapped him up. *A quilt.* Earthy patterns formed and reformed on the giant quilt's surface. Stars, boxes, plantlike tendrils. It was unmistakably one of Janey's, though. Or maybe it was *all* of them, brought together through time, to exist all at once, in all their suffocating, chaotic complexity. The patterns gathered in speed and intricacy, as if they were bees, getting angrier and more sure of their target. Hwaet rose up, a lump under the quilt.

Then Raej struck—biting down with a slavering mouth, through the quilt, just beneath Hwaet's snakelike head. Hwaet tried to shake it loose, but Raej and Thomas knocked the lower portion of his body out from under him with a huge swipe of a back paw.

Along the quilt's patterns, it began to glow with a green and brown light. But the glow wasn't light. More like *cracks*. The true world was seeping through. Things were mixing and melting. But not randomly. Precisely where Janey wanted them to melt. She had established a deadly control.

"Goodbye, Father." I turned, and saw Janey standing right behind me, beside Sarah. "Even though you are still here with me, it hurts me to kill you."

The ghost-snake gave a final lunge upward. Raej did not let go. The quilt muffled Hwaet's energy, dragging him down, inexorably down. Then Raej was on him, clawing through the quilt, mauling him like a grizzly after a backpacker in a sleeping bag. Spots of black bile appeared on the quilt, and the stench of fields of dead bodies rose up. Only the random, natural wind blowing up, and dissipating some of the stink, kept it from being completely overpowering.

From under the quilt came the muted sound of a gurgling aspiration, like the last hiss of a kettle, after the water is all boiled away and the metal is about to burn.

Then Raej rose up on his hindquarters, and, with a roar that must have echoed throughout Jackson, and perhaps all the way to Doom, came down with all his might on the thing under the quilt.

I was scared for my own safety, twenty feet away. I backed up against something soft, turned, and found Sarah holding on to me. I put my arms around her, and shielded her from the terrible sight, until the roars had become growls and snufflings, then were gone altogether.

I turned around. The quilt was seeping away like water after a rain, the world was twisting back to normal. Thomas stood over Corazon's body, and Raej was only a blue flicker around him. He reached down and took the clay from the priest's pocket, and crushed it between his fingers.

"There," Thomas said. "Done."

Yesterday, I had a vision. I know that those are usually reserved for Indians who do a little too much sipsi in the Gathering Hall. But mine was pure Mississippian, as authentic as Kentucky bourbon.

In my vision, Thomas was still the Great Sun of Doom. He ruled wisely and, now that the war was over, happily. Doom needed a new Wanderer, and my old friend asked me to take the job. So, one cold spring morning, I'd taken my birchbark canoe, called up my old chocalaca friend Dagum, and paddled off into the stars, never looking back. At the back of my mind was the thought that I would not be returning to Candle, that there was a galaxy, a universe, out there, and I wanted to see it. Or at least that my time and use on Candle were past, and I was free.

I was not at all sure that I wanted to share in the new order that was coming. Raej's way was becoming a reality, as Effect scientists, analyzing the strange happenings on Whimsey Apple's ship, found easy, cheap ways to access and inhabit the true world. When we knew enough, and were ready, Raej and his chocalacas would help us take the last step. Hwaet's plan was defeated and, without Hwaet's leadership, there was no hope of it resurfacing. Raej had won the political stakes in the true world.

So the planets would become pools and perches for humanity. The stars would be ours, and we would use them wisely. The change would be good. But I wasn't so sure my frail soul could handle another world-altering change. I was stretched five hundred years thin, and there must be a limit to a man's ability to adapt.

So I took off. I imagined myself a romantic hero, under no obligation, except to himself. Lonely, but with a great nobility to his aloneness, so that he wore it like a mantle of honor, a signature of his power.

But then I heard a startled cry from inside my house, and I stepped back through the open door and found Sarah, standing over a broken urn, wringing her hands, tears in her eyes. It was the Indian urn the house had used to speak to me, in Janey's voice, when I'd returned from Earth. Sarah had accidentally knocked it over, and the house had not been able to keep it from breaking. Sarah didn't understand, as she didn't understand so many things. The sound had frightened her.

"It's okay," I said, taking her hands in mine. "Don't worry. Everything is okay, my love."

And my voice calmed her, although she continued to cry. I led her over to the couch, and the house, without my asking, wheeled out a cart and cleaned up the broken shards. Sarah watched, and soon her bewilderment turned to a kind of uncomprehending wonder, and I dried her tears.

Most days she's like this. Janey killed the WORM, and she's all alone in there. It must feel like an enormous room in some castle or cathedral does to a little child. In so many ways, Sarah is a little child. I have to be careful not to treat her like one, though. I know, in my heart, that if I don't treat her as if she were the old Sarah, my Sarah, then all hope of her becoming that Sarah again will be gone.

So I spend my days in hope and frustration, not really that much different from before. Fleeing to the geothermal vents, then being speared by Hwaet took their toll. She is even less than she was before. She's a child, a baby, and I am her father now, and not her lover. Yet now I can reach out and touch her. I can take care of her, like I did when she broke the urn. And when I listen to the wind, her lonely cry is not what I hear.

But on Candle, every day is *still* an animal. Frank Oldfrunon has seen to that. The new weather algorithm is a duplicate of him, made with the Clerisy's fancy machinery. So when he dies, if the old man ever dies, for all intents and purposes, he'll still be the mayor.

And, thanks to Oldfrunon, I'm now mildly famous. The Westnet *Daily Locals* would not, of course, carry my rather startling story about the Ideal conspiracy to subvert Westpac. After all, Westnet is run by a partially government-owned corporation, and its Oversight Committee is chaired by an Ideal. But Oldfrunon used his pull with the Territorial rep from Mumba's Reef to make sure my story got out on the Wire. Every tramp freighter, along with the *Irrelevance* and the other big ships, spread the news. And small, locally-owned newspapers all across the Territory picked it up, displayed it prominently, beating the pants off the *Daily Locals* once again.

Soon, there will be a *real,* instantaneous Wire. Then, if I understand what the Effect scientists are saying correctly, instantaneous travel from world to world. Westpac is in contact with the chocalacas. Raej has shown the way and left the details to others who followed him. It should have been Dagum, but Dagum is gone. But the *Cold Truth* remains, and somewhere in the true world, I have faith that there Dagum and my halfsent's progeny is growing, getting ready to hatch.

Thomas and Raej are Wandering again. Metay-andi has chosen another Great Sun, at Thomas's request. He is Thaddeus Wala-andi, the former Lawgiver. He was always a moderate, and with the support of Laylay Potter, whom Thomas insisted be the new Lawgiver, there is peace. It didn't hurt that Wrenny Calhoun made good on her promise and gave back the Loosa clay deposit. Janey lives at home now, and I see Wrenny when I go to visit. She still drinks like a fish, but at times her beauty flames forth and leaves me breathless. The atmosphere is almost exactly the opposite at the Calhoun house, and Wrenny is the better for it.

Clay is more important now than ever. The Territory is still tense. But the war on Candle did not spread far, and where it did, it was put out quickly. Maybe that's why Thomas felt justified in giving up his position. He and Raej were needed to spread the word among the Indians of Hwaet's doings, and his downfall. When he returns, I expect him to have another year's worth of stardust in his wrinkles, another year gone by in his slow transformation into a creature that has seen too much to contain in a mere human soul. I don't know what my friend will become, but I'm sure it will be strange and wonderful.

This universe is strange and wonderful, even when it is perverse and awful. I'm still not sure what to make of it. Outside, the sky is brindled over with cirrus clouds, scattered like glass shards in a kaleidoscope. I'm sitting in my office, in the *Cold Truth,* banking this story, waiting for lunch. In my pocket is my good-luck clay. And within it is the guidebook quartersent. I've given it as much freedom as is possible for such things. Perhaps it's busy constructing socialist utopias and dreaming of ways to fight injustice. Maybe it will alight on something useful, after all. From time to time, I hook up to it with my optic flasher, and we have long, meaningful discussions. Well, mostly I listen.

I am filled with terror and wonder these days, and I don't really have much to say. Janey has promised to come by and see me. She is perhaps the strangest and most wonderful thing I've ever come across. She has already reached that plateau that humanity seems destined for under Raej's way. She's no longer wholly with us, here in the regular world, I mean. I suspect she could reach out and instantly be with Thomas wherever he might be. She could be anywhere, and so I am happy, and a little bit proud, when she chooses to be with me.

I don't know what it is I feel for Janey. I have Sarah to care for, and I love Sarah. Yet there is a place in my heart for Janey—*because* Sarah is back—that is wholly separate. Well, who knows what'll happen? And it's just as much Janey's choice as mine. So life is not a lonely romantic adventure, and my vision was false. Life is complicated, and making the right choice is problematic. But I think that always moving with a purpose holy and sure is best left for the afterlife. Who knows? After all, for me, this life *is* the afterlife—my third, depending on how you count.

Ah hell, every day is an animal. Those kaleidoscope clouds are hinting of a snow shower, and something else too. What animal do we have here? This is a hard one.

Other than the sky's antics, there isn't much happening today, so when Janey shows up, I may hand it over to the halfsent and take her to the Goosedown for a drink. The old sun is straining its way up in the east, about to pull itself over the roofs of Jackson's buildings. God, it makes me tired just waiting for it. But what is Oldfrunon's weather algorithm up to?

The clouds are flitting about most peculiarly, gathering in swirls and eddies that hint at meaning, almost like they are preparing for something, trying to say something. And now the old, cold ball clears the roofs and feebly winks down through the clouds onto the world. And I find that I am chuckling, then laughing out loud. Oldfrunon's ghost has brought back the stuff of legend, and made the old myths true. For Candle's sky is flickering, just like the stories said it did back in the old days, back when the Indians and settlers had first met, and we were all going to live in peace. I realize what animal we have here. A human being.

Now Janey steps in with the red sun in her hair. It's time for me to get my parka and go back out into the cold.

You know, I was thinking: maybe it's enough. Maybe that's always the way it is with us. When everything else fails, we still have the flicker.